Tor Books by J. A. Pitts

Black Blade Blues
Honeyed Words
Forged in Fire

Forged in Fire

Forged in Fire

J. A. Pitts

TOR®

A Tom Doherty Associates Book

NEW YORK

FORGED IN FIRE

Copyright © 2012 by John A. Pitts

A Tor Book
Published by Tom Doherty Associates, LLC
175 Fifth Avenue
New York, NY 10010

www.tor-forge.com

Tor® is a registered trademark of Tom Doherty Associates, LLC.

ISBN 978-0-7653-2469-6 (hardcover)
ISBN 978-1-4299-4637-7 (e-book)

First Edition: June 2012

Printed in the United States of America

0 9 8 7 6 5 4 3 2 1

This book is dedicated to those adventurers
who question societal norms,
explore the dangerous and forbidden,
push the limits, risk greatness,
and dare to dream.
Never give up, never lose hope.

Acknowledgments

Forged in Fire is the latest installment in the Sarah Beauhall series. It's definitely been a steep learning curve, this professional writing gig. There are a lot of folks who have helped me along the way.

First I'd like to acknowledge my family for all their support and the occasional boot in the rear that it took to make this the novel that it is. You make all of this worthwhile.

My support network stretches out to a huge array of friends. You are all wonderful people who help me get through my days. From the occasional gaming session, movies, e-mail, lunches, and even phone calls—each of you makes my life richer.

I would be remiss if I did not mention the writing family I have been lucky enough to join. You friends who are on the same journey as I are all a wealth of love and support. Thank you for the midnight sanity checks, the convention decompression, and the moments of exhausted camaraderie.

My editors, Claire Eddy and Kristin Sevick, are wonderful people who deserve accolades beyond this silly little acknowledgment. I love working with you. You make the publishing aspect of this journey a joy.

To my most excellent agent, Cameron McClure, who has a

keen eye for story, good solid advice, and a sharp wit, thanks for all the help.

To Dan Dos Santos, thanks for another astounding cover, and for making folks stop and look at my book. You create magic.

And finally, thank you to the fans, bloggers, critics, and book reviewers who help spread the word of Sarah and her adventures. Thanks for boosting the signal.

Forged in Fire

One

I kept Katie back and to the right of me as we followed the she-troll into the clearing. Here the snow was deep
enough to see the paths the troll had made and to see where she
was heading. Even with the sheep slung over her shoulder and
one of Katie's crossbow bolts in her right thigh, the she-troll had
stayed ahead of us, weaving in and out of the trees, climbing for
the last mile or more. Not for the first time this winter, I swore
over the loss of my Doc Martens. The trainers sucked in this
rough terrain.

"Be careful, Sarah," Katie called to me in a hoarse whisper.

I glanced back at her, letting a grin grow on my face. We so
had this.

Halfway across the clearing, the troll spun around, launching
the sheep at us. I barely got my head turned around fast enough
to dive to the right. Katie wasn't as quick. She dropped her crossbow while trying to avoid the ovine missile, but went down under
two hundred pounds of meat and wool.

"You okay?" I called, rolling to my feet, keeping between Katie and the troll.

The she-troll roared, overwhelming Katie's reply. I drew my
sword Gram and squared to face the beast, expecting her to fall
on me, but she stepped back, ripped the bolt from her leg, and

screamed once again. Blood ran down her rough britches and stained the snow beneath her huge feet.

"I know you, berserker," the troll growled. "I will not let you destroy what is mine."

"You're one of Jean-Paul's beasties, then?" I called. Her only answer was to scoop a fallen tree limb from the ground and lumber at me.

I caught the downward stroke of her cudgel against Gram. She was strong. I nearly fell beneath the sheer power of the blow. I slid backward on the ice, barely keeping my feet.

"Not anymore," she grunted, swinging at me again.

I parried, spinning around. It was a beautiful move, at least in my mind. It should have caught her in the neck, smashing through the arteries. Instead, my shoes slipped on the ice and I stumbled, missing her by half a foot. She lunged forward, punched me in the chest with the cudgel, and slashed my right leg with her claws.

Lucky for me, the universe is random and capricious. The wound in her leg kept her from putting her full strength and balance in the blows, so I didn't lose my leg. As it was, she punched through my chain mail and sliced into my upper thigh.

I screamed with the pain and fell backward. Luckily, rocks and ice broke my fall. I clamped my right hand over my thigh and kept Gram up between me and the killing machine. She loomed over me and roared. Spittle flew over me, and for a moment she looked like King Kong raging on Skull Island.

"Oh, shit," I said, trying to scramble backward with one good leg. She had me dead to rights, only we'd both forgotten about Katie.

Katie smashed the crossbow into the side of the troll's head, causing her ugliness to lumber to the side. I rolled up onto my good knee and shoved Gram upward, sending six inches of black steel into the troll's neck.

The troll jerked backward, flailing with both arms. She caught Katie a glancing blow. She staggered backward to fall against one of the old oaks.

I forced myself to my feet as the troll fell to her knees, clutching her throat. She looked at me, really looked into me, pleading. I could see the pain and fear in her huge green eyes. She opened her mouth, gasping something through the foaming blood. I couldn't make out the words. Tears rolled down her pocked face as she tried over and over to say something. I think it was "mercy," but I couldn't be sure. After a minute her eyes rolled into the back of her head and she fell backward. The forest shook with her falling.

"Damn it," I shouted, looking around to Katie, who was limping toward me.

"Hang on," Katie called, pulling her pack and guitar from the underbrush. She fell to her knees at my side and pushed me onto my back. "Let me stop the bleeding," she ordered.

I leaned back on one elbow and watched as she peeled the chain and cloth from the wound. I grunted as she pulled several links out of the rent flesh. "Fuck, that hurts," I growled.

She looked around, picked up a small stick from the ground, and thrust it at me. "Bite down on this," she said and pushed me onto my back.

I bit down onto the stick and tried not to make too much noise as she dressed the wound.

"Not too deep," she assured me, pulling her first aid kit from her pack. She'd been training with our doctor friend Melanie for weeks—basic wound care and treatment. She used an irrigation syringe to clean the wound with distilled water. Then she had me hold it partially closed while she applied four wound closure strips.

"Gotta keep it open some," she said, grimacing. "Can't risk infection."

She slathered the wound with antibiotic ointment and applied a sterile bandage over it. I held that down tight, applying pressure to help it stop bleeding while she tore off several lengths of muslin and duct tape to finish off the dressing.

"At least you didn't wreck the runes," she said, cupping my calf.

I had runes running down my left calf—Thurisaz, Dagaz, Kenaz, Gebo, Tiwaz—the same runes that ran down the length of the fuller on my sword, Gram. I inherited them when I became tuned in with the blade. Just popped up on my calf one day, pretty as you please. Damn funny thing about magic swords. They mark you in some ways. I just never figured it would be so literal.

She did a quick and efficient job of binding the wound. Within a few minutes, I was standing. I wouldn't be running any marathons, but I could get around.

I cleaned Gram and sheathed her before examining the troll.

She was dead, for sure.

"What was that at the end?" Katie asked, looking around for a branch long enough for me to use as a cane.

"I think she said 'mercy,'" I said. "She was already dying, knew it by the look in her eyes. Why would she ask for mercy then and not when we had her cornered?"

"No idea," Katie said. "But she was definitely making a stand here. We should look around."

We hadn't gone very far across the clearing when we heard crying. I looked at Katie, who shrugged and pushed forward, her short sword out. I pulled Gram from her sheath and hobbled forward, leaning on the staff.

Beyond the clearing, where the rocky slope pushed upward, we found the troll's lair. The opening was fairly low, but firelight shown from inside. Katie went in ahead of me. The opening jagged to the left and expanded into a huge, dry cave.

The place was amazing. Most of the floor was covered in

sheepskins, and several pieces of crude furniture were placed around a central fire pit. The cave went back about thirty feet. The smoke from the fire wound its way upward, being pulled out through a natural chimney of some sort.

A spit was erected over the fire and several cook pots sat off to one side. Katie and I looked at each other in astonishment. It was dry, warm, and homey.

"Christ!" I breathed. "How long has she been here?"

That's when we heard the cry again. I'd forgotten it in the shock of seeing the way the cave had been made into a home.

"Oh, no," Katie said, walking to the back of the cave.

I hobbled after her, expecting the worst. What I saw, however, was beyond even my worst nightmares.

In the back, buried in shadow, was a handmade crib. By the time I made it around the fire, Katie had lifted a troll baby out of the crib and was holding it to her chest, trying to quiet it.

"Sarah," she started, her voice thick with tears. "There's a second one here."

I stumped over to her and looked down into the crib. A second troll baby lay sleeping. I looked at Katie, stunned. "What the hell do we do now?"

"I think he's hungry," she said.

I took two more steps and collapsed into a rough-hewn chair. It gave a little, and I realized it was a rocker. This was where she nursed them.

"What have we done?"

Katie handed me the child. "Hold him. I need to find what she used for diapers."

I held the kid out from me, eyeing the drooping cloth diaper. "Great," I said, rocking forward and holding him over the floor. I did NOT want any of that leaking on me.

He looked a lot like a human baby, only longer, like he'd been stretched. He had the normal eyes, ears, and mouth you'd expect on any humanoid.

The thought stopped me. How utterly bizarre my life had become. Humanoid, indeed. Just a year ago, I'd had a normal life as a blacksmith in Seattle, one of the coolest cities on the planet. I was shoeing horses and making swords for the local ren faires. I had taxes and lattes, too much traffic and not enough income. Then I reforged a magic sword and the dragons took notice of my sorry ass. Now I'm plagued with troll babies and dragons, giants, dwarves, magic swords, and ancient Norse gods. How had the whole damn world managed to miss all this hiding in plain sight? Why wasn't this front-page news all over the globe? Instead, I sat with an orphaned troll and was wishing for nothing more than a hot shower and a thin crust pepperoni pizza.

The child's fingers were long and thin with no talons. I guess they grew in later. Made me wonder if you could trim those back like fingernails. Really, he pretty much looked like a normal kid. His skin was a bit knobbly, thicker than mine, I'm sure.

"Any luck?" I called back to Katie. When I looked back, he had the greatest little smile. Probably gas. That's what my ma would've said.

Katie found a stack of cloths we assumed were diapers and changed the little monster. His nappy was heavy with urine. Katie rolled it up and took it to the back of the cave. "This clears things up," she said, carrying a shield back into the light. "This is one of ours."

It bore the emblem of Black Briar. Nidhogg had been right, damn her icy heart.

"So she was a survivor of the battle back in May," I said, looking down at the mewling troll baby in my lap. "She probably killed some of our friends."

"Good odds," Katie said, taking the child from me and sitting on the edge of a pallet of sheepskin that looked like a bed. "But she only took sheep and such since then. And didn't try to head back north or harass us further."

"True enough. But the farmers who lost those sheep weren't too happy." And Nidhogg, the dragon who claimed these parts, was none too pleased to have a beastie raiding her territory.

The second baby woke then, and we repeated the diaper routine. I ended up on the makeshift bed with the first troll baby beside me while Katie carried the second on her hip. "I don't see any bottles or anything," she said. "I guess she could've been nursing them still." She held the second one and looked into its mouth, worming her finger around past the tight, rubbery lips.

"Plenty of teeth," she said, pulling her finger back quickly and wiping it on her shirt. "And sharp."

"Maybe they're already eating meat," I offered. "They're not like human babies."

So Katie returned to the clearing and dragged in the sheep the mother had been bringing to feed her children.

"If they weren't hurting anyone, why'd Nidhogg want you to look into this?" she asked me as she began cutting small chunks from the sheep carcass.

Both troll babies were sitting on the bed with me and actually giggled and clapped as we fed them cubes of raw sheep.

"Oh, if I had to hazard a guess, I'd say she was testing me, testing my loyalty. She has high expectations for her servants. That and I'd wager a punishment for causing Qindra to be locked in that house out in Chumstick."

"Not your fault the witch got trapped with all those ghosties," Katie said.

"Fault doesn't come into it. It's spite and obligation."

She didn't reply to that, just worked in silence. We'd had that conversation too many times—what with Julie's staying at my apartment since the dragon attack in May and my volunteering to help cover Qindra's duties for the last few weeks. The only plus to it all in Katie's mind was that I was sleeping at her place pretty regularly now.

I rubbed my eyes. It didn't have to be this hard. I loved her; she knew it. There are just times when you have to stand up and do the right thing, even if it isn't easy. Yes, Nidhogg was a dragon. But she had a kingdom to run, and the witch Qindra had been her face to the world. With her incapacitated, I had to step up. It was quid pro quo.

Qindra had helped our people—had come to our aid during and after the battle with the dragon Jean-Paul. Hell, she'd agreed to try and cleanse Anezka's property in Chumstick as a favor to me. It wasn't her fault that my substitute blacksmith mentor, Anezka, was bat-shit crazy. Nor was it her responsibility that Anezka's home and smithy had been built on the vortex of a major ley line that ran down from the wilds of the Cascade Mountains. No one knew the whole place was a haunted house waiting to explode. Well, maybe the evil necromancer dude Anezka had dated and dumped. I'm sure he'd had a clue, bastard.

It felt right, standing in for Qindra. She was locked inside that magic dome she'd thrown over the property, protecting everyone from the demented and nasty spirits that were being drawn to Anezka's place. My running a few errands for Nidhogg paled in comparison. Of course, I'm sure the troll I'd just killed would've rather I stayed out of things.

Katie butchered the sheep with efficiency. Taking out some of her frustration, I'd bet. When she turned, however, she was nothing but grim determination and sunshine. Even with bloody hands and her hair askew, she was the most beautiful woman I'd ever met.

I looked from her to the babies. They were cute, too.

"Frick and Frack," I said as they chewed noisily.

"Nice," Katie said, wiping her knife on the sheep's wooly back. "Since you've named them, I guess we're keeping them."

I watched them a minute. Were they condemned by their species? Did we have the right to slaughter them? "Well, I don't think we can kill them, do you?"

Katie looked over at me; I was lying with a bloody bandage over one thigh and two troll babies nestled into the thick sheepskins.

"No, we can't kill them," she said. "You're right."

"So what then?"

"I don't know."

She found a large barrel in the back filled with rain water, and we cleaned up.

I limped to the entrance of the cave and looked out over the frozen clearing. "It'll be dark long before we can get back with me hobbled and carrying two troll babies."

Katie stepped up and hugged me from behind. "We can sleep here tonight. It's safe enough. Frick and Frack went right back to sleep."

I kept watching the clearing, seeing the blowing snow begin to cover the troll mother. "Wish I hadn't killed her," I whispered.

"Aye," Katie said.

Soon enough, I was back on the bed and Frick and Frack were back in their crib. Katie kept the fire stoked up for another hour or so, long enough for dark to set outside, then crawled into the bed with me.

"Smells pretty strong," she said.

I reached for her, pulling her to my chest. "Smells like sheepskin. Doesn't stink like you'd think for a troll bed."

"Maybe they're clean by nature," she said against my shoulder. "Never knew a troll until we fought them in May."

I wondered about the troll mother, the life she'd led that took her into Jean-Paul's servitude. I can't imagine living under the regime of that brutal bastard. Jean-Paul was one of those dragons who, like a nasty dictator, played with his food. I can't even begin to imagine the brutality that any of the special creatures had experienced under his rule. Hell, I'm not sure what to call them: trolls and giants, elves and dwarves. Was it a blessing for us stupid humans, who had no clue of the dragons? Did our ignorance make the difference?

Then I thought back to Skella and Gletts, the young elves we'd recently met. They spent their whole lives living in Stanley Park under Jean-Paul's violent rule, and they ended up being decent enough folk.

Maybe this troll momma was just in the wrong place at the wrong time. And here we'd killed her for trying to take care of her children. Yeah, Nidhogg was concerned when the sheep farmers started talking about Wendigo and how something terrible was killing their stock. But, damn it. The troll didn't need killing. She needed helping.

"You ever thought about having kids?" Katie asked me after the fire had burned low.

"I've never been all that interested," I said. "I just never considered it something I needed to do. Don't get me wrong, I think kids are fine."

She made a noise beside me that I couldn't interpret.

"But I just never figured on getting pregnant, bringing a child into this world. Especially now, with everything I know about the dragons and worse."

"I thought I'd have a daughter," Katie said sleepily. "Someone to teach to play guitar. Someone to have tea parties with and play dress-up."

"You never know," I whispered. She didn't answer, and before long I heard her steady breathing that let me know she'd gone to sleep.

Katie may very well be the best thing that ever happened to me. I cared more for her happiness than damn near anything else on the planet. I'd thought about living the rest of my life with her, back when I thought I was gonna have a long one. Now with the dragons, and the sword Gram, I wasn't sure I'd live out the winter. Put a totally different spin on things.

I tried to keep it together, not to let things spin out of control. But I'm not sure how well that was working for me. Let's forget the fact that I fought giants and trolls, killed a dragon, forged an ancient sword, and had to deal with a crotchety and half-crazed homeless guy who either was Odin or channeled him on a regular basis. Magic really existed in the world. There were some nasty things out there that wanted to kill me. Hell, some of them wanted to eat me.

And now, filled with a righteousness that blurred the lines of right and wrong, I'd killed this troll. She was a living, breathing, thinking, caring entity who wanted nothing more than to keep her family safe. Isn't that what we all wanted? How did this make me any different from the fucking dragons?

I lay awake for a long time, the throbbing in my leg dull compared to the one in my heart.

Two

It snowed overnight, deep, hard-blowing snow. We ended up spending several more days in that cave, tending to the babies. Mainly Katie tended to all of us. She butchered the sheep, putting it out in the snow to keep, and cooked a bunch of it for her and me. The troll babies would eat it cooked but preferred it raw. They didn't do much but sleep, eat, and fill their diapers with the most god-awful foulness that you cannot even imagine.

Katie was such a trooper. She changed the diapers, cleaned the babies, and even took the diapers out into the clearing so they wouldn't stink up the joint.

I woke up late that first night when the little ones were squalling. Before I could as much as roll over, Katie had her guitar out and was singing a lullaby to the little monsters. Soon enough they went back to sleep. Or, I suppose they had, because her singing put me right out. The next thing I knew it was morning.

As the fourth day dawned, cold and clear, we packed up. The swelling in my leg had gone down quite a bit, mainly due to packing it with snow.

I hobbled out into the clear morning. It was surprisingly cold after the coziness of the cave. I hated that we'd left the troll mother to the coyotes and wolves, but when I got to the clearing, I saw that Katie had spent an amazing amount of time covering the body in stones. The cairn was easily nine by four and at least three feet tall. She'd twisted a wreath of holly and pine and placed it on top of the mound. God I loved that woman.

I turned, catching her watching me, a sheepish look on her face. "I knew you were upset," she said. "What else could I do?"

I didn't say anything, just limped over to her and hugged her. I never wanted to let her go again, but the babies needed attention.

Katie made a sled from the big Black Briar shield she found, rigged it with long straps, and settled the babies in it, covering them in sheepskin. We filled our water bottles from the rain barrel, filled Katie's pack with extra diapers and cooked mutton, and then headed back down the mountain toward Black Briar.

They weren't expecting us.

We hadn't told them where we were going. I hadn't felt the need to explain to Jimmy and the crew how I was working for Nidhogg off and on. Katie wasn't too happy about it overall, but she was tolerant. She understood the obligation I felt for the whole Qindra debacle. She loved me enough to see how important it was for me to pay my debts.

Jimmy got twisted around the axle anytime something about Nidhogg or Qindra came up. So we just avoided the conversation.

I was conflicted. Jimmy and Katie lost their parents when Katie was just a kid. They'd been mixed up in all this dragons and giants stuff, magic and swords. Jimmy considered himself on the side of good and right. Dragons were on the side of darkness and pain.

Just as no two people are exactly the same, I felt that maybe, just maybe, dragons weren't all the same either. Now, I'm not stupid. I was under no illusions that they were fluffy bunnies or anything. And I had the scars to prove otherwise. It's just that

Jimmy took his role as clan leader pretty damn seriously. "What wasn't fer us was aginna us" type of thing.

He had a good heart. He just kept his anger in a tight little ball and nursed it along with his courage and his goodness. A good guy to have in your corner. Not someone you wanted to go up against.

So I didn't want to mess with it.

We'd trailed the troll for the better part of a day before catching her in that clearing. It had been slow, grueling travel. Even so, I didn't realize just how far up into the national forest we'd gone. It took a surprisingly long time to get off the mountain and back to Black Briar territory. Travel was getting difficult as the sun went down and the temperature dropped.

Trisha and her squad were on patrol today. Keeping an eye on the wild country that backed up to Black Briar proper. Mostly mountains in the north and east—federal lands. But you never knew who or what was going to come down out of those mountains. Jimmy had an arrangement with the local rangers. Black Briar didn't hunt or fight on their land (as far as they knew), and we helped out with search and rescue, as well as keeping the local kids from heading into that stretch of the national forest and partying. It was a symbiotic relationship.

They must've heard us coming. Trisha stood a little ways away from her squad, out in the open enough to not scare the hell out of hikers or rangers. The rest of the crew was in a defensive position with crossbows, pikes, and hunting rifles. Ever since the battle, where we learned just how badly magic screwed with complex things like electricity and gunpowder, Black Briar made sure to have backups. Enough rifle fire could take down a giant, but only if the gun would actually fire. That's what the pikes and crossbows were for.

Katie called out to them and they responded with a shout. Soon, we had Trisha and her squad swarming us, offering help.

There was a lot of chatter and surprise over the troll babies. Trisha thought they were as cute as could be. Nancy didn't have much to say, and Benny and Gary just looked confused. All of them had been in that battle, knew the truth of the world. Still, troll babies were not something you saw every day.

We rested with them for a bit and then got the babies cleaned up, fed, and back on the sled once more. They escorted us toward the big house, where Jimmy and Deidre lived.

I was flagging fast.

Jimmy was Katie's older brother and the seneschal, or leader, of Black Briar. Deidre was Jimmy's wife, a retired software designer who'd struck it rich in the late nineties. Together they'd raised Katie after Katie and Jimmy's parents disappeared on a trip to Iceland.

Publicly, Black Briar was a mercenary house in the Society for Creative Anachronism, a group of people whom the world thought played war games fueled by overactive imaginations. Even in that crowd, very few people knew about the dragons, giants, and assorted mythological creatures that haunted our world. Up until a very short time ago, I'd been blissfully unaware, and it boggled my mind to find out just how much this group knew.

When we got back to the farm, things switched into high gear. Trisha insisted that they get us all the way up into the big house, where Deidre took over. She set the base crew to getting us unpacked and cleaned up.

After I'd had a long, hot shower, Deidre redressed my wound. Katie had done a good job, but I'd be needing some antibiotics.

Katie called Melanie—our doctor friend and Katie's old lover—who sent a script up to the pharmacy in town. She said she'd swing by our place after her shift to check in on me. I was beginning to like that girl, in spite of her and Katie's past.

Nathan's crew went out on patrol, and Trisha's group hung back at the house, anxious to hear our story. The great room had a large couch and enough chairs to hold most of us. Katie and I gladly took the couch, so I could keep my leg elevated. Trisha's crew stayed in the kitchen, drinking coffee, but Trisha sat in a chair next to Deidre. The troll babies lay on a blanket on the floor.

Jimmy made a production of adding logs to the embers in the big fireplace, deliberately not looking at the babies. Once everyone was settled, we told the full story of going out on Nidhogg's orders, tracking the troll, killing her, and then finding the babies.

"Nidhogg's orders?" Jimmy asked, his face purple with anger. "What the hell were you thinking?"

"Paying a debt," I said. "I'd expect you to understand that. Qindra is trapped in the house out in Chumstick, keeping the nasties locked inside that dome with her. I owe her, Jim. You know about obligation."

"You should've talked to me first," he said, his anger barely in check. "How dare you?"

"This is why we didn't tell you," Katie said, her own anger rising to the fore. They were definitely related. "You keep things from me all the time. Have done for years. I'm a grown-up, Jim. I don't need your permission."

He looked at Deidre, who kept an impassive face. This was not a new topic.

"Damn shame about that troll mother," Deidre said, shaking her head. "She was just protecting her babies."

Smooth subject change.

"Screw 'em," Jimmy barked. "Trolls are bad news. Better dead than haunting our backyard."

Katie got up, walked over, and picked Frick up off the ground. He was mewling and fussing. He had a clean diaper and wouldn't need feeding for a while yct, so I figured he was reacting to all the anger in the room. She set Frick down in Trisha's lap, then grabbed Frack and gave him to Deidre.

"Nature beats nurture," Jimmy spat, but Deidre wasn't hearing any of it.

"We will NOT kill these babies," she said to many head nods. "There's been enough killing here."

"That was not our fault," Jimmy growled.

Katie got up and paced across to the fireplace. I hadn't moved, letting the family bicker. "When the farm was attacked, things changed here, Jim," I said, breaking into the flow. "We can't be like them."

"You should've thought about that before you killed their mother," he said.

Katie whirled. "We know, Jim. Believe me. You know what she said to us, as she was bleeding her heart blood out onto the packed snow? She begged Sarah for mercy. Not for herself, but for her babies."

Jimmy looked down at the floor. Deidre held Frack tighter against her chest and blinked back tears.

"Let me take them," Trisha said quietly. "Please?"

Jimmy looked up at her and Katie turned, dropping to her knees at Trisha's feet. "Are you sure, Trisha?"

"I've got nobody," Trisha started, her voice cracking. "Since Bob and Chloe died." She took a deep breath, the tears streaming down her face. "Chloe was my best friend . . . and Bob." She sighed. "Bob and I had gone out a couple of times, ya know? We'd talked about kids, if we'd be good parents. Now I've got nobody."

Jimmy turned away, a sour look on his face.

"We'll take 'em out in the barracks," Trisha said. "Me and my squad can look after 'em. It takes a village and all that." She looked around, hopeful.

"Seems reasonable," Deidre said, looking over at Jimmy. "What do you think, Jim?"

"What happens when they get big? You took more than a few down, Sarah. How big do they get?"

I glanced at the babies. "Pretty big. Would be nice to have that kind of power on our side the next time we get in a tussle."

Jimmy barked out a laugh. "You think they'd be on our side?"

"I'd say they could make a choice when they're older," Deidre said. "But we should give them a chance to make that decision."

Most of the heads in the room nodded. Gary seemed hesitant. He was waiting for Jimmy to make up his mind. Nancy was with Trisha, though, as was Benny.

"They killed our friends," he argued.

"Not these babies," Trisha said. "No more than all us poor humans are responsible when one of our own goes off and starts a war. We can teach 'em. Show them how to be good, decent."

"Your mother would not allow these babies to be killed," Deidre said, her voice as low and menacing as I've ever heard it.

"What happens when they go out on patrol?" Jimmy asked, throwing his hands into the air.

Deidre looked up at him. The battle was won, I could see it in her face. "I can babysit them, and the others will chip in, especially if *you* ask."

Jimmy harrumphed and crossed his arms, building a wall between him and the rest of the room.

"I take that as a yes," Katie said, smiling.

"Awesome," Trisha said, standing and handing Frick back to Katie. "We'll need all kinds of supplies. Diapers, wipes, food. Oh, god. What do they eat?"

Katie laughed. "Slow down, Trisha. They eat meat, raw is preferable, apparently. We didn't try any fruits or vegetables, since we didn't have any with us."

"And they like to be sung to," I piped up. "Especially when they're going to sleep."

Katie smiled at me and I let the warmth flood through me. I loved the connection we had, the looks and knowing glances. She was something special.

Three

WHILE EVERYONE SAID THEIR GOOD-BYES, I HOBBLED INTO the kitchen and took out my cell phone. All the stuff about the babies and their mother begging me for mercy had me missing my own mother. I punched in the house number, well aware that Da may be home, but I had to take the chance. It rang a few times, then went to the machine. I clicked the phone off before it got to the beep.

"One of these days, someone is going to answer," Katie said from the doorway. "Then what are you going to do?"

I slid the phone in my pocket and shrugged. She walked over, wrapped her arms around me, and pulled me tight to her. "Might be easier to reach out to them than to carry around all this guilt."

"Probably," I said, kissing her on the cheek. "But not something I'll deal with today."

My parents would freak if they could see me now. Not the haircut, or the way I dressed. Not even the fact that I was a blacksmith. They would totally and utterly come unglued if they knew about Katie. Knew what I was.

I took a deep breath, smelling her, letting my heart settle a bit.

I didn't fit into their cookie-cutter world of a wrathful god and his intolerant flock.

Katie smiled at me, knowing full well how I was feeling. "We're almost done here," she said, stepping back.

"Good. I'm wiped out."

She kissed me quickly and dashed back into the living room. Trisha and Deidre were in full-on baby mode, and Jimmy was grumping down the hall, muttering under his breath.

"Be good, Jim," I called to him.

He turned, looked back at me, and shrugged. "Overwhelmed by women," he said.

I waved at him and zipped up my coat.

"Hey," he said, remembering something. "You may want to talk to your buddy, Bub. He took a trip out to the homestead."

That got my attention. The homestead was Anezka's place—the one where Qindra was trapped. Bub was the kobold I'd inherited from Anezka. He was a creature from the plane of fire, and he could sorta teleport. It was complicated.

He stood about four feet tall, covered in fine red scales. His ears were little nubs on either side of his face, and his nose was two slits over a cavernous mouth. Think a cross between a komodo dragon and Kermit the Frog.

He was tied to the amulet I wore around my neck. For the last thousand years or so he'd been helping the amulet's various owners, blacksmiths all, work their forges. The amulet claimed me when Anezka flipped her shit.

With the amulet came Bub.

I'm a blacksmith. It made sense. Anezka was supposed to be filling in on my education while my regular teacher, Julie, recovered from the dragon attack. Anezka had been well thought of in smithing circles. She was a bit of a recluse but knew her stuff. None of us knew that she'd gone over the edge. Well, to be fair, she was pushed.

I walked across the kitchen. "What happened?"

"Not sure," he said, seriously. "Was gone three days. Looked like he'd been starved near to death. Ate a box of roofing tiles before we could get something less expensive into him."

"Thanks," I said. "I'll ask him what's up with that."

"He's here on your word, Sarah. So far he hasn't done anything too far outside the norm, but I'm watching him."

"Good plan," I said. "I think he's an ally, but it never hurts to be cautious."

"It's just . . ." He sighed, slipping his hands into his back pockets. "I've talked to him a couple of times. I think he's lonely and homesick."

That was the Jimmy I was used to. Concerned for Bub's welfare. "Thanks, boss. I'll check on him."

"Good," he said, brightening a hair. "Don't want him moping around. Brings the whole joint down."

He gave me a little wave and headed down the hall. I scooted out of the house and let the crisp cold wash over me. I limped to the edge of the deck and called down to one of the folks on guard duty. Another newbie. Young kid in his early twenties. Didn't look as if he shaved often, or had a reason to. I'd seen better beards on goats.

Seemed Bub was hanging out in the old barn—the one the dragon burned. Had a place built up in the wreckage. I made my way over in that direction and called out to him.

I had to call three times before he poked his scaly head out of the ruins.

"Hey," I said, shaking my head. "They make you live out here?"

He clambered up some charred boards and squatted down, practically eye level with me. "No, I just prefer it when I want to think. I've missed you," he said quietly. "How was the hunt?"

"Not good," I explained. He was sympathetic. By the time I'd relayed the whole story, he was nodding and craning his head around to the house.

"Babies?" he asked. "Troll babies?"

"Yes . . . is there a problem?"

He waved his clawed hands between us. "No problem, just thought it would be cool to have some others to . . ." He trailed off.

"Someone to play with?" I asked, smiling.

He shrugged again, not looking at me. "It's hard to be different," he said quietly. "They tolerate me, but not even Anezka has time for me these days."

I watched him; there was something more, I was sure of it.

"I do not care for this Gunther," he said finally. "He assumes too much, takes too much of Anezka's time. She tires easily."

There it was. Jealousy after all. It was cute, the little biter was missing his best girl. "Look, I'm sure Gunther is not bothering Anezka. He's good for her. Isn't that what's most important?"

He rocked his head from side to side before answering. "Yes, she is mending and he has stopped banishing me."

"That's good, right?"

"She needs to be working," he said at last. "Needs to bend steel, bank fire, twist the bones of the earth, and create something new and beautiful." There was passion in his eyes then; flames licked along his shoulders and scalp. "She's a maker. She needs to create something to be fulfilled."

I reached up and patted him on the foot that had not yet erupted with flickering yellow flames. "Buck up, big guy. I think I have a cure for what ails you."

He looked up, his face full of expectation. "Do we return home?"

Now it was my turn to be crestfallen. I felt a lump splash into the hollow of my stomach, dread, guilt, fear . . . "No, not yet," I said, trying to sound upbeat. "Soon, I hope."

The smile on his face slipped a little, making him look like a sad Muppet.

"What if we built a forge here?" I asked. "We could work on the farm and keep Anezka safe, and all three of us could work together." I'd been thinking about it for a while now. Someplace controlled.

"Honest?" he asked, the smile beaming from him. The flames that danced along his arms flickered to a mellow blue. "I crave the forge, lament the dearth of hammers and fire."

The beam he was sitting on suddenly flashed with flame. Bright yellow and orange tongues licked upward, dancing around Bub like a cartoon fanfare.

"Careful," I said, stepping back.

"Not to worry," he said. He made a motion with his hands, and the flames rushed up him, blanketing him in a halo of fire. Then, as quick as it had appeared, it vanished.

"Nice trick," I said, smiling at him. "Gotta be careful with flame around here. Dragon fire burned this place down."

"I know," he said wistfully. "I can taste it in the beams and ash."

"About home," I asked, tentatively. "What's this I hear about you disappearing for three days?"

"I could not stand it," he began, shifting from one foot to the other on the beam. "I traveled there. It was difficult and exhausting, but there you have it."

"I bet. What happened?"

"Nothing," he said, falling into a squat once again. "There is a wall of force over everything. I could not get inside. There are dead things there," he said, his voice dropping to a whisper. "I smell the hand of that bastard, Justin."

Necromancer; ex-boyfriend of our mutual friend, Anezka; minion of the twice-dead Jean-Paul Duchamp; all around douche bag and psychopath.

"Yeah. He did something there, corrupted a ley line."

He looked up quickly, scanning the dark behind me from side to side. "Do you mean the well?"

"Sure, it could be a well. Live wire, like electricity, almost. Solid feed of magic or power, take your pick. Runs right under Anezka's house."

He dropped from his perch, landing at my feet, and stood. "That is what happened to my Anezka. His interference broke her mind," he continued, pacing around me in a wide circle. "That is the taint of it. It nearly drove me mad as well."

"You could taste it?"

He shook his head. "Not taste." He waved his right talon back at the ruined barn. "Not like here, where the essence is stirred with the lightest touch." He patted a beam and dust rose into the air. "We settled at that place on the very edge of the broken mountains because of that well. It gave us both power, let us hide from those who pursued us." He stopped, looking up as if he'd said something he shouldn't have.

"Who pursued you?" I asked, turning to keep facing him as he paced.

"It does not matter." He waved a dismissive claw. "Minions of another drake, one far younger and less powerful than those who rule here. It is a shame that you did not meet her first. I would be glad to see the world rid of that one. Spiteful and full of hate."

Okay, mental note: Anezka was hunted by another dragon—a female. And they'd fled here to Nidhogg's territory. Something to ask Anezka about later. Jimmy would want to know as well.

"Back to your little jaunt over the mountains," I said, changing gears. "You couldn't get into the house. Did you know the well was in a cavern beneath the house?"

"Yes," he said, nonplussed. "I have been there many times.

There is a cave you can get to, if you know the way. Or if you can travel as I do."

"Justin knew the way," I said. "He placed a corrupted shield in your well, spoiling the ley line, drawing the vilest spirits to that place like a beacon."

"Things had gone bad before that," he said, quietly. "Justin did many vile things there, things my Anezka did not know about."

"But she could sense them, right? She was sensitive to his dark magic."

Bub nodded, wringing his clawed hands. "Yes. As was the third who lived there for a time. The kindhearted Flora."

I knew a bit about Flora. Justin's first lover. She and Justin had moved to Chumstick to be with Anezka, lovers in a triad.

Bub stopped pacing and looked back at me. "I liked her, as did Anezka," he said. "Flora was a maker in her own right. Not one such as I would love, but she had her skills."

Wood carver, I knew. Damn excellent one at that. I'd seen the carvings she'd done at the house. Anezka said they were to protect her from the nightmares she'd been having. Neither of them realized they needed protection from Justin's dark magic.

"How'd you get back here?" I asked.

"Traveled as I could," he said with a shrug. "There are many vehicles traveling the roads. I just found my way upon one of them, or several, actually."

"If we go back, do you think you can take me to that cave?"

"No," he said. "I am sorry. It is inside the magical dome the witch maintains. I cannot go there."

Well, that was almost too good to be true. "We need to find a way in, a way to rescue Qindra."

"He will also want to find his way inside," he offered. "The necromancer will need to reconnect with the well. That is power too strong to forego."

"Good thought," I said, thinking hard. "I should have Jimmy put a guard out on the house. Let them keep an eye on the place in case Justin makes an appearance."

"If he does, I'd advise cutting him down before he knows you are there."

Good plan. "We'll see how Jimmy wants to handle it."

"He is a good man," Bub said. His confidence seemed to have returned. "He is a good leader. Firm but caring. There is much that preys on his mind, something that is keeping him distracted. I have seen it before. My first master often had that look when something vexed him."

"I'll see what he's up to," I said. "I'm gonna go back inside and mention sending a squad to keep an eye on the house."

"Will you stay the night?" he asked, looking up at me.

I stepped to him and bent a little to hug him. He was surprised at first, but the gesture was not unknown to him. After a moment, he leaned into me and rested his head against my chest. "I'm tired and hurt," I said quietly. "But I will come back and visit you, I promise."

For a long moment he said nothing, just leaned against me, breathing through his mouth, like a broken teakettle. "There are troll babies," he said into my side. "Do you think they will let me see them?"

"Sure," I said, patting him on the back. "Why don't we go in now, and I'll introduce you."

He stepped away quickly, a look of anxious joy on his face. "Truly? You do not think they will fear me?"

"They're trolls. I'm sure you'll fit right into their worldview."

He took my hand and turned to the house. I wobbled along as fast as I could, but still he practically pulled me up the stairs. Guy just needed some friends.

Four

KATIE WAS AT THE BACK DOOR, PUTTING ON HER COAT, WHEN we burst in. She gave me a look but stepped aside as Bub dragged me into the living room. I introduced him all around, even though he knew all the adults already.

He sat down in front of where the babies were lying on the floor, careful not to touch the blankets.

Trisha sat beside him, placing a hand on his shoulder and pointing out the differences between Frick and Frack. I guess the names were sticking for now. I couldn't tell them apart, but Bub seemed to be seeing all the little clues that Trisha had already discovered.

Deidre rolled her chair out into the kitchen, parked it beside me, and looked back into the living room. "He's cute when he's not so damn scary."

I gave her a hug. "He's just lonely. I'm sure he can help out around here. I think he really wants to be a part of things."

"We'll take care of that," she said, patting my hand. "We're turning into quite the menagerie."

"It's a good place to call home," I said. "Makes you feel welcome."

That made her happy. I excused myself and went down the hall, calling to Jim.

He came out of the back drying his hands on a towel. "Thought you'd gone?"

I leaned against the wall. "Wanted to talk to you about an idea we had."

He looked past me, sizing up the room, then nodded. "By we I assume you mean you and Katie?"

"Yep."

"Does it involve working for Nidhogg?"

I grinned at him. "Oh, no. This is much cooler. You remember the elves? Skella and Gletts? The mirror children?"

He nodded. "Not sure I like where this is going."

"It's a good plan, honest."

He sighed. "Do I get an actual vote here?"

"Of course."

"Fine. What's this plan?"

"Hire Skella. Let her take a squad out to the house in Chumstick to keep an eye on things. We could set up a camp across the road from the house."

He looked at me, thinking. "Interesting idea. I've been thinking how we could keep watch out there. Don't want any surprises."

"That's why I agreed to help Nidhogg, Jim. Keep things on an even keel until we can figure a way to diffuse the situation out there."

"Ask her," he said. "But we'll pay her. We're not like the dwarves she and her brother worked for."

That made me smile. "Oh, she'll love it," I said. "Hell, I'm willing to bet she'd do it for nothing, if it meant she had something interesting to do."

He rolled his eyes at me and motioned to the living room. "Run it by Deidre. She'll have to agree on the salary, but I'll work out the schedule with the squads."

"Excellent. Thanks, Jim."

He walked away, shaking his head.

I grabbed Katie and we boogied. Things were coming together. I liked that we had a plan. Now I wanted sleep and a return to my normal routine. I needed to work with horses soon.
The power of them and the grace, that's what kept me going back.
I loved their gentle hearts. Gave me something to look forward to.

Five

OF COURSE, WE GOT HOME TO A MESSAGE FROM ONE OF MY regular clients: Jude Brown. He wanted to postpone my coming out to Broken Axel and shoeing his mules until Wednesday. Something about his sister extending her stay past the weekend.

So I figured to sleep in Monday morning. And I gave it a yeoman's effort. Unfortunately, the image of the troll mother kept intruding into my dozing. That and the wound in my leg throbbing like a hammer on an anvil. I gave up, figured it was a good time to head over and see Nidhogg. She wanted a full report of what was killing the sheep, and I wanted some answers of my own.

If I had to work for a dragon to rescue someone like Qindra who'd been nothing but kind to me, I'd make good use of that time. I'm sure there were things I could learn that I'd never dreamed of. Maybe clear some of the unknown that plagued me.

Katie went off to school dressed in that way I loved so much: hair pulled back, long skirt, frilly blouse. Total kindergarten-teacher chic. I puttered around the apartment for an hour or so longer, giving the tepid sun time to really rise. I'd be taking the Ducati into Seattle, and I'd be cold, no matter what I did. Maybe I needed to buy some heated pants or something. I loved the bike, but, damn, it got cold riding in the November rain.

The guard at the gate to Nidhogg's property knew me by now

and waved me through without even having me take off the helmet. I'm not sure that's a good thing.

Zi Xiu, the head of Nidhogg's household staff, met me at the front door. For an old Norse dragon, Nidhogg sure had a lot of Asian people in her employ. I'd met Zi Xiu on my last visit. She was in her fifties and from Hong Kong originally. She'd been raised in Nidhogg's household and assumed her current position when she was in her thirties. The last matron of servants had met an untimely end at the same time Qindra's mother had passed. No one would give me any more details, but I speculated it was Nidhogg going on a rampage, just like she'd done in the spring after I'd forged Gram.

Dragons were funny creatures. Nidhogg looked like she was eighty, but was surely several thousand years old. She represented an order of dragons that wanted to keep control of us poor, misguided humans—help us maintain our upward trek to prosperity and comfort, while keeping to the shadows and not letting us know where the real power lay.

Her last broodling, Jean-Paul, had ruled the Vancouver area. I never got a clear idea of his territory. I just knew it was above the Canadian border. Nidhogg ruled the entire state of Washington, more or less. Seattle was her home base.

Jean-Paul had been a member of the ruling caste, like his momma, but he played with a second, more sinister team. He was mixed up in a different political faction: one where the dragons called for an open rule, putting the humans in their place, letting us know in no uncertain terms that we were prey.

Jean-Paul was scum. I'd killed him (twice), but Nidhogg did not begrudge me the acts. Dragons live a brutal life. Apparently they kill each other more often than they want to admit. She told me on my last visit how Frederick Sawyer had come to rule the

Portland area. Nasty business, that. Intrigue, assassination, and political favors being traded.

Sounded very Machiavellian.

Zi Xiu directed me to the great doors that lead to Nidhogg's inner sanctum—a vault of a room with a tiled floor covered strategically in rugs of assorted sizes and styles, probably from all over the world. The large fireplace set in the west wall had a fire burning merrily in its humongous depths, and the french doors to the veranda were shut tight, with the heavy curtains drawn against the cold.

Jai Li, the small cross-stitch girl, sat at Nidhogg's side again during this visit. She was a cute one, six or seven, and didn't speak. Zi Xiu had explained that the girl did not have a tongue. Total freak show around here, let me tell you. She smiled at me, this little waif child, and bent her head back to her cross-stitch. I could not tell what vision she saw as she slid the needle through the delicate white cloth, but she did not seem to need a pattern.

Nidhogg nodded by the fire, her cane propped against the wall to her right and a quilt thrown over her lap. Her gray hair lay fine against her mottled skull and her face seemed a little misshapen, like a candle too long near the fire.

Jean-Paul had been a small but stout man until he shifted to his full dragon form. That had been sleek and beautiful; eighty feet from tip to tail, with a wingspan to match. He was a sculpted killing machine—powerful and elegant.

How would Nidhogg appear when she shifted?

I bowed when I got within the proper distance (as Zi Xiu had taught me) and waited. One did not wake Nidhogg. One waited for her to rouse herself and notice one's presence.

That lasted about thirty-eight seconds. I'd been on the bike, in the cold rain, and my jeans were a little too tight for this kneeling on the floor shtick. I held that position, trying to clear my head, but I just couldn't do it.

I coughed. The echo fell away, absorbed by the wall hangings and the crackling fire. Twice more I coughed. She did not move.

Finally, I'd had about as much of this as I could stand. I quietly slid over on my knees until I was near enough to the fireplace; then I swung my leg out and kicked over the cane with its thickly carved metal cap.

It slid sideways before it hit the floor, and everyone in the room froze, staring at me. It was a millisecond, maybe less, but when the cane clattered to the tile in front of the hearth, it sounded like the Seventh Cavalry coming over the horizon.

Jai Li looked green around the gills, and the boy near the veranda doors covered his head with his arms.

Nidhogg took a long, shuddering breath, raised her head, and opened her eyes.

"I smelled you, you know," she said, her voice like a silken ribbon.

I blinked rapidly.

"You have no patience, no understanding of your place."

"Yes, well . . ."

She continued with a wave of her hand. "You are quite unlike any who have served me in many a year." She chuckled dryly, covering her mouth with one gnarled hand. "The rest are so afraid; they cringe if I as much as break wind."

I barked out a laugh. Juvenile, I know, but the image of Nidhogg ripping one in front of this crowd was damn funny.

She smiled at me and clapped her hands. Two young women appeared from behind a long curtain to my left. One strode quickly to retrieve the fallen cane, the other offered her arm to Nidhogg, who took it and stood.

Once her cane was grasped firmly in her left hand, she waved at me to rise, then reached out to hold my arm as she strode across the great hall.

As I looked back, the servants had a look of awe and horror on their faces. Way to rock their world, Sarah. I tried really hard not to grin.

"You remind me of another I knew in the long dust of time," she said as we exited the great hall and turned down the long corridor to the right. "There was this boy who teased me when I was very young." She glanced up at me at a noise I made and smiled. "I was young once, even in this broken world."

We reached a large wooden door and a footman peeled himself away from his post where the hallways crossed and opened the door.

Inside was the largest library I've ever seen in my life. It was larger than the great hall where Nidhogg spent most of her days.

"Wow," I said quietly. I couldn't help but crane my neck around as we crossed the threshold. The bookshelves rose in three great stacks, tiered upward, wrapping the room in paper and leather.

You could fit the entirety of the Seattle Public Library and the Bellevue Public Library inside this room and still squeeze out room for the Seattle Storm to play an exhibition game.

"You approve?" she asked me.

I looked down. She obviously wanted to go farther into the room but had stopped when I found myself frozen in wonder.

"I'm sorry," I said, stepping toward a row of couches near the far side of the room. They were set to allow ample angle for conversation and still face the great fireplace at the end of the room.

The fire there was already burning. How much wood did this place go through? That was no gas fireplace.

She sat us on either side of a small table and clapped her hands again, calling out, "Tea."

Soon, several young women were placing a tea setting and

plates of cookies and pastries on the table in front of us. They poured for each of us, then faded back into the shadows.

Nidhogg picked up her teacup and sipped the steaming liquid. I took up my cup and blew on it, afraid for the heat.

"You have news for me," she said, matter-of-factly. "You have solved the problem plaguing my thralls near Wallace Falls?"

"Yes, ma'am," I replied, feeling like I was speaking with my mother about homework. "It was a troll."

"Troll?" she asked. "Here?"

I nodded. "She had fled the battle where Jean-Paul . . ." I froze. Last thing I wanted to do was piss her off by reminding her I'd killed one of her kids.

"He was a toad," she said, setting her cup gently back on the saucer on her lap. "So, this troll was marauding through my lands, injuring my thralls, impacting my commerce?"

"Um, sure."

"And you dispatched this creature?"

A lump rose in my throat as I thought back to the troll falling to her knees, whispering the word "mercy" while her lifeblood flowed into the snow. "Yes," I agreed.

"That is settled then." She reached over and took a fruit cookie from a tiny plate near her. "What are you doing about rescuing my Qindra?"

I took a deep breath. "She remains in Chumstick, holding a barrier over the breach of the ley line that runs through the area. Nothing has changed."

She studied me over her teacup, her ancient gray eyes peering into me. I kept my gaze level, even. She'd know if I lied, could read the intent in my words. I had no fear of her, but I respected her.

"She is strong," she said finally. "You will bring her back to me soon. I have dreamed this."

Dreams scared the hell out of me lately. They were portents, visions of things to come or things that had been. Not all dreams, but when they crossed that line into premonition, it was like trying to hold on to a two-twenty line with lightning shooting out of your toes.

For the next hour, Nidhogg told me of her youth. Of the godling, Loki, who tormented her, teased her with his antics and brazen arrogance.

"One night, as snow fell through the branches of Yggdrasil, he came to me, whispered into my dreams that the gods were jealous of my beautiful scales. How Freya wanted to have a mirror made of my great eyes and how Thor sought to make a suit of armor from my hide.

"For three nights he came to me, each time dripping his poison into my ears. Each morning, when I would wake, Ratatöskr the squirrel would scamper down to bid me warning from the great hawk, Veðrfölnir, who sat upon the great eagle at the top of the World Tree.

"'Loki poisons you against the gods,' Ratatöskr said to me each morning. 'Veðrfölnir sees him with his keen vision, fleeing your nest among the roots. I have heard the trickster myself,' he told me.

"But I was young and vain. I feared the gods, and Loki the first among them. They were spiteful and mean creatures, bent on self-aggrandizing and debauchery."

She looked at me, as if I was going to contest her account. "Sounds creepy," I offered.

A smile touched her creased face and she nodded. "Yes, creepy, as you say, does cover it most vividly. Alas, I hatched my plans from there, cast my words out through the World Tree to my offspring. We waited until Loki tricked the mighty Thor to lay aside his hammer, Mjelinor, and we struck at them, singly and en masse at the end. Freya fell first, under my claws. The rest I left to my brood. I had grown jealous of Freya's beauty and fearful that she sought to steal my own for her vanity."

As the tale wove on, we finished two pots of tea and most of the cakes.

"I have not spoken of such in a very long time," she said with a sigh. "It feels good to unburden myself of these memories that haunt my nightmares."

"Perhaps," I offered, feeling daring and brave beyond my measure, "just a thought, but perhaps you regret the way of things?"

She cocked her head at me, stroking the side of her face as she watched me. "Regret?" she finally croaked. "And more. The wheel no longer turns, the axle is askew. That is what the mad wanderer tells me in my dreams."

I caught my breath. Even Nidhogg was plagued by dreams from Odin. "Is there any chance to fix things?" I asked.

She shook her head, sadly. "It is too late," she said. "Too much blood, too many sacrifices. We live in a world of our making, and we will rule it with justice and right."

It was like talking to that old man in the *Indiana Jones* movie, the one who protected the Holy Grail for centuries. There was no other path, no other options. This is what I was meant to do and what we always did.

It was sad and pathetic.

The world was a mess. How could we not fix it? Was there no hope?

"I thank you for the story," I said, standing. "But I need to return home."

She nodded and waved a hand again. "I will see you out."

The servants who were coming forward to escort me out froze, confused. This just was not done.

We exited the great library and walked back toward the front of the house.

As we neared the front doors, Nidhogg paused by a side corridor. It was smaller than the rest and ended in a plain, white door. Small items lay along the floor in front of the door—trinkets and toys, hand-drawn pictures and needlework.

"The children," she said, waving back toward the house. "They come here, try to sneak into her room." She looked at me, sadness in her ancient eyes. "Qindra's suite."

I nodded, understanding.

"They love her, the wee ones. The older ones, too, I guess," she said with a shrug. "But this is a room fraught with dangers and magic. They will injure themselves, interfere in things they cannot begin to understand."

I'd seen Qindra in action. I could easily believe her room would be filled with things that went boom, in the magical sense.

"I understand," I said, grinding my teeth. "Rescue Qindra faster."

Nidhogg chuckled and shook her head. "You will find the way, I have told you. It is foretold. I have no worries now that I have seen your true self, young blacksmith. If anyone alive can bring her home to me, it is you. But that is not what I mean."

She walked down the short hall and, using her cane, pushed a cross-stitch that lay propped against the door. I knelt and picked it up. It was a beautiful portrait of Qindra.

"Jai Li misses her the most, I fear," Nidhogg said, her voice husky. "Since . . ." She did not finish her thought.

Jai Li, the mute girl who sat at Nidhogg's side, working her needle and thread from morning to night. She'd captured Qindra perfectly.

"I want you to build me a gate," she said, finally. "Something befitting my home that will keep the children from this hall. Protect them from hurting themselves."

I stepped back, gauged the hallway, noting the thick wooden beams across the ceiling and the tiled floor. "And a lock, I presume?"

"Yes," Nidhogg said, smiling. "With two keys. One for me to wear near my heart, to keep her safe. The other for you to keep, to remind you of your obligation."

"A gate. Sure. I can do that."

Nidhogg patted me on the arm. "Go home to your lover, young one. She misses you."

I watched her turn and walk away. Emotions warred in me, fear, sadness, and frustration. I hated that she knew about Katie, likely from Qindra. Made me feel vulnerable. But on the other hand, she feared for the children. That spoke of some level of compassion.

What a complicated creature, this dragon. Nothing like her spoiled, broken child, Jean Paul, had been. And what of Frederick Sawyer? His public persona was one of philanthropy and benevolence. But I knew he was a dragon, through and through. How horrible could he get? I didn't think I wanted to find out.

I took my gear from a nearby servant and pushed back into the tepid light of early afternoon. I had to tell Katie everything.

Six

I SWUNG BY MONKEY SHINES—MY FAVORITEST COFFEE SHOP, ever—before heading back to Kent. I wanted to organize some of my thoughts about the gate Nidhogg asked for and do a little research on the intertubes before Katie got home. Mondays were her long day, so it was all good.

It made me sorta sad, driving by the ruins of the smithy where I used to work with Julie, my blacksmith master. I loved that place. But the damn dragon, Jean-Paul, burned it down along with Julie's home. I felt it was a victory to come back here, thumb my nose at the ruins that couldn't be recovered until the dragon taint had been leached from the land. Two years, we figured, as the fireweed grew wild. Then the elves assured us we could reclaim the land. Until then, it remained a condemned property that reminded me of what we all had lost.

If it wasn't for Monkey Shines, I may have given up hope. I was welcomed in that eclectic coffee shop, a native—family. It made me happy to walk through the doors.

The hot, inked, and pierced barista, Camille, was working, which meant I'd get a cool design in the foam of my coffee. Katie and I both joked that Camille was too much for either of us to handle but that she'd make someone deliriously happy someday. I thought it was the tattoos and wild, technicolor hair she favored, but Katie assured me it was the miniskirts and boots. I could see the appeal.

Camille had been working at Monkey Shines since long before the dragon came, and I'd seen her nearly every day that I worked for Julie.

She winked at me when I walked in. The kids in front of me were eastside punks, momma's boys and trust-fund babies by the look of 'em. They wouldn't tip her. Their kind never did. I always made sure to drop a buck or two in the tip jar. Good karma.

"Usual?" Camille asked, when the angst-ridden children shuffled to the exit with their six-buck coffees.

"Yeah, you got any crullers?"

She smiled and took the last two out of the case, putting them on a little plate before taking my twenty.

"What's new in your world?" she asked, handing me back my change.

I dropped the loose coins and a single into the tip jar while she went over to make my mocha. Gail was working the drive-thru, but the place had hit a lull. Not time for the after-work crowd yet.

I rambled on about the goings-on in the blacksmithing world. She asked about Katie, and we generally exchanged small talk. It was our relationship. She was my dealer. I came to her for caffeine and sugar, and in exchange I let her into parts of my world. It was comfortable.

I grabbed my liquid addiction and went to the back, parked my ass in a great overstuffed chair, and put my feet up on the table. I'd give the coffee a little bit to work its way into my bloodstream before I pulled out the laptop. I took the first sip, let the chocolate and strong coffee roll across my tongue, and gave a wavering sigh. It was nearly as good as sex.

Once I felt the buzz kick in, I pulled out my laptop and began making notes. This had to be the best damn gate ever built.

After an hour, I got up to go pee. Camille was out wiping down tables and offered to keep an eye on my gear. When I got back I decided to do a little research along another line.

When I first met Frederick Sawyer, the dragon from Portland, I'd sat in this very seat and researched him. He was more of a puzzle than Nidhogg. While she sat in her house like a giant spider, pulling her stings, capturing her flies, Frederick was out among the people.

At any time I could find pictures of him at some social soiree or fund-raiser. He'd just recently been given an award for his work with homeless kids.

What was creepy, I knew he'd killed a ton of people—eaten some of them by his own admission. The three dragons I'd met were so different I had no clear idea how to correlate a search. I knew other dragons existed. I just needed to find out where.

I knew from the dwarves that there were dragons in Memphis and Dublin. Maybe I'd start there. How hard could it be to find someone with a lot of power and money?

I flagged Camille down for another mug of coffee. I felt another project emerging.

Seven

Frederick Sawyer breathed deeply, inhaling the intoxicating scent of the young woman who glided at his side. She was elegant, turning the heads of many of the gentlemen and a few of the bolder women. The opera crowd had a pecking order, and this young thing upset the balance of power among the matrons and crones.

"You look wonderful this evening," he told her.

She smiled demurely. "Flatterer."

He laughed, a mellow sound that drew smiles from those around them.

"Guilty," he said. "But you are stunning this evening."

"Thank you," she said, curtsying. "The dress, the hair. It's all a charade. Monday, I'll be back in blue jeans and a work shirt, stocking shelves at the food pantry."

"Ever the pragmatist," he said. "How lucky I was to find a discerning opera fan among the creamed corn and chickpeas."

Then it was her turn to laugh, and he drank it in. She had a beautiful laugh that would capture some young man's heart before long. One musical trill and he would fall smitten into her arms.

He loved the way the light shone on her silky black hair. While he *could* have relations with her, as was his wont, there was more value in enjoying the beauty of her. Even the way she sipped her champagne was a work of art.

She scrunched her face, wiggling her nose, as if the bubbles tickled her.

Her beauty was natural, he surmised. *Not painted on like many of the women in this room. She exuded a certain je ne sais quoi that eluded many women.*

"Isn't *Orphée* wonderful?"

"Quite lovely. I'd heard good things about this performance, and if they fulfill the promise made before intermission, the ending should be spectacular."

The matrons mingling in the vestibule grew suddenly restless, flitting about as if a hound had set upon a flock of geese.

One of the women from the box next to his own nodded at him as she passed them, her agitation palpable.

From the midst of the blue hair and fur coats, the house manager struggled to make his way forward. Once he cleared the flock of opera groupies, the manager bore intently toward Frederick.

Frederick stepped forward, automatically putting himself between the urgent fellow and his date.

"I beg your pardon," the manager said, his face red with a patina of sweat across his balding brow. "There is an urgent message for you, sir."

He held out a piece of folded paper. Frederick took it with raised brows. The man stood by, as if waiting for a response.

The note was brief. Certain assets in Seattle had recently been compromised. Mr. Philips had urgent information that needed Frederick's immediate attention.

It must be serious, he thought, *for Mr. Philips to interrupt my night at the opera.*

"A thousand pardons," he said, turning to the young woman.

"It is my bad luck to be deprived of this fine opera and your delightful company this evening."

He turned to the manager. "Please see that she enjoys the rest of the performance and arrange a taxi to see her home."

"Assuredly, sir," the man said, mopping his brow with an embroidered handkerchief.

Was he nervous? Frederick was a patron of the theater. Was the man afraid he'd offended him by interrupting his date?

"My good man," Frederick said, taking him by the arm and turning to face the girl. "I entrust this beauty into your care, just as I entrust my elusive time to the wisdom of your artistic vision."

The manager blushed and a crooked smile crossed his face. "Thank you, sir. I do hope you can return to see the performance another evening."

Frederick shrugged. "C'est la vie." He turned to the young beauty, took her empty hand, and raised it to his lips. "You will forgive me?"

She giggled as his lips brushed the back of her hand. "I'm sure I can find a way," she said.

He straightened and gave her his most winning smile. "Another night, perhaps, we can pick up where we left off?" He let a bit of his fire flow into his words. Allowed the power to brush against her like a summer breeze.

"Perhaps," she said, blushing. "I would hate to think I wasted this dress."

"You are by far the most beautiful creature here this evening," he said, his tone serious, his eyes filled with flame.

She gasped, but the smile did not leave her lips. He leaned in, kissed her lightly on the cheek, and turned to the door.

He would carry her scent the rest of the evening.

Once he cleared the crowd, he called his driver to have the car brought around front. Then he checked his phone. A message from Mr. Philips. "Number one," he said, and the phone began to ring.

"It was a ritual murder," Mr. Philips said.

"Do you believe it is a message from her?" Frederick asked.

"Nay, it was not she who must be obeyed. It was one of Jean-Paul's surviving lackeys. There was no attempt to hide the evidence. It is as if he wanted you to know his identity."

"I see," Frederick answered, walking toward the car.

Jean-Paul had been such an unfortunate blight on his kind. There was no excuse for his level of depravity. It served the wretch right to be cut down by one of the humans. Of course, the precedent *that* set had unknown consequences. He shook his head. Not many dared to raise a hand against the *Draconis Imperi*. The great council had not been convened in over a hundred years. Would this Beauhall woman cause the members of the august body to slither from their dens?

And what of the rabble, the self-styled Reavers who wished to eschew centuries of quiet control and rule openly? Jean-Paul had been rumored to have dealings with those wild ones. Were his remaining minions lashing out, rudderless, or were they in league with these pitiful excuses for dragonkind?

The chauffeur stood with the door open, allowing Frederick to slide across the expensive leather before closing the door. "I will be in the office as soon as possible."

"My apologies on the opera," Mr. Philips offered. "I know how much you hate to leave things unfinished."

"Not to worry. I will see it again." *And the girl*, he thought to himself. He would definitely see her again.

"Shall I try the witch?" Mr. Philips asked. "She has not returned the last several calls we have made. This is not a tactic we are used to from her."

"No," Frederick said. "I'll make the attempt. It will be better, if she answers."

"As you wish, sir."

He hung up the phone and called a number he'd had memorized for years. "Where are you, my dear Qindra? Why do you no longer take my calls?"

Eight

WEDNESDAY WAS RUNNING INTO LATE AFTERNOON BY THE time I made it out to Broken Axel Farm. Jude Brown only had a couple of mules he used to plow with and didn't see a need to do much more. He was a kindly old man, retired from Boeing while I was still in elementary school. He loved working the earth, and this way he didn't have to answer to anyone's deadlines but his own.

This was my third stop of the day and the last. The air was crisp and clear, which meant cold in the Pacific Northwest.

The mules stood steaming in the paddock. I was writing out the day's receipt while Mr. Brown rambled on about everything from the weather to local crime.

"Damn shame, I was telling Buster over at the Grange," he said. "Never knew why anyone would want to go killing young girls like that."

I stopped writing and looked up. "Who's been killed?"

He laughed. "You young folk don't pay attention enough. I was telling you how somebody killed a couple of party-time girls up in Vancouver and a barista from over in Redmond. Young girls, all of 'em. Damn shame."

I finished the invoice and handed it to him. "Serial killer, you figure?"

Jude Brown nodded once and spat onto the ground by his pickup truck. "Real hoodoo, there. Nancy, up at Pete's Alehouse, said she had a sister that lived in Surrey. She claimed the girls were strippers, ran with a bad crowd. But the girl from Redmond was going to college, had a boyfriend, was making her own way."

I blew into my hands, my breath steaming. The cold still hurt my right hand from where I'd gotten so burned by the dragon fire. It felt like there were bands of steel biting into the hand when I held the tongs or picked up something.

"After the mess down at Green River, I'd have hoped we were through with all that nonsense," he said, taking out his checkbook.

"Did they say where the barista worked?" I asked while he wrote out the check.

"Got something about it in my truck. Hang on." He handed me the check and walked around to the passenger side, pulled out a newspaper, and walked back. "Some place called the Monkey Shines."

I gasped like someone had punched me. I took the paper from him, and he leaned over, pointing out the small article.

Camille Preston, 22, was found murdered in her apartment on Tuesday. Her parents were not available for comment. Redmond police are not releasing much information, but the young woman's boyfriend claims it was a ritual murder.

"It was awful," he said, his eyes red from crying. "She lay in the middle of a double circle with all kinds of markings around the edge. The candles around the circle were still burning and she was warm." He paused, coughing. "They cut out her heart. I don't know if I'll ever sleep again. They took her eyes," he said before breaking down and crying again.

The coroner has not released a report at this time.

"Jesus," I breathed, handing Mr. Brown back his paper. "I knew her."

"Is that right," Jude Brown said. "I'm sorry to be the one to bring you such bad news then."

"I bought coffee from there almost every day," I said. Dear god. She was cute, made it a point of remembering the regulars. Once she gave me an extra cruller when I was having a bad day.

I sat on the bumper of the pickup truck and massaged my right hand. Across the field, two crows landed and began berating the mules, who just turned away.

"Life is a bitch," he said. "Ain't no two ways about it."

"You got that right," I said, standing. I walked over to the fence, leaned on the rail, and watched the two crows squawking and prancing along the opposite rail.

I bet it was the necromancer, Justin. He was a flunky of the dead dragon, Jean-Paul.

Why murder Camille? And who were the girls in Vancouver?

"Cold coming," Mr. Brown said. "Almanac says we're going to have a bad winter."

I could feel it down in my bones. Bad winter was right. But I'm not too sure how much of it was the weather. I needed to start tracking Justin down, stop him from killing again. I just knew it was him.

The crows watched me, cocking their heads from side to side.

"My old granddad used to say when you saw two crows like that, make sure you aren't saying anything against the gods. They report back to them, you know." He laughed as he said it, but the crows were silent, staring at me.

"Yes," I said, keeping them in my sight. "I'm sure if Odin or one of the elder gods wanted to hear what I was thinking, they'd show up and ask."

Jude Brown guffawed at that and trundled back to his house.

The crows lit into the sky, squawking and swearing in their crow language.

"Where is he?" I asked them as they flew off. "Where does the old man hide these days?"

Nine

KATIE MET ME IN TOWN FOR DINNER. I NEEDED TO STOP AT the Doc Martens store and replace my boots, finally. Hitting three farms in one day made for a lucrative paycheck, and, with no one to split it with, I felt like I could splurge on new boots.

They're not like a new car, but they are damn expensive. And, man, I missed my Docs. Hell, I should figure out a way to have Bub pay for them, the pisher. Seeing how the last pair was ruined by his teeth. Of course, I did step on his head and banish him to the hidey place where he goes when he gets killed.

He always comes back, though. And I'd grown to like the biter.

We got bento, which Katie loved, and I drank a couple hits of saki. Rice wine was not as good as beer, but it was a treat—a sometimes food, as my ma would say.

I explained about the killings and how Mr. Brown thought they were related to the killings in Vancouver.

"You might want to check with Rolph," she suggested. "Ask him if he can get any information on the two girls killed up there. See if they had their hearts and eyes taken out as well."

Rolph was my dwarf friend who lived in Surrey. "Yeah, good idea," I agreed. "But that's three young women in the last week, week and a half. Shouldn't the FBI or someone be investigating this?"

"This isn't television," Katie said, smiling. "I'm sure they'll investigate it locally."

"Creeps me out," I said, polishing off my steamed green beans. "Like someone walked across my grave or something."

Katie watched me closely, seeing if I'd freak out, I suppose.

I'd been living with Katie for the better part of the month. Most of my stuff was still at my apartment, but I was basically letting Julie, my old blacksmith master, take over my lease. Didn't bother to tell the landlord, but what they don't know, etcetera.

"We should discuss this with Jimmy," she said. "He called me, by the way. He, Stuart, and Gunther have broken some code that my father left him."

I watched her for anger when she said those words. She was pretty bent at Jim for holding back on information, especially when it came to their parents.

"They have this ring mentioned in the code and they think it's a key to something. Well, Stuart thinks it's a key. Gunther thinks it's something that we are supposed to protect."

"What's Jimmy think?"

She smiled, scooping up a tuna roll with her chopsticks and dunking it in a small dish of soy and wasabi. "He tried it on."

"Holy crap. Anything happen?"

"Nope. Gunther thinks it's girl magic. They want you and me to stop by, look at the ring. See if we spot anything they're missing."

"Girl magic? Seriously?" I shook my head.

"Well, he didn't put it exactly that way, but something in the coded message made him believe the ring was made for a woman. Something about sympathetic vibrations."

So, we wrapped up dinner and trundled down the block to the Doc Martens store. For the longest time, the only Doc Martens storefront in the United States was in Portland, and I'm not likely to go to Portland, voluntarily, ever again. Just because I killed the dragon in Vancouver does not mean I want to mess with the one in Portland. And I'm pretty sure he can smell me.

The guy who found the boots I wanted in my size was stunning. Even Katie thought he was a hottie. We chatted a bit, and he told us he was from Redondo Beach down in LA. He'd only come up here because of his girlfriend, and she'd dumped him.

Seattle is a happening town. He should have no trouble finding someone else, especially with shoulders like a linebacker and wavy, blond hair halfway down to his ass. And, he was funny, too.

We were out on the sidewalk when I realized I wanted a second pair of shoestrings for the boots. I'm hell on footwear, and I didn't want to come back right away. As I was fishing out some gaudy colors, pink, turquoise, and purple, I heard our boy in the back, singing along with the radio. Anna Nalick isn't my cup of meat, but the man had a damn fine voice.

Ten

TRISHA PULLED INTO THE STRIP MALL OVER IN LYNNWOOD and looked into the mirror, frowning. Her hair was too short and the scars too vivid for her to be comfortable. Deidre had told her she looked just fine, but she could feel the way the scars crossed her body. How the swords of the trolls had cut her in half a year ago and how she felt like a scarecrow.

She took a deep, shuddering breath and opened the car door. Once she'd gotten out of the hospital, she'd moved to Black Briar and hadn't left. This was the first time she'd as much as stepped off the property, but she needed a break. All the drilling with her squad and the babies and all the tension with the higher-ups since Katie had bailed on the crew had her exhausted, on edge.

Deidre was the one who suggested she go into town, buy a few things for Frick and Frack, maybe pick up something for herself. She was on salary at the farm, so she had money. What she didn't have much of was nerve.

Frick and Frack were not petite children, so she worked her way through the used baby gear store, scoring a bunch of clothes and some toys she hoped they would love.

Once she had the loot in her car, she noticed the big bookstore across the street. They had a coffee shop, the sign said, a bakery, and miles and miles of books.

She hadn't read a book in a long time. Maybe she needed something to distract her when the kids were sleeping. Something to wile away the long hours of darkness.

She crossed the parking lot, dodged the few slow-moving cars on the road, and jogged into the bookstore.

First thing she did was get a giant hot chocolate and a slice of cheesecake. They were heavenly. She sat at a table near the back of the coffee shop, flipped through a magazine someone had left on the table, and indulged in dairy, chocolate, and sugar overload.

Across the shop, where the bookstore opened up, she noticed a gorgeous Latino guy in a nice suit browsing the magazine racks. Once she thought he was looking at her, but she dismissed it right away.

Unless he was wondering why a freak like her had bothered to go out into public. More likely she was imagining it.

She finished her treats and walked in among the books. First, she browsed the baby section, but the three pregnant couples there just pissed her off. They were such sheeple, chattering their magpie bullshit while killing machines like sixteen foot giants roamed the streets, invaded farms, killed lovers.

She walked past the baby section, head down. She could feel the heat rising as the anger flashed through her. Her stomach started to feel heavy, like the hot chocolate was turning or something. She paused in the history section to catch her breath, calm her nerves. None of these people was staring at her, none of them.

She turned around and saw the hot guy from earlier looking at her, smiling. The smile reached her lips before she could stop it, but it was quickly followed by dread. She ducked her head again, dodged up two rows, and watched as the man started walking up the main aisle toward the front. He'd walk right by her.

Her heart raced and she panicked. Without thinking, she took the first book within reach off the shelf and stuck her nose in it, not even paying attention to the pictures inside.

The man, tall, handsome, and a little scary, was too much for her to contemplate. Three long, drawn-out breaths later, she felt her heart beginning to slow. There was no way he was really smiling at her. He was so good-looking. His smile, she decided. That's what it was. She could see falling for a smile like that.

"That book is quite advanced," a smooth, male voice interrupted her reverie.

Trisha looked up, saw it was the hot guy, and looked down, seeing the book she was holding for the first time. The cover showed two women, tied together with intricate knot work and thin ropes. They were both nude. The title was *Kinbaku*. She glanced around, her heart in her throat, only to realize she was in the human sexuality section.

"It is an acquired taste," he said, smiling at her. "It's so rare to meet someone with such discerning appetites."

She looked down, embarrassed. "I really don't know anything about it."

"I'd love to discuss it. Over coffee, perhaps?"

Trisha felt the heat rush across her chest and up her neck. Who the hell was this guy? "I don't know," she mumbled.

His smile faltered slightly. "I'm sorry. I was being too forward. My apologies. I'm not good at this." He held his hands up and stepped back. "I must sound like a total jerk."

She looked up at him. He looked cute, backpedaling like that.

"It's okay," she said, feeling brazen. "Maybe we can just sit and talk."

"If you're sure," he said, his smile returning. "My name is Efrain. It is very nice to meet you."

Eleven

AFTER WORK ON THURSDAY, KATIE AND I SAT AT THE KITCHEN table with Jimmy and Deidre, while Stuart and Gunther hovered over the room divider. Jimmy had been working for a while now on some code his father had left him. Gunther and Stuart had been helping. Deidre said it was like a constant playdate with three cranky toddlers. They bickered and fussed, but in the end they cracked it—well, most of it.

Jimmy showed us his father's scroll, explaining how it had been stashed inside a clay statue of a Valkyrie.

I got a shiver when he said it. There was a Valkyrie I'd met who made me forget my own name for a minute. I glanced over at Katie guiltily, but she was too busy examining the ring Jim had put on the table.

The ring was fairly plain, as far as the metalwork went. Looked like silver but showed no sign of tarnish. I didn't touch it and neither did Katie.

I looked at her and took a deep breath. "Okay, before we touch this thing, I want to hear everything."

Jimmy rubbed his eyes and leaned back in his chair. He was tired, I could see it in the set of his shoulders. Gunther and Stuart didn't look any better. They'd been working this thing around their regular lives, and it seemed like sleep was the loser.

"Dad knew some of the history of the ring," Jimmy said, keeping his left hand over his eyes. His right lay on the table, and Deidre covered it with hers.

"It's old, that much we know. And there's magic to it, though none of us can really tell what it is."

Katie just watched him, her mouth set in a line.

"Dad knew the ring was recovered from a burial mound in Germany just before World War Two. A guy named Urho Vänskä documented several Nazi attempts to capture magical artifacts. Dad didn't mention if this Urho was a member of any of the shadow organizations known to dabble in this type of stuff."

Gunther grunted. "There are so many sects and cults out there, it's hard to know who belongs to which ones. It's not unreasonable for someone of Vänskä's reputation to be a member of several organizations."

"We know he was not above grave robbing and murder," Stuart chimed in. "Real stand-up individual."

I watched them. They'd been sharing information like this for a long time, since Katie's folks disappeared. Well, Gunther had been raised in a monastery for a chunk of his life and had some tie to an order who knew of such things. I was fuzzy on the details.

Stuart had discovered the real world before he met Gunther in elementary school. That's one of the reasons they became fast friends. His story was not clear either, but he had no love for the dragons. That much was sure.

Jimmy cleared his throat. "Anyway. There are rumors the Nazis intercepted the courier bringing the ring out of the country. They hunted several known organizations to extinction in their desperate search for mystical powers. Hitler was a total loon about the stuff."

"Was Hitler a dragon?" I asked.

Stuart barked a laugh.

"No," Gunther said, giving Stuart a stern look. "It's not an unreasonable question. But our records indicate his rise to power was due to a vacuum caused when the local dragons managed to get themselves killed in a tit-for-tat exchange that had been going on since the assassination of the Archduke Franz Ferdinand, who very well may have been a dragon."

"Right," Jimmy continued. "Apparently the Nazis didn't know too much about the ring when they snatched it. There's no evidence we've found so far to tell us what it's about. The message says a young gypsy girl stole the ring and smuggled it out to France, where it ended up in the hands of a monastic order associated with the Knights Templar."

"How it ended up at Black Briar remains a mystery," Stuart added. "But there is more text to decipher."

Katie nodded and looked at Jim hard. She was pissed to have been left out of something once again. I looked over at Deidre, and she noticed it, too. She'd practically raised Katie. She knew the looks.

I started to reach for the ring, but Katie casually covered it with her hand. "Anything else you'd like to add, Jim?"

Jimmy didn't speak up, just held his gaze steady on Katie. There was a battle of wills there that had the potential to get ugly fast.

"Look," Stuart said from the counter. "I know you're frustrated, Katie, but we are where we are. We're coming to you for help and guidance, bringing you in. Can't you just be open to that?"

Gunther shuffled from one foot to the other with his arms crossed over his barrel chest. "We're all undergoing an enormous amount of change. We're all evolving."

Katie looked over at him. A strange look flitted across her face, but she softened a bit. "Aye," she said, with a sigh. "The world's a mess and we need to stick together." She turned slowly back to Jimmy, her eyes steely once more. "But Jim, so help me god, if you don't stop hiding stuff from me, I swear I'll fucking abandon Black Briar." She coughed, and I saw that she was crying. "I can't stand it anymore."

Whoa. What the hell was that about? I reached over and placed my hand on top of Katie's, but she didn't look at me, just kept her gaze level at Jimmy.

"That's bullshit," he huffed. "This is where you grew up. This is home."

I felt her tense under my hand. "Home is a place where you're welcome and valued. This is stuff about Mom and Dad. I miss them too, you know. They're my parents." She was tensing her hands so tightly, her arms were shaking. "You got to have them a lot longer than I did, Jim. And now you're keeping what little that's left away from me. What gives you that right?"

"Katie," Deidre began.

"No!" she shouted, leaning forward. "You are not my mother, Deidre. I love you, but this is between me and Jim." She pulled her hand away from mine and held the ring out on her palm. "This is the shit that took them from us, you know that, right?"

He didn't say anything, but I could practically see the steam rising off his face.

"They kept their secrets, and one day they just vanished." She hiccuped and took a deep breath. "You've kept things from me, Jim. Things that nearly got me killed, nearly got Sarah killed, and I can't live with that any longer."

"You're being childish," Jimmy said, leaning forward. "What the hell's the matter with you?"

The room was boiling with anger and tension. The twins were studying their feet, and Deidre was watching Jimmy's face. Her eyes sparkled with tears, but she didn't say anything, just let the two siblings square off.

Something had changed in Katie. I started noticing it right after we fought the spirits out at Anezka's place. Maybe it was my being trapped in walkabout, leaving her to face the haints alone; I didn't know. But the nightmares had started again. And she'd been doing so well. The nightmares from the kidnapping and brutalization at the hands of the dragon and the giants had begun to ease. I'd seen them fade over time. I was thinking post-traumatic stress or something. She was hiding something from me, something important, but she wasn't ready to tell me.

Not that I missed the irony here, with Jimmy and his secrecy. Seems the whole family was built in shadow.

"They told me to protect you," Jimmy said, his voice taut and his face flushed. "She made me swear."

"That wasn't fair," Katie said. "But she's gone. Now it's time for you to make a decision."

"We're bringing you in," Stuart said. "Clean slate."

"Is that true, Jimmy?" Katie asked. "Full disclosure?"

He looked down, not able to look into her eyes.

She stood, tipped her hand, and dropped the ring onto the table with a clunk. "That's what I thought." She turned on her heel and stormed across the kitchen. We all looked on in amazement when she slammed the door behind her.

The world dimmed for a minute, like the dark side had gained something here. I got up, glanced at them all, and followed her out. There was no doubt I'd choose her over them.

We didn't talk about it. Not on the ride home, not in bed, not even the next morning. She was like a statue, cold and stiff. I couldn't get inside the wall she'd put up. I knew that look, knew that defensive mechanism, seeing as I was an expert at it.

I lay in bed next to her, listening to her breathe. She hadn't cried. Hadn't done much of anything. It was like she'd gone on autopilot.

Jimmy had only been trying to do what he thought was best, struggling in a world that was a hell of a lot more complicated than any of us had imagined. And he honestly felt obligated to honor his mother's wish to keep Katie safe, no matter what.

Even if that meant losing her, it seemed.

And that's when the universe bitch slapped me again. I'd closed my eyes, drifting to sleep. My mind kept playing the scene with Katie so upset and Jimmy being his typical stoic self.

Then it wasn't Jimmy, it was my da. And it was Ma sitting next to him, crying. And it was me ranting at him, pushing him away, rejecting his attempts to protect me from the world the way he saw it.

I got out of bed and padded into the living room wrapped in a spare comforter—my mind racing. I could barely breathe for the grief and nausea.

I was having a hard time focusing my anger with them. Finding it difficult to hold that grudge. I missed them, damn it. Even Da, with all his patronizing bullshit.

I couldn't let Katie do this. Jimmy loved her, even if he was a douche sometimes. And Deidre thought she walked on water.

Black Briar was home. Safe. And now I had to choose between them and supporting Katie?

I was watching the night fade in the two windows along the front of the apartment by the time Katie stirred. I stood up, folded the comforter, and headed to the shower. No use letting her know I'd been up half the night. She had enough on her mind.

Twelve

I had Motörhead rocking the earbuds while I was browsing at the Emerald City Metal Arts Collective Friday morning. They ran a swap meet once a quarter, like a big-ass, three-day flea market for metalworkers. I liked to walk through and see what other people were doing, maybe pick up some supplies, or more likely ideas.

I needed to build that gate for Nidhogg, and I was feeling the pressure to make it something spectacular. I felt like Qindra deserved it.

Most blacksmiths make a lot of their own tools—tongs, wedges, bits, things like that. But there was always someone who wanted to just purchase the tool, not spend the time making yet another set of tongs. Unfortunately for me, most of my favorite gear was burned up when the dragon torched Julie's place. I was really interested in finding some decent hammers. One guy had a couple of decent two- and three-pound jobbies, but nothing really sang to me.

The hot dogs at the concession area were starting to call to me, and I'd just decided to spring for something smothered in kraut when my cell phone rang. It was Julie.

She was pretty damn upset, and it took a minute before I could understand what the hell was going on.

Mary Campbell, owner of the Circle Q Farm, had called her an hour ago. Someone had broken into her place and killed one of her high-steppers—Blue Thunder. He'd been a beautiful animal.

"Brutal," Julie said into the phone. "Ritual killing, and whoever did it left a message. The cops are here now."

"Holy shit," I breathed, hot dogs and kraut suddenly the last thing I wanted. "Are you with her?"

"Yes," Julie said, and I could hear some voices in the background. "Mrs. Sorenson and I came out as soon as she called. Mrs. Sorenson is making tea, and Mary is lying on the couch. I'm interfacing with the police, but I'd appreciate it if you could come out."

Her voice got quiet, and I had to strain to hear her. "I think this is a warning for you, Sarah."

I slid down the wall I'd been leaning against. My legs just suddenly didn't want me to be standing any longer. "Me?"

"No one else will get it," she said, a sense of urgency in her voice. "But I think you need to see this."

"Okay," I said, letting my legs settle out in front of me, blocking one of the aisles to the food court. "I'm in Seattle. I'll be there as soon as I can."

"Thanks," Julie said. I hadn't heard her this freaked out, ever.

I hung up and thought about who to call. Jimmy, Gunther, and that crew would have a better idea of a lot of cultlike signs and such. But I wanted to call Katie, and she wouldn't come out if Black Briar was getting involved. It was too soon for her pride.

But something had to happen. It was early, eleven thirty. Katie was at her school at the moment, working on lesson plans. She'd knock off around three thirty, and maybe Jimmy and the crew would be long gone before then.

I climbed to my feet, swung by to grab a soda. I needed the sugar and caffeine to fortify myself. Then I called Black Briar.

The phone rang several times before it was answered by Trisha. I was surprised to hear her, but she told me that Jimmy had taken Deidre to her physical therapy.

"He'll be back in a couple of hours," she said. "I'm letting Frick and Frack watch some videos. They really like the music and the motion. They're pretty damned smart."

It would be cute, if I hadn't personally murdered their mother.

"What about Gunther or Stuart?" I asked.

"Stuart's out in the barn working on some gear," she said, laughing. "I'll call him. Bub can watch the kids a minute."

I waited, amazed. Bub had made himself a part of the little bizarre family pretty damn quickly. Pride rose in me. I counted him as one of mine. My responsibility, mine to keep safe.

I'd made my way out of the hall and was heading across the parking lot to my bike when Stuart got on the line. I gave him a brief of the few facts I knew and asked him if he could gather Gunther and Jimmy and head to Mary's.

"Glad you called," he said, seriously. "This tiff between Jimmy and Katie isn't good for any of us."

I ground my teeth. This was a pain in my ass. "Look, Stuart. Jim's being an ass here, you know that, right?"

He didn't answer right away. "He's scared, Sarah. Afraid to lose her, even with everything that's gone on."

I growled, letting my frustration echo out of me. "She was kidnapped by a fucking dragon, Stuart. How much worse can it get?"

He chuckled then, not that it was funny. "Yeah, you got a point. Look, I don't like that they're fighting, but you need to let the man come around as he can. It's been hard for him keeping all this balanced, you know?"

"Yeah, I guess." I rubbed my eyes. "Look, Stuart. The thing is, I need your help, and Katie doesn't know I called you, yet. You know I gotta let her know. Gotta keep in her good books. I just need to make sure we don't miss anything important here. If this is a warning to me, I'd like to have as much input and advice as I can get."

"This is some serious shit."

"Amen, brother. Look, can you work on Jimmy to apologize? That would make it all so much easier."

The line was quiet for a moment. "Baby steps," he said, finally. "I'll do what I can. How soon will you be there?"

"I'll be there in thirty or so," I said. "Cops are still there now, so we'll see what we can see."

"Okay," he agreed. "Gunther is at his shop and it will take longer to get that crazy girl he uses to help around the record store. But I'll text Jimmy and have him and Deidre head to Circle Q from the doctor's. How's that work?"

"Beautiful," I said, pleased. "Thanks, Stuart. I like having the backup."

He harrumphed into the phone. Worried about me? "Just stay out of trouble, Beauhall."

I laughed, and he cut off the phone. He still loved me.

I picked up my helmet, shrugged into my heavy leather jacket, and took a moment to make sure my new Docs were tied tightly. I was feeling pretty bad-ass, but was wishing I had Gram on my back. I didn't like feeling threatened, especially when I couldn't pull her into play.

The bike roared between my thighs as I popped a wheelie ripping down the service road to the main drag. I'd call Katie once I got out there and had an idea what we were up against. Better that way.

Thirteen

I PULLED INTO CIRCLE Q THIRTY MINUTES LATER. THERE WERE two cruisers and a couple of normal cars. I recognized the Taurus that Julie was driving, since it was mine. I guessed the second was a detective or something.

I parked the bike, took off my helmet and gloves, and approached the police officer who stood between the road and the barn. He was fairly short, five six maybe, and thin. I bet he didn't weigh a hundred pounds soaking wet, but the gun on his hip was in a worn holster. He'd used it a long time. There were a few folks down on the road, neighbors, I reckoned, but no one was approaching the farm. The officer had an aura that demanded respect, despite his physical stature.

"I'm sorry, ma'am," he said. "This area is off-limits at the time."

"I understand, officer," I said, using my bestest, sweetest girl voice. "But, I'm the farrier for Mrs. Campbell. I was just here this week, and she called, asked me to stop by and look in on the rest of the horses, with all the excitement and all."

I smiled and even thought about batting my eyes, but the matted-down hair and black eyeliner probably didn't instill much confidence.

"I'm sorry," he said. "Crime scene—I'm sure you understand."

He had a craggy face, pocked from years of acne, but his eyes were kind. He didn't raise his voice or lean into my space or anything, but you definitely knew who was in charge here. I took a breath, ready to change tactics, when I heard tires on gravel behind me.

I turned to see a van pull up from Smythe and Williams Veterinary Medicine. I thought Mary used the Cadiz Brothers, but I could've gotten it mixed up.

The slick young man who walked up to us had a smile on his round, pale face. He had on a stocking cap with blond curls poking out from underneath, a tiny mustache, and not much of a chin. He shrugged into a white doctor's smock and carried a messenger bag. When he got up to us, he nodded to me but turned his full attention to the officer.

"Beg your pardon," he said, politely. "Sorry it took me so long to get out here. We had a foaling out in Maple Valley that took longer than we expected."

He handed the police officer a business card he took from his shirt pocket and stood with both hands on the handle of his bag, looking as contrite and demure as one could expect from a schoolboy.

The officer read the card, looked at both sides, and tucked it into his shirt pocket. "You'll be wanting to speak with Detective Carmine," he said. "Tall lady, black hair. Dressed like Columbo."

The young vet tech looked at him, puzzled, then looked at me. I shrugged. I had no idea what the hell he was talking about.

The cop shook his head, snickering. "I must be getting old. Okay, tall woman in a trench coat. She's directing things up at the barn. You can't miss her."

He stepped aside, and the vet tech took three steps before turning back. "Would it be okay if the farrier came with me? She really does work with the animals more than we do."

The officer just nodded and waved me through. I was stunned. But I wasn't looking a gift horse in the mouth. I grabbed my pack off the back of the bike and scrambled after the vet.

He held out his hand when I got to him. He had a firm shake, not aggressive, but he was definitely not a pansy. "Charlie Hague," he said, smiling. He turned and began walking to the barn.

"Sarah Beauhall," I replied, falling into step beside him.

"Yes, I know," he said. "Folks talk highly about you on the circuit."

Hmph . . . I was getting recognition. The community was too damn small.

"You need to get some business cards," he offered.

I gave him the eyebrows, but he just smirked at me. "Trust me on this one. Makes you official. Cops just need some scrap of authenticity to hold on to."

It made sense. Da called it the clipboard theory. Walk around with a clipboard, everyone assumed you were in charge. "I'll take it under advisement."

The sun was bright and the sky a startling blue that we only get here in the Pacific Northwest. We neared the barn and Charlie slowed down, delaying our arrival.

"What do you know?" he asked me as we walked the long drive.

"Just that someone killed one of her high-steppers. Not sure which one."

He twisted his mouth back and forth, thinking. "I don't know them, personally. I've not visited this farm more than the one time Mr. Smythe brought me out to introduce me around."

"How long have you been with Smythe and Williams?"

He grinned. "About a year. Got my degree from Washington State and did some time in the stockyards in Pullman. You wouldn't believe the amount of experience you can get in a stockyard. I saw more cases in the one month there than I've seen the entire year I've been here."

"Quiet life?" I asked, amused.

"Well, vaccinations and an occasional abscess is fine with me," he said, glancing around. "I just hate being low man."

"Why's that?"

We stopped by the barn, not going in. "Newbie does the lion share of necropsies. Messy work and great experience."

"Lovely."

"Yeah," he said, digging into his kit for a couple of face masks. "Put this on, helps with the smell."

I took it from him and held it up to my face. It smelled like anise, not cloying, but fairly strong.

"Never get used to the smell," he said, hooking the mask over his ears. "Ready?"

I pulled the mask on and followed him into the barn.

It was horrible. I leaned against the stall door, trying to breathe.

"Take it easy," he said, grasping my arm. "Try not to breathe too fast. You'll hyperventilate."

I tried to slow my breathing, but I needed the oxygen and taking deep breaths just filled my head with the stench.

Not only did they kill the horse, whoever did this was a sick bastard. The body had been dismembered. I looked around the stall. It was like something from a bad Santeria movie. There was a ritual circle drawn on the floor with salt and wax. A five-pointed star cut through the circle, and bowls were placed at the lower four points. Flies were thick around the bowls, which told me that they held blood. At the pinnacle of the star was the horse's head.

Charlie stepped aside to talk with the detective, and I walked down the length of the stalls. The horse had been dismembered in the third stall down, and most of the body remained there.

The feet were missing, hacked off with a special blade. I was positive, because it was sticking in the floor of the stall next to a series of marks. I didn't touch it. The thing practically glowed it was so vile. Magic for sure. It was a serpentine blade used in rituals. I knew my blades. I also knew not to touch something that putrid. It screamed bleeder. Something that would keep the blood from clotting while the ritual was being performed. I'd read about them. Allowed for the maximum bloodletting. I'd always assumed they were rumor, but now . . . This had to be the real deal.

Across the back of the murder stall, words were written. "I'm looking for you, little pig."

I walked back to the first stall, where the head remained, and knelt down, keeping a good distance from the ritual site. The horse's eyes were missing. Instead, candles had been inserted into the sockets and burned down to waxy nubs.

In the center of the macabre design was a small box. No one had touched it yet, but one of the detectives was taking pictures of it.

There was magic here. I held my hand out, careful not to touch anything, but allowed it to hover just inside the stall.

I could feel it, a residual taint in the air. Like when I held the honeyed blood mead Qindra had shown me. Holding the vial had allowed me to experience the electric buzz of the power.

I wish she was here for this. I had no doubt she could throw some squiggles in the air and tell me a hundred times more than I could figure out.

The detectives had been here awhile. There were chalk marks in several areas, where the camera guy demarcated sections of the scene. The uniformed officers stayed outside. I couldn't blame them.

My cell phone rang. I stood, brushed the straw and dust from

my hands, and walked out of the barn. Charlie was talking with
Detective Carmine, so I walked around the other side of the barn.
It was Gunther.

"Heather just got here," he said. There was city noise in the
background, so I could tell he was walking to his bike.

"Stuart is driving out now. I asked Trisha to keep an eye on
Anezka, but I asked him to bring Bub."

"Interesting choice," I said, keeping an eye on Charlie and the
detective. "Why, pray tell?"

"I have certain prejudices," he said with a chuckle. "But I see
he wants what's best for Anezka, and lately I've discovered he
wants what's best for you as well."

That was sweet. "Besides," he continued. "He has a nose for
magic and wards and such. He may see or smell something we
miss."

"Okay, then. Cops are just wrapping up and the vet tech is
here. I guess he'll be here a while longer."

"We should wait until he leaves, I think. How about we all
meet up someplace near there and you call me when he leaves."

I nodded. "Good plan. I'll be in touch."

Charlie was done with the detective and was heading back
into the barn with a camera around his neck and his messenger
bag over his shoulder. I jogged over to catch up with him, but he
stopped short and we kind of collided. He didn't drop anything,
but I juggled my phone. It hit the hard packed earth, bounced
over his feet, and landed just to his right.

"I'll get it," he said, bending over. Once he had my phone in
his hands, he rubbed the readout with his thumb, to brush aside
the dirt, then looked over at me. "Nice phone," he said, grinning. "Seriously nineteen nineties. Do you also have a Walkman
at home?"

"Funny man," I said, holding out my hand.

He placed the phone in my open palm and grinned. I closed my fingers around the blocky, silver phone and looked down. For a moment, I got a clear view of a tattoo on the inside of his wrist, but he pulled away, like he didn't want me noticing.

"I should check on the rest of the horses," I said, avoiding looking at his arm.

"Good plan," he said, lifting the camera off his chest. "I'll get some more pictures of the remains."

The rest of the horses were overwrought. I counted six in the barn, but I knew there were two other barns. The paddock was empty and the gate closed. The horses were stomping and prancing around, their eyes wild with fear. They'd hurt themselves if they hadn't already.

One at a time, I opened a stall door and took a shaking and rearing horse by the lead rope. They didn't want to be touched, wanted to run wild, escape the smell of blood and the memories of what had happened in their safe place.

I got them all out to the paddock and shut the barn door. There was water in the trough, and I'd grab some hay to put down. Eating would calm them.

By the time I had the horses settled, the cops were wrapping up. I hopped the fence and made my way toward the house. Julie was talking with Detective Carmine and Mrs. Campbell while Mrs. Sorenson hung back on the porch. The uniformed officers drove away, and the neighbors began to wander back to their homes.

I walked up to Julie and Mary.

"How're you holding up?" I asked Mrs. Campbell.

"The other horses are okay, right?" she asked.

"Panicked," I said. "But I don't think they are injured in any way. I'll inspect them each with the vet tech before we leave."

"Thank you," Mary Campbell said, quietly. "I can't believe someone could come here and do this while I was here all alone."

She shivered, and Julie put her arm around Mary, who then turned and put her head on Julie's shoulder.

"I've called Black Briar to come out as well," I said, mainly to Julie. "They'll get here after the vet tech vacates."

"Good idea," Julie said, patting Mary on the back. I could hear her quietly sobbing. After a minute, Mrs. Sorenson trundled off the porch and down to us. She smiled at me sadly, said something in Yiddish I didn't understand, and pulled Mary off Julie's shoulder.

"Come inside," she said, her accent thick and throaty. "Let the young ones do what must be done. You come and lie down."

Mary allowed herself to be led away. Julie patted her on the shoulder as she walked past, then turned to me, speaking in urgent, hushed tones.

"Did you see?" she asked.

"The little pig message? Yeah. Very pleasant." I rubbed my eyes. "But why did you think it was a warning to me?"

Julie looked puzzled. "Did you not see the other message? The one written down the length of the roof beams?"

"I didn't see anything," I answered truthfully. "Only the one message in the stall where the ritual stuff was done."

She looked at me with that exasperated teacher look and turned me by my shoulders. "Go look again," she said. "And pay attention."

"Geez, yes, Mom," I said, rolling my eyes at her.

I walked away from her toward the barn. Before going in, I turned back to see her watching me with her arms crossed over her chest.

That's when it dawned on me. She wasn't using her cane. That was a bright spot in an otherwise creepy day.

Charlie was taking pictures in the stall where the horse had been butchered. "Hey, Beauhall. You see anything I might've missed?"

I looked around, looking at the pillars and cross-joists. If there was a message there, I didn't see anything.

"Not that I can see," I answered. "You looking for something specific?"

He stood up, holding the camera in one hand. "I thought maybe you recognized that weapon the cops took," he said, motioning to where the serpentine blade had been stuck into the ground. I've heard you had a keen eye and were some sort of weapons expert."

"Collector," I said. "Looked like a stereotypical ritual blade," I said. "Wouldn't fight with it. Twisted blade like that wouldn't stand up to real punishment."

He watched me, waiting for me to say the magic word. I wasn't sure what he wanted. "Anything else catch your eye, besides the blade?"

I walked up and down the length of the barn, looking from one beam to the next—one stall after another.

On the third pass through the place, with Charlie standing in the kill stall watching me, I caught a glimmer of something.

Near the top of the third stall, there was a glamour. That's the only way I could think of it. If I looked directly at it, I couldn't see anything but old wood and dust. But if I turned my head to the side and let the sunlight hang in the corner of my eye, I could see something sparkling, something that looked like runes.

I suddenly didn't want to mention this to Charlie Hague. He of the secret tattoo and cavalier talk of horse necropsies. "I got nothing," I said.

He looked at me skeptically, then shrugged. "Thought you may have caught something there at the last. Something I missed, maybe?"

"No." I shook my head. "Sunlight got in my eyes, that's all. We should see to the horses, don't you think?"

He pulled the camera from around his neck, wrapping the strap around the body and stuffing the whole thing into his satchel. "Let me grab my medical kit," he said, walking out of the stall. "I'll meet you outside."

"Cool." I walked down through the barn, but a tickling caused me to stop and turn. He stood in front of where I thought I'd seen the runes, stood staring at the wall for a good long minute, before jotting something into a notebook and turning back to get his kit.

I hustled out of the barn and walked out among the horses. They were much calmer, but I'd forgotten to get them their hay. I went back inside to grab a bale when I caught a flash from where Charlie stood. He had his back to me, but it had that distinct flair of magic I'd seen from Qindra. Was Charlie Hague a witch?

"Grabbing some hay," I called out.

He startled, quickly grabbed his kit, and turned back. "On my way," he said. A neutral smile painted his face as he walked down the aisle toward me.

Who are you, Charlie Hague? I thought. *Whose side are you on?*

We examined each horse. Two had to have small abrasions cleaned where they'd obviously knocked against the stall in their panic and one I had to walk around for a bit, keeping her head low with the lead rope and speaking calmly to her. I like to pet them on the neck when they are agitated. I feel like it helps calm them, letting them know you are there for them, that you will keep things safe.

"You have a subtle touch," Charlie said from a stack of hay bales. He'd left the last one for me to calm down while he worked on his report. By the time I had the little mare breathing evenly and willing to eat some oats from my hand, he'd uploaded all the pictures from his camera and was sending e-mails off to his office.

"If you give me your e-mail address, I'll make sure you get a copy of everything," he offered.

I gave him my account and watched him send me a zipped file.

"Should be enough for the insurance company, as well," he said, closing the lid on his laptop. "I'll just go inside and have Mrs. Campbell sign a couple of release forms, then I'll send a truck out to remove the remains."

"Thank you," I said. "I'll stay out here until things are cleared up."

"Good idea," he said, smiling. "And here's my card. Call me if something comes up."

He flipped a card out of his pocket with the flair of a three-card monte dealer and held it out to me. I took it from him, and, as our fingers brushed, I got a flash of young Mr. Hague's true self. Just like when I first met the dwarf, Rolph Brokkrson, only this time, instead of the forge, it was books and dust, secrets and sorrow. There's a bit of the cloister in him, I decided. Something quite different from a hotshot vet tech on the rise.

He gave me a puzzled look and bowed toward me, ever so slightly. I guess it was a thing. Lately everyone was bowing to show respect.

I waved as he walked down the drive to his van and turned to the house. I texted Stuart, letting him know they were clear to come see what there was to see.

Now I just had to let Katie know what was going on.

Fourteen

KATIE HADN'T BEEN HAPPY ABOUT THE SITUATION, AS YOU can imagine, but understood my decision to call Jimmy and the others. She didn't want anyone else to get hurt. She just said she'd be home when I got done. Not as bad as it could've gone, but there was definitely a frostiness in her voice.

I was on my second cup of righteously sweet tea when we heard the sounds of vehicles coming up the drive. I looked at Julie briefly and got up. I didn't even wait for Mrs. Sorenson to finish her thought.

Jimmy and Deidre were in his truck, Stuart and Bub in another. Gunther rolled up on his Harley. The sun was low in the sky, casting the farm in shadows. Frankly, I'd been afraid to go back into the barn alone. The magic done there was vile, and I wanted no part in it. Besides, I loved horses. Being around a dead one was not high on my list of fun times.

I thought about the message Julie saw, about the fact that it seemed to have faded, and about the way Charlie Hague had done something like magic when he thought I wasn't watching. I definitely needed answers.

"Hey, Jim," I called as I went out onto the porch. He was taking Deidre's chair out of the back of the truck as Stuart and Gunther walked toward the house. Bub hovered over between the trucks, where folks in the house couldn't see him. Not sure how either Mrs. Sorenson or Mary would react to my little demon buddy.

"Mind if I just head into the house?" Deidre asked. She looked exhausted. Physical therapy was hard work. I knew from when I had them work on my wounded hand.

I took her in and introduced her around, and she settled in next to Julie. Before I was out the door, they were all chattering together like old friends. Good folks.

The guys had waited for me by the trucks.

"It's not pretty," I said, waving them over to the barn. "Smell is bad, burned meat, viscera, stale blood . . ."

"Sounds delightful," Stuart said, hefting a flashlight.

Gunther and Bub went straight for the ritual stall, while Jimmy hung back, taking in the whole scene. I just stood to the side, letting them examine things without prejudicing them. I wanted them to find something I'd missed.

Stuart did more of a security sweep, examining each stall carefully without going inside. Keeping an eye on things while the others did what they had skills for.

Gunther, on the other hand, went about his investigation so specifically, the same as Charlie Hague, that I was startled. He couldn't be following the same steps Charlie did any closer than if he'd been there to watch the first investigation. I'm not sure exactly how to explain it. His examination was as much metaphysical as physical, if that makes any sense.

There was one spot, where a lot of blood had splashed on the ground outside the stalls, like perhaps the killer had spilled a bowl of blood or dropped a body part that was still leaking a lot. He didn't touch the blood exactly, but after a moment he called Bub over. They squatted, heads together, exchanging ideas.

Jimmy watched them a moment and shrugged. I smiled, thinking how much they'd changed. Then I looked down the length of the barn to Stuart. He watched with his arms folded across his chest, his face impassive. After a moment, he turned and looked out into the paddock.

Jimmy nodded once toward Stuart, then went to join Gunther and Bub, leaning against the stall wall, slipping into their conversation. Gunther said something about entrails, and Bub added that someone was scrying.

I walked to the back of the barn with Stuart, put my arm over his shoulder, and leaned my head against him.

"Thanks for coming," I said. "This is pretty damn creepy."

Stuart grunted but didn't move. For the last of the light, we watched the horses moving together along the very farthest part of the paddock. As the darkness rolled over the farm, the horses became more vocal, whinnying and blowing. One of the younger colts reared on his hind legs and cried to the night sky.

"That's us," Stuart said quietly. "Huddled against one another in the dark, fearful we'll be the next one butchered."

I didn't say anything, just held on to him until someone threw on the big sodium lights that blanketed the back of the farm.

Fifteen

I HEADED OUT AND MET JULIE AT JIMMY'S TRUCK. WE MADE mindless small talk while waiting for the guys to wrap up. They didn't take too much longer and came out of the barn huddled in a moving scrum.

"Mary is having a bath," Julie said. "Mrs. Sorenson is washing dishes."

"Good. I don't want to freak them out with Bub."

Julie looked at me and smiled. "I wouldn't put it past Mrs. Sorenson to be hipper to such things than you think. But you're right. Best not to test that just yet."

The guys got to the truck, and we started sharing what we'd seen.

First Stuart gave his impression. For as little time as I saw him look at the two main stalls in this little drama, he'd picked up a ton of details.

"Charcoal marks on the slaughter stall, rubbed out, but still visible if you looked closely enough. Likely used to ward the cell, cloak it from being noticed by the outside world while the killing occurred."

"Explains why Mary didn't hear anything," Julie said.

"And there is a sign on every stall. A warding mark, to keep the secrets hidden from anyone who looks around casually."

"Aye," Gunther agreed. "Probably there to keep the other horses from freaking out."

"Not foolproof," I said, explaining the wounds Charlie Hague and I had tended.

"It wasn't powerful magic," Gunther said. "Just enough to allow our visitor to finish what he was doing."

"Blood magic," Bub spoke up. "And there is a distinct taint to the magic. One I've smelled before."

"Crap," I said. "Justin?"

He nodded. The necromancer who had tormented Anezka, sabotaged her house out in Chumstick, eventually trapping Qindra there.

"And he's looking for you," Bub said, quietly.

"Told you," Julie said with a grimace.

"I didn't see a message," I said, frowning.

Bub shuffled his little taloned feet and wrung his hands. "It was written in pain."

"Nicely put," Gunther agreed. "I've heard of those who could take the energy from a situation and manipulate it, use it for other purposes. This is the first time I've seen anyone use it to leave a message."

"But I can't see it," I said, beginning to get pissed off.

Jimmy shrugged, as did Stuart. "Oh, I see," Gunther said. "Follow me."

"I'm going back into the house," Julie said. "I've seen enough pain and blood for one day, thank you."

Can't say as I blamed her.

We walked back into the barn. Gunther positioned me directly in front of one of the stalls, made sure I was looking at the area he wanted, then, without as much as a how do you do, punched me.

I spun at him, shocked, but in that flash, as the pain jolted into my brain, the words flashed in front of me.

"What the fuck?"

"Julie is in constant pain with her rehab, as am I," Gunther described. "Bub, are you in pain?"

"Only my heart," he said, seriously. "But it suffices."

"I'm sorry," Jimmy said. "I thought you'd seen it."

"You in pain, Jim?" I asked, surprised.

"Same as Bub, I reckon. Must be this fight with Katie." Or the loss of his parents, or the deaths in the spring fighting the dragon and his minions, or Deidre's being crippled in that battle. He had a lot of things to be pained about.

I turned to Stuart, who shrugged and smiled. "We all carry some level of pain. I guess I'm luckier than some others. I could barely see the words."

Great. I had caught something but did not get a clean look at them. "Can someone tell me what they say, without punching me again?"

Jimmy pulled a notebook from his pocket and handed it to Gunther, who copied down the message.

"Sister of the flame. I call to the passion that rises between your thighs, the lust that builds in your loins. I draw forth the moisture from your body so that I may drink at your fountain. You who slew the dragon, who lays with women and is blessed of the one eyed god. How is it I cannot find you?"

Okay, I was the only dragon slayer we knew about, but the message was pretty freaking specific.

"Um," I said, looking up from the notepad. "That's a bit too personal for my liking."

Jimmy laughed. "I was wondering why you weren't pissed off," he said. "Those are things about you, not you. He doesn't know who you are yet. He's just picking up random bits of information."

"Aye," Gunther agreed. "And based on what we see here, he's been responsible for the other killings in the area."

It was all over the news.

"I knew the girl killed at Monkey Shines," I said, chagrined that she died because of me. There was enough of that in the world. This sucked.

"And the girls in Vancouver?" Stuart asked.

I shrugged. "Not sure. I met a lot of people at the concert. Groupies and such. Could be any number of people. Have they released pictures?"

No one knew.

"Okay, one crazy psycho with the ability to do some kinds of death and/or blood magic who is tracing you by at least two different living creatures you come into contact with on a regular basis."

"And he's onto the fact you're a farrier and a lesbian," Stuart added. "That should narrow things down quite a bit."

I thought over to Charlie Hague. He'd known me by sight. I was feeling a little claustrophobic all of a sudden.

"Can we get out of here?" Bub asked from near the door. "The smell is bad."

"Wait," I said, turning down two stalls. "There's something else. I didn't tell the vet tech, but I caught something here. Something that looked like runes."

I pointed to the crossbeam that ran up to the rafter. There, in the corner, I caught another glimmer of glamour. "I can't see it when I look directly at it, but when I look out of the corner of my eye, I can catch something."

Bub and Gunther both looked where I pointed.

"I got nothing," Bub said. "Not my realm."

Gunther turned to Stuart and motioned for him to join him. Stuart pushed off the wall and strode forward, reminding me of nothing more than a bulldog wading through a pack of poodles.

Once he entered the stall, Gunther held out one hand. Stuart clasped it in his opposite and the two looked up.

"I see," Stuart said, startled.

Gunther nodded at him and Stuart left the barn. Everyone else was confused.

"It's like the pain writing," Gunther offered. "Only this one is even more specific. It will only fully display for someone who is intertwined with their significant other."

I looked at Jimmy quickly, his eyes were as round as saucers.

"Um," I began, my mind racing. "You and Stuart are an item?"

Gunther laughed, shaking his head. "Not in a sexual context."

I shook my head. "I don't get it."

"We're blood brothers," he said, holding up his hand. There were many scars on those meaty paws, but down the middle of his palm was a wide scar. "We shared our blood, bound ourselves to one another for the rest of our lives. Warriors 'til the end."

I walked to the barn door and saw Stuart leaning against the truck, his shoulders slumped. Was he crying?

"Is Stuart okay?"

Gunther smiled. "He's had a rough year. I'm afraid he had begun to doubt our friendship, misunderstood my need to share my attention with Anezka."

"He thought you'd ditched him?"

"As it were."

Wow. I guess I'm not the only one who was struggling with self-esteem and feeling like part of the family.

"So, what did it say?" I asked.

"It was a binding, I'm afraid," Gunther said, quietly. "Meant for you and Katie, most likely."

"Binding?"

"Well, more of a geas, a breaking."

I was confused. "In English this time?"

"There are three runes," Gunther said. "Three runes, all in reverse. Kenaz, to represent breaking; Nauthiz, for deprivation; and Perthro, for loneliness."

"Damn," I breathed. "What the hell?"

"It was a trap for you, in case you were here with Katie, your true love. Your soul mate. It was a way to drive a wedge between you, to break your bond."

I looked back at him and then out at Stuart. "Wait, does that mean . . . ?"

Gunther shook his head. "It is weak, callous magic. Stuart and I have seen too much, been through too many rough times to be influenced by this pettiness."

I took a deep breath. This magic stuff was dangerous and tricky. "Is he okay, then?"

He nodded.

"I get it," Jimmy chimed in. "The only way he could see it is if you and he still had your bond."

"Exactly," Gunther said, smiling. "His fear of our bond being riven by Anezka, or anyone else, has been settled. Our bond is as strong as it has ever been."

"If this is the necromancer you name Justin," Gunther said, "he is both bold and foolish. This is a desperate act. Anyone with even the slightest bit of training could uncover the hidden messages here. There must be more to this."

"Maybe he looks for her," Bub chimed in. "But maybe he also looks for me."

I looked around, as if Justin would suddenly appear.

"That could explain that tremor we felt when we came in,"

Gunther agreed. "Maybe it's time we got you back to someplace more sheltered."

"If he has marked me somehow," Bub said with a shake of his scaly head, "it would follow me, allowing him to trace me to you. Better I try something he cannot."

And with that, Bub stepped into the sideways. There was the expected pop as the air around him collapsed into the space he'd just vacated.

"A trace on him?" I asked, looking around for him to return. "Will teleporting remove a magical trace?"

"Perhaps," Jimmy said from the aisle. "He and I have been discussing the difference between this world and his home. I don't believe he goes all the way back to Múspell, back to the land of fire, but he goes far enough away to be undetectable with any means we know of."

"We've been practicing," Gunther added. "Trying to get a handle on Anezka's trauma."

"What about the rest of us?"

Stuart was leaning against the truck, not moving.

"I think we need to split up for a few days," Gunther said. "We'll avoid Black Briar, so this magic can't triangulate us all to one place. The police, vet tech, and even the horse have this same taint. Our necromancer will have a hard time following all of us.

"We'll just go about our lives without congregating at any one point.

"Except you, of course," he continued. "You stay here, help out Mrs. Campbell. That way, he'll likely mistake you for a farm hand or one of the horses. It isn't an exact magic, more of a wide net to capture the most fish."

"Can we de-magic the barn?"

"Easy," Gunther allowed. "Once the body has been removed, clean the stalls down with bleach. After the blood has been removed as best you can, burn sage throughout the barn, making sure to get smoke in every stall.

"Finally, circle the entire building with salt. This will leach away any residual magic that may remain."

Bleach, sage, salt, got it.

"We should split up," Jimmy said. "Deidre and I will head home after dropping you folks off. How long should you stay away from Black Briar?"

"Only a couple of days," Gunther said. "Like I said, the majority of the magic here was in scrying for Sarah. The rest is to track down anyone else who may pose a threat to this man. Recall, he did not go after Mary. She was not a target."

"Good to know." I walked out with them—hugged them individually, making sure to squeeze Stuart extra tight. I think he'd been crying. Silly man.

Once Deidre was in Jimmy's big four-door pickup, Jimmy stopped and turned to me.

"Do me a favor, Beauhall. If you will."

"Sure."

"Tell Katie we miss her, in a way she'll hear it."

I studied him. He wanted to do the right thing, to be the protector. But sometimes you had to let those who love you take some risks. I'd learned that with Katie. If I hadn't brought her with me out to Chumstick, I'd still be stuck in that horror house with Qindra, and Ari would be dead. Hell, I can't imagine how deep the shit storm would've been if I hadn't turned that bike around and taken her with me.

"Jim," I said, putting my arm on his shoulder. "Give her some time. She's strong, stronger than you want to give her credit for."

"I can't lose her," he said, his eyes shiny in the light of the sodium lights.

"And you can't keep her in a box. Let her breathe, Jim. Let her know she's one of the grown-ups. She still loves you, will still look to you for guidance and protection on a lot of levels. Hell, you raised her, took care of her. She's not stupid."

He nodded, his face stern and contemplative. "You're right, of course. And she believed this craziness long before I fully embraced it."

"See," I said, stepping back. "She'll help you think outside the box. Let her know she's needed. Let her be part of the team. That's how you'll win her back."

"Thanks," he said. "You've gotten a helluva lot smarter since when I first met you."

I wasn't sure I shouldn't be insulted there, but I let it go. The man was thinking, changing.

"Sleep on it," I said.

He climbed in his truck, executed a three-point turn, and drove down the drive. Stuart drove partway down the drive and waited. There was a quiet pop and Bub appeared again. He climbed in the truck and they drove off.

Gunther hugged me once and started his Harley.

It had been a long day. Julie came out on the porch as they drove away.

"What's the plan?" she asked.

"I have a list," I said, turning to her. "Think Mary'll let all of us camp out here for a day or two?"

She put her arm across my shoulder. "I think she'd love it."

"Good. Tomorrow, the vet will send a truck to take away the remains. If you can work with the insurance company, I'll see to the horses and getting the barn cleared up."

She looked at me with a smirk. "Does that involve cleaning, or will there be other forms of activities?"

"Nothing super difficult," I assured her. "A bit of this, a bit of that."

"Leave the horses out?"

I looked across the yard to the paddock. The horses were settling in for the night, huddled together away from the barn.

"No way you're getting them back inside tonight," I said. "We'll get them settled tomorrow."

"Good, let's tell Mary the plan."

She turned to go into the house, but I stood there a minute longer, looking at the barn. The horse was still in there, still watching out of the ritual circle.

How had my life gotten this psychotic?

Sixteen

I was up before dawn. No one had slept well, but they were all asleep for the first thirty minutes or so I was up. The farm had a quietness to it that reminded me of home. But it was also lonely. Mary had kept a dynamic household, but the loss of her husband had been hard. And the betrayal of her most trusted hands this year didn't do anything to make things easier. I tried not to feel guilty about Jack and Steve leaving Mary high and dry. At least they waited until after foaling season. Guys were assholes in any case. She was better off without them. I'm fairly sure my tussle with them was only part of the reason they left. Probably.

Maybe we needed to combine forces here. This land was good, the energy felt right, except, of course, where the taint was near the barn. Felt like pain that you anticipate, a known blow that had yet to land. I sipped my coffee and watched the barn, making sure nothing went in or came out without my seeing it.

By the time the sun was up and everyone in the house was nursing their first cup of coffee—my third—I went out to move the horses. It had gotten chilly in the night, and by morning the air was crisper than I wanted the horses to be in all day.

I was able to move them over to the other barns. Circle Q didn't need three barns these days.

The truck arrived at 8:00 A.M. sharp to dispose of the horse, so Julie and I were in the barn with high-power hoses and buckets of bleach water before Katie was at school. She had a fund-raiser meeting in the morning and was going to be grading papers in the afternoon.

She's been a trooper once I explained how things went down. She was safer with me away from her at the moment, and, until we got the magic cleared from the barn, I didn't want to risk her showing up here and being influenced by any residue.

She agreed to come out to Circle Q for dinner. Mary was delighted. Five women around the dinner table should shake any of the negative energy that lingered after we cleaned things up.

We took our time in the barn, making sure to scrub every nook and cranny. Even if we couldn't see anything foul. With the hidden runes and pain writing, I didn't want to take any chances we missed something else.

While we were on our hands and knees scrubbing with good, stiff brushes, Julie began to open up about some plans.

"I'm thinking about working for Mary some," she said, wiping the sweat off her forehead with the back of her wrist. "She needs the help, and I need a good launching pad."

I let her talk, nodding and grunting where appropriate, but I wanted her to talk it out.

"I had the idea," she went on, watching me like I was gonna shy away or something. "What if we took the regular customer list and split it, giving you the lion's share of solo work."

I started to protest, but caught myself. If she saw me flinch, she didn't let on. She'd built this business, damn it. It was her client list, her sweat and tears.

"You and I can work the bigger farms, do the big work together, but if you take all the little places, the ones you already know, it will give me time to work on the ranch here. I already know I can't rebuild on my land until the fireweed we planted has a couple of years to grow and leach away the dragon taint."

"That's true," I interjected. Wanted her to know I was paying attention.

"Besides," she said, sitting back on her haunches and looking at me. "You're damn good at farrier work. And we both know you could use the money."

I nodded, pleased with the compliment. "Thanks."

"I've been thinking on it. Maybe I'll get a couple of horses. Do some riding again. I used to ride all the time as a kid. That's why I got into the farrier gig, you know."

I smiled, making sure to keep scrubbing. She rarely talked about her childhood in Texas.

"My old man kept a couple hundred head of cattle as a hobby," she went on. "But really he worked as a geologist for the oil companies."

I wondered how she got on with her old man. She never gave any indication she had trouble of any kind, but sometimes benign neglect is just as painful in the long run.

"I assume you've talked to Mary about this?"

She nodded. "Some of this came from her, sure. I've been thinking I needed to get back on my feet for a while now. Mary just gave me a good excuse to quit stalling. And this." She waved her brush through the air, taking in the entirety of the stall, barn, whole dragon-infested world. "We need to band together against the crazy bastards."

"Amen," I said, slopping my brush into the bucket of sudsy water. I stood up, stretching my back and rubbing my knees. "Sounds like a good plan."

She stood as well, leaning against the wall, but doing a damn sight better than I'd figured she'd do. The femur break and muscle trauma from where the giants had tortured her had me worried, but she was a fighter. Her physical therapist said she was stubborn as a mule and strong as an ox.

And she thought she was going soft.

"Reminds me," I said, picking up the bucket to pour the sudsy water down the big barn sink. "I want to put together a small forge out at Black Briar. Something to allow Anezka a chance to get back to the hammering and metalwork."

She studied me a bit, cogitating on it. "You think she's ready?"

I thought about the last four months and about how for most of it Julie had been holed up in my apartment, afraid of the world. "How do you feel? Are you itching to have a hammer in your hand? Need the heat from the forge, to smell the sharp tang of hot metal?"

"Like a drug," she admitted with a rattling sigh. "I miss the ringing of steel on steel and the way the forge glows as the coal is banked just right." She gave a little shudder, like she was shaking off something hard. "I get that. She's a smith, like you and me. But can she handle the fire?"

"Bub will help her, for sure, as will most of the others out at Black Briar."

"Seems like you have a handle on the situation. Why are you asking?"

I scuffed my boots on the floor, letting the anxiety rise up from my belly and out through my fingers. Deep breath. "I didn't want you to think I was leaving you, that I'd abandoned you."

She studied me the way she does, with a critical eye tempered with compassion. "Sarah Jane Beauhall," she said, her voice a little too throaty. "You are a piece of work."

I tried to read her, see if she was mad or something, but she had a look on her face I hadn't seen before. "Yeah, I guess I am."

She stepped forward and pulled me to her, wrapping her arms

around me and squeezing. "Thank you," she said into my shoulder. "Thank you for being my friend."

I hugged her back, blinking away the stinging tears.

We finally broke apart, and each pretended not to notice the other one was crying. "Let's get this barn finished," she said, wiping her face. "If we don't jump in to help, Edith will have cabbage boiling."

"I take it that's Mrs. Sorenson," I said, grinning.

"Lose enough rummy to her and she'll let you call her Edith," she said, returning my smile. "Got a big heart, that one."

"Excellent. Guess we'll have to keep her, then."

The rest of the work went along faster. I don't know if it was the fact that we'd obliterated all the heavy magic that had corrupted the place or, more likely, that we'd let a lot of angst about our relationship go. I dearly loved Julie. She was the best teacher I'd ever had. And the fact that she thought of us as friends just made it all the better.

Katie arrived just after five. Julie was in the kitchen, bickering with Edith and Mary over the concept of too many jalapeños in chili.

I met Katie at her car, let her scold me for all the wrongness in the recent days, then let her hold me until she felt safe again. We might have made out a bit, leaning against the car. Could've happened.

She opened the trunk of her Miata and brought out several large bundles of sage and lavender. "Sage is good," she said, pushing fragrant bunches into my arms. "But lavender is just as important. Helps keep the negative energy from reforming."

I didn't argue with her. I'd dismissed her fantasy theories most of the time we'd known each other. The funny thing was, in spite of Jimmy's keeping so many of the family secrets from her, she'd been closer to the truth than all of us.

We set up three small hibachis in the barn, one in the middle and the other two halfway down each of the long rows of stalls. We burned the sage first. It was interesting the way it drew down the length of the stalls, flitting into each one, as if directed.

Next we burned the lavender, and while the sage cleansed the place, stripped the last vestiges of hoodoo, the lavender brought an easing to the barn. Like a deep sigh after a fright or a good long stretch when you're tired.

Before dinner we got the horses back into their stalls, and while they sensed where the death had occurred by memory, they weren't agitated. The lavender calmed them, allowed them to settle in.

She's a smart one, that Katie Cornett. I grabbed her ass on the way to the house, and she squealed. Yep, the lavender was the right thing.

Dinner was full of laughter and warmth. It was almost as if Justin and his twisted, sick shit hadn't gone down at all.

Seventeen

Trisha waited at the University Bookstore near the coffee shop, fidgeting with her purse. She'd gotten there a little early since the traffic gods had been kind. She was excited to see Efrain again. They'd been getting along well so far. He had a nice voice, and their phone calls were great.

It had been his idea to go to the book signing. She'd never read much beyond what she had to for school. It gave her a thrill to discuss things like literature, politics, and psychology with someone who really cared about what she had to say.

"You look lovely this evening." Efrain approached her from the front of the store, a small bunch of carnations held out to her.

She took the flowers. When their hands touched, a tingle ran through her—a shiver of joy. "Thanks," she said, smiling. "It's been a while since a fella brought me flowers."

He flashed his best smile, all teeth and sunshine. "There are so few who appreciate beauty these days." He held his elbow out to her. "Shall we go up?"

She took his elbow and sighed. "Sure. I've been pretty psyched about this all week."

They made their way up the stairs to where the bookstore had chairs set up for the author event. Efrain let her sit down first, then took the seat next to her. Her mind was alight with the fact that his thigh was pressed against hers in the close arrangement.

The author discussed her recent trip to the Middle East and how she'd been welcomed into several homes of women who'd lost their husbands in the revolution. Trisha thought she may have said Egypt, but it could've been something else. She had a hard time concentrating when her mind kept wandering around to the way Efrain was casting sidelong glances at her.

It had been a long damn time since someone had paid that kind of attention to her, and she wasn't sure how she felt about it. Part of her was wary, cautious, looking out for the danger, but another part of her brain wanted her to let him be nice to her.

Afterward, he bought a copy of the woman's book and had it autographed to Trisha. She took the book graciously but insisted on buying dinner after. She had to keep this on equal footing.

They ended up at a little Greek place down on the Ave. The moussaka was heavenly, and the wine wasn't too bad.

"Tell me again why you are so guarded," he said as they shared a dish of garlic-stuffed olives.

She felt freer with him than she had since getting out of the hospital. It was like a block of ice in her chest had begun to melt. All he did was look at her, listen to her, but really, isn't that what everyone needed?

"Life is just too out of control," she said. "I wake up some days totally freaked, just wishing that someone else would make the decisions, you know?"

He smiled at her, rolling an olive between his thumb and forefinger. "It takes a very strong person to give up control like that, you realize?"

Trisha shrugged. "I don't know. I mean, I know I'm strong, physically. I can knock out a hundred push-ups without breaking a sweat." She looked at him to see if he'd have a reaction, but he just nodded. "So, yeah, I've got strength. But there are moments I'd like to stop worrying, let someone else take the reins."

She was watching him. That book she'd picked up, the one about bondage, had intrigued her. After they'd had coffee that first day, she'd gone back and bought the book. It had some interesting ideas, some things she thought maybe she'd like to try.

He popped the olive in his mouth and chewed slowly, staring at her. "There are many forms of power," he said, finally. "Allowing someone else to control things for a while can be quite liberating."

She took a long drink of wine, emptying her glass. "That could be hot," she said, setting the glass on the table. Her head was swimming a little.

He reached out and touched her hand on the glass, steadying it as he poured her more wine. There was a flash of heat at his touch.

"Is it getting warm in here?" she asked, lifting the glass to her smile.

"Maybe we should take a walk," he offered. "Clear our heads."

He let her pay, as she'd insisted, but when he slipped his hand in hers on the way out the door, she didn't argue.

They were several blocks from their cars when she pulled him into an alley and kissed him, pushing him against the brick wall, pressing her body against his.

She didn't know if it was the stimulating conversation or the wine, but at that moment she wanted him more than she wanted anything else in the world.

Eighteen

Jimmy had a meeting over in Pasco on the following Saturday, so Katie agreed to go out to Black Briar to see Deidre. I don't know what I would've done if she said no again. Likely knock her on the head and put her in the trunk.

When we got out there, the place was practically deserted. Well, compared to normal days. Most of the troops were in town, leaving a skeleton crew on the farm. Deidre and I sat out on the porch, enjoying the unseasonably sunny sky, while Frick and Frack trundled after Bub, who was having the time of his life.

"He visits them every day," Deidre said, sipping her coffee. "Been a real help to Trisha. She's totally loving the mom thing and damn good at it, mind." She looked at me as if I'd argue. "You never know who'll end up making a good parent."

I laughed. No telling indeed. Some of us just know before we start. There are some mistakes made by my parents that I'd rather end with them.

"Trisha had been pretty depressed," she told me, watching the kids. "Frick and Frack were a strong pull back to the light, but," she lowered her voice, like anyone could hear. "She's been seeing this guy. Gaga all of a sudden."

"Really?" I asked. "That's great."

"We all think so. She's keeping up her shifts with the troops, keeping the kids on a regular bedtime, and even making time for a little nookie break."

I choked on my coffee, spewing a wide spray across the wood of the deck.

"Jesus, Deidre. Don't say shit like that. You're gonna kill me."

She was laughing when Katie came out of the house with a fresh carafe of coffee. "She torturing you about something?" she asked.

I gave Deidre an evil look and leaned over to kiss Katie in front of her. I'd show her.

Katie was surprised, but kissed me back.

"Trisha has a boyfriend," I said, sitting back.

Deidre shrugged. "Hey, we all need to get laid from time to time."

Katie moaned and covered her face. Deidre had practically raised her and was married to her brother. Anytime she talked about sex Katie got squicked out. Ever since Deidre had been hurt and confined to a wheelchair, neither of us had gotten around to thinking about how the sex was impacted. I know I didn't want to know.

"How'd you get Jimmy out of the house?" Katie asked, carefully watching Deidre for some ploy or other.

"He and the twins have been locked in the basement, researching that ring and the code all week," she said. "I finally convinced Stuart that Jim was getting buggy. He worked on Gunther, and before you know it they were all going out to Spokane for a day of research and kicking back."

She sure knew how to manipulate all of us. Like an evil overlord or something. I'd be sure to watch her for telltale signs of interference with Katie. Not a woman you'd want to be on the wrong side of.

"Why Spokane?" Katie asked. She had her hands wrapped

around a steaming cup of coffee and was leaning over it like it was the only thing keeping her from freezing to death. Granted, it was only forty-three degrees—in the sun.

Deidre looked over at Katie, debating on spilling a secret. That much I could figure out. Her good sense must've overcome her fear.

"Your mom and dad had a place out there. A safe house, some-place to run when things got wacked in the world."

Katie's mouth went hard, her lips so narrow I could barely see them. "We were going to tell you, but you freaked out and left."

"A week ago," Katie said through clenched teeth.

"Don't start, young lady," Deidre said, spinning her wheelchair around to face where Katie was sitting. "He's given his whole life to keeping this place safe for you. Don't judge him harshly, Katie. He may have some rough spots, but in the end he loves you more than anything."

I reached over and put my hand on Katie's shoulder, not heavy, just a light touch to let her know I had her back.

Only she didn't explode. She just slumped back and let her breath trail away to nothing.

"I know that," she said so quietly I could barely hear her. "But he's keeping them from me, hiding the things I could cling to."

"Dangerous things," Deidre said, rolling back a foot or so, to not cramp Katie's personal space. "Were you aware your mother kept a diary?"

Katie sat up, her eyes alight. "Diary? No. Can I see it?" The dark side caught up with her thoughts half a second later. "Of course, he's read it already."

Deidre watched her for a second, then shrugged. "No, he never read it. Wanted to save it for you, when you were mature enough to handle it."

Katie looked back at me, then to Deidre. "Can I have it, then?"

"No, I'm afraid not," Deidre said. "Jimmy only took it out of the case she kept it in once. That's before he and I were married. You were with friends, a sleepover. He opened the case and touched the cover."

We waited, but she stopped there.

"And?" I asked.

"As soon as his fingers touched the cover he began to shake, like electricity was shooting through him. I thought he was joking at first, but smoke started coming out of his mouth, so I tackled him, knocking the diary and case onto the floor, landing on top of him." She shuddered, either from the cold, or the memory. "He almost died. I had to do CPR on him for fifteen minutes before the EMTs arrived."

"What?" Katie asked.

"It killed him, Katie. Sent a jolt of power through him so strong it stopped his heart. If he'd been alone, he'd still be dead. As it is, we got him to the hospital in time. He ended up in there for a week. Full-on heart attack at nineteen."

"Wait. Where was I for that week?"

"I picked you up the next day and took you out to my parents in Bellevue."

Katie sat back, stunned. "I was twelve," she said. "I remember that week as one of the best in my life. That's when I met Melanie for the first time." She put her hand on top of the one I had on her shoulder.

Deidre nodded. "And we never told you."

"More secrets," she said, heat filling her again. "How could you not tell me?"

"You were twelve," Deidre said. "And you'd just lost your parents not so long ago. He didn't want you to think you'd lose him, too, that there was any chance. Made me promise not to tell you. After the battle you two have been having, I've decided that you're being selfish, so I told you."

Katie mostly deflated. She'd asked for it, pushed Deidre to tell her.

"And the diary?" Katie asked.

"Stashed away," Deidre said. "Can't risk it killing anyone."

I looked at Katie, questioningly. With all the crap we've been through lately, with the dragons and the blood mead, the ghosts and dwarves, giants and trolls, magic amulets and magic swords, how could she be so quick to want that diary?

Of course, it *was* her mother's. I don't think she had anything of her mother's. Just memories of smells and songs. I guess that's why she became a skald, to embrace the songs from her mother.

And now that I remembered it, her mother loved lavender. No coincidence there, I'm sure.

"And Jim's worried about Anezka's place," Deidre continued, letting the subject of the diary drop. "They're gonna stop by on the way home tonight."

"Bub said Qindra's dome is holding strong," I reminded her.

She looked out at the yard, where Bub was chasing Frick and Frack, who were laughing like hyenas.

"Yes, he went out there. Damn near killed him," Deidre said. "Ate like a horse, then slept for two solid days. There's something going on out there, something he can't figure out, and he's agitated all the time."

"What's Jimmy think?" Katie asked.

Deidre studied her a moment to see if she was digging for a fight. "He's not sure, but thinks we shouldn't leave it unattended." She turned to me. "Sarah, I know you have an obligation to that witch who's trapped in there, and we all heard the tale of your battles with the ghosties." She turned to encompass Katie as well.

"He's scared, hon." She covered Katie's hand with hers. "But he's damn proud of you."

Katie had earned a good amount of cred around the farm with that event. Pissed Jimmy off beyond belief, but proved she had the chops. That she wasn't a little girl anymore.

Course to Jimmy, she'd always be his kid sister, even when she was eighty.

"I may know a way to ease some of Jimmy's worries." I waited until they both looked at me. "What if we arranged for Skella to provide travel services for Black Briar the same as she was doing for the dwarves before we wrecked their happy home? Traveling by mirror is a damn sight faster than driving over the mountain."

Katie's face lit up and Deidre seemed pleased.

"We'd need to pay her," I started.

Deidre didn't even let me catch my breath. "Done, what's next?"

I looked to Katie. "It won't be exactly cheap," I said. "Specialized service and all."

Deidre laughed. "You let me worry about the cash flow. I think we can afford her."

Who was I to argue? I know Jimmy and Deidre were sitting on some serious cash, what with the insurance from his parents being declared dead and Deidre's money from selling her software company. Must be nice to be that flush.

"Well," Katie said. "We could set up a watch station out on Chumstick Highway, near enough to the house to keep an eye on things, but far enough away to be out of danger."

Deidre thought about it. "Good plan," she said. "Sarah, if you can arrange it with Skella, we'll use her to travel between the mirrors here and a mirror out in Chumstick. We'll get her a cell phone in case we need a special delivery, but we'll have a normal schedule."

She was already into heavy project-management mode—thinking of ways to make this work while keeping some modicum of control over it all.

"Three shifts," she continued. "I'll help schedule it all. What do you think?"

"Brilliant," Katie said. "Jim will hate it."

"True enough," Deidre agreed. "But what do you think, Sarah?"

"Seems reasonable. Let me get with her, make sure she's even vaguely interested."

"Fair enough," Deidre said, and gave us a grin.

We spent the next couple of hours watching Bub and the kids while making plans for how we were going to set up an encampment out at Anezka's place. Someone had to know when things went even more hinky than they were now. Besides, I know I could use all the intelligence we could gather on the place.

A ley line ran down from the mountains, right under Anezka's place out in Chumstick. Quite a few lines ran through the Pacific Northwest. It was a regular nexus of power. This particular line came to the surface in a cavern below the house. That's where Justin had blocked the line. It burned me that he'd used my shield—the one I'd gotten from the Valkyrie, Gunnr. The very shield I used to help kill the dragon, Jean-Paul Duchamp.

I'd left it on the battlefield and Justin had recovered it. He'd worked his dark magic on it and shoved it into the ley line, disrupting the flow of energy and flooding the region with tainted magic. Of course, he'd been murdering people on those grounds for a year or more by that time.

Now, I just needed to get past the dome Qindra had over the place, remove my shield from the ley line, and bring Qindra home.

Piece of cake.

Nineteen

We left messages on the mirrors at Black Briar and at home. It took a few days, but Skella finally saw one of the notes. I knew she was keeping an eye out for contact. We arranged to meet at Monkey Shines. I hadn't been there since I heard about Camille, and we wanted to pay our respects.

The place was fairly packed. Gail was working the drive-thru as usual, but there were a couple of new girls running the front and the line was pretty long. We knew what we wanted and had more patience than some of the idiots in front of us. At one point, I thought I was going to have to kick some guy's ass, but his girlfriend got him under control. Did no one have any patience these days? Didn't they know how fine this coffee was?

"Look," Katie said, pointing to a small stand-up on the counter when we got near the front.

There was a cardboard sign with Camille's face on it. In front of the placard was a fishbowl half full of singles. The sign read: HELP US REMEMBER OUR FRIEND. CAMILLE PRESTON MEMORIAL FUND. HELP SEND GIRLS IN AFRICA TO SCHOOL. IT WAS CAMILLE'S FAVORITE CHARITY.

"Damn," I said, fishing in my pocket for my wallet. "I talked to her for years. I never knew she supported kids in Africa." I dropped a twenty into the jar, and the angry guy in front of us glanced our way. At least he had the decency to look abashed when he walked away with his coffee. He didn't donate any money, and I bet he didn't tip.

The new girls were perky and solemn at the same time. It was a little creepy. We ordered coffees and worked our way to the back of the shop, hovering over the good chairs until they were vacated; then we claimed them before anyone else could.

"What the hell are we going to do about this necromancer guy?" Katie asked, leaning forward with her elbows on her knees, her cup cradled in her hands.

I looked around at the other patrons. A vital part of this place had been brutally murdered and people were sitting around doing crosswords, texting and chatting like the world was safe.

"I don't know," I answered, trying to keep the frustration from my voice. Katie's look told me I hadn't succeeded. "I think once Skella gets here, we might be able to get some answers."

Luckily we didn't have too much longer to wait. I had barely dented my huge mug o'mocha when Skella walked out of the hall leading to the bathrooms. The mirror down the hall was fairly secluded. It was also one of the ones Gletts had kept tuned to when he'd been stalking me, before I'd really met them.

I waved Skella into a seat we'd been saving—much to the annoyance of the other patrons—and she beamed at us.

"I'll grab you a coffee," Katie said, standing.

"Hot chocolate, please," Skella said.

Katie nodded and began to swim her way back upstream of the crowd at the bar. I put my feet in Katie's chair, to keep the guys behind us from taking it.

"I have a proposition for you," I said, launching right in.

She didn't say anything for a bit, just listened with wide eyes.

"Of course I'll help," she said, bouncing in her chair. "Gran is making me crazy. All we do is sit with Gletts and mope. All those families sitting around the infirmary, hoping their loved ones will wake up someday. It's like being at a funeral all the time. I mean, come on. The battle was only a month or so ago. Give the people time to heal. But just sitting around all the time. I'd kill for a diversion." She grinned at me. "Gran said some days she has a hard time believing I'm an elf."

Katie arrived at that moment with a vat of hot chocolate and three plates of blueberry crumble.

"We hope it's all pretty mundane," I said, sliding a plate of crumble to my side of the table. "No real excitement."

"At least I'd be helping the good guys," Skella said, picking up her drink. "Thanks," she said, inclining her head to Katie.

Katie nodded back. "We're hoping for dull and boring, actually. We've had enough excitement."

In the end, we settled on a salary I thought was criminally low, and Skella thought a king's ransom. That and we promised to provide her a cell phone and cover the monthly bill. She was in heaven.

I finished the crumble and set my mug aside, considering the young Goth elf. "How's your brother?"

"Fine," she said, her face suddenly neutral. "No change, really. Gran insists we sit with him every day, so he knows we need him to come home."

"What do you think?" Katie asked.

"He's out there, somewhere," she said, wistfully. "I just can't find him."

I looked at her, suddenly nervous. "You're looking for him? Like where?"

"The sideways," she said, lowering her voice. "His body is strong. I know he could come back, if he could find his way home."

"So, he's a ghost or something?" I asked.

"Something like that. If he doesn't come back soon, his body will begin to die. Then he will be lost to us forever. Gran is getting quite desperate."

I thought back to how the dwarves of the Dragon Liberation Front had forced Skella and Gletts to act as their taxi service while they kidnapped Ari and used him to make their blood mead. Not all dwarves were evil, but that crew definitely had bought a franchise into bat-shit crazy land.

"Your gran isn't thinking of doing anything drastic, is she?" I asked.

Skella just shrugged. "She doesn't tell me. But I know she has no love for dark magic, nor blood magic, if that's what you're thinking."

I shrugged. "No. She seemed like a lovely person. I just know that grief and fear can drive rational beings to do some pretty stupid things."

"Which brings us back around to the necromancer," Katie said.

There was a sudden lull in the conversations around us, so we all paused. Once things got back to their usual dull roar, we huddled close over the small table between our chairs, and spoke in earnest tones.

I explained everything that had been happening, from the death of the girls in Vancouver, to Camilla's murder, and even the horse, Blue Thunder. Skella hadn't heard anything, alas.

"I'm almost positive it's the guy from Anezka's place," I explained. "The one who worked for the dragon up your way, the necromancer."

"Blood magic, yes." Skella looked very uncomfortable. "Before you killed Jean-Paul, Gletts had met the necromancer a couple of times. That's how we knew to find you at the house in Chumstick. Gletts had taken some of the dwarves out there to meet this blood mage, Justin." She paused, toyed with her cup. "He never liked it, you know. No matter how he may have come across to you. Gletts hated them. Hated what they forced us to do." She sighed, look-ing up at us in turn. "He said we had to fight fire with fire. I think he may have dabbled in a few things he wasn't proud of."

I thought back to the crap in my life, the current relationship I had with Nidhogg. How could I argue?

"They never included Gletts in their conversations, but the dwarves, Kraken and Bruden, let things slip from time to time." She set her cup on the table and scrubbed her face briefly. I could see the tears in her eyes. "They were arrogant and cruel. I'm happy they're dead."

Katie reached over and patted her on the knee. I loved that about her. Always reaching out to make sure others were okay.

"Well, we may have broken up the blood cult, but Justin is still out there wrecking havoc. Unfortunately, we don't have a lot of facts," I said. "We just know that he's killing people around me. We think he's trying to figure out who I am."

Skella looked at me for a long time, a look of resignation on her face. "Sarah. I don't know much, but based on what Gletts shared with me, I'd guess he already knows who you are. I think if he wanted to kill you, he'd have already tried something." She shrugged. "I'm just guessing, but based on the things Gletts had picked up, I think he's doing something else. Something he doesn't want you messing with."

"You think he's trying to scare me?"

Katie pulled a face, but didn't say anything.

Skella thought for a moment. "He knows someone killed the dragon. To do that, they'd have to be pretty damn powerful." She smiled at me.

"Which we know is totally true," Katie said with a laugh. "Kick-ass warrior chick."

I shot her a look. "Seriously?"

Skella snickered when Katie leaned over and kissed me.

"So," Skella went on, "I think he's still on the path he was on before, only now he knows you're out there and he's trying to keep you going in circles."

Made a kind of sense. "Any clue to what he was planning?"

"Not much," she said, glancing at Katie. "He was always looking for an item of power. Gletts never could figure out what it was, but they think it's down here somewhere, in your neck of the woods. Whatever it is, the dwarf, Bruden, always claimed it was a game changer."

"And they were in league with dragons who want to rule openly?" Katie asked.

Skella nodded.

"Why the hell would anyone want to help the dragons rule openly?" I asked. "It would be mass murder."

"He thinks he's getting something out of the deal," Katie said.

Skella shook her head. "I can't imagine what would be worth all that."

Katie grimaced. "He's a necromancer. I'm thinking he'd love a lot of death. It buys him something."

"If he just wanted massive carnage, he could blow up a building or something." I sat back and ran my hands through my hair. "There's something else he's after, I'm sure of it. We're missing something crucial."

We let the subject drop, each lost in our own thoughts.

Justin had been in league with the Dragon Liberation Front. And they were in league with the psycho dragon cult that wanted to rule openly.

How did I play in all that? Could he be after Gram? She was built to kill dragons. Maybe he needed her to tip the balance of power somehow—take out one or more of the ruling dragons, start a civil war. It was a thought.

Damn scary thought.

Twenty

We were home doing laundry on Saturday a week later. I was whining about how much I hated doing laundry, which explains why most of my clothes were jeans and T-shirts. I rarely took them out of the laundry basket once I'd washed them. Katie decided I needed to be retrained, so we played strip laundry. It was pretty fun. We were folding clothes, and if we both took out a similar piece of clothing, the first one to get that piece folded and in the basket got to make the other remove something.

I was down to one sock, panties, and a T-shirt. Katie was wearing nothing but a stocking cap and thigh-high boots. I'd just about given the laundry up in favor of other activities when my cell phone rang. Katie made me answer it and ran around the other side of the bed, away from my reach.

I answered the phone. The number was out of area, which likely meant it was a sales call.

"Smith," a gravelly voice said on the other end. "You should turn on the news."

"Who is this?" I asked.

Katie was busy on the other side of the bed doing something rather intriguing with a bottle of baby oil.

"There's a report coming on right now that involves a girl getting murdered that may interest you."

I walked out of the bedroom and into the living room. Katie called to me, but followed. I sat on the couch, flipped the remote, and the news came on.

They were just finishing up a segment on traffic, when Katie joined me, confused and mouthing something at me I couldn't understand. I couldn't read lips. Why did she think I could figure out what she was asking me?

"I'm watching," I said into the phone.

"Hang on," the voice said. It was familiar, like I'd heard it before. I just couldn't place it. Not Rolph, or any of the other dwarves I'd met in Vancouver. But definitely something that made me think of Canada.

The news spoke of a kid in her early twenties who'd been murdered. I recognized her as one of the groupies that was doing Ari the night he got kidnapped. It was the girl who'd helped me by whacking one of the bad guys with her big-ass purse. On the television they listed her as an exotic dancer. As the newscaster spoke, they flashed up the pictures of three other young women.

Katie sat by me, and the baby oil slipped from her slick fingers and hit the floor with a thunk. She was pointing at the screen. "We met her," she said. "She was at the concert. The one who thought she was going to marry Ari, remember?"

I did remember. Big girl who wanted to meet the singer with all her heart. We'd promised to pass her message on to Ari. I felt pretty sick about it all of a sudden.

"Someone is gunning for you, sweet cheeks," the voice growled. "You want to be watching that pretty backside of yours."

Before I could tell the guy to get bent, the line went dead. I put the phone on the coffee table and turned up the volume on the television. They linked the new girl with the others I'd heard about lately and showed a couple I hadn't heard about. All in all, six girls had been murdered the same way. Brutal, nasty murders like the way the horse had been killed.

By the end of the news report, we recognized several of the women in the string of killings from Vancouver to Everett, Lynnwood down to Redmond. Someone in the police leaked to the press that they believed the murders to be the work of a serial killer. All the deaths were caused by similar weapons, and all the women had been ritually murdered.

It had to be Justin, had to be that sick fuck doing his blood magic to find me. Killing all those girls who'd run into me at some point in their lives.

I needed to call Rolph. See what he knew about what was going on in Vancouver. Then I needed to start looking for Justin on my own. I didn't have magic to fight him with, but I had friends and contacts. And I knew Nidhogg. She may know something. And there were the dwarves in Vancouver. Some of those who'd worked with him had to be alive. They couldn't have all been killed when we rescued Ari.

Definitely needed to engage Rolph. Call Skella and maybe see if her gran knew anything that would help here.

Someone had to stop this bastard.

Katie picked up the bottle of baby oil and trundled back to the bedroom, only to return wrapped in a bathrobe. She'd looked so freaking hot with the oil all over her breasts, but even that was tainted with all this.

That was the final straw.

Rolph answered on the second ring.

"Rolph, dude," I said into the phone. "What the hell's going on up there?"

"Smith?" he asked.

"Yeah, it's Sarah. What do you know about the girls that have been killed up there? You have any idea who's behind it?"

I heard him yawn. It was early; the sun hadn't gone down yet. Crap, I'd probably woken him.

"I've heard something," he said. "But nothing more than you probably already know."

"Someone just called me, warned me to watch my ass. I thought I recognized the voice somehow. Made me think of Canada. Any of your cousins up there in the know?"

He didn't respond right away. "Just because I am a dwarf," he said, his voice a little cold, "does not mean I am the spokesmodel for my race."

Definitely cranky. "Sorry if I woke you. Everything okay in your world?"

I heard him take a drink of something. "We are fine, thanks for asking. Juanita is with child."

Holy crap. "Um, seriously? Is that safe and everything?"

He laughed, a harsh croaking sound that told me he was not well. "And I have the flu," he finished. "She is staying with her sister in Bellingham while I am sick. Doesn't want to risk anything this early in the pregnancy."

"Yeah, sure. Makes sense." I looked at Katie and mouthed "Pregnant." She looked at me, puzzled, so I mimed having a very large, round belly and pointed to the phone. A look of under-standing dawned on her face.

"Anyway," he continued. "I can inquire about the girls you mentioned."

"I think I know who is doing this," I said. "That necromancer that was working with Jean-Paul. He's the one that mucked up the ley line down here."

"Where you battled the spirits?" he asked. "And wrecked an ill-conceived scheme by my brethren here in Vancouver?"

"Yep, the same."

He went quiet again for a bit.

"I will call the King of Vancouver," he said, a note of resignation in his voice. "This necromancer cannot go unchecked. The king will be disheartened to hear how his minions are being slaughtered."

"Cool," I said. "I'd like to get ahead of this freak. I'm sick that these girls all have me in common."

"Hmmm . . ." he mused. "Perhaps I will call Juanita first. Make sure she takes precautions. Knowing you has become both a blessing and a liability, Smith."

"Geez, thanks."

"We are not helpless," he said. "Caution is a way of life for those of us who follow the blade."

Ah, the blade. Gram, harbinger of dragon doom and the tickle that rides in the back of my brain morning, noon, and night.

"How is the blade?" he asked, quietly.

"She's fine, Rolph. Sleeping, actually. Waiting for the next battle."

He laughed. "Sleeping? Like a child?"

I shrugged, even though he couldn't see. "I feel her like she's alive," I said. "Like she's this entity that has a will of her own."

"Formidable magic, indeed," he said. "Your skill as a smith may exceed even my first impression."

"Thanks." What else could I say? I'd fixed a magic sword that was originally forged by the famous smith Völundr. That's what exposed me to this strange new world. Who knows what magic it held at that making? But rumors had it that Odin himself broke the sword at least once. Maybe she was too dangerous if given her head too much. Like a spirited horse who did what she wanted, and damn the consequences.

"Get with your king, Rolph," I said. "I'll start some inquiries down here. Let's get back in touch in a few days, exchange what we've found."

"Seems reasonable," he said. "It is an honor to serve the blade at your side."

I rolled by eyes. "Take care of yourself, Rolph, and tell Juanita we said congratulations."

"My thanks, Smith. Be careful."

"Thanks."

I hung up and looked at Katie. "Human girl, dwarf father. Is that gonna work?"

She gave me a funny look. "Why wouldn't it?"

"How am I supposed to know? Just seems odd."

"More importantly, did he know anything?"

"No, but he'll get back to me."

I hated the not knowing. Hated even more that Juanita was a target, just like Katie, Julie, heck, even Melanie and her EMT girlfriend, Dena. Only women. That was important. Even the horse had been a mare. I'd have to mention that to Gunther.

We finished the laundry with a few more clothes on than I'd anticipated, but the tone had shifted. There was fear in the air and it sucked.

I took Gram out from under the bed while Katie took a shower. She'd used a lot of baby oil, apparently. Next time, damn it.

I opened the case and took Gram out by the handle. The minute I touched her, the light shifted and I saw the room more clearly than usual. What do you think? I asked in my head. I closed my eyes and held Gram out in front of me. "Can you find the bastard?" I asked out loud. There was a twinge, a wobble, but nothing more than that. Gram was made to kill dragons. I'm not sure she understood necromancer. No clues there. I put her back in her case and slid it back under the bed before Katie got out of the shower. One thing, though. The niggling worry and fear had vanished.

Twenty-one

I DIDN'T HAVE ANY SMITHING WORK ON THE AGENDA FOR THE day, so after Katie went off to school, I decided to head over to Nidhogg's and get the measurements I needed for the gate. It was forming pretty well in my mind; I just needed some parameters to make it all come together.

I put on the new leather pants Katie'd bought me. She also bought me those assless chaps but decided I had to try them on when our cell phones were in the freezer, the television remote hidden in the microwave, and the front door intercom disconnected.

Sometimes a girl wanted some playtime that did not get interrupted by crazy phone calls warning of serial killers.

I'd seen the chaps. They were pretty smoking. I'm sure they would make my ass look big, but whatever turned her on.

Once I was in my leathers, I grabbed a bottle of water and an energy bar and added them to my messenger bag.

The ride over the water to Seattle was cold but I was getting used to it. It only rained part of the way, but with the right gloves I did just fine.

Zi Xiu met me at the door when I arrived. "The mistress is indisposed," she informed me. I guess that meant she was in the can.

"Just need to take some measurements for the gate."

She nodded and ushered me in. As we crossed the foyer, I spotted Jai Li, the young girl who haunted Qindra's room.

"The mistress has banned her from Qindra's room," Zi Xiu assured me. "The child has grown willful. I fear for her."

"Any idea what's causing her to disobey?"

Zi Xiu looked at me for a moment, then ushered me over to the hall to Qindra's quarters. "It is not for me to speak out against the mistress, but as you are a surrogate for Qindra, it seems fair for you to know the truth of things."

"Jai Li pines for Qindra, as do many of the household," she whispered. "But the mistress has been having nightmares of late. She calls out to Qindra as if to a daughter, cries ofttimes." She watched me, her eyes wide with shock at her own words. "I think we are all in danger. If she rages as she did in the spring, who will calm her? Who will bring her back to her true self?"

I shuddered to think of a raging dragon among the small children here. Jai Li watched us from her hiding place behind one of the floor-to-ceiling wall hangings. "Did she see her twin killed?"

Zi Xiu shook her head. "No, she had been in the kitchen getting tea. She only heard the mistress rage. We all cowered where we stood when that roar shook the house."

I remembered Jean-Paul's roar as we battled. It was horrifying. No wonder Jai Li had attached herself to Qindra. Safest port in a storm. And with her twin gone, she had no one else.

The measurements went quickly. I agreed to have tea with Zi Xiu. The woman was lonely in her position. The other servants feared her for her power. Qindra had shown her kindness, however. By the time we were sipping our tea, Jai Li had crept into the kitchen and sat with her back to one of the industrial ovens, watching us with hungry eyes.

"Hello," I said to the young girl as we finished tea. I paused in

front of her, kneeling down to be on her level. "I love your needlepoint." I smiled at her. "You are a beautiful artist."

The girl looked from me to Zi Xiu over my shoulder. Apparently she saw approval. For one moment she sat frozen as a mouse
hunted by a great hawk. The next, she'd flung herself against me,
wrapping her arms around my neck. I was too shocked to respond.
Before I could move, she was gone, a wisp of yellow and red silk as
the kitchen door swung back and forth.

I stood and glanced at Zi Xiu, who shook her head in disbelief.
"She has not allowed anyone to touch her except Qindra," she
said, awed. "You have been paid a great honor."

An honor I'm not sure I deserved.

I thanked my host and left the house. It wasn't until I was on
the bike did I find out I had a missed call. The house was cavernous; it was no wonder I hadn't gotten the call.

I didn't recognize the number and there was no message. Katie hated it when I did it, but I called it back. I couldn't stand not
knowing. It rang three times before a bright young woman answered, "Family Martial Arts."

I hung up, panicked. That was my old Tae Kwon Do school.
Why would they be calling me? And how'd they get my number?

The ride back across the water was cold and miserable, but not
because of the weather. Someone from my old life had tried to
contact me, and I'd freaked. Hadn't I been calling home, refusing
to leave a message on the machine?

If I thought a missed call was maddening, what was I putting
Ma through?

Twenty-two

"IT'S JUST A GAME," EFRAIN SAID. "ROLE PLAYING. WE ONLY do what you want to do, and we have a safe word. Something you can say that stops everything, understand?"

Trisha watched him, her mind racing. This was nuts, crazy. Part of her wanted to leave, take her things and go, but another part of her was intrigued.

"I'm afraid," she said, quietly, pulling her robe close around her. They were both in silk pajamas. He'd given them to her as a gift. They were green, while his own were deep red. They had matching robes, and she felt like it was Christmas. She knew what she wanted to unwrap. If she just had the courage.

He studied her a moment, crossing his hands on his lap. "Sex is like magic," he said, smiling. "It only works if done properly. If anything is off even a little, it just doesn't work."

She shrugged. "I'm pretty sure it'll work for you. Guys have it easy."

Efrain chuckled. "It's not all about release, though that in itself has its own power. I'm talking about real magic, Trisha. The power to transcend who you are for a moment, to meld the two into one."

She sighed. "I'd settle for an orgasm." She blushed. He did nothing to make her uncomfortable. On the contrary, he'd been patient with her, letting her ask all the questions, letting her direct their first steps toward intimacy.

"I'm sure we can arrange many of those," he said. His tone was even, but his face was bright with excitement. "It would be an honor to bring you to such pleasure."

Honor? He was like some dream date. "I want to," she said, wringing her hands. "I really, really want to. It's just . . ." She paused, taking a deep breath. "I don't want you to think I'm some kind of freak." There, she'd said it.

He laughed, not a mocking laugh, but a tension release. "How in the world would you believe I could think less of you? You are a beautiful woman who knows what she wants. That kind of strength is intoxicating, arousing."

She looked at him, saw the way his face was flushed, saw how taut his body was. "You promise it will be magical?"

He sat back, grinning. "If you will indulge me a moment." He pulled a blindfold from the pocket of his robe. "Let's try something simple. I'll blindfold you, and then we can just kiss a bit. See how your other senses react."

She felt a hunger rising in her. "And if I like that?" she asked.

"It is up to you, my flower. The world is yours to take. I am but a willing partner on your journey."

"Okay," she said, sitting up and holding out her hand. "Give me the blindfold." She slipped it over her head. It smelled of lilacs. For a moment she practically vibrated, expecting his touch, but nothing happened for several long heartbeats. Then his lips brushed hers, and she could smell him, the musky scent of him. She could taste the mint of his toothpaste.

When they paused to catch their breath, he whispered to her. "I could show you real magic, Trisha." His hand stroked her arm, and she leaned into him, letting her lips find his again.

Twenty-three

GUNTHER AND ANEZKA WALKED THE GROUNDS OF BLACK BRIAR. It had only been a month or so since she'd escaped the madness of her home, just ahead of the catastrophic break that forced Bub to snatch her and take her with him into the sideways. Bub had brought her back days later, nearly catatonic. She was recovering and showing miraculous progress.

"It's hard to think some days," she said, leaning on his arm for support. "I dream of that place, the whisper of voices, the dark things that came for us, tried to steal me away from Bub." She trembled against him.

Gunther squeezed her against him. "Hush now. That has passed. You are safe here with us, with me."

She looked up at him, a smile ghosting the corners of her mouth. "You are a kind man."

They walked on in silence a bit longer. She rested her head against his arm. Gunther watched the area for interruptions, signs of danger.

"I have had the same dream for three nights in a row," she said, breaking the silence. "I dream about a man crucified to a great tree. Lightning plays in the heavens above him, and he cries out into the wilderness."

Gunther had heard this before. She was not the only one dreaming of the one-eyed god. Sarah had spoken of this dream, as had Deidre. "What does he say?"

She laughed, the edge of mania still coloring that raucous cacophony, but it had lessened with time. One day, he hoped to hear her laugh for the pleasure of living, instead of the answering call to the madness that threatened to consume her.

"He asks for his children," she said, breaking into a cackle. "He believes I know them. I barely know myself." She tapered off, the last words a whisper.

"It is not yours to fix," Gunther said, finally. "Your road leads elsewhere."

"Easy for you to say," she chided. "I can no more find up from down than I can north from south. I am lost, brave warrior. Lost and afraid I will never find my way home again."

"Home is relative," he said with a gentle bump of his shoulder to hers. "You are safe here, among friends."

She squeezed his arm. "Are you my friend?"

"Most definitely," he said, and they continued their slow trek around the circumference of the barnyard. "When was the last time you did something creative?" he asked.

Anezka studied him, turning her head from one side to the other. "Define creative."

"Fair enough. When was the last time you made something with your hands?"

"Before Sarah came into my life. Before she wrecked everything."

Gunther paused, pulling her to a halt. "You think it is Sarah who has brought you to this?"

Anezka looked down, avoiding his eyes. "My life was fine until she showed up."

He took her hands in his, turned her to face him. "She saved you from Justin and his vile plans. You realize that, don't you?"

She squirmed at Justin's name. He'd done things to her, evil things that Gunther hated to even speculate about. "He would have killed you, if she hadn't rescued you."

"Perhaps," she said, pulling back from him. "He liked to hurt things, hurt me. That's a truth." She turned, walking three steps from him, before turning her gaze back on him. "You would never hurt me, would you?"

Gunther shook his head. "Never."

"Not even if I asked you to? Just a little?"

She threw her head back and laughed.

Gunther did not react. Just let her laugh until the madness trickled down to a titter, then a final wheezing cough.

"I think you've had enough pain in your life," he said, quietly. "Perhaps it's time for you to try living with joy."

She covered her face with her hands and wept. After a minute, he stepped forward and drew her to him, allowing her to cry herself out against him.

When the storm had cleared, he walked her back to the house. Took her up to her room, the only place she felt safe these days. He'd made sure to add little wards as he had the skill. Quiet things that would allow for peace and reflection without the anxiety that frequently overwhelmed her.

He sat with her as she lay down and fell asleep. She slept a lot, but she was still recovering. The nurse they kept on shift took over for him after thirty minutes, and he left the house, confident that she was safe.

As he crossed the yard, near the old barn, the one the dragon had burned down, he paused. Bub was trundling across the yard from barracks A. He'd been playing with Frick and Frack when Gunther and Anezka first began their walk. There was a sense of joy surrounding the imp, which seemed at odds with his demonic appearance.

"Bub," Gunther said, capturing the imp's attention.

Bub froze, startled. There was fear there, suddenly. Fear and resentment. Gunther took a deep breath and pressed onward. "I wish your opinion," he said.

This was not what Bub expected, apparently. He seemed taken aback. "My opinion?" he asked. "From one such as you?"

Gunther assumed he meant someone who could banish the imp for a short time, but hesitated to speculate on the meaning. "Do you love Anezka?"

"Of course I do," Bub answered, indignant. "For longer than you have."

And it was Gunther's turn to be surprised. Certainly he cared for her, but love? He'd never truly loved a woman. He had friends, and Stuart was chief among them, blood brother that he was. But love for Anezka?

"Be that as it may," he continued, "I worry for her sanity. I believe we need to find something for her to do. Something to capture her imagination, something to fire her curiosity and give her hope."

"There is only one choice," Bub said, matter-of-factly. "She must work iron, hammer steel, brighten the forge."

Dangerous, Gunther thought. "Do you think this wise?"

Bub considered, pondering his answer. "She is a child of the flame, capricious and maddening as a dancing fire. It calls to her soul. She is a maker. It is in her to create."

"Could you help her?" Gunther asked. "Keep the flames from getting out of control? Protect her from herself?"

Bub bowed to him. "I have it within my power to keep her safe, as long as you provide me a place in which to work my skills."

"Sarah said as much. She would like to build a forge here, make a place for the three of you to work together."

"She has spoken of this to me," Bub said. "It is an excellent idea."

"You truly believe it will help Anezka? It won't feed her madness?"

He did not hesitate. "It is the only thing that can free her mind from the spell the necromancer wove in her, the chains he bound her with."

Gunther looked up, surprised. "He bound her with chains?"

"Not of steel, but spirit and pain."

"Speak with Sarah on this," Gunther said. "I need to do some research on these spirit chains. Perhaps we can help break the bonds that warp her mind."

"Fire and forge," Bub answered. "You may ease the transition, for when the shackles are finally removed, she will be frightened and weak. Perhaps you can ease the transition back to her true form."

"I will study on this," Gunther said, "but if you have any ideas, please let me know. I value your insight."

Bub bowed again. "As you wish."

Gunther walked toward the new barn to grab some gear. Sparring would help clear his mind. He looked over. Stuart and Sarah sat on the deck, conspiring something mischievous, likely.

He waved at them and made his way into the barn.

Twenty-four

I sat on the deck out at Black Briar, watching Gunther and Anezka walk around and around the farm, each lap taking about twenty minutes. They were on their third lap when Stuart joined me with two mugs of hot chocolate. It was fairly cold out, but I'd traveled here by mirror instead of riding the bike. Much more civilized.

"I just don't understand why you feel honor-bound to serve her."

I looked up at him as he set the mugs down on the small table. He was still angry about the battle where we'd lost so many to the damn dragon. But Nidhogg was not Jean-Paul. No more than I was Stuart.

"They're not all the same, you know?"

He didn't answer. Didn't even look at me.

I waited him out, sipped my cocoa, and practiced my patience. I wanted to shake him, to make him see the way things had shifted, but he didn't have it in him to forgive. Not yet, not with so much blood spilled.

"You could kill her," he said, finally. "On one of your visits. If you can't take Gram, I'm sure you can find something large and heavy enough to bludgeon her with."

"Nice," I said, turning to face him. "Is that what we're down to, now? Killing an old woman in her home?"

"She's a dragon, damn it. You know she is. It's only a matter of time before she turns on you, on us." That was the real trick. He felt helpless to protect the folks of Black Briar. I had the proven record of killing a dragon and surviving. It was ugly business.

"There's another way," I offered, "if we're open to the possibility."

He watched me out of the corner of his eye.

"If I can rescue Qindra, it will put Nidhogg into my debt. That's gotta count for something."

He harrumphed and blew on his drink.

"Besides, I'm learning a ton of stuff. You want to lose that level of intelligence?"

"True," he admitted, grudgingly. "That information about her helping kill the gods, how Loki stirred the pot. All very interesting. And her thought that the wheel is broken, like Odin said to you. Makes it all weirder. Who is on whose side?"

I nodded. "Exactly my thought. What if we could make Nidhogg's domain a safe haven? We know this Joe/Odin guy has lived in Nidhogg's domain for years, even though he's disappeared lately." I thought back to the last time I'd seen Homeless Joe, the sometimes god, Odin. I hadn't figured out if he only channeled Odin from time to time, or if he really *was* Odin. It wasn't unreasonable that he'd forgotten who he was through the loneliness and grief for his lost family.

"Besides," I reasoned, "we don't know that the other dragons are like Jean-Paul. You can do the research; Frederick Sawyer is a regular philanthropist. Patron of the arts, all around pillar of his community."

Stuart groused, mumbling something foul under his breath, and generally caved. "Fine," he said. "Just like no two people are exactly the same, I'll grant you that maybe the dragons are not cut from the same cloth, but you cannot sit here and tell me you think they're harmless."

I covered my immediate reaction by sipping my drink. I knew better, at least with Nidhogg. She'd killed some of her own household in a rage. I wasn't sure if it was Alzheimer's, or some other form of dementia, but she seemed very lucid when I spoke with her. If anything, she seemed to crave some intellectual conversation and the company of someone who did not quake when she twitched.

"I'd go as far as to say that they are not all crazed sadists like Jean-Paul was, but I am under no illusions that they are benevolent rulers. They are manipulative and self-serving."

"There you go." He wasn't rubbing it in, because he knew we weren't keeping score.

"But, can you tell me a politician in the world, or any significant leader, even a CEO of a company, that isn't arrogant and self-serving at some level?"

"Touché," he said. "And I don't care much for the lot of 'em."

"Aye, but you aren't advocating we hunt any of them down and kill them, either."

He growled at me, but his shoulders sagged a bit. The fight was leaving him for now. The episodes of anger and rage were diminishing, but he would not be forgiving the breed for the loss they'd dealt us.

"What about her?" he asked, pointing out to Anezka. "And her little demon buddy?"

"I think she's desperate for companionship and Gunther fits the bill."

"He's breathing, you mean?"

Nice. "No, I mean he's been kind to her and that isn't something she's used to."

"And her old lover, the lunatic that's killing girls and animals in two countries just to find you?"

"Oh, she hates him," I assured him. "Whatever he did to her was not pretty. I'm not even sure if he doesn't have some long-term, deep-seated tether on her somehow. She's definitely a few crayons shy of a full box."

"And Bub?"

I looked for the little pisher. He was mostly sharing the company of Trisha and the twins: Frick and Frack. "He has a good heart," I said, meaning it. "He's not like us, that's for sure, but he loves Anezka like a daughter or something."

Stuart looked over at me, perplexed. "I'd say he's in love with her, but he watched her grow up. More of a protective figure at this point."

"Wasn't he more violent when you first met him?"

I reached up to touch the amulet under my shirt. His shift had begun the second I touched it. "He's aligned to me as well, through the amulet," I told him. "He was tuned only to the CRAZY.FM that Anezka was broadcasting on all channels. Once he switched to me, he began to settle down, to become more reasonable, tame."

Stuart choked, coughing and laughing at the same time. "Nothing personal, Beauhall, but you are not the pinnacle of calm and collected."

"I know, right?" I was as stunned as he was. "It's like out at Mary's place. I was the only one who couldn't see the pain writing. I assumed I was carrying buckets of it around, and it turns out I'm the only one on the farm who was pain-free."

He smiled at me. "Maybe you just have a better set of shields."

Maybe. I didn't argue with him, but ever since deciding to move in with Katie, a level of low-grade angst had vaporized.

"Of course, I'm still carrying a trunk full of psychosis about my family."

He chuckled. "That's just normal living. Hell, if I let all that get to me, my marriage would've killed me."

Whoa . . . Stuart had been . . . "When were you married?"

He glanced at me sideways, squinting. I guess he was seeing if I was busting his chops. "I was a young pup. Got married to my high school sweetheart before shipping out to Iraq in the first war. Didn't do much other than chew sand and live in boredom. But, when I got back, she'd hooked up with a few of my other friends."

"A few?"

He waved his hands to clear the air. "We got married too young. She needed to sow her wild oats. Just didn't figure I'd come home from serving my country to find my wife knocked up by some guy I counted as a friend."

He looked down, studying the cocoa in his cup. I didn't press the situation, but I could tell it still bothered him.

"And look at them," he pointed out to the yard. "Gunther and I've been thick as thieves since elementary school. I trust him with my life." He took a long draw on his mug, draining the last of the chocolate. "If he wants to fall in love with a wacked-out blacksmith, I'm all for it. As long as it doesn't interfere with our sparring and the occasional drinking binge."

He winked at me and grinned.

"Gotta tell ya," I said, laughing, "I've seen Anezka drink. She'd give you a run for your money."

He turned back to the yard and watched them. "Is that so? Maybe she's gone up a notch in my book."

"She's a damned fine blacksmith as well," I assured him. "She just needs to find her way."

"Aye, don't we all?"

I finished my chocolate and stood, picking up the mugs. "Refill?" I asked.

"Nah," he said. "I've had enough sweet for one day." He gestured out across the lawn to where Gunther and Anezka were standing, hand in hand. "If I need anymore, I'll just watch them."

I laughed and took the mugs back inside. Deidre was napping on the couch and the house was quiet. Jimmy must have been down in the basement, working.

The house had a different vibe when I was here without Katie. I felt more like I was visiting my grandparents' place or something.

Not that I'd ever visited my grandparents. Both Ma and Da had distanced themselves from any family they may or may not have had. I wasn't even sure if either of them had brothers or sisters. I could have a whole passel of cousins and I'd never know it.

Stuart came back inside, making sure the door did not bang in the frame and wake up Deidre. He watched me, smiling. "Place feels funny without Katie, huh?"

I nodded. "I was just thinking that."

He glanced around, shrugging. "Been coming here a lot of years, but every now and again, it reminds me of my grandmother's place up in Blaine."

"That's what I was thinking, only I don't know any of my extended family. Not like Da was open about much."

The spark was back in his eye. I could just feel a lecture coming. "You know, Beauhall, for a dragon slayer, you sure have a lot of fear around your old man. He beat you?" He stopped, like he'd gone too far. "Sorry, none of my business."

I sat down on the barstool at the big island in the kitchen and dropped my hands on my knees. "No, it's a fair question." How to begin with him?

"He was a kind man. Amazing, really, all the way until I could start asking questions like why we moved every year until I went to high school. He was always moving from job to job, and we didn't have a lot. Ma kept the house together, but when Megan came and I was pushing things too far, we got to fighting."

He sat and listened. I'd never really shared any of this with him, but it seemed like the right time.

"There was something he was running from," I said, feeling it out as I went along. "I can see that now. Sometimes the phone would ring late at night, and the next day Ma would take me out of school and we'd be moving right then."

"Hard on a little girl."

"Yeah, but I had a few special things, an emergency pack in my room that I could grab and run. I kept a stuffed rabbit as well, carried it around so long I'd worn the fur off its arms."

He smiled.

"But when Megan was born we had a pretty rough time. Da woke me in the middle of the night, and we disappeared. Ma was still in the hospital with Megan, and we didn't go for them. We spent three weeks living in our car, moving from wooded lot to abandoned farmhouse. Anytime he heard the slightest noise, he'd grab everything and we'd run for it. I thought we were gonna die."

I stood up and paced over to the cabinet and grabbed a glass. Then I went and got water from the fridge.

"I cried a lot. I really wanted a sister. Never could keep friends long, so I figured if I had a sister, I'd at least have someone to be friends with, even if she was a crying poop machine for the first year."

Stuart chuckled at that.

"Around midnight one night, it was cold and blowing, snow and ice beating down on the roof of the car. I lay awake in the front seat, freezing and exhausted. Neither of us was sleeping much, but I knew he was keeping me safe. I'd stopped asking about Ma and Megan. He only got angrier every time I asked, so I clammed up."

"Harsh."

"Yeah. I was lying there, thinking that some hit men or something were after us, when I started my period."

"Oh, crap. That's not good."

"No, not at all. I was only twelve, and, while I knew it was going to happen soon, I had no idea it would be while my dad was sacked out in the back of our station wagon. I started crying. We didn't have any sanitary napkins or anything, and I was so damn embarrassed.

"I finally woke him up, begged him to take me to a gas station so I could try and get cleaned up, but he lost it. First time I ever saw him cry, to tell the truth. He just sat there in his sweatpants and a wife beater, unshaven and unbathed. We were both a little too ripe, in my opinion, and for the last three days we'd been eating cold beans out of cans.

"I think he'd been so sick with worry for Ma and Megan and so equally scared that we were going to get caught by whomever he was running from that the little detail like his daughter getting her first period was too much for him. He hugged me, told me how sorry he was, and drove straight to an all-night truck stop. We went in, and he went with me to pick out the product I needed. I was horrified, and I think he was, too, but he stuck with me until I had what I thought was the right thing.

"He ordered coffee while I went into the restroom and got cleaned up. I changed into my only other set of clothes from my emergency pack and went back out to meet him. He got his coffee to go and we drove straight home. Mom had returned to the place we were staying when she left the hospital. I found out we'd run to keep me safe. Not sure what that was about, but Ma wasn't in any danger, he told me."

"So, he didn't hit you?" Stuart asked.

"No, he never hit me," I admitted. "But he kept secrets and didn't like questions. It was not too long after that time that I gave up believing in him."

I sat back down, letting the nervous energy bleed from me. "I told him I wanted a real life, wanted someplace where I could have friends. Someplace where we didn't have to leave Ma and Megan behind ever again. I told him if we didn't find someplace to call home, I was running away."

"Oy, I bet that went over well."

"I'd read Vonnegut and a bunch of other authors he didn't know about. I'd squirreled away maps and tour guides whenever I could find them. I told him I was going to run away to Seattle because it was so green. We were living in Kansas at the time, and I was sick of the flat lands. I wanted trees and mountains and the ocean. I'd never seen the ocean, but I was only twelve."

Stuart watched me, let me work my way through it.

"We moved out here, first to Bellingham for a couple years, then out to Crescent Ridge. Something about being in the shadow of Rainier calmed him down. Never figured out why, but we'd pretty much stopped talking to one another by then."

"Running from somebody seems fishy, sure, but it sounds like he was trying to protect you from something."

I rolled my head, trying to relieve the tension in my neck and shoulders. "You see, that was the problem. He was protecting me from everything. Everything terrified him when it came to me. Up until that year, he'd been the best dad, always hugging me, reading me stories, even helping out with whatever Girl Scout troop I landed in at the new house. But something changed on that trip. Something scared him so bad he was willing to abandon Ma and Megan, even for a little while, to protect me."

"Sounds like he loved you."

And he was right, of course. "Loved me with his heart and soul. And smothered me to the point I couldn't breathe. He picked the books I could read, chose my friends, even went so far as to homeschool me in case I learned something he didn't want me knowing."

"When did he find out about you liking girls?"

I looked up and shrugged. "Don't think he knows, honestly. Didn't need to say anything to him to know how he'd react. He was clear on his beliefs. Heard it from the pulpit two or three times a week. Heard it from his own lips more than I care to recall." I rubbed my temples. "I love him, never claimed different, I just can't stand the man he became."

Whatever Stuart was going to say disappeared when Anezka walked into the kitchen. She'd been sleeping. For a moment she didn't have her shields up, and she looked happy for the first time in a long while. When she saw us, however, she let the mask fall back into place—cold, aloof, and protected.

"Hey," I said, smiling. "Did you and Gunther have a good walk?"

She shrugged. "Fair enough."

Stuart winked at me. "At least the company was good."

The look she gave him was a cross between knowing and disdain. "He's a gentleman," she said.

Not sure she thought it was a good thing.

Stuart laughed and stood up. "Well, I can see how that wouldn't appeal to everyone."

Uh, oh. I watched her for a reaction, but she just smiled at him. "He's unique, I'll give him that."

"Fair enough." Stuart nodded to us and went toward the back of the house. Once we heard the door to the basement open and close, I patted the chair he'd just vacated. "Come sit with me a minute."

She eyed me, but sat.

Twenty-five

AT ONE POINT, I THOUGHT ANEZKA WOULD MAKE A FANTAS-
tic mentor, but then her world went to hell and I got swept up in
the mess.

"I have a proposition for you."

She got a wicked grin on her face and started to say something, but I forestalled her. "Nothing naked, geez."

There was an evil twinkle in her eye. "Afraid I'd make you
forget that perky little brunette you're banging?"

Oh, yes. She was a real charmer. That hadn't changed. "I
thought you might want to work. Do some smithing."

"Fuck, yeah," she grunted, looking at me with a different kind
of lust. "I've been jonesing for that for a good while now. Only,
they won't let me near anything that could burn the place down,
or explode."

Good. She'd nearly killed me at her worst. And she wasn't exactly stable yet. "I need to make a gate, real intricate job. You want
in on the deal?"

"I've made tons of gates," she said. The weirdest thing happened. It was like a veil had been parted and I saw the real Anezka.
The thought of working iron, building with fire, pushed aside
the crazy, or so it appeared by her demeanor. She was suddenly
calm.

I showed her my drawings and my specifications. We worked for nearly an hour making adjustments for weight and accurate swing of the gate, etcetera. It was probably the most rational conversation I'd ever had with her.

"If we could get to my place, I have some specialized gear that would make parts of this go really smoothly," she said. It was the first time she'd mentioned her place that I knew about. "But that's fucked up beyond all recognition."

"Aye," I agreed. "Something we'll need to get cleaned up sooner rather than later."

"I'll sell the place, as soon as I can get back to it," she said.

I watched her, but she seemed sincere.

"Soon," I said, patting her on the arm.

She glanced down to where I'd put my hand on her arm and she very gently covered my hand with hers. We sat like that for a long while. It was very sweet.

"I've been having dreams," she said to me, taking her hand off mine. "I haven't told anyone but Gunther, but I think you'd understand."

"Try me," I offered.

"It's always the same," she said, staring at something I could not see. "I'm standing on the side of a mountain. I think it's Mount Rainier, but I can't be sure. I've never been up there."

I was getting a tingling in the bottom of my stomach.

"There's a tree, huge, like something I've never seen. It had branches that seemed to reach up to the stars, and the roots reached down to the gates of hell. It was that big."

I didn't interrupt her, but I knew where she was going.

"He's calling to me," she said, lowering her voice. "The one-eye'd god is crucified on that tree, and lightning is flashing across the sky, cracking down against the mountain, striking the tree.

"'Where are my children, Smith?' he screams at me. 'Why

does no one miss their presence? Where are the kith and kin? Why do you shirk your duty?'"

I listened to her, sick with dread. I knew that dream. Knew the one-eyed god, Odin, and the way the mountain began to come apart, crashing down around the crucified man, burying the world in rock and snow.

"Am I crazy?" she asked me. "What does he want? Why does he come to my dreams?"

I took both her hands in mine. She was shaking. "It's not just you," I assured her. "I think it's been bleeding over to anyone who can hear him." I took a deep breath and let it out slowly. "I've had that dream myself."

Her eyes widened in surprise and a little relief. "He's not angry with me?" she asked, nay begged.

"No," I assured her. "Not you. Me." How had I blocked the dreams? What had I done to stop picking up the Norse god emergency broadcast signal?

Her shoulders slumped, and a smile blossomed across her face. It was moments like this where her inner beauty shone through. "I thought it was something I'd done, a debt I owed, you know?"

I nodded at her. There was a debt owed, but I'm not sure by whom. "You know there's weird shit in the world, Anezka."

She nodded slowly. Of course she knew.

"There is something he wants me to do, the one-eyed man. A geas he put on me."

"I don't want to know," she said, emphatically. "I will tell him to seek elsewhere when next he enters my dreams." She lowered her voice. "Like Justin," she looked ashamed. "He used to come to my dreams, to my bed." She shuddered.

"But, no more?" I asked.

She looked up. "Not since I've come here. He can't find me here."

"That's good."

"You bet your ass," she said, straightening up and clearing her throat. "Now, I need a nap."

She stood and made her way to the back of the house. I waited until she was in her room before I took out my cell phone and called Skella. Time for me to go home.

Twenty-six

JIMMY, OBLIVIOUS TO THE COLD BITE OF THE MOUNTAIN AIR, sat on the deck long after the rest of Black Briar was asleep. He rolled the ring around his palm, over and over, thinking. There was some piece he was missing. He could feel it—something tied to the Valkyrie statue his father had hidden the ring in, but he couldn't place it. Or had his father picked the figurine at random?

He thought about the coded note that had been hidden in the Valkyrie statue with the ring. The double-blind code was based on the writings of Marcus Aurelius and a mathematical skip pattern involving a complex key that they'd only partially solved. Something about Katie niggled at him. She was seriously pissed at him for excluding her, but he was only protecting her.

Unfortunately, there was a connection there that kept eluding him. What was he missing?

He put his head in his hands, massaging his temples. He needed to do something. Spending every waking moment in the basement poring over ancient records and breaking the code his father left was maddening. The daily goings on at Black Briar had fallen off his radar, and he needed to correct that.

Beauhall had set up a watch schedule out in Chumstick, even arranged that elf girl, Skella, to provide transportation. Maybe he needed to go out there, check on the setup. What kind of leader was he? Things were definitely out of control.

He picked up his cell phone and checked the time—two thirty. Shift change had been at midnight. Trisha and her crew were on duty.

He glanced over to the barracks where they lived. Maybe they should make some small apartments or something. They had plenty of room on the farm. Some of the members only stayed here when they were on guard duty but went back to their real lives. Trisha lived here full-time, and now with Frick and Frack she would have a hard time reintegrating back into normal society no matter what.

His life had become a menagerie. With the troll twins, Bub, Anezka, and the Black Briar regulars, he wasn't sure the world wasn't tilting right off its axis.

Skella answered on the third ring, but she'd obviously been asleep. She agreed to transport him, though he thought she might not be too happy about it.

"I'll add a bonus for this type of thing," he assured her. "And I'll come back with the next shift change."

She hung up and he went inside the house. She'd appear there in the next five or so minutes, and he wanted a few things.

He went back into the house, checked that Deidre was asleep, and slipped into the basement. The sword he'd used in the dragon battle hung on a coatrack ensconced in its scabbard, and he felt the need to carry it. Magic screwed up modern machinery, which included guns at some level.

The shotgun Sarah had taken from Anezka's house was covered in crazy carvings that Bub had insisted would allow it to work in the most heavily infested magical areas, but he wanted to leave that for Deidre, in case something happened while he was gone.

Putting on the sword reminded him of his own father. He'd

only seen him don this weapon once, but it had been to protect
the farm and refugees from marauding giants when he was a wee
lad. It was the deepest part of the night when he missed his parents the most. He leaned against a long display case and took
several deep breaths. Tears were not welcome. Once he had it under control, he climbed the stairs, shutting the door to the basement with a quiet click.

"Ready?" Skella asked him from the living room.

She had on a pair of jeans and a long white T-shirt that obviously did not belong to her. The band on the front was something that Beauhall would like, so he speculated it had been her
shirt at one time. Katie told them how Gletts, Skella's brother,
had stolen a bunch of clothes from Sarah before he had been
injured in the battle in Vancouver. Ghosts, it had been, or some
form of spirits. He didn't argue semantics with Katie. She had a
dozen names for different types of haunts.

"Sorry about the time," he said, grabbing his heavy coat, gloves,
and a stocking cap.

She shrugged. "Don't make a habit of it." The mirror rippled at
her touch, and, within seconds, he stood at the Black Briar encampment in Chumstick.

Nancy Butler whirled around when he stepped through the
mirror, her crossbow loaded for bear.

"Don't shoot," he said, holding up his hands.

"Jesus, Jimmy," she said, aiming to his left. "What the hell
are you doing out here?" She paused, then added, "sir."

He shook his head. "Felt the need to see how things were
going. Where's Trisha?"

"She and Benny are doing a circuit of the place."

"And I'm right here," Gary said, stepping out of the shadows.
He had his crossbow loaded as well.

"Glad you folks weren't sleeping," Jimmy said, smiling.

They returned to keeping watch, and Jimmy walked across the road to stare at Anezka's place.

The energy dome over the house and grounds was still intact—strong as ever, by the looks of it. He bent down, grabbed a handful of gravel, and chucked stones at the wall for a few minutes, thinking. Not everyone could see the dome, frankly. It had the effect of diverting the eye, forcing the attention to focus elsewhere. He had to really concentrate to keep it in view.

He didn't like being in the dark, didn't understand Qindra and her magic. His own mother had been a witch of middling power. Not that he had any specific details. There were hints, notes left behind, remembrances of a young child. But this. He tossed another rock against the dome, annoyed and relieved that it bounced off.

Spirits went in but did not come out. What kind of magic was this, and how was Qindra keeping it going after all this time?

The unknown scared him more than all the dragons and trolls combined. He hated feeling helpless.

Everything in the world was sliding off the cracker, and he was sick of his family and friends being in the thick of it. This year had been so off the charts, he was afraid for the new year coming. Hell, Christmas wasn't that far off. The years were slipping by faster and faster. His parents had been gone now for thirteen years. For most of them, he'd had very little interaction with the "other" world. Now, since the spring, they'd been attacked by dragons and visited by gods. There was definitely a shift happening, and he couldn't get ahead of it. Was it Beauhall, that sword of hers, or maybe it was he and Katie. Hell, he had no real answers, but plenty of questions.

Snow began to fall around him, dampening the sounds of the world. He watched the white flakes fall around the house, but not through the dome. It kept even the snow and rain out. But not the cold, he bet. He could see spirits trapped inside, wispy things that were drawn to where he stood. It was as if they could sense him, body heat, living spirit, something. On the other side of the domed wall, they grew thick, like hot breath on a cold window.

How was the witch surviving inside there? And what would happen if she finally succumbed? Spirits were still drawn here, angry things, violent things. Trisha had reported hearing them battling inside, hunting and consuming their own kind. Katie and Sarah had described it before, and he shuddered to think of his baby sister, alone inside there, while Sarah and Qindra were trapped by whatever it was that had held them there.

Of course, Katie had saved Sarah, but Qindra had stayed behind, sacrificing herself to keep the nasties locked inside. He respected that. It's what he would've done.

She continued to maintain the dome, but he knew it was more than that. She had a dedication, a driving conviction to keep the world safe; he saw that. And his crew had things under control on the outside. Or, at least, they had the illusion of control. What he could do, besides figuring out the meaning of the ring, was to help find the bastard necromancer, Justin. What a pussy name for a serial killer and overall wicked badass. But that didn't stop those girls from being dead. Didn't stop the fact that he was hunting Sarah and by extension, Katie.

He hated feeling so fucking helpless.

Tomorrow he'd get with Gunther and Stuart. Maybe it was time to do something more, something daring. Stuart would be happy, he was sure.

Skella knew about this Justin prick. He'd check her for information. The freak was a protégé of Jean-Paul, the Vancouver dragon, Sarah had snuffed. Maybe Skella's people would have some leads.

He just knew he couldn't sit back and do nothing.

Twenty-seven

FREDERICK SAWYER LOUNGED IN THE PENTHOUSE SUITE AT the Fairmont Hotel in downtown Seattle, sipping a cup of English breakfast tea and watching the sunrise over the mountains to the east.

He let the morning wash over him, keeping his chi balanced with the rhythms of the waking city. *Soon*, he thought.

A quiet knock broke the silence, and he allowed a smile to touch his face. "Come in."

Mr. Philips strode into the room, his presence as reassuring as always. How ever had he lived without this paragon of efficiency?

"I have news," Mr. Philips said.

Frederick nodded once to his servant and went back to his tea, listening.

"Your sources have confirmed your understanding of recent events," he said, referring to a small notepad he pulled from his jacket. "One of Jean-Paul's minions has attacked and killed your operative in Bellevue, the young barista you had hired to keep an eye on the special subject, Sarah Beauhall."

Frederick sat his tea to the side, careful to not upset the pot of tea on the small table. "She was quite pretty, as I recall."

"Yes, sir. You do have an eye for a certain type of woman."

Ah, women. He considered how his life was enhanced by their

subtle curves and willing spirits. And so many baristas. Was there any wonder the smell of a strong cup of coffee could give him an erection? "That must be rectified," he said. "I cannot have those in my employ become the victims of some deranged lunatic. How does that make me look?"

"Quite right, sir," Mr. Philips agreed. "The twist, however, will interest you."

"Go on."

"Word is that the fair Qindra has not been seen in weeks, perhaps as long as six to eight."

That was most interesting. "And?"

Mr. Philips turned the page in his notepad, jotting down several check marks before continuing. "Her grace Nidhogg has apparently decided it prudent to bring Sarah Beauhall into her employ."

Frederick leaned forward, steepling his fingers together in front of his mouth. "Now, that is delicious news. The smith, a lackey for her most bloatedness." He stood, paced over to the desk, and opened a file folder. "I would have believed, after the incident with Jean-Paul, that Ms. Beauhall had chosen sides against our kind."

"None of my sources indicate the level of interaction with the community that Qindra had exerted. But it is known in many circles that she is Nidhogg's and to cross her is to cross the grande dame herself."

"Impressive. I believe we have been played, Mr. Philips. This Beauhall is either one of life's anomalies that bumble along, falling into success without even trying, or she is more attuned to the game of thrones than I'd given her credit for."

Mr. Philips nodded. "She is indeed a cipher. One we are well advised to underestimate at our peril."

Frederick didn't react to the bluntness of Mr. Philips's reply. That was one of the things he valued most highly—the ability to get a clear assessment of things. More than once, Mr. Philips had an insight into something that Frederick himself had misread. He knew dragon kind, that was for sure. There were moments where he considered the man almost a peer, at least intellectually.

"Arrange to handle my business from here for a few days," he said, pacing back to the windows. Seattle was a concrete and steel island amid turbulent waters. How would they weather the storm to come? "And arrange for a meeting with Nidhogg, or whichever functionary she deems appropriate. No need to have her discover our little jaunt northward on her own. We will be open and forthright in our business here. Allow her to extract her pound of flesh. But believe me," he said, turning back, "I will have answers from this so-called necromancer. He does not serve Nidhogg's interest. Perhaps it is time the old cow and I had a common goal, something to endear me to her. What do you think?"

Mr. Philips flipped back through several pages of notes before answering. "I believe it prudent to uncover the motives and goals of this necromancer. If we can win points with her eminence, it would serve your cause well. If I may say so, sir, I find myself most interested in how this may all tie in with Ms. Beauhall."

"Yes," Frederick agreed. "That is a most interesting connection. See what you can find."

He turned back to the window and watched the sheep pursuing their petty lives. They packed the roads like lemmings. Would they not be better off under his loving wing?

The irony of the thought was not lost upon him. The soft click of the door closing told him that Mr. Philips had gone to his duties. "I wonder what the art scene in this deprived community has to offer one as discriminating as myself?"

He called down to the concierge. Let the city entertain him while his minions sifted through the crumbling pieces of Nidhogg's domain. Soon enough he would stride onto the scene, rescuing her people from a century of malaise and neglect.

"Yes," he said into the hotel phone. "I'd like to inquire as to the available performance art options for this evening."

He patiently waded through the young man's questions.

"Another thing," he asked before disconnecting. "Where might I find a truly decent cup of coffee in this city?"

Twenty-eight

TRISHA AND EFRAIN SAT NAKED IN THE MIDDLE OF HIS LIVING room. Efrain had drawn circles within circles upon the bare wooden floor, each drawn with blood, salt, and wax. Trisha sat in one, while Efrain sat in a second. Those circles were wrapped in two other circles intertwined, like a number eight, or an infinity symbol.

Finally, all of it was in a greater circle drawn with chalk runes and other arcane symbols.

When he first started speaking of real magic, she thought he was being coy, speaking in metaphor. But when he offered to show her, she hesitated. Now, she was glad he persisted.

She knew of magic from the horrors of that night with the dragon and his minions. But the witch had helped them, and she wielded magic. Maybe she could learn from him. Magic had been fiction until recently. Why not take advantage of it? Then, maybe, she could save those she loved, instead of seeing them cut down.

She'd never felt more alive. There was a sexual energy in the air unlike anything she'd ever known. She could feel her body reacting, her nipples stiffening and trills of pleasure running down her abdomen and into her groin.

He chanted words she did not understand, but the power of

them was like raindrops of ecstasy. As he wove his magic, she saw how excited he got, how his manhood rose with each word, until he was rigid.

"You see?" he asked.

Her breath became rapid and her heart raced. He hadn't touched her, yet she neared climax. "Yes," she breathed.

"Not everyone appreciates the power, nor revels in it the way I do. Can you feel it, Trisha? Does your blood quicken?"

"Oh, God. Yes!" She struggled not to touch herself, to bring herself to that final peak. He had insisted she wait. Promised that it would be beyond anything she could imagine.

She yearned for release, but watched him, waiting for his signal. Letting all this be in his hands. And they were such beautiful hands, she thought. Untouched by the scars that criss-crossed his body. She loved his body, there was no mistaking it, but the scars were startling in their abundance and intricacy.

"Blood," he said, drawing her attention back to his mouth. "Blood is the key. There is more power in a thimble full of blood than in a ton of uranium. Imagine being able to wipe out your enemies without destroying the world with nukes."

Part of her rebelled against this, the blood magic he spoke of, but another part of her thrilled with the thought of it all. Being that powerful, controlling the energy needed to defeat your enemies and save your loved ones.

Between them, in a smaller wrought circle, sat a woven basket holding two doves. He took the basket and carefully plucked out one of the shaking birds. Before Trisha could react, he snapped the bird's neck, chanting words she'd never heard before. A white mist rose from the murdered dove, and he inhaled it. She watched intently as the glowing vapor slid into his mouth and nose, vanishing in his long inhalation. When he exhaled, the vapor was gone—incorporated into his spiritual reserves.

He nodded to her, taking the second dove from the cage. "Just inhale when I hold it to you," he said, smiling like a thousand-watt billboard. "I promise you it will be okay. When we are done, we will restore the birds, as the power of life is greater than the power of death."

She nodded once, terrified to move a single muscle.

He snapped the bird's small neck and held it to her. The mist began to dissipate under her face. In a panic, she inhaled quickly, and the vapor filled her nostrils, her head, her spirit. She could feel the dove, understood his joy for flying free, experienced the amazing sensation of absolute freedom.

Then it was gone, like a memory of glory. She flagged a moment, desperately craving the taste of the mist.

"You can revive them?" she asked, desperate to believe him.

"Raising the dead is within our grasp," he assured her. "There are those who fear it, fear the loss of control, are horrified by reviving the dead, but it is not only feasible, but practical."

He held up the broken dove, spoke an arcane word, and threw the bird into the air, where it cried once and began circling them, beating its wings with panic.

"You see?" he asked her a third time.

And she did see; she accepted his power and wept for the joy of it. So many had died at Black Briar when the dragon and his minions invaded. Her best friend, her would-be lover.

She looked at Efrain guiltily. They had not consummated their relationship, but they'd done things, she'd done things, that she never dreamed of.

"Save the best for last," he told her when she begged him to make love to her the last time they had been together. How many times would he bring her to the brink, right up to the very edge of climax, and then leave her, allowing it to settle back, leaving her frustrated and angry.

"But it is vital," he told her, "that we do this right. This cannot be something you throw away, to be forgotten in the gutter. This will be beautiful beyond your wildest dreams."

So she waited, frustrated and anxious. Would this be the moment he allowed her to touch him, to feel him inside her?

He spoke more words of power, and the lust in her was so great, she thought to crawl to him, to ravage him against his will.

But he knew of her need, felt her pulsing through the magic, she could tell by the way he looked at her. He knew exactly what he was doing, and she wanted the release more than her next breath.

She felt helpless in front of him, naked and wanting, so very frustrated and urgent in her needs. There was no way to reach him while in her circle, and he had impressed upon her the need to remain within the confines he built, to protect her.

In the end, her mind could no longer withstand the physical need, and she blacked out. There at the last, she saw him smile at her before the world faded to black.

When she woke, he leaned over her, chafing her wrists and wiping her face with a cool rag.

"Oh, good," he said when her eyes fluttered open. "Welcome back to the living."

She stared down, but he had covered her in a blanket. He had put on sweatpants, but his scarred chest was bare in front of her, within reach of her questing fingers.

For a moment, she let her hand rest on his chest; then she noticed the birds flying in the air above the couch. He pushed the hair from her face, and she saw he had bandaged his right hand. Red blotches showed through the bandages.

"As I said," he held up the hand. "I brought them back, and I am no worse for the effort."

She took his hand and kissed the back of it, where the bandage did not cover flesh.

"Magic is powerful, my dear Trisha. Powerful and terrible. Something that only the wisest and strongest utilize for the greater good. I have friends who are very loyal. Very interested in making things right."

She smiled at his touch as the birds flew silently around the room.

"You should sleep," he said, stroking her forehead. "You are exhausted."

"Maybe just for a bit," she replied, closing her eyes, slipping into unconsciousness.

Justin rose, sloughing off the Efrain personae like a snake shedding its skin. He chanted in a language of bruises, and the final vestiges of his alter ego faded with the flashes of collapsing quasars.

He held his wounded hand above her body. The blood rose in a thin red mist through the bandage, creating an intricate net that settled over her in layers, allowing the knots and strands to settle onto Trisha and seep into her.

"Soon I will take what is rightfully mine," he crooned to her. "We will rise up and rule together. First, I will bring forth your greatness; then, I shall transform to match you. It is only a matter of time." He chuckled. "And the death of a dragon or two."

Overhead, the doves continued their lazy circling of the room, their dead eyes seeing nothing, their broken necks askew.

Twenty-nine

I TOSSED AND TURNED THROUGH MOST OF THE NIGHT. THERE was something niggling the back of my brain, some avenue I hadn't pursued. The talk I'd had with Skella came to mind, the way she and her grandmother were so sure that Gletts was out there somewhere, waiting to come home.

I woke with a start. Of course, how had I been so dense? I had a way to go exploring on my own. I'd done it before, even if I was too out of control to really have a handle on things.

Sure enough, the answer was clear. All I had to do was go walkabout. Shy of being hammered, or poisoned, I had no real idea how to get there again, but I was willing to bet Skella's grandmother may have a clue. Ancient elf, lived for years under a dragon without being caught. She had to know something about it, being all magical and stuff. At least, Katie figured she was. What the hell did I know, really? If I could figure this out, maybe I could get out and talk to Qindra, scout the place out in Chumstick. Take some action instead of sitting on my ass and feeling useless.

I called Skella.

"Hey, girlfriend," she said, as soon as she picked up.

"Hey," I replied. Girlfriend I wasn't sure about, but whatever. "I need to talk to your grandmother, I think."

Skella laughed. "Seriously? She's not touching a cell phone. She hates modern technology."

Great. "Okay, I need to talk to her, all the same. Could I come visit, maybe?"

"Let me check with her and get back to you," she offered. "She's over with Gletts right now."

"Call me back."

" 'Kay."

I nuked the leftover coffee and took out my knitting. My hand had improved dramatically from the dragon-fire injury in May. I could probably get away without the physical therapy the knitting provided, but I was beginning to like it. I was working on a hat now. I'd given away three scarves. Well, Julie had taken the first two to stop me from trashing 'em. Katie asked for the third one. It was sweet.

"Ready?" Skella asked.

I looked up to see her climbing through the mirror in the hallway. "You should bring the knitting," she suggested. "Might put Gran at ease. You're a little high energy for her."

"Let me finish this," I said, counting off the completed row. I packed the yarn and needles into my knitting bag and got my jacket. "Did she say anything when you told her I wanted to speak with her?"

Skella shrugged. "No, but she's still willing to talk."

"Great. Let me text Katie, tell her where I'm going in case something comes up."

Five minutes later, we were walking through the woods of Stanley Park.

"Any change in Gletts?"

She shrugged and dug her hands deeper into her jeans. "One of the others died last night."

I stopped. "Damn, I'm sorry."

"You didn't even know his name," she said, walking on. "Gran wasn't sure he'd come back to us, in any case. He had other problems."

We broke through the tree line and into the village they kept hidden from the outside world. Skella lived with her grandmother in a house that ran into the side of a hillock. There was plenty of room for guests, as I'd discovered.

But we were heading to the common house, almost a longhouse from old Norse culture. Only this one was a place of healing and peace. Several people watched us as we crossed the open spaces, some smiled and waved, but most watched us, well, me, suspiciously. Strangers rarely brought them anything but pain.

Inside the building I found most of the pallets set up in the middle of the great room still held the wounded. Family and friends tended to them. Those physically wounded had all gone back to their lives, but those who had suffered spiritual damage battling the ghosts and wraiths remained. They were whole, unscathed to the naked eye, but their spirits had been damaged, some severely. Riven from their bodies, Skella's grandmother, Unun, had explained.

"Their spirits will find their way home," she'd assured me when we first arrived after the battle. "He's a good boy. He'll come back to us."

She meant Gletts, of course. Skella's brother and her grandson. He'd fallen protecting Skella, Katie, Melanie, and Ari as they tried to escape the battle.

A spirit in the form of a *Tyrannosaurus rex* had attacked him. He saved the others but fell, his spirit damaged or fled.

I bowed when I stood before Unun. She bathed Gletts, wiping down his lithe limbs with a gentle touch.

"You needed something from me?" she asked, not taking her attention from her grandson.

"Knowledge," I answered. "I would ask if you could help me understand something, some magic I wish to perform willfully."

She glanced at me, then to Skella. "What do you know of this, Granddaughter?"

"Nothing," she said. "She's my friend. She asked to speak to you, but she did not go into details as to why. I expect that she has a good reason for seeking answers."

Unun studied her a moment more, then turned her gaze upon me. "It is rare that one of your race has a need for what you call magic that goes beyond seeking power or revenge."

Except for Qindra and Justin, I didn't know anyone else who used magic. I'd have to take her word for it. "Fair enough. Let me explain what I need and you can decide if you deem me worthy of your time."

She nodded, motioning Skella to take her place at Gletts's side.

Skella moved there and raised her eyebrows at me once she was behind Unun. I smiled and diverted my attention to the old elf.

"Walk with me," Unun said.

We left the building and walked around to a large garden full of covered beds. Harvest had been a month earlier, and the soil had been tilled and covered for the spring planting.

"You saved us and have been kind to my granddaughter," she began. "But I am not pleased with the cell phone you have given her, nor the method of her employment with you and your clan."

Blunt enough. "We are protecting the world from the same spirits that wounded Gletts." It was mostly true. Protecting seemed a bit of a stretch. More like watching so we could react if something happened.

She thought on this a moment and nodded. "We will set that aside for now. Tell me of this magic you seek."

We walked among the orderly garden, and I told her of the times I'd gone walkabout. I didn't sugarcoat any of it, but left out the parts that didn't matter, like how I'd gotten myself into trouble with a couple of rough cowboys. But I explained how I'd been dog drunk the first time I went astral. Then I explained about the time Skella and Gletts came to our hotel room, having poisoned Katie and me. Finally, I ended up with Anezka's place, the house of horrors, where I'd been sucked from my body and down to the hidden cavern.

"You see," I said. "Each time, I'd been influenced by other things. I want to go walkabout on purpose. I think if I can learn this, I can cleanse the ley line that runs under Chumstick. This is a good thing, right? Better for all of us." It would also allow me to free Qindra and stop the house from being a collector for horrible energy. Somehow, I knew Justin was going to use that like a battery to perform some significant magic that we would all regret.

"I may be able to help you," Unun said. She had her hands folded in front of her as she walked, looking totally like a monk or something. She exuded peace and tranquility. I, on the other hand, must have glowed like a roman candle.

"Let us go back to the infirmary and gather some herbs we'll be needing," she said. "We are familiar with a similar magic. One not unlike how Skella and Gletts travel the mirrors."

I hadn't put the connection together quite that way, but it was an interesting thought. We walked around the garden one last time. I tried to keep my thoughts mellow, my actions cool, but I was anxious, jumpy. If I could make this work . . . holy crap. This could change things, big time.

When we finally walked back to the infirmary I was about out of my head with anticipation.

"This will take awhile," Unun said. "And I would appreciate it if you were not here while I work. Your presence agitates me."

Wow, that was harsh.

"How long do you need?" Skella asked.

"A few hours. You are as bad as she is," Unun said. "I will be done when I am done. One cannot rush this type of thing. Honestly, do either of you ever breathe?"

Skella grinned at me as Unun worked her way through the infirmary. She spoke with everyone she passed, even placed her hands on the wounded, giving each a moment's concentration, praying maybe.

"Come on," Skella said when she noticed I was fretting over the delay. "Let's go someplace else."

"I thought you had to stay with Gletts," I said.

"Oh, right." She pouted, the young girl she really was coming through the goth makeup and the stoic demeanor.

"I'll call Rolph," I suggested. "See about meeting him for dinner somewhere. Then I'll come back here. Sound okay?"

It was early. Likely Rolph wouldn't be able to go out for a couple more hours, but Unun had an air about her that told me she was not rushing anything. Partly to teach me a lesson, I was fairly sure.

"I'll call you when I'm done. That okay?"

She shrugged. "Sure. I'll just go back to singing to Gletts. He seems to like it."

She had a lovely voice. I'd heard her sing on several occasions. I stood to the side as she began a quiet tune of coming home. I let myself out, crossed the village and went into the woods where I'd entered on several previous occasions. I could leave, but I'd need a guide to get back.

By the time I'd made my way out to the edge of Stanley Park it was getting closer to dark.

Rolph was finally over his flu and agreed to meet me for dinner. He gave me the name of a local Thai place he liked, and I grabbed a cab. I hadn't seen the guy in a few months. And with Juanita down in Bellingham with her sister, I bet he needed some company about now.

Thirty

Rolph and I weren't exactly friends in the truest since. He had tried to wound me once. I'd have said kill, but I had the feeling if he meant me dead, I'd be dead. The sword Gram was his obsession. Had been since he'd reforged it several hundred years ago as a child, after the dragon we know as Frederick Sawyer had wiped out his village back in the old country. These days it's called Sweden.

Rolph had quested for Gram ever since it left his possession. I had no idea how he'd lost it. When he'd forged it from the shards of the original sword he'd done a bad job. The blade had not been as strong as it should have been and the magic—the spirit—hadn't been there.

Not until I reforged it this past spring. While I'd repaired the physical blade, I'd somehow managed to imbue it with the magic it had once possessed. Gram was a dragon-slaying blade, and she'd claimed me more than I'd claimed her.

Rolph was jealous. He coveted Gram beyond reason. Of course he wanted to kill Frederick Sawyer for killing his family. But there was also the fact that he was a dwarf and dwarves covet things of power. It was in their nature.

He was better than some dwarves I'd met, so in the end he managed to fight his instincts. He respected my smithing and weapon skills, especially after I'd killed the dragon Jean-Paul. So we were at a truce: common enemies, common obsessions. Enemy of my enemy and all that.

He was a good guy, overall. I just wouldn't trust him with the family jewels.

The Thai place was packed, but they turned the tables quickly. We got a place in the back, and he ordered beers for us. I'd never had Thai beer, but he knew what to order.

The meal was delicious and the beer adequate, if a little too light for my taste. We settled back and ordered a third round of beers while we exchanged news.

While he was seriously worried about Juanita, she was doing well. It was sweet to see him fuss about it. He even had pictures of her on his cell phone. The six months or so since she and Rolph had been together had been good for her. She looked thinner and oh so much happier than when she was hanging out with the actor JJ as one of his three regular hookups. Here she had one man's attention and seemed to have blossomed for it.

"You're going to be a papa," I said, holding my beer up to toast him. "May you have a happy and healthy family."

We clinked bottles, and he drained his in one long pull. "Skoal," he said when he slammed the empty bottle onto the table.

Rolph had been my first "other" friend. He came out to me in the spring, let me know that he was a dwarf, helped me forge the sword. He had all kinds of inside knowledge into this world. No reason not to pump him for info on the whole astral-project thing.

He was patient, listened to me ramble about the other times, some I'd discussed with him before, but he let me find my way through the telling. Helped sometimes, repeating things, finding connections.

"This walkabout, as you call it. Will you try to reach the witch this way?"

"Yes," I told him. "That bastard Justin is out there killing women and horses, looking for me. And all the time more spirits are drawn to Anezka's place, collecting like a huge battery."

"Interesting thought," he said. "Perhaps he is planning an extraordinary spell of some sort, something that will utilize that much power."

"That's my thought. Can you imagine what he'd be trying?"

He shrugged and flagged down a waitress. "Two more?" he asked me as she came over.

"Sure, why not. I'm not driving."

He grinned and ordered a couple more beers. At the last second he added crab wontons. The man liked to eat.

"I think you should be careful," he advised. "The house traps spirits. You in walkabout would be a spirit, would you not?"

"Yeah," I agreed. "I'll need to go slowly. Test the waters. Maybe do a couple trial runs where someone can wake me and pull me back into my body."

"Is that possible?"

Good question. Not like I had much experience at any of this. "I'll test that, too."

The last beer and wontons vanished and Rolph still hadn't asked about Gram. I took that as a good sign.

"I spoke with someone in the king's organization," he said, peeling the label off a beer bottle. "You are known to them."

"How so?"

"They were once part of Jean-Paul's organization. I am not sure in what capacity, but they had no love for him. As a matter of fact, they feel a debt of gratitude to you for ridding the world of his vile depredation."

"That sounds promising."

He nodded. "They consider you a liberator. A hero of the realm, as it were."

"Cool. I think maybe I should meet this King of Vancouver."

Rolph thought on it long and hard. I let him have his space, waiting with hands crossed on the table in front of me, emulating Unun in her patience.

"They offered me certain opportunities as a compatriot of yours," he said at last. "Some I would have been more than willing to explore before Juanita found she was with child."

"Being a dad is serious business," I said. "I'm sure you'll do the right thing."

He sat back, pushing the wonton plate away. "I have to take many things into consideration. My life span is different from your kind. It concerns me that I will outlive Juanita and perhaps the child."

"Will this child not carry your traits as well? Including life span, at least living longer than my folks, for example?"

"I do not know. And I believe that is the crux of my worry."

"Do you love her?"

He didn't hesitate. "Of course."

"Then spend the time you have with her. Let her know how you feel and raise your child to be strong and open-minded."

The words seemed to settle him a bit. We paid the bill, and he hailed me a cab. Ever the gentleman. "Keep in touch," I told him. "And let us know if there's a baby shower or anything."

"Damn," he swore. "Another thing I had not considered. Perhaps her sister can do this for her. Does that seem fair?"

I patted him on the arm. "I'm sure the two of you can work it out, big guy."

The cab arrived. He held his hand out for me to shake, and on impulse I hugged him. I think it was because of how scared he seemed about the baby. I rarely hugged anyone.

The look on his face was worth it, however.

"Be safe," he said to me, holding the cab door open. "I will be sure to send you any knowledge I can find about this necromancer."

Oh, right. I'd totally forgotten to ask. Too many competing thoughts.

"Please do," I said after the door was shut and I rolled down the window. "He's a crazy one. Watch your back."

He patted the side of the cab, and we pulled away. "Stanley Park," I said, leaning back with my eyes closed. He was basically a good guy who had a hard life. I really did wish him the best.

Now to see what Unun had cooked up for me.

Thirty-one

My meeting with Unun was short. She gave me the herbs, explained the proper way to prepare the tea, and shooed me on my way. I was in and out of the village in under fifteen minutes. I could really feel the love.

Skella apologized when she dropped me off at the apartment. She was embarrassed. Katie was very polite to her, and I gushed about her help, so in the end she left happy. Katie, on the other hand, was pissed. "That took way longer than I thought," she said. "I've been worried."

"I met with Rolph," I said, as if that fixed everything. "We had dinner."

I looked over to see she'd cooked, of course. She had the skills. Tuna casserole was one of my favorites. I'd have it for lunch.

"Did you eat?" I asked her.

"No. I was worried about you."

I took her hands in mine and walked her to the table. "Then eat. I'll tell you what happened while you were at school."

"Okay," she said, sitting where I guided her. "Did you learn what you needed?"

I explained what I'd learned from Rolph. She asked a few questions, and we discussed sending a gift to Juanita. Once we were cleaning up the dishes, I explained about my ideas for walkabout and what I'd learned from Unun. I was anxious to try the tea Unun had prepared for me.

Katie was excited. This was right up her alley. She laughed as we made preparations for my first, deliberate walkabout. We moved the coffee table out of the middle of the living room and built a nest out of a sleeping bag, pillows, and blankets. That was for me. We made a bed for Katie on the couch. She got her guitar out so she could sing to me as I went to sleep.

We lit several dozen candles around the room and cut off the lights. Unun had insisted on natural light. None of the fancy technological contraptions. I steeped a cup of tea from the blend she'd made for me—careful to follow the instructions precisely. The water had to be a certain temperature before I could pour it over the ball of loose tea I had in my cup. I could add no more than a teaspoon of sugar, and the tea must steep for exactly one hundred and fifty heartbeats. I think I got it right.

Katie stopped singing long enough to whistle at me as I shimmied out of my jeans and panties, so I wiggled my rear end at her before stripping my shirt over my head.

Once I was naked, I picked up the perfectly steeped tea and carried it to the nest. I sat with my legs crossed and blew on the tea to cool it.

It was bitter despite the sugar. Luckily I only had to drink a few swallows for it to take effect. I guess I got about half the cup in me.

Katie took the cup as I lay back. She pulled the blankets over me as sleep took me.

In what felt like a split second, I was up and out of my body. I could see pretty well, and I was indeed walkabout. My body lay on the ground at my feet, my chest rising and falling in a very deep sleep. Totally cool. I wasn't dizzy or lightheaded or anything that Unun warned me could happen.

The entire world, or at least the apartment, was in black and white. Like an old movie. It was both cool and unsettling at the same time. That is until I turned around and saw Katie asleep on the couch.

There, much to my delight and annoyance, was a colorful rainbow of light arcing from Katie's sleeping form to my own. I felt like a commercial for the national GLBTQ campaign to prove that gay people love just as deeply as straight people.

Frankly, I found the irony thick. I avoided rainbows in an effort to distance myself from the crusaders, and here was a vibrant manifestation of one.

Then I noticed that the candles were burned down to stubs. Maybe it wasn't as quick a transition as I'd thought.

Just like the first three times, I had difficulty moving around. Unun had told me I could will myself into a direction if my mind was centered and my thoughts clear of distraction.

That being the case, I hovered where I was for nearly fifteen minutes. I wasn't sure how long the tea would last, or how long I could stay in this form, but I didn't want to waste the time I had.

Finally, I found the ability to move. I'd moved during my other walkabouts, but it was like swimming upstream through molasses. Here, I was just thinking I wanted to touch Katie, even though I couldn't actually feel her. I wondered if she could feel me. And just like that, I found myself flowing across the room toward her. It was only three feet, but when you've been hovering in one spot, craning around, unable to move, three feet is like a miracle.

I tried to brush her hair from her eyes, but her hair didn't move. It was strange, though. I could feel her when I touched her, but inside, like an emotion.

She didn't react outwardly. Total bummer. I'd totally hoped for one of those Patrick Swayze *Ghost* moments.

Now that I'd figured out how to move, I explored the apartment.

I could see places I didn't know existed before my eyes had opened in the astral form, but I didn't have X-ray vision or anything.

Not much different from the real world, only everything remained black and white. As I thought about it, I don't think things were black and white the other times I'd gone astral. Maybe it was the tea. I'd have to look into that as well.

The bedroom was just like the rest of the house. I poked around, looking for secrets, but beyond the box of toys Katie kept beneath the bed the room was pretty blasé. I turned to leave, but something behind the bed caught my eye. I could barely make out a shadow of a door behind the headboard. There was no door there in the real world. Perhaps it was the memory of a door.

I floated above the bed and examined it. I'd traveled between solid objects on other walkabouts, so I figured I could probably put my hand through the wall where the impression of the door was. I had a feeling the door had been in that space long before the apartment had been built. An older building, then. It had a presence beyond its physical existence. I had no idea how I knew that. It just felt right, ya know?

The apartment on the other side of that wall should be a mirror image of this one, and it had been vacant for a while now. I pitied anyone who moved in there. Katie and I tended to get a little rambunctious. The occasional hollering and banging about.

The thought made me all tingly. It was strange. I was definitely a little turned on despite the fact that I had no physical body that could react at this moment. Spiritually aroused, I guess.

I reached for the doorway, feeling a bit of a daredevil.

I pushed my hand into the wall to the right of the doorway, and it felt like I was trying to push through oatmeal. Thick and viscous. I could do it, but it would take some effort. Next, I tried the doorway. There was more resistance than when I moved through the open air, that's for sure. The space wanted to be a doorway, so it was easier, if that makes any sense.

I leaned my head forward next, pushing through to see the other side before I committed my entire being. I'd been able to pull my hand back with no problems. As I slid across the threshold something odd happened. Unlike crossing from the living room to the bedroom, this had a different feel.

A sucking sensation pulled me sideways into the wall. I fought it, struggling against the force. I flung my arms out, grabbing either side of the narrow gap between the wall, and halted my forward motion. My mind raced back to Skella and her description of the sideways. This was it, in the raw.

The sideways was not the narrow point between the walls. Instead, it was a whole wide world. A world full of sharp angles and crystal. If I flowed against those shards that made this new world, I knew my spirit would be shredded. Danger, my mind screamed. This is not where you want to be.

I redoubled my efforts to pull away and felt myself moving a fraction of the way out of the slipstream. *Clear your mind, Beauhall*, I thought to myself. *Keep your head and will yourself out.*

I was locked in a balance, part of me being pulled forward like taffy, the rest held back in the real world.

Something tiny scuttled across the crystalline landscape— a many-legged thing with pincers half the size of its body. Crap. A wave of spindly, many-legged creatures swarmed over the distant hills. And, following in their wake, came the mack daddy of eaters. Skella's warnings had not done it justice. My mind flashed to Shelob from *Lord of the Rings*, but even that beast paled in comparison to this monster. Here was a predator on par with the dragons, only this creature had only one thought: eating. I could feel its hunger washing over me in great putrid waves. I might have started screaming.

The slipstream pulled at me as I struggled, losing strength and hope. "Help me," I whispered. I could do no better than that.

"Fool!" a voice blasted into my psyche. I looked around, and a streak of light sped toward me. I had no idea who or what it was, but there was color there, a golden glow that was warm and welcoming.

"Get back," the voice echoed across the crystalline world. I was shoved back across the threshold.

I woke screaming. The eater had been nearly upon us. Yet, somehow, I was free. I knew who the other was. The second he touched me, I knew.

Katie was at my side, her arms wrapped around me, shushing me. I stopped screaming but shook in her arms for a long time. I kept muttering his name. She couldn't understand me.

"It's okay," she kept saying. "You're safe. I'm here." Over and over until I stopped shaking and could think straight.

"It was him," I said, urgently. "I need my phone."

She sat back, shocked as I launched myself from her and snatched my phone from the counter. I dialed and danced around impatiently while it rang.

"Come on, answer."

Finally, Skella picked up. "What the hell?" she asked. "I gotta sleep sometime, geez."

"It was Gletts," I shouted into the phone. "He just saved me from an eater."

"What?" she asked, obviously not awake. "Gletts, what?"

"I was going walkabout," I explained as slowly as my pounding heart would allow. "There's a doorway here, old and barely a memory. I tried to go through it and got sucked into the sideways."

Katie gasped behind me, her hands over her mouth. "Holy shit," was all she could say.

"That's bad," Skella said. "How'd you get out?"

"That's what I'm telling you. I was being drawn into the vortex, pulled into the world of crystal and sharp things. Eaters began to flock toward me, mostly small ones, but then I saw this monster." I shuddered thinking about it. Katie went and took a blanket from the couch and draped it over my shoulders.

"It was horrifying," I whispered. "It wanted to devour my spirit."

"Yeah," Skella said. "That is what I warned you about."

"Gletts saved me, Skella. Seriously. He called me a fool and pushed me back across the threshold. He was a streak of golden light. You've gotta tell Unun. She'll know what it means."

Skella was crying. Not deep sobbing or anything, but I could hear it in her voice. "Thank the maker," she said, her voice thick. "I'll go now. I'd about given up hope. If he's in the sideways maybe we can draw him home."

The line went dead and I turned to Katie, pulled her to me and let her warmth settle me. "Come on," she said, pulling me to the nest of blankets on the floor. "Lie down with me. Let me hold you."

So we lay together, our bodies intertwined, and I just let her presence soothe me. Here was safe; here was home. I fell asleep in her arms and dreamed of crystal worlds.

Thirty-two

JULIE WAS FINISHING THE LAST OF HER BREAKFAST DISHES
when there was a knock at the door. She dried her hands on
a dishrag and grabbed the cane that leaned against the counter.
She'd been using it less and less, but she was afraid to be without
it. Okay, to be fair, she was just afraid. The killing out at Mary's
place had her on edge. She'd come back to the apartment for
a night, just to get some space, but she'd be going back later in
the day.

"Just a minute," she called as the knocking persisted. "Hold
your horses."

When she got to the door, she looked through the peephole. It
was a woman, but the distortion was too severe for her to tell who.
She opened the door and was stunned at the woman in front of
her.

Here was a proper lady, dressed in a fine flower-print dress,
white gloves, and even a small hat that sat atop her flowing blond
hair. She had the most beautiful blue eyes. Julie knew who this
was immediately. There was no doubt this woman was Sarah's
mother. Same eyes, same mouth, set and stubborn. Her whole face
said she was stubborn and worried all at the same time. Julie
almost laughed, the look was so familiar.

"May I help you?"

"You're older than I thought," the woman said.

Julie winced a little. "I'm sorry," she said. "We do tend to age. You're Sarah's mother, right?"

Mrs. Beauhall blinked rapidly then nodded once, curtly, producing a half smile. "Well, since we already seem to know one another. I assume you are Katie."

Julie couldn't help but laugh. Here stood Sarah's mother, and she not only knew that Katie existed, but assumed that she was Katie . . . and Sarah's lover to boot.

"Oh, Mrs. Beauhall," she said after a moment. "I'm Julie, Sarah's . . . "—she almost said boss, but that relationship had been on hold since May—" . . . a friend of Sarah's," she finished.

Mrs. Beauhall looked confused. "I take it Sarah is not here?"

"No, she's," she paused. Was it her place to tell this woman anything about her daughter? She waved her hand. "Likely at work. You know Sarah, always off somewhere."

"Are you her lover then? Has this Katie moved along? This is Sarah's place. You live here as well, I presume."

"Please come in," Julie offered, stepping aside. "It's not as sordid as all that."

Mrs. Beauhall did not move, but Julie could see the conflicting emotion on her face.

"Mrs. Beauhall. If you'd like to come in, I'll make some tea and we can chat," Julie offered.

The decision clicked into place. It was just exactly like watching Sarah. "Yes, that would be nice," she said and crossed into the apartment. "Please call me Meredith."

Thirty-three

SKELLA CALLED US JUST AFTER HER MORNING SHIFT CHANGE and arranged to bring us back out to Vancouver. We got to Stanley Park and set up in the healing lodge before I had my first cup of coffee. Unun was excited to hear the news I had and a little worried not only that Gletts was roaming down our way in spirit form but also that he had somehow crossed over into the sideways.

"Probably using the shortcut to get to Sarah's place," Skella offered. "You know he's in love with her."

Unun nodded, her lips pressed together tightly.

"He saved her," Katie added. "I'm glad he took the risk."

"Let us prepare," Unun said in response. "I would know what you can learn."

We set up for the walkabout. I took one of the empty pallets and sipped the tea. Unun prepared it this time, whispering words in a language I didn't know.

"Elvish," Katie said, in awe. "She's wishing you a safe journey."

Skella was shocked. "You can understand her?"

"Some of it. I've studied it for years, but it's more like Latin to me. No one really speaks it."

Skella said something in Elvish, grinning.

Katie was thrilled.

I fell asleep with Katie and Skella making small talk in Elvish and Unun hovering over me, her eyes tired and shining.

The transition was much quicker this time. I sat up, away from my body, and floated upward to a standing position. All around me the world was beautiful. Unlike our apartment, where the only color was in the connection between Katie and me, here everything glowed with light. There were connections between each of the others in the room, a kaleidoscope of emotion and love.

I walked around, enraptured by the way every object resonated with energy. How had I not seen this the other times? Was it because here things were handmade with loving care? More natural than the cold, machine-made world I lived in?

Katie glowed the brightest, of course. I loved her. I could see the connections the others in the room had to one another, various mingling of colors and intensity of light. After a minute I was able to adjust my vision to tone down the overwhelming spray of colors and see the world a little more basically. The colors were there if I wanted to see them. It was like looking at those 3-D illusion pictures where if you screw your eyes just right you can see depth in a flat picture. Like that.

Gletts had a silver tether flowing from him—a wispy thread that snaked upward and through a large mirror that hung on one wall. He was in the sideways right now. Others had tethers as well, some strong, like Gletts, while some were more threadbare. I willed myself around the great room, examining each of the fallen. There were several dwarves in the back, tended by the elves and visiting dwarves. I recognized them from the battle. They'd taken up arms to protect the elves, unlike some of their brethren. Those who had abandoned the elves to their fate were mostly dead, in any case.

One of the dwarves, a burly young man with a braided red beard and rosy complexion, had the weakest tether of them all. He had no desire to stay here, I realized. His tether was straining, being pulled on the other end. The only reason he had not moved on was the anchor two dwarf women had to him. They had their hands on him as if he were going to float away.

I brushed the tether with my hand, and I could feel the pull between them. He yearned to move on to the next place, a happier place. Opposing this was the love of two women—a mother and a sister—trying desperately to keep him with them.

I could feel the tether like a braided cord in my hands. The yearning was so strong on the far end that I knew I could pluck the three remaining strands, breaking the tether, freeing the man's spirit to go onward.

But the women held him so tightly, I couldn't do it. It was not my place. The tether would unravel on its own before too long. That much was obvious.

I drifted onward, looking at the others. Some had the strength to return, while some were lost, wandering in places where no return was possible.

I moved back to the mirror where Gletts's tether flowed and looked through into the crystal world. There were no eaters that I could see, only a plane of clarity and beauty corrupted with the webs of discord.

Gletts had gone into the sideways, and not for the first time, I was sure. He couldn't be lost; he could follow his tether home. Why was he dithering? He should be back here by now.

I placed my hand on his tether and felt it was strong. At my touch, a pulse ran in both directions, one to his body, and one through the mirror.

I glanced over. His body arched for a moment, as if an electrical charge had gone through him, and then he settled again. Back into the quiet state he'd occupied for weeks.

The other pulse had gone into the mirror and disappeared. Would he feel that on the other end?

Skella was watching me through that mirror, her eyes full of wonder. She waved at me, smiling, and Katie looked confused at her side. Skella touched the mirror, causing its surface to waver, and suddenly Katie could see me as well. She looked back from my body to where I stood just behind her, and she turned.

"I can't see her," Katie said. "Except in the mirror."

"I can," Unun said. "She is a spirit, is she not? It takes practice to see one such as she."

Unun dripped several drops of honey against my lips, and I felt a tug back to my body. "Come home," she said to me. "Let us talk properly."

I allowed myself to flow back to my body, willing the walk-about to end, which it did. I sat up feeling refreshed and a bit sad. I could hear the dwarf women crying on the other side of the chamber.

"He is so desperate to move on," I said to Unun, who looked at me with her ancient eyes. "They're keeping him here, causing him grief. They should free him."

"They will let him go soon," she said quietly. She helped me to my feet. "Let us go back to our house, have some tea, and discuss the ways of the world."

Katie took my hand as we walked out of the house. "That was so cool," she whispered to me, squeezing my hand. "What was it like?"

"Beautiful and sad," I told her. "It's different here. Alive. Our apartment is cold in comparison. Inert."

Her face fell, and I wished I hadn't told her. "Maybe we should move," I said. "Find a new place, one where we aren't over a gun shop, you know?"

That brightened her. "That's probably it," she said, emphatically. "Too many items of destruction between us and the earth."

We walked through the village, hand in hand. Part of me was content to just be with her and part of me missed the vibrancy of the "other."

Thirty-four

Frederick Sawyer paced along the trails of the Alpine Rock Garden. Most of the flowering plants were dormant, but the rhododendron had a few straggling blossoms. They would be gone by the time winter actually arrived. He checked his phone for the time. Mr. Philips had arranged to meet him well over an hour ago. It was not like his most able servant to be late for any meeting or obligation.

A group of schoolchildren entered the Bellevue Botanical Gardens led by a wiry, gray-headed volunteer. They cackled and tittered in their childish ways, each a nattering bundle of energy and optimism.

They did not bother him. Unlike some of his kind, he saw children as beneficial parts of society. And, on occasion, a sometimes snack.

He chuckled to himself. He had not eaten a child in nearly a hundred years.

Perhaps he would visit the Yao Garden portion. It would take the children a while to reach that section of the grounds. Besides, he quite enjoyed the Japanese maples.

Forty-five minutes later the children had made their way to where Frederick sat. He wanted to enjoy their antics, but the absence of Mr. Philips had become too much to bear. His ire had risen to the point that several of the closer children began to move away, whimpering.

The tour guide watched him as if he had done something. He rose from his seat and walked briskly to the gift shop. There, he dropped two fifties into the donation box and strode out to his waiting car.

Mr. Philips had never failed to show. Frederick was beside himself. What could have possibly detained him? He dialed Mr. Philips for the seventh time and slammed his phone closed when it went to voice mail. "Damn it," he growled.

The chauffer who had been leaning against the car, reading on some electronic device, straightened up at Frederick's outburst.

"Take me to Redmond," he ordered the man. "Crankshaft Tavern. I have a need to visit a tragedy." Time to take matters into his own hands.

As they drove through the quiet neighborhood surrounding the gardens, a sliver of fear insinuated itself into his belly. He did not like surprises and did not take failure easily. Mr. Philips's sudden and uncharacteristic disappearance was unnerving in a way he had not experienced in many a century.

Once they'd arrived at the tavern, he stepped from the limo and crossed the road to the burned-out smithy. Jean-Paul had spread his fire here in the spring. No fire can be controlled on land cursed by dragon fire. He pace through the wreckage and spotted a growth of fireweed. He knelt and brushed the long red stems. Someone knew their lore. A couple of seasons and this ground may be salvageable.

He rose, pacing toward the ruined smithy. Sarah Jane Beauhall had worked here in the spring. Now she was a willing servant of Nidhogg. What had she done here that so upset Nidhogg and set Jean-Paul in motion?

He opened himself to the carnage. The destruction sang to him; the scars of kin-flame raised the hackles on his neck—danger. They were territorial beasts after all.

"What was so important about this place?" he asked aloud.

The trailer that had burned held nothing for him, nor did any of the outbuildings. It was the smithy proper that pulled him. He stood among the blackened timbers and filth, stirring the ashes with his oxblood Berlutis.

There was a taste of something here. He knelt, running his hands across a mound of metal slag. This had been an anvil once. Its form cried to him. The dire flame of his kin had destroyed its shape, but the intent of it, the intrinsic being, remained. "Here," he whispered. "This is where something was reborn. What did you bring into the world, young Beauhall? What memory did you stir?" He opened his senses, searching for the ancient magic that somehow frightened him.

A blade.

He stood, suddenly very aware of his surroundings. The Berlutis would be ruined and the ash might forever ruin the pants. But there was knowledge here, something Jean-Paul had known, or guessed at.

The sword. He'd been in its presence, felt a nudge in his direction when Beauhall held it. But there had been no evidence of its power. He laughed. He'd tried to buy it from her on a whim, not understanding what it truly was.

It was the blade that had drunk deeply of Jean-Paul's blood. His was not the first. This blade, this relic of a long-forgotten past, had risen from the dust to return to hunt his kind.

He shivered as a cold wind stirred the months-old debris. Here was death for his kind. He fled back to the limo, stomping his feet as he crossed the street to remove as much of the ash as he could.

Beauhall. Her face rose in his mind, young and brash. Did she know what she'd wrought? The ancient ways had been snuffed out by the systematic efforts of the dragon high council. They had performed a careful elimination of certain elements, collection or destruction of texts, items, even whole languages.

How had this sword been reborn, and just who was this Sarah Beauhall?

He settled himself in the back of the limousine and took out his phone once more. This time he called up a number he'd never planned to dial. The thought of contacting the smith wrapped the trickle of fear that rode in his belly with a razor wire of lust and power he would always associate with Sarah Jane Beauhall. He hesitated, unsure of the words he should use. It was not like him to hesitate so. He snapped the phone shut, leaned back, and closed his eyes.

Maybe it would be better to visit the young woman in person. He opened his phone and read an address to the driver, who turned at the next intersection and headed back to Bellevue.

Thirty-five

Skella left our apartment just after eleven in the morning, exhausted and begging for sleep. She'd ferried the Black Briar crew out to Chumstick and returned to pick us up from her place in Vancouver.

"I need to be up in time for the next shift," she groused. "All this extracurricular work is really wearing me down."

"Okay, sorry," I said. "Thought this was important."

"It is," she agreed, stifling a yawn. "We'll talk later." She stepped into the mirror and was gone.

Katie pulled me to her, hugging me for a very long time. "Let's go to bed," she said. "Maybe even get some sleep."

"Sounds excellent," I said, kissing her. We worked our way to the bedroom with one or more parts always in contact while simultaneously stripping off each other's clothes. When we got to the doorway, however, I froze, stepping back.

Behind the headboard was that doorway with the unstable threshold—a vacuum that could suck me into the ether—into the land where the eaters lived and hunted.

Suddenly I wasn't really in the mood any longer.

"What if you'd woken up and I was just not there anymore?" I asked her, pulling away. "What if I was a hollow shell, my spirit eaten by the things out there?" I pointed to where the doorway had once existed.

She looked at the wall and then to me. "We've been in this bed for a long time," she said, patiently. "And while I may have lost consciousness a few times, neither of us have left our bodies during sex."

I shrugged. "Yeah, I know. But that first time could really suck."

There was no mistaking her arousal. Her brain was working overdrive to get things moving. But she loved me and relented, if somewhat reluctantly.

"Fine, we'll sleep in the living room," she said. "Help me."

We moved through the house naked, pushing the dining room table against the wall and clearing the middle of the great room. Then we carried the mattress from the other room, lay it in the middle of the room, and set it up with sheets, blankets, and pillows.

"Better?" she asked.

I nodded slowly and allowed her to pull me down onto the new bed. For a while we let the world fade away to nothing but each other.

Afterward, tangled in sweaty sheets, we spoke of a new place. A house where we could start from scratch, make our own mark.

"We could move north, be closer to Black Briar," I offered, but she didn't like that answer.

"No," she said. "We can't go too far north. I don't want to leave my kids. It's hard on them when teachers leave in the middle of a year."

"Well, it will take awhile for us to find a place. Maybe we can move next summer, after the school year ends."

She sat up, running her fingers down my rib cage and over my hip. "We can't keep the bed in the middle of the living room," she said. "We'd never be able to entertain."

I squirmed under her touch. "The only people who come over are Melanie and Dena." I grinned at her. "I'm sure they'd find some use for this setup."

She smacked my thigh and covered my mouth with hers. I guess the problem didn't need to be solved right this moment.

Thirty-six

TRISHA SAT ON A MAT ON THE FLOOR, NAKED AND BOUND. Intricate knots and thin ropes wrapped around her torso in such a way as to encircle her breasts. From there, a line trailed down her stomach to a complicated array of lines and knots that wrapped around her waist and down across her naked and shaved pubic mound, the thin rope parting her labia and running back up the crack of her ass to meet the loop dropping down from her shoulders.

Justin sat in a chair across from her, naked as well, with a large book in his lap. She contemplated his pale skin, his light eyes. Had they always been so? She thought for a moment that they had been darker. And hadn't there been another name? Why was it so hard to remember?

"Your scars make you beautiful," he said. "They are a way of marking your life, bringing out the inner light that yearns to be released."

Trisha whispered. "I see that now, master. Thank you for showing me how beautiful I can be."

Justin put the book aside and picked up a small sheathed knife from the table beside him. "Are you ready for me?" he asked her.

She lowered her torso forward, cocking her head to the side and putting her right shoulder against a large cushion with her knees under her and her rear end in the air. "Yes, master. I am yours to do with as you wish."

He knelt behind her and unsheathed the small, silver knife. He reached under her and dragged his hand from her stomach, following the rope. She gasped as he crossed her mons and gave a moaning shudder. He continued to follow the rope up over her ass and to the connecting knot at her lower back.

She cried out as he pulled the rope tighter, forcing it deep between the folds of her labia, and set the knife beneath the taut line, edge upward. He sawed across the bond three times, eliciting grunts from Trisha, before the rope parted. Once the cord dropped to the floor, he leaned forward, entering her with one swift motion.

She rose from the floor, her back taut, and cried out in ecstasy.

He held his place, not moving, just allowing her to feel him filling her for a moment. Then, as she found some moment of control, a stilling of her earnest thrusting, he began to make the first cut across her left buttock.

Thirty-seven

FREDERICK ARRIVED AT YOUNG SARAH'S APARTMENT, HORRI-fied at the low-budget arrangements for one of her stature.

The chauffer opened the door, and he stepped out, straightening his jacket. He walked briskly up the stairs to her apartment, his heart beating quicker than he wanted. *Calm*, he told himself. She had no reason to kill him. He was not a coward and not without his own powers.

Still, a bit of uncertainty assailed him as he approached the door. Nidhogg had the smith in her employ. What did that portend? He raised his fist to knock on the door and paused. He picked up two distinct voices inside. The close proximity to so many others, like rats in a warren, confused even his outstanding hearing. With a sigh, he knocked three times and stepped back, allowing the people inside an opportunity to see him through the peephole.

A woman approached the door, her steps hesitant, her smell strong in his nostrils. Middle-aged, lonely. Strong and fiery. A smith, he determined. She smelled of fire and forge.

Julie Hendrickson opened the door, smiling at him. "I guess it's a day for visitors. How may I help you?"

There is something about her scent he realized: fear. Not fear of him, that would be more distinct. No, this was fear in general, like something had been taken away from her—a festering fear that debilitated the mind and crushed the soul.

"I'm very sorry to disturb you," he said with his most winning smile. "My name is Frederick Sawyer. I'm looking for Ms. Sarah Jane Beauhall."

Julie froze, the smile on her face rigid and stiff. Another woman appeared behind her, a dozen steps back. She looked and smelled like Beauhall. *Relative*, he thought. Perhaps her mother. How amusing.

"Sarah's not here," Julie managed to say.

He glanced past her into the tiny apartment. The other woman, this matron Beauhall, crossed her arms and looked at him as if he were something oozing and pestilent.

"My pardon," he said with a slight nod. "Perhaps you could let her know I have urgent need of her?"

"I'm sure I can pass along a message," Julie said, a bit of steel returning to her.

This amused him. Both women suddenly became much more dangerous. Protecting their young, he surmised. Interesting indeed.

He reached in his jacket, removed his wallet, and handed Julie a business card. "Please have her contact me at this number. It is a matter of some urgency."

Julie took the card from him, the steel in her eyes growing stronger with every breath. "It may be a day or more before I see her, but I'll be sure to pass this along the next time she checks in."

Bluff, he read. She'll call her the second his limo leaves the lot. He bowed, thinking of Mr. Philips. "As you will," he said. "Thank you for your time."

She had the door shut before he straightened. It had been a very long time since he'd had such a strongly negative reaction from one of the chattel. Had she known who he was? It was not unthinkable, being a compatriot of young Sarah, but he knew he had never met either of these women before in his life.

The other woman, however. Sarah's . . . he sniffed. Mother, if he was not mistaken. There was something about her. It wasn't until he had climbed into the limo that he placed the feeling. She was marked. He was absolutely sure of it. Marked by another of his kind, ownership established, brand burned into her skin somewhere. Neither Nidhogg's nor Jean-Paul's.

Very interesting. "Take me back to the hotel," he told the driver. He leaned back, poured himself a scotch, and let the whiskey burn its way down his parched throat. Better to flush out the stench of that place, the overcrowded life they led, these furtive humans. Did none of them have a sense of smell?

And Sarah's mother, marked by another dragon. Did she know? Did Sarah? Did Nidhogg understand there was a fugitive in her midst? Perhaps it was time to contact some of the others— see if there were similar events happening in other realms. It would be good to get news of the Reavers from others. Who knows what wickedness they worked while their betters looked inward to their own kingdoms or, in some cases, to the magic of their torpor. The full might of the conclave may be required to quell a simmering revolution.

Frederick shuddered. Such was not an idle fancy. Calling a conclave; waking the slumbering ones would have dire consequences.

The last council had spawned the great migration and the settling of this new land. Would the thralls suffer as they had half a millennium ago?

Thirty-eight

I HEARD THE PHONE RINGING, BUT I WAS SPOONED UP AGAINST Katie, and she felt too good to move. I pulled her tighter against me, cupping her left breast and closing my eyes. I recognized the ringtone. It was Julie. I couldn't take any more bad news just now. Besides, we were only resting.

I managed to wake Katie up by licking my way down her side and across her bottom before the phone rang again.

Julie again. I ignored it, keeping focused on the task at hand, but the phone rang again and again.

"Damn it," Katie said, pushing my head away from her. "Will you either answer that fucking phone or turn it off?"

I grinned up at her and nipped her thigh. "Sure, hang on."

It was cold outside the blankets, so I padded across the room quickly. I snatched the phone off the counter and started to turn it off, when I saw the text message she'd sent.

"Jesus," I said, punching the voice mail and then the speaker button.

Katie sat up, disheveled and anxious. "Aw, come on. Come back over here and finish what you started."

I must've looked pretty freaked out because she stopped teasing and got up. "What is it? What's the matter?"

I keyed my voice mail on speaker. "Sarah, why don't you ever answer the fucking phone?" It was Julie. Someone with her gasped.

"Sorry," she said. "Listen, you have to call me as soon as you can. He was here, Sarah. Jesus. Frederick Sawyer came here to the apartment looking for you."

"Damn," Katie said, sitting down on a bar stool.

The next three messages were similar, with less cussing.

I punched in Julie's number and set the phone on the counter. As it rang, I picked my T-shirt off the lamp and slipped it over my head. I was freezing all of a sudden.

"Sarah?" Julie answered. "Where are you?"

"I'm at home," I said into the phone. "I'm with Katie. You're on speaker phone. What the fuck is this about Sawyer?"

Then my world fell to the side like I'd been hit by a truck.

"Sarah Jane Beauhall," a voice I recognized shouted into the phone. "How dare you use that kind of language?"

It was my mother. My knees gave out and I collapsed onto the floor.

"Sorry," Julie said. "You're shouting."

"Is everyone okay?" Katie said into the phone. "Are you safe?"

"Yes," Julie said. "He left, but he wants Sarah to contact him."

I climbed to my feet looking wildly at Katie. I hadn't spoken to my mother in years. What the hell was she doing at my old apartment with Julie?

"That's all he wanted?" I asked once I'd managed not to fall over again.

"He left a card."

I jotted down the number and began getting dressed. "I'll call you back," I said and punched the off button without waiting for a reply.

"Was that your mother?" Katie asked, covering her breasts with her arms.

"Yes," I said, slipping on my panties. "And she can't see you."

She dropped her arms, but I could see she was embarrassed. "What are you going to do?"

"Easy answer," I said, pulling my jeans off the coffee table. "Where are my boots?"

She pulled them out from behind the couch and dug the socks off the top of the television. "You can't just leave me here," she said, searching for her own clothes.

I sat down and stomped my feet into my boots. "I'll need to call Nidhogg first, I think. He's in her territory. I'm sure there's a protocol for this."

She walked into the other room and came back out with a dress over her head. I walked up to her, pulled her to me, and kissed her, cupping her naked ass through her dress. "I'll have to finish that later," I said, squeezing her cheeks in both hands.

"You know," she said, squirming in my hands, "you could finish up now, then call Nidhogg."

I kissed her and slid to my knees, pushing her dress up her waist. She leaned against the doorframe, put one leg over my shoulder, and cried out as I parted her with my tongue. She held onto my head, crying and shaking until finally collapsing over me, spent and whimpering.

I stood with her, helped her to the couch and lay a blanket over her. "Go to sleep," I said. "I'll come back when I can."

She mumbled something and rolled over, the blanket pulled to her chin.

I grabbed my helmet and jacket, picked my keys from the rack, and slipped my phone into the jacket pocket. I'd make the call from outside so I wouldn't bother her.

The rain was coming down sideways in the blowing wind by the time I stepped out in the vestibule of our apartment. I hated the fact that I was going out in that rain, especially with what I'd

just left, but Frederick Sawyer was one predator I was not willing
to ignore.

Zi Xiu answered the phone. Was she the only one left who
spoke English? "I need to speak to Nidhogg," I told her.

"She is in the library," she said. "Is this urgent?"

"Yes," I said. "She'd agree with me, I'm sure."

"I will have her return your call," she said. "There is no phone
in the library."

I hung up and waited. It only took two or three minutes for
the phone to ring again, but it felt like forever.

"Yes?" Nidhogg said into the phone when I answered. "You
have an urgent matter?"

"Yes, ma'am," I said. The image of my mother hearing me say
"fuck" was vivid in my mind. "I'm very sorry to disturb you, but
something has come to my attention that I believe will be of
interest to you."

There was a pause, then a warm chuckle. "How formal of you,
Ms. Beauhall. Do we trade on formalities now?"

She seemed to prefer my bluntness, my straightforwardness.
And she wasn't my mother, damn it. "No, sorry. Listen. Frederick Sawyer is in town. He went to my apartment." I started to say
old apartment, but I wasn't sure she knew I was living with Katie.
"He spoke with my mentor, my teacher, Julie Hendrickson."

"I know of Ms. Hendrickson," she said. "She has done an
excellent job with your tutelage so far."

"Thank you." What the hell did she know about my life, exactly?

"You are very welcome, dear. Now listen. Here are your orders."

Basically, with Qindra out of commission, I was in charge of
things like this. I was to contact Frederick and see what his needs
were. She warned me to be careful but advised it was in our best

interest to keep a civil relationship with him, as he was a neighbor, if a scheming, power-hungry one.

I was just putting on my helmet when Katie came rushing out the door of our apartment. The dress was barely on her, and she showed a lot more than most kindergarten teachers would in public, but no one was there to see her. I did enjoy looking at her breasts, though.

Then I saw what she had in her hands. Gram. At least she was still in her sheath. Unlike Katie.

"You forgot your sword," she said, a bit discombobulated. "You are taking Gram, right, Sarah? He is a dragon."

It was tempting, but that would not be friendly, and Nidhogg said to keep it friendly. "I can't. It would be a threat."

"Damn, right," she barked. "I want you coming home to me."

I laughed. "He's in Nidhogg's territory. He has to adhere to a certain decorum."

Then it was her turn to laugh. "Like the decorum Jean-Paul showed? He was her kid and he didn't care what she thought."

True enough, and the argument was compelling, but Nidhogg had warned me about Jean-Paul that night when we first spoke.

"Dragon, Sarah. Remember? Teeth, fire, eating people."

"He's not Jean-Paul," I said gently, walking up the stairs. I took Gram from her, wrapped my other arm over her shoulders, and steered her back into the apartment. "I need to do this right, without weapons. Until I can rescue Qindra, this is my responsibility."

"This sucks ass," she said, pouting.

"Amen, sister." I kissed her and directed her back toward the apartment. I opened the door, and gently pushed her inside.

"Careful," she said, grasping my hand. "I'll wait up for you."

Thirty-nine

I CALLED THE NUMBER JULIE HAD GIVEN ME, AND THE CON-
cierge at the Fairmont Hotel in Seattle told me I was expected.
Great, another ride in the freaking rain.

I was shivering my ass nearly off by the time I took the exit
from I-5. Traffic was heavy, but I was on the Ducati. I took advantage of the size difference and wove between cars, edging out
lights and generally raising the ire of every taxi in the metro
area. I had to signal one guy with my middle finger, but he let me
cut over.

By the time I pulled onto the circular drive in front of the
hotel, I was pissed off and frozen. I parked the bike on the far
side, near the loading dock; then I tossed my helmet to the valet
and told him I'd be right back. I didn't give him my key, though.
No way I wanted him on my Ducati.

A lovely young woman in a purple dress and way too much eye
makeup greeted me at the front desk. I guess I was not her typical
clientele, especially with my jeans, T-shirt, and nontraditional hair
cut. When I mentioned Mr. Sawyer, however, she fell into line.

Soon enough I was watching her sashay in front of me, her
hips swinging like a saloon door, all the way down a long corridor
to a private office. I guess if you had enough money you could
have a private office in a public hotel. She held the door open and

waved me through. She had a great smile, even with all the makeup. I bet she was hell on wheels.

The runes along my scalp began to tingle as soon as I moved across the threshold, pulling my attention from the girl. There was something here. Not an ambush, surely, but something new, possibilities yet unnamed.

These were different from the runes on my leg. These were a gift from Odin. His touch had marked me, put the berserker in me. They helped me to cut through the clutter in times of danger and stress. Like now, for instance.

Sawyer sat at a large table strewn with papers. An open briefcase sat on a side table, and a cell phone lay broken on the ground near the door.

"Please bring us water," Frederick Sawyer said, a slight tremor to his voice. The young woman nodded and let the door swing shut.

He rose from the table, strode across the room, and held out his hand.

I shook it, feeling the power of him, the fire just beneath the surface. He looked haggard, fussed. I'd never seen him so off his game.

"Nidhogg sends her greetings," I said, following the script. "And asks to what she owes this visit?"

He sniffed, looking at me quizzically. "You came here from your lover's bed?"

"Yes, as a matter of fact," I said. He already knew it, bastard. Probably smelled her on me. Dragons were freaky. "Would you have preferred I waited to shower before answering your urgent request?"

He waved his hand in the air, dismissing my comment. "You are a joy to know, Ms. Beauhall. I am glad we have the love of women in common. Gives us a place to build a relationship."

I bit my tongue and smiled. "Why are you here?"

"I have business in the city," he began, sitting on the long leather couch and gesturing to a leather chair. "One of my—operatives, let us say—was killed recently."

"Killed how?"

Patience was not his strong suit, and he didn't see me as an equal. But he respected me. I was surprised by that insight.

"Murdered by most foul means," he said. "Ritual murder. Not unlike several others in the region."

Of course my mind went straight to Justin. Why did Frederick Sawyer have an employee working in Nidhogg's territory? And if she was one of those Justin had murdered, did that mean Frederick Sawyer was spying on me?

"I'm sorry for your loss," I said, mustering as much sympathy as I could.

"My thanks."

He seemed to mean it, too. That's what seemed wrong with him. He was flustered and somewhat confused—out of his element. And where was his businessman, Mr. Philips?

"As it is," he continued, leaning back and crossing one knee over the other, "I wanted to ensure that her eminence was aware of my little visit to the Emerald City. I do not want to cause an incident like we had in May."

Incident? Well, from his point of view, sure. He lost his stake in Flight Test, which I ended up getting half of. Nidhogg kept the other half.

For the rest of us, however, the events of May were a catastrophe. Except the killing Jean-Paul part. That was pretty righteous.

We exchanged pleasantries for a bit: opera, which I knew nothing about; the art scene; philanthropy. Obviously we had nothing in common.

"On another subject," he continued. His hand shook as he held a letter out to me. "I received this just before you arrived."

I stepped over and took the embossed document. It was from the Dragon Liberation Front. Son of a bitch. Didn't I wipe those bastards out several weeks ago?

Dear Mr. Sawyer,

Our last venture involving the mead has run into a snag, as you may have heard. For this, we offer our humblest apologies. It further pains us to bring you news most unsettling. We have opted to exercise other options in our quest for betterment. Be advised we have acquired something that belongs to you, some-thing we believe to be of value.

If this is the case, perhaps we can come to an arrangement. I'm sure the sum required to release this valuable commodity would pale in comparison to its worth. We do hope you agree. We will be in contact with you in the coming days to arrange for said com-modity's release. For one such as yourself, we are sure the mone-tary sacrifice will be a blip on a balance sheet.

Yours in freedom,
The Dragon Liberation Front

I looked up at him and he grimaced.

"I believe they have taken Mr. Philips," he said, his voice qua-vering.

My runes flared again, warning me of imminent danger. His fire was close to the surface. He was close to raging.

The young woman appeared with a pitcher of ice water and two glasses. I took the tray from her and waved her out.

"That is most unfortunate," I said, pouring two glasses and taking one to him.

He drained it in one, and I thought I saw steam escape his mouth. I refilled his glass before sitting.

"We will be happy to help in returning your servant," I said, thinking of how Qindra would react. "Nidhogg does not condone this type of activity within the boundaries of her kingdom."

This settled him a bit. The tension ebbed from his shoulders, and he sat back with a sigh. "My thanks to your mistress." His eyes gleamed. "I saw your mother today, it would seem."

I stiffened, and he noticed immediately. Bastard. That caught me by surprise. I let a smile settle over my face and tried to breathe quietly. Lower the heart rate, quiet the battle instincts. He hadn't touched her, and, hell, I had no idea what she was doing at my place in any case.

"I tell you what," I offered, leaning forward. "I'll do what I can to find Mr. Philips. He seems like a nice guy. And you asked so nicely. But my mother is not on your agenda, today or ever. Are we clear?"

"Are you sure?" he asked, his face quite amused. "There is something you may find intriguing about our meeting."

The rage was rising in me despite my best efforts. I took a long draw on the cold water and set the glass on the table beside me.

"Are we done here?" I asked, standing.

"As you wish," he agreed, standing to match me. "I will be in touch if I hear anything further."

"Excellent," I said. "I'll find you here, I presume. For the next how many days?"

He shrugged. "I have no idea. At this point, I would assume to be in town until Mr. Philips is returned to me."

Good enough. "I'll be in touch."

His gaze followed me out of the room. There was something there, something I'd missed, but he shouldn't have brought my mother into this. I needed to call Julie, to see what was going on. Was something wrong with Da? Was Megan okay? Crap, this sucked.

Forty

I MADE GOOD TIME OVER TO BELLEVUE. I DIDN'T CALL KATIE or anything, just went straight to my old apartment. I needed to know just what was going on.

Julie opened the door and pulled me in, looking behind me like she expected us to be attacked.

"What happened?" she asked. "Katie called me after you left, said you had gone to meet Frederick."

"Where's my mother?" I asked, pushing past her, looking from room to room.

"She's gone," Julie said, spinning around to keep me in sight. "She left an hour ago, not long after Frederick was here."

I sat down on the couch, let my helmet roll on the floor, and covered my face with my gloved hands. "Christ, Julie. What was she doing here?"

She sat beside me, put her hand on my knee, and waited until I looked up. "Everything's fine. Your family is safe." She hesitated a moment, looking at me. "You look just like her, you know."

I laughed. Holy shit. Of course I looked like her; she was my mother. I took a deep breath, peeled off my gloves, and shucked out of my jacket. Those I left on the couch, when I stood. "You have any coffee?" I asked. "I'm frozen."

She got up and went past me into the kitchen. She ground

fresh coffee and set up the machine. I sat at the table, and she took out cups, saucers, cream, and sugar. "Want some cookies?" she asked. "Mrs. Sorenson made a batch for Mary the other night, and I brought some home."

They were fine cookies, but I really didn't taste them. The coffee was hot and sweet, though. That's what I needed.

"I met with Sawyer," I told her, looking into her face for clues. "Someone killed one of his people up here, and he thinks it was the necromancer."

"Interesting," she said, stirring cream into her coffee. "Since the necromancer has been killing people somehow associated with you, does that mean he had someone watching you?"

"That's what I figured, but he didn't come right out and admit that. Now that group I smashed up several weeks ago, the Dragon Liberation Front, have snatched his right-hand man, Mr. Philips."

She sipped her coffee, holding the cup in both hands. "Do you think the necromancer Justin and the Dragon Liberation Front are in league?"

"Oh, yeah," I said, waving my hand in the air. "The whole lot of them worked under Jean-Paul. I'm sure of it."

The color drained from her face, and she fell silent. I knew about her trauma, the pain and torture. But I didn't know about the fear. I'd had some time to come to grips with all this, pieced things together with Katie and Skella. This was all news to Julie.

"You okay, boss?"

We sat in silence for a couple minutes while she gathered herself. "I can't imagine more of them, darker, more vile than Jean-Paul."

I took her hand, just held it for a bit.

"You gonna call Katie, tell her you're okay?"

"Damn it, yeah." I got up, pulled out my cell, and called her.

Julie sat with her coffee, pretending not to overhear my conversation.

"She's only a little pissed," I said, sitting back down a few minutes later. "But she thought coming here was a smart move."

She nodded her head once and picked up a cookie from the plate. "She and I had quite the conversation. I hear you may be moving."

Talking to her calmed me, gave me back balance and a sense of normal. "Maybe in the summer. We'll see."

"Going to spend that check Sawyer gave you, finally?"

Honestly, I hadn't thought about it in a while. I was flush with money. That's what I needed for the smithy out at Black Briar. I could get a new forge and everything.

"I'll do something with it, I'm sure."

I sipped my coffee a bit, thinking. Too much had gone down in the last twenty-four hours, and I welcomed the calm. The second cup of coffee was even better than the first, and I could feel my fingers and toes again.

"Okay, we're all safe and sound. Dragons are where they need to be, and the world has not fallen into the sun."

Julie looked at me, waiting.

"So, what the hell, Julie. Why was my mother here? Did someone die?"

"No, nothing like that." She toyed with her cup, trying to think of a way to tell me something hard; I knew from experience.

"Just spill it," I said, throwing my hands in the air. "Christ on a crutch."

"She apologized to me several times for that f-bomb you dropped earlier."

I rolled my eyes. "Great, whatever."

She took a deep breath and looked at me with that boss look. "She came about Megan."

Megan, damn. "Was she in trouble?"

"Nothing specific, but yeah. Your mom thinks she's heading for trouble like nothing you ever did. They're out of their minds with worry, and she's slipping away from them in ways you never could."

I shook my head. That made no sense. "I left. What more could I have done?"

"They're worried she may be getting into drugs. You never did that."

Drugs, crap. "No, not even in college. I had no desire to go through life wacked out on somebody's poison."

"And you went to college."

"She's not old enough. Fifteen," I said. "They had me under an iron fist when I was fifteen. The only thing I had going for me was Tae Kwon Do."

Julie got up and walked to the coffee table. "She left these for you."

They were pictures of Megan. Dozens of them. School plays, yearbook photos, belt awards. "She's a black belt?" I asked, surprised. "Took me to seventeen."

"They let her start sooner," she said, shuffling through the pictures and showing me one of Megan, maybe ten, getting her first rank.

I'd missed so much. Her whole training career to black belt. That was huge. Some of the pictures reminded me so much of me as a kid it hurt. But the rest, the ones where she got taller, prettier, coming into her own. Those gave me an ache I did not know was possible. God I missed her. Missed Ma, too.

"Your father is thinking about moving," Julie said. "Something happened this summer that has him freaked out."

The fear was back. Suddenly I was twelve, sleeping in the back of our car while sleet beat down on the roof. "Why? What happened?"

"Your mother wouldn't say. She just thought you should know. Maybe thought you could come home, talk some sense into him. It was because of you they settled in Crescent Ridge. You knew that, right? He risked whatever scared him so badly so you could have a normal life."

How many times can you say "fuck" in a day before you use up your allotment. I squeezed the bridge of my nose, trying to keep the tears from coming.

"She'll run," I said, looking at the most recent pictures of her. "If he tells her they're moving, she'll disappear. That's what I was going to do."

"That's what your mother is afraid of." She reached over and took my hands in hers. "Sarah. Your family needs you. Your sister needs you. Can't you find some way to make this right?"

I pulled away from her, stormed over to the living room, and started throwing on my jacket and gloves. "I gotta go," I said, feeling like a coward. "I can't. Not now."

She followed me to the living room and handed me my helmet. "What are you afraid of?"

I stopped, looked at her, and felt the fear tight and hard in my chest. "I can barely fix myself. I have dragons and necromancers screwing up my world. How can I bring that down on them? They have enough problems."

"I see." She walked to the door and opened it, giving me a free escape route. "I'm sure Megan will understand that when she's living on the streets, hooked on heroin."

Not fair. The runes tattooed on my body flared to life. The berserker rose in me: fight or flight, what's it gonna be? I sat down on the couch, collapsed really, slamming it back against the wall. I put my fists on the sides of my head to hold in the scream I felt building. Keeping that in your head was the hardest thing in the world. So why try?

I shrieked, and Julie shut the door. I wailed, stamping my feet and slamming myself back into the couch, over and over. It only lasted a minute or so, and I only quit when the couch broke. It collapsed under me, broke the main support beam or something. My ass was on the floor, and my throat hurt from the screaming.

"Feel better?" Julie asked. I looked up and she was sitting in a kitchen chair she'd pulled into the living room to watch me. I'd knocked over the coffee table, somehow. I didn't even remember touching it.

"Quite the tantrum."

I took slow deep breaths, or slower than I'd been doing. It took me almost three minutes before my heart beat began to stop hammering in my head. It was possible I pulled something in my neck, or maybe my back.

"What am I supposed to do?" I asked. "Jesus, Julie. If Da's set on running, how can I possibly stop him?"

"You faced a dragon, for fuck's sake," she said, her voice rising for the first time. "You faced that bastard while the rest of us lay broken and mangled. Even when he fled, you chased his sorry ass down to his lair and took the fight to him. You're stronger than anyone I know, Sarah. Why can't you give some of that to them? Go to them, or at least go to Megan. She's drowning, and they're both terrified they'll lose her and then they'll have nothing."

"I'll figure something out." Sure, why not? Not like I had anything else going on. I climbed out of the ruins of the couch and rolled my neck. Something definitely strained there. The runes were itching, the ones on my scalp more than the ones on my leg. I needed clarity. Maybe I needed to take Gram out. When I held her things always seemed clearer. Of course, that was usually in the way of problem solving through violence.

Julie stepped to me and pulled me into a hug. I let her hold on for a brief instant before I hugged her back. It was exactly what I

needed. The runes started to fade. No battle, no need for immediate action. Just a moment of quiet support and comfort.

I stepped back, and she held on to my shoulder with one hand
and wiped the tears from my face with her other. "You can do
great things, Sarah. You just need to figure what's most important here."

"I can't bring this down on them," I said, quietly. "I hate letting Katie go to work each day. I'd feel safer if she was out at
Black Briar, but that hasn't totally mellowed yet."

She nodded.

"I need to find Justin, stop him from killing people around
me. Hell, I'd tell him where I am, let him know how to find me,
just to have that final confrontation, but I don't know how."

"Would it do you any good?" she asked. "Don't you think,
maybe . . ." she shrugged, stepping back farther. "I don't know
about anything really, but necromancers deal with death and
fear. Maybe he's just messing with you."

Crud. That made total sense. "You know, Jean-Paul liked to
play with his food, too."

She cringed, and I regretted the comment immediately. I started
to say something, but she held up a hand.

"No, don't." She took a shuddering breath and looked up, defi-
ant. "He's had enough time in my head. I realized that today,
after Frederick came. After your mother." She waved her arm
around, taking in the world. "I've been hiding here. Afraid to
step outside these walls, to tell the truth. Going to see Mrs. Sorenson was the best I could muster most days."

Now it was my turn to listen. I stepped back and sat down on
the arm of the broken couch.

"That plan we discussed out at Mary's. I'm going to do it.
Start back to work, get some steel in my hands, touch some horses,
have a life again."

"Excellent," I said. About time! But I didn't say that out loud. I'd never been helpless like that, had no way of knowing the battle she'd undergone all these months. "We should start a support group," I offered.

She laughed. "I was thinking about seeing a therapist, but how do you explain to one of them about abuse at the hands of trolls, giants, and a dragon?"

"Good point. We'll just have to support each other."

She looked earnest again, resolved. "That's my exact point," she said. "We have to support those we love, and your family should be at the top of the list."

"Da would never approve of my lifestyle," I said, resigned. "He would hate my hair—my clothes—my friends."

"Maybe. But don't you think you should make the effort, find out for sure?"

"I'll try," I said, giving in. "I'll think of something while I'm figuring all this other stuff out. If Justin went after them?" I had no idea what I'd do. I already wanted to kill the bastard, and I could only do that so much.

"You'll think of something."

I hugged her again before I left, just quickly, and promised to contact them, somehow. I didn't say when, though. My head was swimming.

There was one thing I needed, however. I went to the desk where my computer still sat and pulled the cashier's check out of the bottom drawer. Blood money or no, there were some things I could be doing and that fifty thousand dollars would make a helluva lot things simpler.

I needed some help, and the only crew I trusted was out at Black Briar. Katie needed to be there as well. I called her, told her I was heading to her brother's, and that I needed her there. She agreed, reluctantly, which was good enough for me.

Forty-one

I MADE A LIST IN MY HEAD OF ALL THE SHIT I NEEDED TO DO as I rode out to Black Briar. Dealing with Frederick and Mr. Philips was on the list, but not the most urgent priority in my hierarchy of needs.

I needed to find Justin; free Qindra; make a freaking gate for Nidhogg; get Anezka back working at a forge, which would also help out Bub; reconcile Katie and Jimmy; oh and what—world peace?

All the members of the brain trust were there: Deidre, Jimmy, Stuart, Gunther, Anezka, Bub, and Katie.

The meeting went well. Even Katie got into the conversation. We discussed everything but my mother.

They let me lead the conversation, as I had all the pieces in my head. They filled in a few places, even Bub and Anezka chiming in, and by the end of the day, we had a plan.

Some of the things on the list were out of our control, but there was one thing that would benefit a lot of us and that we could begin immediately.

We were going to build a smithy on the farm. Nothing fancy—more like what Anezka had up in Chumstick rather than the slick setup we had with Julie before the dragon came.

Stuart knew a guy selling a pickup that would fit the needs of a farrier. He could get it for about ten grand. I'd done enough research on forges, anvils, and such to know I could outfit a forge pretty well for about fifteen grand more.

Jimmy and Deidre would cover the building itself. They'd already planned to expand the outbuildings more, so this fit right in.

It felt good to have a plan for something. And this way, in a week or so, I could start building that gate for Nidhogg. Anezka and I had already started the design, and she was working my math skills pretty hard. I had to do all the planning, but she checked my work. Everything had to be documented on paper. It was crazy.

Working things under my control felt good, liberating. I'd find Justin, somehow, but there was nothing stopping me getting Anezka into some fire-and-steel therapy. Would be nice to do some hammering again.

Between the contacts the Black Briar folks had and the free labor provided by the troop volunteers we had the ground cleared, a cement foundation poured, and the place framed by the next weekend. It was crazy. Everyone was excited to be working on something constructive.

Meanwhile, I continued the farrier work. Needed to keep the customers happy. Katie continued her teaching, and we both spent weeknights at Flight Test working on the prelims for the next movie shoot. Sleep was hard to come by all of a sudden. I loved it.

We made lists of all the women I possibly knew, and I checked on as many of them as I could. I didn't want anyone else murdered for me. Luckily, things had gone quiet on that front. Maybe he'd figured out who I was already.

The Mr. Philips thing wasn't going as well. I had no clues, and no contacts with this Dragon Liberation Front. Rolph and Skella were asking around in their circles, but so far they'd turned up nothing. Frederick was not a happy camper.

But Black Briar was euphoric. For the first time in a while, when I walked among the people of Black Briar I felt joy. Folks needed something positive to do, and watching a haunted house in Chumstick was really not as uplifting as it sounds.

It took another couple of days to get the smithy set up the way we could agree to, but by early December, despite the crappy weather, we were christening the new smithy. Julie, Mary Campbell, and Mrs. Sorenson came out for the big party as well.

Stuart kept a look out for Odin. The crazy one-eyed god had shown up at our last party a month or so earlier. How the time had flown.

The smithy was set up for two smiths to work at the same time. Anezka and I had worked it out ahead of time, and we'd begun working on separate projects a few days ahead of the official christening.

We presented our first works at the party, to much applause and adulation.

Anezka handed Jimmy a set of hinges and a new latch to be used on the old barn when we rebuilt her. Deidre loved them, giving Anezka a lot of public praise, which tickled her to no end.

Bub got in on the joy, as he'd helped both of us. For three days, that little monster was so happy he collapsed each day with the greatest smile on his face.

I built a twisted metal lattice that would connect the barracks to the new barn, where the troops worked out and kept their gear. In the spring we'd plant wisteria, and in a couple years it would be thick and fragrant, adding a nice bit of calm to the farm.

All in all the party was a huge success. It felt good to be doing something positive, moving in a good direction. Don't get me wrong, the fear of murder and mayhem hung over all of us, but for a few weeks it had abated.

Didn't hurt that no new women were found murdered. Maybe the murdering bastard had tripped in the shower or something. Whatever the reason, everyone was breathing a sigh of relief. Well, most everyone. Jimmy had that look of overwhelming responsibility and fear of failure. Stuart looked like he was ready to wrestle a troll to the ground, and Gunther watched Anezka like she was going to collapse at any minute.

And Katie, she watched me. The intensity was strong, but I cut her some slack. She was worried about me in general, mostly concerned that I hadn't come up with a plan to get with my family. All in good time.

Forty-two

THE MOUNTAINS PRESSED IN AROUND THEM, ADDING A SENSE of foreboding to the day. Justin paused at the entrance to the cave and cast a glance back at his faithful minions. Dane, a brutish man that Justin was sure had troll in his lineage, was an adept of the vilest magic, while Tobin was more refined in his practices and tastes. The two of them made an odd pairing though their strengths were greatly enhanced for their willing cooperation. Tobin did not let his Elvish heritage sway his desires for the meaner aspects of this shallow world. The fairness of his visage did not speak to the true madness beneath his brow.

Justin waved at the two. "They were here," he said. "I can smell the sword wielder." And there was definitely troll spawn here, he thought. It was weeks old—maybe older. Death had occurred here. The lingering energy of battle and blood were unmistakable.

Dane knelt by snow-dusted cairn and ran his hand above the stones. Power crackled from his hands, sending blue and yellow sparks into the air. He nodded. "Dead less than a month. Definitely a troll—female."

"Breeder," Tobin said. He leaned against the bole of a tall oak and scanned the trees along the edge of the clearing with practiced vigilance.

"Shall I raise her rotting corpse and send her down to the enemy?" Dane asked, his voice gravelly and deep.

Tobin chuckled, but Justin cut across him. "Don't be a fool. Would you give away the game so early?"

Dane stood, the power fading from his shimmering fist. "No, you're right. I was merely asking."

Justin let his smile return. "The chaos would be delicious, but no. Let's finish here. I need to see the girl again tonight."

Dane grunted.

Tobin frowned. "Why is it you always get the pretty toys?"

This time Dane chuckled.

"There will be more than enough for you and your predilections," Justin said, motioning toward the cave. "You will have a world to choose from once we succeed."

Tobin pulled a small pouch from his belt and raised a pinch of gray powder to his nose and snorted it. He shook his head like a dog flinging off water, and a manic expression fell across his visage.

"Let's get this over with," he growled. "I'm freezing my ass off out here."

The three entered the cave, seeing the homely home that had been built there. Justin walked around the room, casting small runes in the air, letting intricate red and gold spirals flit about the room.

"She was here," Justin said. "She and another." He licked his lips. "Another woman. Her lover."

Tobin went into the back of the cave but returned with a shake of his head. "Stores, nothing remarkable."

Dane pulled the bed apart, casting the animal furs into random piles. "She was wounded," he declared, holding up a blanket.

Justin took it from him, pulled the fur to his face, and breathed deeply. "Blood for sure, and fear," he said, grinning. "We can use this."

"To what end?" Tobin asked, his face a mask of frustration. "Jean-Paul got his ass handed to him by a girl, and you've spent all your time banging some crybaby who's afraid of her own shadow."

Dane looked up, sensing a line being crossed.

But Justin only laughed. "You cloud your mind with that foul drug, and then you to preach to me?" He stepped toward Tobin, punching him in the chest with two fingers. "We need to know her, need to understand her motives and her intentions. Only then can we go forward with the final solution."

"A glorious day that will be," Dane said.

Justin glanced at him, expecting more derision, but found the appropriate look of fealty and exaltation. "When I ascend," he said, "it will be those closest to me that will follow. We will rise up, take the dragons in their beds, and take their places."

"You're a fool," Tobin spat. "Jean-Paul let himself be ambushed. None of the others will be so arrogant, nor as stupid."

Justin flushed. He'd worshipped Jean-Paul—admired the man, loved the beast. "If it were not for Jean-Paul, we would have nothing," he said, his voice steely. "I remind you of the debt you owe him, Tobin. Your blood oath."

Tobin blanched. "You may be a powerful mage, but you are no drake. Do you truly believe you can transform into one of them? That we"—he pointed to Dane and himself—"can follow the same path, to rise to such heights?"

"Without a doubt," Justin breathed. "We will fall upon them with flames and claw. I will lead the dragons from the shadows and claim my rightful place as the master of all. The countries of men shall cower in the shadows of our mighty wings." He paused, looking at them both. "And those loyal to me will have glory beyond reckoning."

Forty-three

FREDERICK SAWYER PACED THE LENGTH OF HIS SUITE, THE
fire rising in his belly. The letter lay in the fireplace, a dusting
of ashes. He needed no letter—the words were burned into his
brain.

> *If you ever want to see your able servant alive again, you will fol-*
> *low our orders to the letter. We want no money; this has moved*
> *beyond mere greed. This is about liberation for the rightful rulers*
> *of the world. We will rise up and shatter the shackles this ancient*
> *order has placed on us for far too long.*
>
> *We will rise, the true rulers of the world, Draconis Imperi.*
>
> *We request your presence, in all your glory at a time and place*
> *to be named. Do not be afraid to show your true magnificence. It*
> *is time to rise up and greet the new dawn of civilization.*

"Reavers," Frederick spat. "Power-hungry idiots who should all
be hunted down and killed. They will destroy everything the
high council has built."

Did Nidhogg know the renegade dragons were on the move?
Beauhall needed this information. He needed to contact her,
warn her. How ironic that she would be the one he relied on,
after everything.

He paced the room, impotent and fuming.

But no. He would not call just yet. No need to succumb to panic. If Nidhogg did not quite understand what transpired in her own kingdom, he just may have an opportunity to turn this to his advantage.

If he could best this little band of malcontents, the great bitch would be in his debt. She could not very well dismiss him if it were he who preserved her kingdom.

He sat again, pulling pen and paper before him. Allies needed to be contacted. Sanctuaries needed to be insured. And as a last resort, he would call the most sacred of troops to his aid. But the cost there would be dire indeed.

His cell phone rang several times before the voice on the other end answered. "Mount Angel Abbey. How may I help you?"

Yes, a wise ruler ensured his people's well-being. Even at the cost of his own. "I need to get a message to Father Ignacio."

"I'm very sorry," the young novice squeaked into the phone. "We have no Father Ignacio."

"My pardon," Frederick said, the full weight of this action bearing heavily upon him. "Perhaps you could inquire with the abbot. Inform him of an inquiry for Father Ignacio. He may know how to reach him."

He mumbled the formalities for ending the call. His mind had nearly frozen with the implications of what he'd just set into motion. It may cost him more than he was ready to pay. But his people would be preserved, no matter what Nidhogg did within her own borders.

Forty-four

I drove the truck out to Nidhogg's place so I could install the frame for the gate. I had it nearly done and wanted to make sure the supports were in place before I brought out the gate itself. It was heavy, heavier than I thought it would be, and the support structure had to be strong enough to handle the weight. Anezka had experience with it, though, and helped me work it out.

The whole time I worked, Jai Li watched me. How she'd escaped Nidhogg's side, I didn't know, but it was cute. Whenever I looked directly at her, she would scamper away, but when I got back inside from carrying in a piece or bent to choose another tool, she would be back, watching me with huge eyes.

I tried talking to her, but if I looked at her she'd vanish. So, after a few attempts, I just talked to the air around me. Nothing too specific, just about the way the gate was going together or the color of the sky today. She didn't flee if I just talked, so I kept up a running monologue.

Once, when I bent to pick up a mallet to tamp down a cotter pin, I noticed several of the other house children were hanging around, listening to me talk. I smiled, pleased. They were so earnest, so enraptured by the things I said, or maybe just my voice.

"As I drove over the bridge, heading home the other night,

Mt. Rainier was so clear, it looked like I could reach out and touch it."

It didn't matter what I said. They hung on every word.

The frame had to be self-supporting, since I didn't have architectural guidance to attach to the house's internal structure. I'd anchor the frame to the beams of the house, but the weight of the gate would be managed by the frame alone.

Once I had the frame installed, I packed up my tools. I was reaching for a hammer when Jai Li crept over and picked it up. I pretended not to notice and gathered the other bits of detritus. It was a small thing, three pounds at most, but allowed me to move things without marring them.

I stood, admiring the installation, hands on hips, head back. It was good. It felt good. I looked down at a tug on my jeans. Jai Li was standing there, holding the hammer out to me, grinning. I took the hammer with one hand and patted her on the head with the other. "Thank you, Jai Li."

Her eyes got as big as saucers for a moment; then she turned and fled through the crowd of children. The looks on their faces made my stomach ache. They craved that touch, that smile, that familiar acknowledgment.

I walked among them, placing my hand on their heads, like a priest answering his supplicants. As I passed through them, touching each one, I noticed Nidhogg standing with her cane by the library. She had a smile on her face that was at once tender and terrifying.

As the last child scampered away, I approached her, careful to bow properly. "How are you today?" I asked her.

She studied me, turning her head this way and that. So bird-like in her demeanor. "You do them no service," she said, finally. "I do not need a passel of simpering snotlings. They are raised to serve me. It is not their needs that are paramount here."

I was horrified. They were children. They needed nurturing. How else were they to be productive, happy? Nidhogg believed otherwise. The predatory look was back on her face, and the moment of joy died in my chest. They had no hope of being happy. Their lot was to serve and serve willingly or pay the consequences.

The reality of the situation came crashing back home to me. While she found me entertaining and seemed to enjoy my company, I was more like a favored pet. I was nothing to her, just as these children were less than nothing.

"Come," she said, turning to the open door. "I would discuss Frederick Sawyer and his business in my domain."

I explained the news as I understood it. The news of the necromancer disturbed her, as did the murder of her citizens.

"And you say this necromancer was a protégé of Jean-Paul?"

"Yes, I believe so. And you may be familiar with a group calling itselves the Dragon Liberation Front? I believe they are working together."

"Reavers," she spat. "Qindra and I spoke of this. She had made moves to see to this group. The mead they promised would have helped my cause in the council the next time we met."

"Council?"

She eyed me warily. "You are not so much a trusted servant as a convenient substitute. I will not entrust all of my business to you yet. In time, perhaps, if you have atoned for your sin against my flesh and proven your worth, I will trust you further. For now, be contented I have not destroyed everything you hold dear in vengeance for my loss."

Bitch. What the hell was going on with her? The last time we met, she was like a grandmother, sharing memories and giving me cookies. Today, it was threats and innuendo.

"If I have offended you," I said, bowing my head, "I ask your forgiveness."

She grunted, tapping the ground with her cane. "You are wasting my time. Is there further news?"

"No," I said, standing. And I walked away.

"I have not dismissed you," she raged at me. "Come back here."

I kept walking, thinking how much I wished I had Gram with me at that moment. She did not follow me, nor did she change. When I reached the door, I turned and pulled it closed. I had one last glimpse of her leaning against her cane, her anger a frothing aura surrounding her.

Forty-five

THE TRAFFIC ON THE 520 BRIDGE WAS SO BACKED UP, I turned off on Montlake and drove over to the University Village. I needed something to drink. Instead of alcohol, which was my first choice, I opted for a cherry cola from Johnny Rockets. I walked over to the covered courtyard and sat, shocked at what had gone down. No wonder the whole household was constantly on edge. She was out of her damn mind. And how in the hell had I just walked out of there. Total disrespect on my part. It's a miracle she didn't kill me for pissing her off.

I pulled out my cell phone and called my old Tae Kwon Do school. I needed to take an action on the home front, in case something drastic happened. I was also carrying Gram with me from now on. This was too much.

A pleasant young woman answered the phone. I think it was the same one who answered the last time I called.

"Family Martial Arts," she said, sweetly. "How may I help you?"

I got the mailing address and almost hung up then, but I had to know, had to ask. "I'm wondering if Megan Beauhall is training today?"

"Oh, Megan. Sure. She's on the floor now, taking the kids through a warm-up. Can I take a message?"

She was an instructor. How great was that? "When does she get done?" I asked. "This is a friend of hers."

"Not until seven. Would you like to speak with Sa Bum Nim Choi?"

Oh, wow. That was not on the agenda. My mind did a couple of flips: don't do it, do it—couldn't have been more than a second or two to go through a million iterations. Finally, I decided to do the thing that scared me the most. "Sure, that would be excellent."

I waited a minute, imbibing a cherry sugar rush. The adrenaline was beginning to crash, and I thought I might start shaking.

"This is Sa Bum Nim Choi. How may I help you?"

I froze. This was one of the most influential women in my life. I'd walked out of her dojang almost ten years ago and had never as much as set foot in the place since.

"Hello?" she said. "Is anybody there?"

I cleared my throat. "Sa Bum Nim. This is Sarah Beauhall. Can we talk?"

"Sarah?" she asked, more surprised than I'd ever heard her. "Is there a problem?"

I let my head fall into my right hand. "No, ma'am. I just need to talk."

She covered the phone and spoke to the girl behind the desk. "Have Megan take them through their forms when they are done with warm-ups," she said. "I need to take this call."

I heard her walking across the tiled floor by the front door, then heard the bell tinkle as she went outside. There was a place between her school and the BBQ joint next door where you could stand out of the rain and talk on the phone while still seeing the training floor through the windows. Da used to stand there sometimes, when I was testing and the dojang was too crowded.

"Sarah, what is going on?"

Of all the grown-ups I knew, she was the first beyond my parents that I ever trusted. She taught me dignity and respect—let me see myself as a viable human being with valued opinions and a valid purpose.

"It's Megan," I said. "I'm worried about her."

We talked for thirty minutes. Most of the class. Twice the girl at the desk came out and asked for further instructions, but Megan kept the class together.

In the end, she agreed to keep an eye on Megan. She didn't think there were drugs involved, but there was some bad blood with a few boys at school. And things at home were not ideal. Again, a huge amount of it came down to hero worship of me, she said. There were pictures of me at the school—board-breaking seminars, sparring tournaments. I'd loved the whole art, and Megan was better than I was.

"She's competing with you," Sa Bum Nim said. "Even though you have been gone so long, she's haunted by your ghost."

"I know, I'm sorry. But I've got problems of my own to deal with." I know it sounded weak, but I did. I needed to figure this shit out before I thought about taking my crazy life back to them.

"You are welcome here at any time, Sarah. I told you that the day you left, and it has not changed. Come visit us. Watch her on the floor. She's quite the young woman."

"I miss her, you know." Okay, now I missed her. I'd put her out of my mind as part of the leaving home thing. I knew that now. Totally unfair to her, above all else.

"I should go teach some of this class, to be fair to the paying students," she said.

"Of course. Thanks. I'll be in touch."

I sat and finished my drink, feeling like a teenager all over again. That woman scared the hell out of me with her intensity. I thought she could give Nidhogg a run for her money.

Forty-six

By the time I got home, I'd played the conversation over in my head a hundred times. My life was fairly chaotic. Sa Bum Nim Choi's best advice had always been to quiet my mind. Work in the now. It reminded me of some of the things Skella's grandmother, Unun, had said when I was in Vancouver.

I downloaded a podcast on meditation and sat listening to it while Katie graded papers. I needed to learn how to go walkabout without all the ceremony or the herbal enhancement.

I thought about how it felt when I was walkabout. Especially the way it felt when I moved in the astral state. If I could find that place, maybe I could use that as a guidepost. Unfortunately, all I had thirty minutes later was a throbbing headache. I'd just decided to bag it for the evening when I felt a stutter. The thread that was anchored deep inside me came into focus, catching me off guard. I reached for it, hoping to catch it while I could see it. It was like picking up a dropped stitch when knitting. I almost had it when Katie called to me from the living room.

I dropped the line with a resigned sigh and opened my eyes. Things were not exactly normal. The room around me glowed with a fuzzy tinge, and my eyes buzzed slightly. It was like when I was holding Gram—colors were brighter and the connection between things was more obvious.

Katie walked into the room, and it was like a unicorn exploded. Rainbow colors danced all around her. Much stronger than the night I'd seen her while on walkabout. I squinted, she was so bright.

"You okay?" she asked, kissing me on the nose.

"Yeah," I said, squeezing my eyes shut. It was overwhelming. The kaleidoscope of colors made me nauseous. "Just a little queasy."

"Keep up the good work," she said, laughing. "I'm gonna take a shower."

After she left I opened my eyes a crack. The world was just as vivid. Katie just wasn't there blowing the bell curve. I wondered if she glowed so brightly because I loved her or if there was something special about her beyond the general awesomeness.

I got up and walked around. The apartment looked mostly the same as last time, only with an overlay of muted colors. I wasn't sure if it was because it was daylight or if it was because I wasn't using the tea. I'm not saying it looked like the inside of a cotton candy machine or anything, but the apartment was a lot more cheerful.

I ducked my head into the bedroom. I'd avoided going in there since the incident with Gletts and the eaters. I could see the doorway behind the bed frame, but I wasn't willing to get too close. I was still in my body, but I was not risking getting sucked into the sideways.

After a couple minutes, though, the headache blossomed to the point I could barely stand. I made my way to the kitchen and downed a couple of aspirin and a tall glass of water. Then I stumbled to the living room, crawled into bed, and passed out.

Forty-seven

I NEEDED TO GET THE GATE INSTALLED AT NIDHOGG'S PLACE, but after the incident the day before, I was hesitant to go back out there. I'd walked out on her, and she was not someone to piss off. Screwing up my courage, I called Nidhogg's place. Better to scout the territory ahead of time. Zi Xui answered and seemed reasonably happy to hear from me.

"It is good you called," she told me. "The mistress gave orders that she is not to be disturbed, but that you are free to visit the house. She wishes you to finish installing the gate." She paused. "She has also given you free use of the library."

Wow. That was generous. "She's not upset?"

"Oh, she was in a state all through the afternoon, but when she saw the children later in the day, they were happy and laughing for the first time since Qindra left. I believe that was what lightened her mood. She is an old woman, with tendencies to see the blackest parts of life. I think your presence is forcing her to see differently."

I was shocked. If anything, I thought she'd have some form of punishment for me, even if it didn't include being burned alive, or eaten, mangled, or generally mutilated. I felt suddenly light-hearted myself.

"I will need to arrange for a couple of folks to come with me to install the gate. It weighs more than I can handle by myself. Will that be a problem?"

"I will inform security. Please make sure they understand to be polite and try to keep the noise to a minimum? Loud noises upset the mistress."

We wrapped up, and I called Black Briar. I'd need a couple strong backs and a rolling hoist to get the gate from the smithy to the house in Seattle.

I called a construction rental place, arranged to pick up the hoist in a few hours, and got dressed.

Three hours later, Robbie, Dave, and I had wrestled the gate through the huge front door of Nidhogg's estate. The children of the house kept mostly out of sight, but I could feel them watching. Even the adults managed to breeze by a few times as we maneuvered the huge load into the house. Luckily, the hoist was powered, so we drove it, very slowly, into the house.

It took us another two hours to get it into position and aligned with the frame. Anezka was a genius, though. She'd badgered me about accurate measurements and wouldn't let me be satisfied with less than impeccable precision. I knew I would've totally botched it on my own. Too impatient. Every moment of grief and frustration I'd had working with her—measuring again and again, tamping, heating, and in some cases grinding—had paid off.

When the gate slid home for that first time I did a little dance. Rob and Dave joined me, grinning like fools. I held a finger to my lips and they nodded. Dave gave me a thumbs-up and Robbie hugged me.

I escorted them out of the house. "Steaks on me," I told them as they loaded up.

"You're on," Rob said.

I watched them drive off before going back inside to clean up.

I got the hoist back into my truck by myself. It was like a really big remote control toy.

When I had everything put away and the entry way cleaned up, I stood in front of the gate—the two keys clenched in my fist—and let the satisfaction of a job well done swim over me.

I slipped the keys in my pocket and turned to find Jai Li standing there holding two braided leather cords. She handed them to me, and I threaded the twisted leather through the keys. I took the first and put it over my neck, slipping the key into my bra. I didn't want it to knock against the amulet. That trinket had come at too high a cost, transferring its allegiance from Anezka to me before her house fell into ruin. I held the bauble a moment, thinking of Bub and how he'd come to my service at the same time.

I wound the second cord around my hand, holding the key in my fist. This was for Nidhogg, and she didn't want to be disturbed. Maybe I'd give it to Zi Xiu instead. That wasn't the bargain, but we'd see. Jai Li stood there watching me. On a whim I sat down in front of the gate and held my arms open to her.

She looked behind her, as if to see who may be watching, then crawled into my lap. I held her against me, feeling her warmth against my chest—felt the fineness of her hair brush against my chin.

For the next thirty minutes we sat there while I pointed out the different aspects of the gate, from the worked leaves and flowers to the runes for protection and the twin dragons along the top of the gate.

I didn't mention how badly Stuart wanted me to make one of those drakes on its back, with a young woman over it, stabbing it in the chest. It had an appeal, granted, but I didn't think Nidhogg would appreciate the sentiment.

The feel of that child in my lap triggered something in me. Whether biological or just social, I had no idea, but I wanted to

protect her from the life she led. There was no justice if a child
this sweet had to live in a place with such psychosis and fear.

After my butt had long gone to sleep, I shooed her back to her
duties. I needed to get into the library and do some research
while the offer was open. Who knew when the next breeze would
blow the fickle Nidhogg into indignation?

I hobbled into the library, my ass spiked with the pins and
needles of returning circulation. Just like the last time I'd been in
the great room, I was overwhelmed with the beauty of it all.

I spent an hour walking up and down the library, trailing my
fingers along the leather spines. Many of the books were classics
I recognized. There were whole sections in languages I couldn't
begin to read. Twice I found a book that contained real power.
The touch of them was a gentle tingle, like touching your tongue
to a nine-volt battery.

One was in Arabic, so I let it alone after flipping a couple of
pages. The other was in English. Well, mostly English, but there
was French; German, I think; and runes in several different dia-
lects. I set it aside to be looked at in more detail later. First, I
wanted to explore some more.

I spent a good hour researching symbols related to the tattoo
I'd seen on Charlie Hague. The individual parts could be inter-
preted in various ways, but together they seemed to represent an
order. Similar patterns were represented in several books on co-
vert religions and ancient orders. I didn't understand why Charlie Hague would have the symbol of a secret society tattooed to
the inside of his wrist where anyone could see it. It just seemed
reckless.

Before long my bladder decided I needed a chance to stretch.
I got up and walked back to the hall. As I reached for the door I
saw that Jai Li had fallen asleep curled on a chair to the right of
the door. She'd snuck in and watched me while I studied.

I left her and stepped into the hall. One of the scullery maids was just coming down from the laundry with a stack of crisply folded sheets. I called to her. She was startled but didn't drop the sheets. I can't imagine how much time she spent ironing them.

After a brief conversation in broken English I convinced her to follow me to the library. Upon seeing Jai Li, she nodded and mimed me picking up the girl.

When I lifted her she snuggled close, burying her face into my shoulder. I followed the maid to a part of the mansion I'd not visited before and found one of the servant's quarters. It was nearly a barracks. By the size of things, it housed mostly children. The maid directed me to where the girl slept, and I gently settled the child into her bed.

Jai Li looked up at me as I straightened, blinking rapidly. I bent over and kissed her on the forehead. She smiled, pulled the blankets up to her chin, and rolled over. The maid watched the entire scene with shock and amazement. I smiled at her, and she returned it shyly before trundling off.

I lagged behind, staring around at the small personal space Jai Li commanded. She had a small bed, a locker of sorts that was made of carved wood, and a chest at the foot of the bed. Each of the children had a similar setup. Not much space for personal effects, but Jai Li had the wall behind her bed covered in pictures. Many of them were done in watercolors, but there were pencil sketches and two different needlepoints that had been framed.

Most were of people. One was a sad picture of two girls, hand in hand, flying over a field of red flowers. The girls were obviously Jai Li and her twin, Mei Hau. They were so alike, yet I could tell a difference in the two girls by the subtle differences in the colors.

Next to Jai Li was an empty bed with two pictures on the wall, both of flowers—hyacinths and tulips. The bed was made and the locker stood open, empty. This was Mei Hau's place, and the emptiness of it was like a spike in my chest.

I left the quarters, my heart heavy. Several other children were at their places, quietly reading or playing with simple toys. Most were empty as the children were off performing some duty. Mei Hau's was not the only abandoned place. I counted five others that were vacated, forlorn.

I couldn't leave there fast enough. The maid stood outside the door waiting for me. When I emerged she bade me follow her. She paused at a large walk-in closet and deposited the sheets she'd been carrying and then led me back to the kitchen.

Once I was ensconced with a cup of strong, black tea, the maid hurried out, motioning for me to stay. In a couple of minutes she returned with Zi Xiu in tow. The two women sat with me, sharing a plate of sliced apples and more of the dark tea.

Through Zi Xiu's interpretation we discussed Jai Li: how she has grown melancholy since the death of her twin and how she'd been more and more rebellious, even openly defying Nidhogg. Not once, but twice.

They feared for her, feared the retribution Nidhogg would impose on the girl when she finally crossed the line. None of the other children had ever transgressed—not in the lifetimes of these two women. It was not Nidhogg's way to be indulgent, but since the black day when mistress had taken her true form and killed so many, things had shifted in the house.

Qindra had held the house together, kept a balance between the kind Nidhogg, the gentle grandmother of them all, and the angry, spiteful monster she became, sometimes quite literally.

I was amazed to hear them speak so bluntly about the situation in the house. When I inquired, they both spoke at once. It was the girl and the kindness I'd shown her. If not for that they would have remained silent.

When we had run out of things to speak about, the scullery maid returned to her duties and Zi Xiu showed me back to the library. I needed to wrap up soon. Katie would start to worry.

I spent another hour looking through the grimoire I'd found. I copied down several sets of runes to discuss with Jimmy and Rolph. There was so much here. We could've studied this book for a long while and not figured out everything it had to offer.

My eyes had begun to burn, and I really needed to go to the bathroom. I got up and flipped through the rest of the book just to get a glimpse of the rest. Near the back I found a little song. The words didn't make any sense, but the notes were clear enough. I copied down the stanzas, totally oblivious to their meaning. I was sure Katie could figure it out. A note scribbled in the margin stated the song would show the truth of things. That sounded like a cool thing to know.

I put the book back where I'd found it and headed to the bathroom. It had been a good day, in many ways.

Minutes later, as I made my way through the winding halls toward the entranceway, Nidhogg stepped from her grand hall. She did not say a word, just held her hand out to me. I stepped to her, fished the second key from my pocket, and handed it over. She slipped the braided cord over her neck, tucked the key inside her blouse, and turned, dismissing me with a wave of her ancient hand.

I didn't look back, just turned on my heel and walked across the foyer. I paused once to look over at the gate that blocked the rest of the world from Qindra's rooms.

Soon, I promised, I'd be handing the key to her. She belonged here. This was her domain, not mine. The people in this house needed her too much.

Forty-eight

THE WHELP, CHARLIE HAGUE, SAT IN THE STUFFY HOUSE SIP-
ping the too-sweet tea the old woman had insisted he drink.
Madame Gottschalk sat buried in cats and nattered on about the
weather. The formalities were irrelevant; it was the ritual that
mattered. Best to cleanse the traveler before engaging in clan-
destine conversation in case someone had discovered their meet.

When the tea was drunk, Madame Gottschalk waved at the
boy. "Begin," she ordered.

"We bugged the main house out at Black Briar just after the
ritual murders. If their planning anything specific, it's not obvious to our agents."

She listened intently, stroking her favorite tabby.

"While they have stumbled around in the last half a year or
more, they have uncovered a new artifact of some ilk. We do not
fully know the nature of this item, but it is tied to Paul Cornett
in some fashion. There is a safety deposit box we are aware of.
James Cornett, the son and current leader of the Black Briar
clan, visited that box recently and retrieved an item. If they are
utilizing it, we have no indications."

"And the girl?"

"She remains a mystery. We know the necromancer is targeting those around her, whether to elicit fear or to reduce her sup-

port base. We have not been able to determine the connection between all those murdered in similar fashion." He paused, considering. "There is other news. We have word that Frederick Sawyer is in the city."

"Well, well," Madame Gottschalk said, tapping the arm of her chair. "A king moves onto the board. Shall we see a response from the queen?"

Charlie shrugged. "We do know there is a connection between the girl and Nidhogg. I do not get the impression she loves the great beasts, especially if the rumors of her hand in Jean-Paul's demise prove to be true."

Madame Gottschalk cackled. "Easier to believe Nidhogg or Sawyer killed him than believe a simple girl had the power to take down one of their kind."

"I beg to differ," Charlie said, obviously agitated. "We have underestimated things in the past. What if it's true?" He leaned forward, elbows on knees. "Can you imagine?"

"Blasphemy," she bellowed, sending cats scrambling off her lap. "Speak no foolishness in this home, silly boy."

This was not a new argument. Charlie lowered his gaze, grimacing.

"You are young and eager," she went on, settling back in her chair. "Revolution appeals to your generation, as it did mine, when I was as wet behind the ears as you are." She paused, considering other revolutions, other powers vying for control in a world of chaos. "Trust me. They killed Rasputin, the fools, and we see what happened to the Romanovs in the end."

"Shall I contact the blacksmith again, or do you have other orders?"

"I want you to contact young James Cornett. Perhaps it is time to bring him into the fold. They are a menace where they are. Either we bring them in and allow him to replace his father in the order or we need to eliminate them as a threat to Bestellen von Mordred."

He stood and knelt at her feet, taking her hand and kissing her knuckles. "It shall be as you say, Seiðr."

Once the door shut behind him and the room no longer reverberated with his energy, the grey tabby jumped atop the table and spoke.

"This haven is at risk, grandmother. I fear all our plans may be destroyed by this foolish clan of ruffians."

"Perhaps you are correct," Madame Gottschalk offered. "I will consult with my sister, Jaga."

The cat yawned, stretching her entire body. "Does she still live in that ridiculous hut outside Minsk?"

Madame Gottschalk shooed the cats away. "Mind yourself."

She sat back and sipped her tea. Things were amiss in the realms. There were echoes of energy she had never felt before. First in the spring, just before Jean-Paul was killed, and twice more in the last several months. She needed to perform a scrying, throw the runes, maybe even read some entrails. She looked at the cat a moment and dismissed the idea. Chickens told better futures, in any case.

Forty-nine

I CONVINCED KATIE TO JOIN ME FOR DINNER OUT AT BLACK Briar so we could discuss all the notes I'd taken at Nidhogg's place. She had mostly forgiven Jimmy, but there was still something niggling there, something she wouldn't open up to me about. I figured she was due some privacy. It just wasn't like her.

We had a full crew for grub: Anezka, Gunther, Stuart, Deidre, Jimmy, Katie, and me. Oh, and Bub. Gunther thought he'd make a good addition to the conversation, even though Deidre was not sure their dishes could afford his indiscriminate definition of food and foodlike substances.

I was pleasantly surprised when Gunther and Anezka cooked for us. They made tacos, which went over well with Bub. I'm not sure it wasn't his idea originally. He loved Mexican.

The meal went by quickly. I cleared the table while they passed my notes around. I'd made a couple of copies, so we didn't have to share all the way around.

The first thing I wanted to know about was the symbol I'd seen on Charlie Hague. Visions were something I would've laughed about a year ago. But no more.

"Definitely the symbol of an order," Gunther said. "I'll run it by some of my friends in the monastery, but I believe I know this group."

"Aye," Jimmy said. "I've seen this mentioned in one of Mom's journals. It was pretty sparse, mostly short, cryptic notes about meetings. But I thought it funny that a group would use something so obviously linked with the Illuminati."

Neither Bub nor Anezka had a clue, and neither Katie nor I could add anything. Deidre just went into the other room, declaring a hoodoo-free evening for herself. "I've got better stuff stacked on my DVR," she said and showed us the back of her.

The song I found caught their attention, though. Katie got out one of her guitars and plucked out the tune. It was a bit discordant, low tones, with a steady rhythm that felt like drums in the deep. That's how she described it. Conjuring up something best left unsummoned. Once she thought she had the basic through line down, she added the words.

For a moment, things got really creepy. My vision shifted, like the other morning. Everything in the room had a different level of energy, a different color palette and hue. Bub glowed, as did Katie.

"Can you see that?" Katie asked the room. Everyone shook their head. Everyone but me. Katie smiled at me and motioned with her head. Katie walked down the hall, and the door to the basement was outlined in sparkling squiggles. She laughed. "It's like in Dungeons and Dragons," she said, pausing in her singing. "It reveals hidden things."

We compared notes. She saw the highlight around the hidden door, but not the glow around her or Bub. That was interesting. The song had triggered my walkabout vision, but she could see some of it while she was singing. She wanted to continue down the hall to the bedrooms, but Jimmy put a stop to that. "Some things are personal," he groused. I didn't want to know what he and Deidre had hidden in their bedroom, and after a second it dawned on Katie that she didn't either. Stuart just sniggered at us.

The music was haunting, not unlike that song by Objekt 775 I loved so much. They were an obscure band but had a wide range of punk and rock in their repertoire.

We had a big time with it, laughing and kidding around about what folks wanted to keep hidden, when Katie noticed something else. There were three points in the house that glowed faintly when exposed to the song. It wasn't a long song, so Katie had to sing it over and over.

The three spots were surprising: the smoke alarm in the hallway, a spot over the back door, and one in the living room, over the fireplace.

Stuart pulled down the smoke alarm and found a tiny camera installed. The spot in the kitchen held a listening device, and the living room had both.

Someone had bugged the damn house. Katie stopped singing after twenty-seven times through, saying her throat was hurting.

"Unbelievable," Jimmy said, taking a pocket knife to the drywall above the fireplace. "When could someone have bugged this place? We're always here, or at least someone is."

He looked to Gunther and Stuart. "Pretty sophisticated stuff," Stuart said. "Not government issue, but damn close. Private market, but high-end."

He dropped them on the tile floor in the kitchen and ground his boot down on top of them. "Somebody's in for a surprise," he said.

We grabbed Deidre and filled her in. She agreed to go around with Katie and me to search the house, but shooed everyone else out. "Too crowded in some of the rooms," she said.

We worked our way through the top of the house. Deidre's nightstand glowed, but she opened the drawer before we could stop her. We didn't need to see whatever sex toys she kept.

There were no other bugs in the upstairs, but there was a book in the den that glowed. Deidre flipped through it and found three loose pages tucked in between the pages of the book. They were written in a small, tight script that Katie recognized as her mother's.

They were lists of Christmas presents from when Katie was two. She sat down in the living room and cried over them.

I sat with her, taking the guitar and letting her cry. This was something even Jimmy didn't know existed. "Keep them," Deidre said. "They can be your secret."

In the margins were little notes and measurements. Dresses for Katie, books for Jim. And some things for her father that made her smile. A new flashlight, underwear, and silk pajamas. She folded the pages carefully and put them in her shirt pocket.

I let her cry on my shoulder, but when she pulled away she was covered in blood.

"Jim?" Deidre called, rolling her chair to the kitchen. "Get in here!"

The others piled back into the house and went into crisis mode. Katie had a pretty serious bloody nose, and she and I were both covered in it. Luckily, we got it stopped with pressure and an ice pack.

Katie kept clothes in her old room, and I borrowed a T-shirt from Jimmy. We got cleaned up in the bathroom, and I decided to keep my bra on even though the blood had gotten that far. "No way I'm going out in that crowd without a bra."

Katie snickered but didn't protest. I was a bit horrified to be wearing a John Deere T-shirt. At least it fit.

"It was the song," Katie said. "I could feel it working on me but didn't really make the connection until the end there."

"Well, it's not something I want you singing again anytime soon."

She looked at me, one eyebrow raised, but I stood my ground.

"Unknown magic, Katie. Who knows what kind of damage that can cause."

She leaned in and kissed me. "Yes, ma'am. Whatever you say."

We walked back out into the kitchen and joined the others again.

"Well, we can sweep the rest of the farm another time," Jimmy said. "Stuart knows of some gear we can get to sweep for bugs." He looked at Katie, his face taut with fear. "I can't let you do that again. That song is dangerous."

For an awkward minute they stood there. Katie's face was flushed. She was getting pissed at him again. I started to say something, but she relented and hugged him. Everyone in the room breathed a sigh of relief, including Bub. The tension had even gotten to him.

We called it a night. Katie promised to leave the song for now. At least until we could research it more. I could always get more contextual information from the grimoire out at Nidhogg's.

No magic is without cost. I had to remember that.

Before we left, we went to visit Trisha and her crew in the barracks. Nancy, Gary, and Benny were playing cards, while Trisha read stories to Frick and Frack. They were getting bigger and filling out. Soon they'd be the size of two-year-olds. But they loved Trisha, and they loved stories. We hung out, listening to a second reading of *Goodnight Moon* before she could get them into their cribs.

"Gotta do everything twice," she said, leading us to the end of the barracks where the card game was going on. "They'll sleep through the noise, but if we're too close, they think they can whine and we'll come running."

We watched the four of them playing euchre and chatted about how things were going out at Chumstick.

"Boring," Benny said.

"Useless," Gary added.

"Critical," Nancy said, giving the other two evil looks. "Boring is good. No action is good. Total surrender is fine, as long as nothing happens you regret."

"Yeah, like I said," Benny mouthed around a long pretzel stick. "Total yawn fest."

"It's something to do," Trisha said. "And we're good at our jobs."

The others grunted their assent.

"I wish I had these folks at my back when the giants hit our line back in May," Trisha said, then went quiet, not looking at anything but the emptiness in her memory.

"We held our own," Gary said. "I helped defend the wounded."

"I recall," I said, smiling at him. "You saved lives that night."

"I was finishing grad school," Benny said, shrugging. "Sorry I missed it, but glad at the same time, you know?"

"I hear you've been seeing someone," Katie said, all innocent.

Nancy looked worried for a minute, like a trust had been betrayed, but Benny chuckled.

"I've been out," Trisha said, blushing. "He's like no one I've ever dated."

"Sex ain't bad, either," Gary added. "Am I right?"

Trisha didn't answer, but the smug look on her face was enough for me.

"Good for you," I said, patting her on the arm. "Must be hard getting out with the twins."

"Not too bad," she said. "The crew takes turns babysitting, and we're flexible on when we go out. Sometimes it's not until after we get done out at Chumstick."

"Morning nookie," Benny said, smirking.

Nancy hit him. "Mind your manners," she said. "None of your business."

"It's okay," Trisha said, smiling. "He's just jealous."

They laughed in a way that spoke of trust and camaraderie. It was good to see.

"We should go," I said. "I need to get this girl to bed."

Benny started to say something, but Nancy kicked him under the table.

Trisha walked us out. We paused by the cribs and kissed the twins good night. This place felt safe. Felt like home. We left them to their banter.

"Good folks," Katie said as we climbed into her Miata. "Glad they're on our side."

"Got that right," I agreed. "I'm just glad to see Trisha getting out, seeing someone. After her wounds, I was worried she'd freeze up, hide herself away."

"We're all pretty lucky," she said, leaning over to kiss me. "Put on some music; I feel like driving fast."

Fifty

We were approaching Bellevue when my cell phone rang. It was the Kirkland Police Department. It seemed a young Asian child was spotted walking around down by Juanita Beach. When the girl was picked up, the officers learned the child couldn't speak as her tongue had been cut out.

What the hell? "We'll be right there," I told the dispatch officer.

"What is it?" Katie asked when I'd hung up. "Someone in trouble?"

"It's Jai Li," I said, disbelieving. "That mute girl I told you about. She's at the Kirkland Police Department."

"Why'd they call you?"

I thought back to my visits to the house, how Jai Li had followed me around. How the hell had she gotten to Kirkland? "Not sure. Guess we'll find out."

She concentrated on the roads, and cut across two lanes of traffic to get us into the turnoff for downtown Kirkland. "Why is she in Kirkland?"

I was stumped. As far as I knew, she'd never set foot out of that house in her life. "Guess we'll find out shortly."

We whipped around a couple of corners more quickly than I was comfortable with, but the car handled it like a champ.

Within a few minutes we had parked the car and were running into the police station.

No matter the urgency, we managed to be stymied by the bureaucracy. Ended up, we waited in the visitors lounge for almost twenty minutes before a stoic-looking policewoman came out to greet us. "Ms. Beauhall. I'm Officer Simpson. We met a few months back."

How could I forget? She's the one Melanie called to report my rape that never really happened.

"What's this all about?" I asked. "How'd you know to call me?"

Officer Simpson handed me a stack of papers. They were hand-drawn pictures of me. Seven of them altogether. Different aspects of me working on the gate, studying in the library, speaking with a shadowy figure that had to be Nidhogg. These weren't mere sketches, however. These were lifelike portraits. It was the most amazing thing I'd ever seen.

"I recognized you from when we spoke in the spring. I tracked down my notes and checked your contact information."

"Wow," Katie said when I handed her the pictures.

"Can I see her?" I asked.

Officer Simpson had a soft spot. I could see it. "She can't leave, not until we establish custody," she said. "But you can visit her. She's back in interrogation room two. It's private and quiet. She was pretty upset until we gave her the crayons and paper. Then she's done nothing but draw pictures of you and point at them and then the phone. It was pretty clear what she wanted. She understands English well enough."

Dread filled my stomach as we followed Officer Simpson down the long hallway. What the hell had happened? How'd she get out?

Before they opened the door, they let us watch her a moment. She sat on a metal chair with her legs tucked under so she could reach the table in front of her.

"We offered her soda, but she refused," Officer Simpson said. "She took water though. First kid I ever met that turned down soda." She smiled at me. "Bright kid. Hangs on every word, picks up more from adult conversations than I'm used to as well. What is she? Four? Five?"

"Six," I said. "She's small for her age."

"We need to call someone," she said, quietly. "Either we get her back to her parents—"

I shook my head.

"—Guardians then. Or we have to call Child Protective Services."

"I can make a call," I said. "But I want to see her first, see if I can see why she was wandering around in Kirkland."

"Yes," Simpson said. "We'd like to know that as well."

There were pictures covering the table and most of the floor between her and the two-way mirror. Made me think of Skella and Gletts and how they'd watched us in secret.

"I need to go in there," I said. Katie took my hand and gave it a squeeze. "She needs me."

Officer Simpson nodded.

I opened the door and stepped in. Apparently other folks had come and gone, because she didn't even look up, just kept frantically drawing. As I stood there, she shoved aside a stunning picture of me holding a hammer and snatched another piece of paper from a stack on the table.

"Jai Li?" I said.

She looked up, surprised, and a smile exploded across her face. She pushed the chair away from the table and scrambled to me. I knelt, and she threw herself into my arms, sobbing. I sat on the floor and rocked her while she cried. Katie watched us with the strangest look on her face.

When she'd cried herself out, we coaxed Jai Li back to the table. Katie offered to color with her while I talked with the officer. At first she was hesitant, but when I explained that I loved Katie, she got a grin on her face and bent to it, drawing like a fiend.

I made a few phone calls, first to Nidhogg's place, where I got Zi Xiu. She practically begged me to keep the girl, said that Nidhogg was furious at her absence and that she was afraid for Jai Li's safety if she returned.

Next I called one of Nidhogg's cadre of lawyers. Zi Xiu had given me the number. She said that there were times when Qindra had needed a lawyer to make things work properly.

I was not fond of lawyers in general. Anyone who thought themselves that important worried me.

In this case I was not disappointed. The woman who got on the phone asked me exactly three questions and hung up, not even waiting for me to ask anything.

"Is anyone dead?

"Do you need bail?

"Where are you?"

I stared at the phone as the dial tone blared out at me. "They don't mince words," I told Katie when I walked back in. "There's a lawyer on the way. Everything should be okay."

Jai Li sat in my lap as she and Katie drew. I asked quiet questions, which she ignored, so I stopped. I watched the pictures, fantasies now, rainbows and ponies, kittens and a cow jumping over a moon.

"You are very talented," Katie said, looking at her own sketch of a dog. "Very, very talented."

Jai Li smiled and took another sheet of paper. She studied the white page for several minutes, then looked up at me. She set her mouth like she'd made a tough decision. She tapped me on the chin, pointed to the paper, and began to draw.

First she drew a picture of her watching me study. Then she drew Nidhogg watching in the shadows, red lines coming off her head.

"Angry?" I asked. She nodded.

Then she showed a delivery truck arriving to drop off supplies for the house. She drew boxes of vegetables, meat, wheels of cheese, and sacks of rice.

Next, she drew three quick pictures of a little girl hiding, then climbing into the back of the truck, then snuggling down in a pile of burlap bags.

"You?" I asked, knowing the answer. She smiled and nodded. This was a game to her, and she was delighted.

She drew a picture of the truck stopping at a restaurant in Kirkland and her climbing out of the back and running toward the lake.

"You are very clever."

She smiled, but took another sheet of paper. I was shocked by the speed at which she drew and the clarity of her pictures. It was like Katie singing, only with lines on a page.

The next one was Nidhogg sitting in her chair, head bowed and weeping. She very specifically set this picture to her right, in front of Katie.

"Is Nidhogg getting worse?" I asked.

She nodded once and took another sheet of paper.

She drew another girl, like her, only sleeping.

"Is this you, honey?" Katie asked.

Jai Li looked at me, expectantly.

"No," I said. "It's her twin, Mei Hau." I looked around, hoping no one was listening. "She's gone."

Jai Li nodded, her eyes swimming with tears.

"And now Qindra is gone," I said, understanding.

Jai Li lowered her head, wiping the tears with the back of her hand.

Katie looked up at me, bewildered. "She loves Qindra?" she asked, her voice a whisper.

I stroked Jai Li's hair. "She's always been kind to the children, even when things were bad."

Jai Li bobbed her head, peeling the paper off a yellow crayon. She was so tiny, so vulnerable it made my heart hurt.

"Did you run away to find me?" I asked.

Jai Li looked embarrassed, but slowly nodded yes, then shook her head no. She took another sheet of paper and drew a picture of herself, only larger than she was, big like me, with a hammer in her hand, breaking the bonds that kept Qindra trapped.

"That's pretty clear," I said, looking from her to Katie. "She was going to rescue Qindra."

Jai Li shook her head vigorously, tapping the paper in front of her.

"You are very brave," I said, giving her a squeeze.

Talk about a kick in the gut. This little girl had escaped the only place she'd ever known and left a mistress that had literally eaten her twin, all to rescue a woman she loved like a mother.

I felt about the size of a pill bug. I needed to get off the dime and find a way to bring Qindra home. This little girl deserved nothing less.

Fifty-one

THE LAWYER ARRIVED, A WOMAN OF MIDDLE YEARS, SEVERE AND professional. I debated whether or not she had a personality under that no-nonsense exterior.

She demanded a private meeting with me, away from two-way mirrors and eavesdropping. Officer Simpson didn't like her tone, that much was pretty obvious, but she let us use a different room to talk.

Katie stayed with Jai Li, who was cool with it once I explained I'd be right back.

The lawyer, Anne Rokhlin, sat across from me with a legal pad and several pens. She looked me up and down, made a face that spoke of disappointment and judgment.

"I cost a very lot," she said, taking up one pen. She jotted down the date and time on the top of the page in red ink, then took up a different pen to write down my name.

"Explain the situation to me," she said, her face closed and her voice clipped.

Definitely not Ms. Congeniality.

I gave her the story as far as I could piece it together. Girl runs away, girl needs help, I get called. She wrote everything down in a sort of code I didn't recognize. Dwarvish shorthand for all I knew.

"And you are not the legal guardian, I take it."

"No."

She wrote several more sentences.

"That's a lot of words for a simple no."

She looked at me, eyes flat, and tapped her pen on the page. "With this particular client, nothing is simple. I get paid to make problems go away." She grinned at me for the first time, and it was like being in front of a hungry wolf. "I make observations, perceptions of things that may serve me in the future. Especially when I meet someone new." She jotted down a few words and laid the pen aside. "I sense you could bring difficulties," she said, finally. "I don't like difficulties."

She opened her briefcase, deposited her notebook, and took out a cell phone. She pulled a Bluetooth headset out of her jacket pocket and hooked it on her ear. Then she dialed the phone.

She spoke quickly, relaying all the details I'd given her from memory. The description she gave of me was a bit disconcerting, but apparently the person on the other end needed confirmation.

"Yes. One minute," she said. "We will call back."

She took a second phone out of the briefcase and placed it on the table between us. I started to reach for it, but she slid it back a couple of inches, shaking her head at me.

She pulled a penknife from a pocket and slit open the plastic casing on a new headset she pulled from her briefcase. It had two sets of wires running out of it, a splitter. She plugged the headset into the second phone, held one piece to her ear, and slid the second over to me. "Put on the headset."

I held the headset up to my ear, and she punched a button on the phone. It rang once, and a familiar voice answered.

"Ms. Beauhall. You are a blessing and a menace."

It was Nidhogg. "I beg your pardon?"

She laughed. "I have granted you pardon on several occasions already. Now I need to know what you intend to do about this latest upset you have caused."

I looked at Anne Rokhlin, who looked at me like I was something she'd stepped in.

"Are you referring to Jai Li?" I asked.

Nidhogg hissed. "You know full well what I mean. The girl is your responsibility now. I can no longer trust her in my presence. Not while Qindra remains detained."

What a stupid bitch, I thought. Anger flashed through me. "She's a harmless child." I had to stop myself. The words I wanted to say would only cause more trouble. Anne sensed it and nodded slowly.

"Broken and useless," Nidhogg said, her voice full of venom. "Tainted by your interference."

Because I hugged her? Showed her compassion? Jesus, this was one stone-cold bitch.

"Fine, I'll keep her," I heard myself saying. "If you think she's too much for you to handle, I'll gladly give her a place that is safe."

Anne's eyes went wide. That was not what she expected.

That shocked Nidhogg as well. "She is not yours," she said, her voice icy. "When will you free Qindra? When will you fulfill your bargain?"

"I built you the gate you requested," I said, trying to breathe through the anger. "I've done everything you've asked since Qindra fell."

"And you are still lacking," she said. "You are not worthy of Qindra's shadow. Do your task. Bring her home to me. Then we will discuss your fate and the fate of the renegade child."

The phone cut off, and I sat staring at the lawyer, my mind numb with shock. She disconnected the phone, rolled the headset around her fist, and took a pair of wire cutters from her briefcase. She cut the wires into several pieces and put them into a plastic baggie. Then she took the battery out of the second cell phone and dropped the shell on the floor. With one quick stomp, she shattered the face of the phone and swept the pieces into the bag with the battery.

Finally, she took out the notebook again and began writing.

I sat there, breathing, trying to find my center. I wanted to pick the table up and throw it through the wall.

"You do not lack for chutzpah," Anne said. "Do you intend to harbor this waif?"

"Absolutely," I said. "You heard Nidhogg. She's not welcome there. Not until Qindra is rescued, if ever."

She nodded, pulled out several pieces of paper, and slid them in front of me. "Sign these. This will grant you temporary custody of the child until the rightful guardian can be contacted."

They were full of legalese, but I scanned them, making sure I wasn't giving away my kidneys. Basically, they gave me power of attorney over Jai Li. For the interim, I was her legal guardian. It was temporary, but there was no specified end date.

The documents were real enough, but how legal they were, I had my doubts. I signed them, of course. What else could I do?

"What now?" I asked.

She took them, pulled a metal contraption from her briefcase, and crimped the signed pages, notarizing them. Then she signed them in several places, each signature different—forgeries. Some laws were meant to be bent, I guessed.

"Simply speaking . . . ," she said, separating the papers into two piles. The first she placed in a battered manila folder and slid it across the table toward me. The rest she slid into her briefcase. "You are now the child's temporary guardian. Have been for the last six months." She smiled at me, a toothy shark's grin. "Legal in the state of Washington. Don't try to take the girl out of the country or across state lines. Other than that, take her home, give her a bath, read her a story, and tuck her into bed."

She stood and held her hand out to me. "Congratulations. You're a mommy."

She swept out of the room, leaving a cold wake behind her. Ice princesses could take lessons from this woman.

I took the papers back into the observation room and sat next to Katie. Jai Li was lying on the floor, playing with some building blocks that had appeared while I was gone.

"Officer Simpson brought them," Katie said, taking my hand. "How was the lawyer? What's the plan?"

I brushed the hair out of her face and kissed her gently. "Looks like we're mommies," I said, handing her the papers. "At least until we get all this straightened out."

She looked at them for a moment, then hugged me. "Oh, God. Are we ready for this?" She got up and paced around the room. "Jimmy will freak. What about work? And all this crazy stuff going on." She whirled to me, lowering her voice. "What about that serial killer? Will she be safe with us?"

I got up and walked to her, enveloping her in my arms. "We can take her out to Black Briar. Camp out there for a few days. Until things settle down, you know?"

She didn't look completely convinced, but I could see something in her, a hunger, perhaps.

"Wow," she said, looking over at Jai Li. "She's so tiny."

"And," I said, squeezing her, "she's amazingly talented in some areas."

Katie looked back at me.

"But she hasn't had a normal childhood," I said. "I'm not sure how well she'll adapt to what passes for normal in our lives."

We stood there, watching her. This was a moment I wanted to last. That child needed me, and I think we needed her—at least for a little while.

Fifty-two

DEIDRE WAS ALREADY ASLEEP WHEN WE GOT BACK, AND JIMMY didn't wake her. "She'll flip," he said as he made up the couch for Jai Li to sleep on. Katie and I would sleep on an air mattress by the couch so Jai Li would feel safe. We got bunked in, and Jai Li went to sleep as happy as I'd ever seen her.

Jimmy and I sat up, drinking coffee for a bit longer. I was watching the clock. I wanted to be ready before midnight. Katie needed to go to work the next day, so she was fast asleep. Or faking it well.

I gave him the rundown on Jai Li, and he kept looking over at the living room.

"She's so damn small," he said finally.

"Yes. We've noticed."

"Smart-ass."

It was nice to be talking to Jim again like normal people. He was relieved that the tiff with Katie had blown over, and I got some of the credit for that.

"I need a favor," I said. "Nothing huge, but important."

He nodded. "Sure, what?"

I explained about walkabout, let him in on all the events around that of late. "I want to go out to Chumstick, set up with the squad out there. Have them watch over me."

"Trisha and her crew are on tonight," he said.

"Who's watching the twins?"

"Gunther, actually. A bunch of folks rotate in and out, but he's spending more and more time out here with Anezka." He grinned with half his mouth, raising the opposite eyebrow—like a Vulcan shrug. "Can't see what he sees in her, but he's a grown-up."

"You only have eyes for Deidre," I said, patting him on the hand.

"Deidre's one helluva woman, that's for sure."

He lapsed into silence, his mind churning. I let him work through it.

"Skella will be here in about thirty minutes," he said, looking at the clock.

"I'll need her to take me home first. I need some things."

"Ask her," he said. "Tell her to put it on our bill."

"Thanks. But we need to think about some options there. We've been working her too frequently, wrecking her sleep patterns. Might want to think about driving some crews out for a few days, give Skella a break."

He looked thoughtful. "Good point. I'll call a meeting with her, negotiate some downtime."

"Good. She's so eager to help out, I'd hate for her to start feeling like we are taking advantage of her."

He laughed. "You helped negotiate a damn good rate for her," he said. "She's making bank."

I thought of the irony of a young elf from deep in Stanley Park, Vancouver, making "bank." It's not like she had a lot of material needs. Jai Li, on the other hand, had more needs than I'd even begun to fathom.

"I'm worried how Jai Li will react if I'm not here when she wakes up."

"Sarah. She lived with a dragon. She's small, but she's not naive. We'll cover things if you aren't back before Katie has to go to school."

"Thanks," I said, getting up.

I crept into the living room and kissed Katie, grabbed my kit, and headed out the door. I needed to chat up Trisha before Skella got there. Make sure everyone was on board.

She was in the kitchen part of the barracks, making sandwiches, when I walked in. Frick and Frack were in the back, asleep, and Gunther was asleep in the room with them, sacked out on one of the bunks.

"Hey, Trisha," I said quietly when I went in.

She waved at me with a knife covered in peanut butter. "What's going on up at the big house?"

I stepped into her assembly line, helped put a stack of sandwiches together. "Katie and I have gotten temporary custody of a kid." I didn't want to tell her she was one of Nidhogg's. Trisha had real anger issues with dragons. Not that I could blame her. She'd been stabbed a bunch. Only Qindra's magic had saved her in the end. I was still pissed at the dragons myself. It was complicated.

Trisha glanced back to the sleeping quarters. "Kids are great," she said, smiling. "They teach you so many things." She pointed at me with that knife again. "Like for instance, did you know young trolls can eat damn near anything?"

"Like grown-up food?"

She laughed. "Yeah and alcohol. They love alcohol, and I can't see it affects them in any way. Frack snuck out of bed one night, only time it's happened, mind. We were getting ready for another shift out at Chumstick, and he took a half-empty beer Benny had left over and drank the whole thing down before we could stop him. He's strong, the booger, and fast. We got him cornered, and he went into total baby mode, crying and wanting me to pick him up."

She had a wistful look on her face. "Totally makes everything worth doing, you know?"

"I'm learning," I said.

"Like this stuff out at Chumstick. I'm keeping the world safe for them, keeping the bad things away from those I love."

I knew the sentiment, trust me. "Sacrifice anything to save those you love."

"Damn right," she said, screwing the lid back on the jar of jam. "Not like you. No offense," she said, looking a bit embarrassed. "But not all of us are bad-ass dragon slayers."

"You played your part," I said.

"Whatever." She shrugged at me, but I could feel some resentment. "There are some damn scary things out there," she said. "Having some power wouldn't be a bad thing."

The frustration was palpable. I shared it. There were so many things I couldn't fix—like my family. I sighed and rubbed my face. My hands smelled like peanut butter.

"I need to come out with you tonight," I said. "I need to do a scouting mission of a different sort."

While she got in her armor and collected her weapons, including swords and guns, I told her my theories on walkabouts.

"That's pretty damn cool," she said once the team had assembled in the rec room. "We'll definitely help out."

"Thanks. I appreciate it. Now to break the news to Skella when she gets here."

Benny laughed. "That one's a wild child."

"You don't know the half of it," I said.

Skella took Trisha and her crew out and brought back Jonathan's group. They were tired and cold to the bone. It had been snowing out in the mountains, and the fire they kept going just didn't do enough to beat the cold.

Skella and I popped over to my place, where I traded my city clothes for long johns and other things I'd wear while camping out in this weather. Then I put together a box of things I'd need to infuse the tea to help me trigger walkabout, even though it would give me a headache the next day. While I could sometimes shift my sight, going full astral was not happening without some assistance. Finally, I grabbed Gram. I could go walkabout with her; I'd done it before. I wanted her with me in case something went wrong and I got sucked into the house. That was not someplace I wanted to be unarmed.

Fifty-three

BENNY AND NANCY WERE OUT CHATTING WITH THE LOCAL sheriff when I got there. He was part of Nidhogg's in-crowd. He didn't mind us being out there, as long as we kept him informed.

Trisha and I walked across the road to stand in front of the dome.

"It's easy to see once you know to look," she said, quietly. "Sometimes I can see things moving inside. Spirits and such."

I stared into the dome. Things did move inside, and I'd fought some of them. Destroyed a bunch, but more and more flowed out here from all over. Who knew how far the spirits were traveling, drawn here like a moth to a flame?

"I've wondered," Trisha said, staring into the dome, "if any of the Black Briar crew are in there. Maybe Chloe or Bob?"

Her pain was raw still, and who could blame her? She'd lost her lover and her best friend less than a year ago. It was all pretty rough.

"I don't think so," I said, patting her on the shoulder. "When I was in there, I got the impression that only the more malevolent spirits were drawn here. Hungry things, big and angry."

"I'm pretty angry," she whispered. "All this watching isn't helping either. I want to do something." She looked at me, her face full of desperate hope. "You know what I'm talking about. I have to protect Frick and Frack. Keep them safe. The world is full of monsters, Sarah. And it sucks being so fucking powerless."

I put my arm across her shoulders and stood there. She leaned her head on my shoulder and we let the cold settle into us as we watched the spirits bump along inside the dome.

"I wish I was powerful," she said.

"You are mighty," I said, squeezing her. "Don't kid yourself. I've seen you on the field. You have the fire."

"I need magic," she said. "Magic and might. Just to keep us safe."

How could I argue? I totally understood.

"Tell me about this new beau," I said.

"He's nice," she said, her eyes staring at the dome, unfocused. "He's really kind to me. Listens to me, ya know?"

"That's important," I agreed.

"He makes me feel important," she continued. "Like maybe I could be somebody."

Her fear pained me. She was a strong woman, full of love and courage. "Don't let a man be your strength," I said. "He can be a partner, but don't put everything in his hands. Stand on your own."

"Yeah, well . . ." she turned her head, looking away from me.

"As long as he's kind to you, doesn't hurt you."

She flinched when I said that.

"He doesn't hurt you, does he?"

She stiffened and pulled away.

"I should get back to the station," she said, turning away. She had an expression on her face I recognized from my own mirror. I'd stepped on something that was none of my business—insulted her. I should've known better than to pry. I know how I used to feel about my relationship with Katie. None of anyone's damn business.

"Sorry," I said. "I didn't realize it was a sensitive subject. Forget I asked."

We got back to the tents without saying another word. I felt bad I'd made her uncomfortable.

I took my time prepping the tea on their little camp stove. Getting the water to a boil was easy—the measuring and steeping had to be precise.

The tea was bitter, but I drank a full cup and lay back with Gram in her sheath across my chest.

"I'll be out a few hours," I said, lying back. I tried to clear my mind. What had I done, exactly, the last time I'd nearly done this without the tea? Think about flying.

"Be careful," Trisha said as the world began to fade.

Fifty-four

THIS TIME IT HAPPENED MUCH FASTER. TRISHA SAT OVER ME, reading a book by a headlamp, and Gary was drinking a cup of coffee. I stood, leaving my body, and slipped out of the tent. Nancy and Benny were making the circuit. Trisha and Gary would go out in a couple of hours.

I rose, pushing my way out of the tent, and looked out on the crazy. The world was glazed in frost, even from this ethereal perspective. I wasn't cold, not exactly. But the area hummed with a sort of wildness that was both distracting and energizing. If I wasn't careful I knew I could get lost here, fade into the background noise of the region.

The ley line spasmed beneath us, feeble and thin. I could sense the residue of power, feel the earth's impotence. The flow was blocked upstream. Somewhere under Anezka's property, the ley line came to an unnatural blockage. Justin's doing.

The dome Qindra kept over the property was easy to see. It throbbed with power, a trap for the unwary spirit. I had to be extra careful. It would totally suck to be drawn into the dome. I floated ahead, crossing the road, edging close, but not too close. I waited three breaths, although technically I wasn't breathing, and moved ahead a few more feet. There was no pull, no rushing sneaker waves in the black tide that crashed against the dome. It was like a giant roach motel—spirits go in, but they don't come out.

I could see them clearly in this state. They were horrific. Some were people, or had once been. Others were so far beyond us I no longer recognized them as anything other than hunger, anger, violence, and fear. They were the nightmares Lovecraft and his ilk drew from.

I reached over my shoulder and stroked Gram's hilt. She slept with my body, but somehow she was with me here. How powerful did you have to be to exist in both the physical and spiritual worlds?

As I got close to the dome, the siren call grew stronger. The ley line tugged on the back of my psyche. Luckily, it was faint enough to ignore. At least for now. I skirted around the dome, keeping my distance. Somewhere to the northeast there had to be an entrance to the caverns beneath Anezka's property. I'd visited Qindra there during my botched rescue attempt back in October. That's how I found out about the shield and Justin's involvement in this whole debacle.

Twice I had to stop and hold my shit together as something horrible passed close by, heading into the dome. I could sense the barrier, see it in my mind's eye. It wasn't a dome, exactly, more like a sphere that went down into the ground, encompassing a great deal of earth. I had a sinking feeling the caverns were inside the sphere.

I worked my way around as close to Anezka's back bedroom as I could get without going through the dome and tried to sink into the ground. It was like pushing through oatmeal. The earth was pretty solid stuff, even in the ether.

"Pathetic," a voice said from inside the sphere. I stopped trying to sink into the ground and flowed toward the dome. Inside was a man. Unlike most of the spirits he hadn't given up his original form. I assumed the monsters I saw were the individual spirits taking on the form that best suited their nature—hunters and killers.

This man, or once man, stood with one hand on the dome, and his other held a bloodied axe.

"You lost, lass? Shall I show you the way home?"

He had a bowler hat on his head and a long coat covering his lean frame. There was something familiar about him. Some picture I'd seen before.

"Who are you?" I asked, careful to avoid getting too close to the dome.

"You ain't like the rest," he said. "I bet you'd be nice and sweet."

I flipped him off. "Get bent, psycho."

He laughed, beckoning to me. "Come and play, wee one."

I drew Gram. The whole world shifted. Inside the dome the proper gentleman was a ragged corpse with meat hanging off exposed bones. At his feet lay several dismembered bodies.

"He's going to enjoy you," the spirit said. "He comes here and talks to us from time to time. His will be a time of renewed glory. A revelry of the best sort."

I reached out with Gram, and she hit the wall like striking glass.

"Lucky for you," I said, smiling sweetly. "If I could get through that shield, I'd be happy to feed you to the eaters."

He cackled. "My kind are growing stronger, whelp. His will be done. You will suffer under his knives, and I will relish every scream."

I turned, stalking away from him. I didn't need his crap in my head.

"There is only one way in," he called after me. "And when you die, I'll be waiting for you. Waiting to play."

Bastard. Made my skin crawl. He didn't pursue me, and I realized he was stuck where he was. Partway around the dome I noticed other spirits stuck in place, sentries of some sort, watching the outside world. Was this something Justin did? His way of keeping watch?

I got to the back of the house without further incident. The other spirits took no interest in me. All I got from them was hunger. Always with the hunger.

As I followed the dome around to the back of the house, I could see the statues inside the dome. The metal warriors and the half-built dragon Anezka had built by hand. Too bad for her, Justin had been killing people and trapping their souls inside the statues.

Unfortunately, I had firsthand experience fighting one of them. Hard as hell to stop. They stalked the grounds, hunting.

I looked away from them, up the mountain, and drew in a breath. There, like a slash of neon, the ley line ran down from the mountains and into the ground under Anezka's house.

It ran through Qindra's protective sphere and through the earth. That was my path. The line was deep here, angling down. Higher up the slope of the mountain, the line rose to the surface, exposed by a recent rockslide.

As I pushed myself up the mountain, I began to feel stretched. I was moving too far from my body. That's not at all how Doctor Strange did it in the comic books. He could travel all around the world. Of course, he was a wizard and a cartoon character. I was only a blacksmith.

I swam up to the rockslide, fighting the weakness that flooded me. I felt for the ley line. It was like dipping my fingers into an icy stream—painful but doable.

One second I was looking down from the mountainside, the next I was captured by the rushing ley energy. The current was swift—not at all like swimming in water—more like drowning in lightning. I cried out, the energy flowing around me, through me.

For one quick moment I was drowning in it, overwhelmed by the sheer magnitude of power. Then, like a hammer on an anvil, I smashed against the blackened shield that blocked the line and fell to the floor of the cavern.

Not exactly graceful, but I was in.

Fifty-five

NOTHING HURT. THAT WAS A BONUS. I ROSE UP—WELL, floated more than stood—and glanced around. The room was pretty big, a thirty-foot-diameter cavern with the shield floating on the north side, hovering in the ley energy, like a ping-pong ball floating above a hair dryer. The whole place glowed with the power, like using a Tesla coil as a lamp.

"Sarah?"

I spun around. Qindra's spirit sat in the center of the room, encased in a prism of power. Her body was up in the house—in stasis. I had no idea how she fared physically. If her spirit was any indicator, we may be too late to save her.

I could see where she'd siphoned a trickle of the ley line, draw-ing the power to keep her alive and shielded from the eaters. That's how she was keeping the dome intact.

"What are you doing here?" she asked. "I thought Katie got you out."

"That was weeks ago," I said, overjoyed to see her. "I'm trying to figure out how to rescue you."

She looked at me, her eyes flat and her face neutral. Even with the ley energy, she was failing. I'd seen better-looking ghosts. Maybe tapping that energy directly was too much for her.

"You are not trapped in the house?" she asked. I think she was confused.

"No, I'm in a tent across the road from the house. Outside the dome."

"Good," she said, nodding. Her attention was definitely elsewhere. "This is not a good place to be."

"I figure if I can get to this room physically, remove the shield from the energy flow, we should be able to stop the spirits from being drawn here, and allow us a chance to bring you out of here."

She glanced at me, her eyes stark white, reflecting the sparking ley energy of the well. "There is no hope," she said. "All is lost."

That was bullshit. I had to get her focused. "There has to be a way down here. Where is the entrance?"

"Blocked," she said. "Covered with magic and hate."

"We can beat this," I argued. She was freaking me out.

"They test me," she whispered. "He has guardians around the perimeter of the dome, trying with their unique skills to crack the outer defenses."

"I met one of them," I said. "Real charmer."

She faded for an instant, like a poorly tuned television.

"Hey," I shouted. "Qindra. Stay with me. We gotta beat this necromancer scumbag."

She waved an ethereal hand at me. "I will survive awhile longer," she said. "Though I'm not sure for how long. He has been here a few times, drawing power from the shield."

"He has? You mean, physically?"

"Yes," she said. "He cannot penetrate my barrier, but he knows some of the energy is being diverted, and it frustrates him."

Justin had come out here. Recently? By her comments, she didn't seem to have a real sense of time. Had Justin been here since Black Briar had begun patrolling? I'd have to alert Jimmy. Maybe we needed to beef up the patrols.

"If he could get here physically, I could reclaim the shield."

"True. But he has the entrance protected. I can sense it. It will be difficult to find in the mountains, but it's there. A narrow crack in the rock that opens to a wider cavern and eventually a path down to this room."

"I'll find it," I promised.

She lost focus then, not seeing me. I had to keep her attention. Needed to distract her.

"I need to talk to you about Jai Li," I said.

That caught her attention.

"What of the child?" she asked. Shimmering dead flowed around her like moths circling a flame.

I gave her the rundown as best I could. How she'd run away. How Nidhogg had given her over to me until such time as Qindra came home.

"My mistress is not well," she said. "It pains me to know things have gone so far."

"I'm doing the best I can," I said. "We're keeping things together, more or less."

"Where is the child?"

"We have her at Black Briar for the moment, until I can free you and make things right with Nidhogg."

Qindra became focused, looked more solid. I think it was the anguish that painted her face. "Nidhogg will never accept her now. Ever since Mei Hau was killed, Nidhogg has become harsher to Jai Li. The fact that she fled our home will only bring her pain. Our mistress is not the most forgiving."

"We'll make it right," I promised. "I just need to get you out of here and stop Justin."

"I cannot protect them, Sarah. She loves them and hates them.

I fear she will kill them without my being there to keep them safe."

"She's not the most stable individual I've met," I said. "I think she's depressed. Maybe we could get her on some medication."

Qindra studied me a moment, really seeing me, I think.

"If it would not cause the suffering of so many, I would relinquish this effort and let the eaters have me," she said, waving at the swirling spirits. "They hunger for my life force. Perhaps it would be easier to succumb to their will."

"No!" I drew Gram and scattered several spirits that had appeared through the wall. "We'll find a way to solve this."

"Protect the girl," she said, sounding more defeated than before. "Love her, Sarah. She is worthy of love."

But am I worthy of her? "I'll do what I can."

The tea must have begun to wear off, because suddenly I felt pulled. I staggered back, and the world shifted between scenes of Qindra and the dark of the tent.

"Sarah?" I heard Trisha calling to me. "Wake up."

I sat up. Light glowed beyond Trisha—the harsh gray light of morning.

"Come on," she said. "Katie called. She's pissed."

My head was swimming. "I needed to find out," I said. "I told you."

"Yes, yes. You told me. Now you need to get up. It's morning. Shift change. Your family needs you. Your new foster daughter woke up screaming."

The headache bloomed behind my eyes as I tried to stand. "What time is it?"

"Eight, come on. Skella's here. We gotta go."

I forced myself onto my feet, the world swaying. Benny caught me, pulled my arm over his shoulder, and helped me back to the second tent, where the mirror was kept. Faster than my brain would reconcile, I was back at Black Briar, staggering against the wall of the barracks.

"I need sleep," I mumbled as we worked our way out of the barracks and into the house. "Lots of sleep. Maybe some aspirin." Benny and Gary supported me on either side, half-carrying me up the ramp to the deck and into the house. They placed me on the air mattress, and I rolled over and went to sleep. I think Jai Li crawled into bed with me.

I slept eighteen hours, got up, spent some quality time throwing up, then collapsed again, sleeping for another twelve hours. By the time I was able to sit up without tossing my cookies, Katie was home. She was too worried to be pissed at me. I considered that a small blessing.

Fifty-six

FREDERICK SAWYER WALKED THE STREETS OF SEATTLE, LET-
ting the physical manifestation of his frustration clear the side-
walks around him. He had no real goal in mind. At first, he
thought to stroll along the waterfront. The crowds had proved
that effort fruitless. He did not want to be surrounded by gawk-
ing yokels. What he craved was order.

Twice he walked by the Seattle Art Museum, but he did not
go inside. While the collection was reputed to be acceptable, he
had no desire for the merely average either.

As he climbed the hills back toward his hotel, he noticed an
old man sitting on a stoop. There was an air of hopelessness about
the man—a sudden and visceral intuition of death. He paused.

"For whom do you mourn?" Frederick asked. The stench of
the man was nearly overwhelming. He had to be in his sixties,
perhaps older. One never knew with the wastrels, the lag-abouts.

The bum looked up at him, his face scarred, one eye socket
hollow and gaping. "Nobody you'd be concerned with, all dressed
in your Sears and Roebuck suit and your smug look."

Frederick bristled. How dare this cretin talk to him this way?
This was a three-thousand dollar hand-tailored suit. "You know
nothing of me," he said, suddenly concerned with this man's
opinion. *How odd*, he thought. "I, too, have tragedy in my life."

The old man waved a hand at Frederick, his broken and filthy nails like blackened tombstones. "You reek of money and privilege," the old man said. "What do you know of suffering?"

What indeed? Frederick found emotions inside himself that he did not recognize. He at once felt queasy and angry, anxious and forlorn. He could not stand here, not like this. There was a void in him. What he needed was a stiff drink—something to take the edge off his thoughts.

"You are a piteous wretch," Frederick said, and turned on his heel. He'd gone no more than a dozen steps when the man's voice rose behind him.

"My children," the man called out.

Frederick stopped, turning his head to see the man. He stood now, thin and ragged. There was a dignity about him that surprised Frederick. He leaned on a rough-hewn staff, obviously favoring a damaged leg.

"What about your children?" he called back.

"They're gone," the man said, "all gone."

The loss of his children had obviously impacted the man in negative ways. How strange to allow oneself to sink so low. But why should this be any concern of his? This man was so far beneath him as to be disposable. And yet there was something compelling in his stance, in the way he held his filthy head high, looking at Frederick with his scarred face and his single remaining eye.

"There is much suffering in the world," he said. Suffering and chaos. "What has happened to your children?"

The old man studied him, shaking his head. "They are lost to me," he said. Frederick found his voice to be haunting. "What do you suffer?"

Frederick considered not answering. This peon had no right

to even talk to one of Frederick's station. But still. "There is one who is lost to me as well," he said, finally.

The old man nodded once. "The world is fickle," he said. "We grieve and love, yet the world turns without so much as a care."

"Indeed," Frederick said. "We each carry our burdens."

The old man snickered. "Some have lighter burdens and more hands to carry them."

Frederick studied the man for a moment. Was he poking fun at him? What an absurd thought.

He made a polite farewell and left the man with a cloying feeling swelling in his chest.

Frederick realized a thing he never thought possible. He was lonely. So lonely that for the briefest of moments, he thought to turn back, to seek more of the old beggar's time, something, anything to relieve the uncertainty and emptiness he felt at the loss of Mr. Philips.

How could that possibly be? Mr. Philips was an able servant, that was without doubt. But nothing more. If that were the case, why did he have this gaping ache inside himself?

And at that moment, he was visited by a flash of clarity. Qindra was not ignoring him. The young and oddly compelling Sarah Jane Beauhall was a stand-in, and a wild card at that. Nidhogg had reached for the nearest flotsam in turbulent waters. This Dragon Liberation Front has done something to Qindra as well.

Helplessness was not a feeling Frederick Sawyer was used to, and Nidhogg, the old sow herself, had been on this muddy ball of a planet for an eon longer than he.

What kind of madness must she be undergoing with the loss of her dearest confidant?

Fifty-seven

Jimmy was scared. I could read it all over him. My report of the trip to see Qindra had him really spooked.

"We need to walk the fence," he said when I'd finished. "Spend a couple days working the perimeter of the farm, securing the barrier."

Katie, Deidre, Jim, and I were sitting around the remains of breakfast. I'd found my appetite, and the headaches had faded.

"It was something Dad did," he told Katie. "I'm not sure if the old magic is holding with the invasion in May and Odin showing up here recently."

"Doesn't sound very secure," Deidre said. She scraped a good deal of scrambled eggs onto Jai Li's plate and winked at the girl. Jai Li loved eggs, who knew?

"I'd like you to go with me," Jimmy said to me.

"What about me?" Katie asked, hurt. "I'm not good enough?"

Deidre rolled her eyes and filled her own plate with eggs.

"Actually," Jimmy said, putting his fork down and crossing his hands in front of him. "I'll need you here to anchor the magic."

"Really?" She practically squeaked. "No bull, Jim."

"Honest," he said. "One to hold the center. One to set the weave. Has to be blood and blood or it won't work."

"Not even me," Deidre said. "It's always been you."

Katie looked skeptical. "When?"

"Remember when you were little? How you and I would wrap Christmas presents while Jimmy, Stuart, and Gunther would go out and repair the fence?"

"Oh, yeah," she said, memory dawning on her. "I always thought it was better to wait for spring, but we had to wrap presents."

It was a fond memory that I was glad that Katie could call up. She needed to feel a part of things here. As it was, I wasn't sure how much she was over being mad at Jim and how much she just didn't want to be out of the center of action.

"What about Jai Li?" I asked.

Katie patted me on the arm. "We're in this together. I'll be here. She'll be fine."

I watched her for a few minutes, sitting in the living room working a new needlepoint. The girl was crazy talented. She just needed things to do with her hands.

"Okay, I'll talk to her, let her know I'll be back."

Katie smiled at me, and Deidre squeezed my arm as I passed her. Lots of love and support here.

We set out that afternoon. Jimmy had plenty of camping equipment, and I had enough stuff with me to survive a few days in the wilds of the farm. I took Gram with me. I practically slept with her these days. Jimmy brought along his sword, the dwarven-made one he'd used in the battle back in the spring. I hadn't seen it since Stuart had hidden all our blades, before Qindra or any of her people could get a look at them. Better safe than sorry.

Cold was the biggest worry, but I knew to dress in layers. Just no cotton.

There were forty-nine markers—seven times seven. We started just to the left of the driveway and worked our way along the front road. It felt silly, but I'd seen enough craziness to just go with it. At each post we pricked our thumbs and dropped a single drip of blood onto the roughly scored surface. There was no physical fence connecting most posts, but there was a connection. I could feel it.

We worked the whole road in front of the property—worked our way west toward the setting sun. The posts were not exactly close together, so we only got six done that first day. Of course, we'd gotten a late start. We made camp behind a long row of aspen trees that had been planted as a windbreak. They didn't keep people from seeing past them, however, so we made sure to set the tent back off the road a ways.

Jim boiled some water, and we made tea. The night was clear but cold. I had a lot on my mind, with the murders and kidnappings. Jim didn't exactly tell me what was on his mind, so that first night ended early with a minimum of conversation.

Camp food is not that exciting. I'd given up doing anything fancy years ago, though Da could whip up a mean omelet over an open fire. We had granola and coffee for breakfast. Not haute cuisine, but filling.

We hit another fourteen posts before lunch, working our way along the westernmost reaches of the property. The place was a lot bigger than I'd realized. Jim remained locked in his funk until lunch.

Then, over canned stew and coffee, he began to open up. I did a lot of listening, not wanting to interrupt his flow. He spoke about his parents, about his speculation on Nidhogg, Frederick, and the Dragon Liberation Front.

I was pretty blown away. When he finally started talking, he didn't hold back. Well, not much. There was another layer, one that took a second full day of speculation and banter to break through.

He talked about how scared he was on the third night as we

camped in the woods north of the farm. The snow was thick
on the ground there, but we sheltered under the copse of trees
where I'd met the Valkyrie and their winged horses. Jimmy never
knew he had such things visit his farm, but with helicopters, giants, trolls, ogres, and one bad-ass dragon showing up, a pretty
winged horse likely didn't measure up.

I loved them, however. One in particular had captured my
heart. She was so beautiful. I woke some nights from a flying
dream, thinking I could almost feel Meyja carrying me into the
cold clouds of the dawn.

Katie had been talking about Christmas before we left, and
I suddenly realized it was coming up to the solstice.

"Oh, yeah. Huge deal," Jimmy said when I asked. "We have to
have this done before then, or the magic fades."

"Fades like, until the next solstice?"

He shrugged. "Not sure, and I'm not in the mood to test it."

Fair enough.

"It always worried my mother," he went on as we made our
way to the next post. "She kept the house lit with candles for
three days around the solstice. Even insisted on a bonfire in the
yard. She said electricity was lovely, but it was prone to outages,
especially on weakly controlled days like the solstice. Equinox
was the same in her book. Too evenly split to be trusted."

By the last night, I'd even begun to tell Jimmy about Da and
how he and I had done a ton of camping until I reached twelve.
That was the end of the end for us. I was too cynical, and Da had
given up hope.

"Why'd you ask me out here, Jim?" I really was curious. "You
don't trust Stuart or Gunther anymore?"

He stirred the coals with a long stick and didn't answer right
away. I drank my coffee and let him stew.

"It was Stuart's idea, actually," he said. "Something about your love for Katie acting to strengthen the bond." He looked up, considering. "And I think you have something about you, some magic, or, I don't know . . . something."

"Cursed, most likely," I offered.

He chewed on it a minute before shaking his head. "We discussed that as well. The way I see it, you are either one of the old gods come back, which seems unlikely, or you have some other connection, some other well of power that we can use to protect the place."

I understood. Needs of the many and all that jazz.

"Good to be needed." I grinned at him, and he smiled, shaking his head.

He was right, of course. Odin had come to me, put the berserker in me. If that could help protect the farm, then so be it.

"Katie really does love you, knucklehead," Jimmy said. "That counts for something."

I smiled ruefully. It counted for everything, actually.

Fifty-eight

THE SECOND NIGHT THAT JIMMY AND SARAH WERE OUT WALK-
ing the fence, Katie and Deidre were on kidlet duty. Trisha had a
hot date. When she'd dropped off Frick and Frack, Trisha practically glowed.

"You look amazing," Katie told her. "Whoever this guy is, he's
one lucky bastard."

Trisha blushed, but her smile only added to her radiance.

"If that outfit doesn't get you laid, he's a monk," Katie said.

"A blind monk," Deidre added.

Trisha laughed, a sound that stopped Frick and Frack in their
steps. "Go on," she said, shooing them into the living room. "Bub
is dying to play."

Sure enough, Bub and Jai Li were both very happy to see the
twins arrive. They'd been playing cards quietly, but the twins
would add a level of chaos that only toddlers could bring.

"Behave," Trisha told them, but they were too far gone. There
were blocks out on the table, and they both dearly loved stacking
things.

"We're taking a couple nights off from guard duty," she said to
Katie. "Gary needs to do some things with his kids since his ex
is going out of town, and Benny is off to Vegas for a couple of
days."

"What about Nancy?" Katie asked.

Deidre laughed. "She's off at a women's retreat down in Lacey. Something about a weekend of silence."

They all laughed.

"He must really make you happy," Katie said. "I haven't seen you smile this much since," she got quiet, waving her hand. ". . . you know. Before."

Trisha nodded. "There is definitely something about him. Do you ever have the feeling something is too good to be true? Ever look at Sarah and wonder if there was something there that could wreck everything, but then she smiles and the doubts vanish and the sun comes out?"

Katie glanced at Deidre, who shrugged, pulling a worried face. "Um. Not really, but maybe you just don't know this guy that well."

Trisha's smile faltered a bit, but she recovered. "I'm sure it's all the shit that's gone down lately, you know. Makes me see the worst in people."

The sound of laughing children echoed from the living room.

"But those little monsters," she said, a fresh look of relief on her face. "They make it worth getting up in the morning."

"Amen," Deidre said.

Silence fell over the three of them. Katie debated changing the subject, but the thought of this new guy being less than good enough for Trisha was weighing on her mind.

"Have you thought," she began, but at the same time Trisha reached for the door. "I'd better get going," she said. "Hate to be late."

"Don't do anything I wouldn't do," Katie called to Trisha as she pulled the door closed behind her. "Too late," they heard her say as the door shut.

Katie and Deidre exchanged a look. "What on earth is there to do that you haven't done?" Deidre asked.

"Boys, for one thing," Katie said, smiling.

Deidre rolled her eyes, and Katie went to look in on the kids and refresh her coffee.

They were getting along like a house on fire. Jai Li was a roughhouser. Sarah was going to be so surprised. Katie and Deidre sat in the kitchen and gabbed over coffee. They only had to intervene a couple of times, when Bub began eating blocks. The kids thought it was hilarious, but Deidre was pissed about having to go buy another set.

"I'm trying to get the twins used to letters, so they can start reading at some point."

"They're pretty young," Katie said.

"Vowels are very important," Deidre argued, stashing a couple of saliva-covered blocks on the counter.

"But the twins are growing at an amazing rate," Katie pointed out. "Maybe we should be taking notes or something. Tracking the different stages of their growth, you know?"

"I think Nancy and Benny are already on it."

Later, after the kids were in their pjs, they put on a movie and let them sack out in front of one of Pixar's finest.

"Sarah and I are thinking about moving north," Katie said over the saccharine music. "Thinking we should get our own place, maybe, with a little land attached. Ya know?"

"Oh, I heartily agree," Deidre said. "Especially with the chance you'll have Jai Li in your life. You're gonna want the room to send her outside to play. Can't do that where you live now."

"True, but we can take her to the park to play."

Deidre patted her on the hand. "Katie, hon. If you go with her to the park, then you can't be having sex with Sarah while she's playing."

"That's not very safe. Wait. You mean, all those times I got sent outside when I was young?"

"Yup."

"It was raining a lot of those times. I froze my ass off."

She shrugged. "Hon, sometimes you gotta take one for the team."

Katie didn't say much after that, just sort of stewed, thinking. Jai Li was going to cause huge changes in their lives, but wasn't the sacrifice worth it in the long run? Hell, they may not even get to keep her. Was she willing to fight for her? Was she ready for that?

After the kids were all asleep—even Bub—Deidre decided to head to bed.

Katie sat up awhile, finishing her coffee and thinking about the craziness in their lives. She cleaned up the coffee cups and was thinking about crashing on the couch herself when she heard a buzzing on the counter by the back door. Sarah had left her keys and her phone there when she went off with Jimmy.

The number was out of country, so she answered it. Could be Skella.

"Smith?" a gravelly voice asked from the other end.

"No, I'm sorry," Katie said. "This is Katie. Who is this?"

There was a pause. "Good evening, skald. I am Rolph, of Durin's folk. I have news."

Katie chuckled. "I remember you, Rolph of Durin's folk. I can take a message, if you like. I'll be sure Sarah gets it."

"Of that I have no doubt. Listen. This concerns you as well. I have received word from the King of Vancouver. I thought it best to inform you as soon as possible.

"It seems the Dragon Liberation Front is not a new society, but something that Jean-Paul concocted decades ago. The king had specific information about its creation and original mission.

Basically, it is a group working to overthrow the high council and install the dragons openly as the rightful rulers of mankind."

"Geez," Katie breathed. "That's pretty ballsy."

"Quite. The king expressed his particular distaste for the group and has worked to eradicate it from the Vancouver area.

"While some of my brethren were members, most of the local clan does not appear to be involved. They are too worried about falling afoul of the king and his proclamation," he assured her. "They survived under Jean-Paul. They do not relish falling to this king."

"What about the necromancer?" Katie asked. "This Justin guy."

"That is more sordid, I'm afraid. He was a protégé of Jean-Paul himself, not just a common thug. He has delved in mighty magics that even the King of Vancouver fears."

Katie sat down, looking over at the sleeping children. "Why is he targeting Sarah?"

"Most likely because she is powerful in her own right."

"She has Gram, sure."

"No," Rolph said, interrupting. "Gram came to her for a purpose. The sword was lost, crippled by my inept skills. But there is something about your young Sarah that goes beyond my reckoning. Even the king mentioned her by name. He seems to know a great deal about her and expresses a significant amount of respect."

Katie had to think about that. How did the king play in all this?

"Any clue what we should do?"

"Unfortunately, no. I worry for Juanita, but I cannot go to her for fear I will lead him to her. No one who is in Sarah's orbit is safe."

"What about men?" Katie asked. "So far, he's only killed young women and animals."

"I can only speculate, but it seems logical that killing the horse was an attempt to flush Sarah out. I am sure that he was able to gain some information, but it is my belief it was a ploy to see how she would react.

"The women he killed were not in her inner circle. I have spoken with someone who shall remain in the shadows. She believes that he weaves an intricate web around Sarah to keep her off guard while he performs something more insidious elsewhere."

"What about Mr. Philips," Katie said, suddenly remembering. "Frederick Sawyer is in town, and this cult has kidnapped his assistant."

"Peculiar," he said. "My source mentioned something about a fulcrum to move the world. I wonder if this is what she meant. If Frederick is involved, the conspiracy runs deeper than I thought. I must consult the oracle once again. Though I am loath to pay her price a second time."

"Be careful," Katie said. "You've been a strong ally."

"Thank you. I will do what I can. One final thing," he said. "He seeks an artifact of great power. No one knows what, but he has a thirst for the darkest arts and will stop at nothing."

"Oh, great. That's helpful."

"Tell her," he said, urgently. "She must keep Gram from him no matter the cost."

He hung up, and Katie sat the phone on the counter. Did he tell her anything they hadn't already figured out? Maybe, or more likely he helped get a glimpse at the top of the puzzle box so they could begin to put some of the pieces together.

She turned off the light and went around the house to check all the doors and windows. Once she was comfortable that the house was secure, she crawled onto the couch. The kids were sleeping in a great scrum on the floor. The twins really did love Bub. Jai Li was a little to the side, but they'd made sure she had a pillow and a good portion of the blankets.

Family is family, she thought as she closed her eyes. *We make of it what we can.*

Fifty-nine

THE MORNING BROKE BITTERLY COLD. THE MOUNTAINS WERE being pounded with snow. We were low enough to only get a couple inches. The tents held up, and my sleeping bag was toasty, but my boots were damn cold when I stamped my feet into them.

Jimmy got a fire going pretty quickly, and we huddled over it while the water boiled for coffee. Instant was fine for camping, but I really wanted to head to Monkey Shines and grab a triple-shot mocha and about two dozen crullers.

Then I thought of the young barista there who'd been murdered because of me, and the coffee turned bitter in my mouth.

"Home, soon," Jimmy said, slinging a half a cup of coffee into the scrub. "I want to go up to that cave first."

I froze. The cave where I'd killed the troll, where we'd found Frick and Frack. The cave where I'd killed that troll mother who was doing nothing really beyond caring for her babies.

"Why?"

"I don't like when some beastie sets up home that close to the farm. Call it professional curiosity."

We were pretty close this far out. Probably only a couple hours' walk there. I shrugged. "Yeah, sure. Why not?"

We packed the camp but made sure to eat an extra large helping of my favorite oatmeal. I loaded it down with our remaining dried fruit and plenty of sugar. It would provide enough calories to see us through the cold morning.

The woods were thick, and the air absorbed sound. I didn't remember it being this quiet the last time through here, but I'd been focused on catching the troll on the way up and trying not to fall over on the way down.

I knew there was something wrong before we got to the clearing. Jimmy stopped when I held up my hand. There was a taint in the air. Not quite a smell. More like a feeling.

I squatted down on the trail and looked through the trees. I could see the cairn across the snow-covered clearing. There were no real signs of disturbance, but the runes in my hairline began to itch.

Jimmy squatted down next to me. "I don't see anything."

I cocked my head to the side and picked up a stone. He watched me with an amused expression on his face as I tossed it toward the cairn. Nothing happened. Maybe I was just feeling guilty.

We stood, drew weapons, and entered the clearing. My senses were alert, pinging. "There's something here," I said, turning slowly. "Or there was."

He had a long sword in one hand, the one from the battle way back, when the troll under that cairn and her friends had invaded the farm.

"If anyone's been here," he said, glancing around, "the snow's buried any trace."

I grunted and approached the cave cautiously. Inside, the invasion was apparent. We'd left the place in good shape. Things as packed away as they could be, bed put together, even the wood stacked neatly for future fires.

Now it was a disaster. The bed had been scattered, the furniture smashed, and the fire pit scattered about.

"Someone searched the place," Jimmy said. "Kids, maybe?"

He didn't look like he believed it any more than I did.

"Maybe." I walked to the back and saw something. A hand-print burned onto the wall of the cave. "Someone with power, it seems," I said, passing Gram in the air before the mark. A spark like static electricity jumped from the handprint to the blade, sizzling and popping for a split second, before dissipating. The print faded as I watched.

"Residual magic," Jimmy said, watching from several feet away. "Someone was loaded for bear, and must've stumbled or some-thing, braced themselves against the wall there."

"Gee, and how'd you figure that?"

He looked hurt. "Hey, I know stuff. I don't just sit on my ass all the time. Since my parents left, I've read a bunch of stuff, you know . . ." He blushed. "Spell books."

"Something else you never told Katie?"

His face got stony. "I can't use magic," he said. "I also can't build airplanes, but I know how they work."

I laughed. "Don't get your knickers in a twist. I was just com-menting."

The rest of the place was without magical residue, at least as far as we could tell. I didn't like the fact that someone had been up here, because I thought I had a pretty good idea who.

"You don't think Justin and his evil minions could get onto the farm, do you?"

"Nope," he said, confident. "That's what the barrier is for. No one gets in and out without me knowing it. Perimeter sets off an alarm. Loud thing, sounds like an air-raid siren."

We scouted the place for another hour but, in the end, had to give it up. Jimmy was satisfied and promised to send a squad back up here to secure the place—whatever that entailed. And then we trudged back down the mountain.

So Jimmy was studying magic. But he couldn't do any himself. That was good to know.

We got back to the fence and wrapped the last seven posts just after dark. I was relieved to hike the final quarter mile back to the farmstead. When we crossed that last rise and saw the house I had to take a minute to enjoy the view. From up here, near the road east of the place, I could see the big house with smoke pouring out of both chimneys. The barn and barracks also hung heavy with wood smoke. The fields on all sides glowed white with the snow. It was beautiful. Not because we'd just donated a lot of blood—and sore digits—to secure the perimeter, but because that's where our families were. Those we loved.

A wave of grief rose in me, and I coughed to cover the sob that had burst out of me. God I missed my family. My eyes burned, and the scene before me blurred as tears betrayed me to the cold day.

Jimmy made himself busy retying his boots, but I wasn't convinced. I let out a deep sigh and scrubbed my face.

"You still miss your parents?" I asked when I could breathe without crying.

"Every day," he said, standing. He kept his hands in his jacket pockets and watched the homestead. "I wake up some nights sure they've come home. But they never do."

"So you think they're alive?"

He shrugged. "No one knows. I believe it, though. Katie seems to have accepted that they're gone. I can still feel my father's hands on my shoulders when things get tough." He sniffed loudly and cleared his throat. "When Deidre was in the hospital and I was alone in the house for the first time since they'd gone, I woke up thinking I smelled mom's perfume. I know it's crazy, but I was so damn sure of it." He scuffed the snow with his boots. "What about you?"

I pulled off my wool hat (that I knitted) and ran my hand through my hair. "All the crap that's been going down lately has got me thinking I need to reconnect, learn to forgive some, ya know?"

He looked up at me, his face set. "I'd cross heaven and hell to find them," he said. "If they were just in another town, no matter how boneheaded I thought they were being, I'd be there with them. And don't you have a little sister?"

I nodded, feeling the heat rise in me. He'd sacrificed everything for Katie. I knew his answers there. "Megan," I said. "She's fifteen. I miss her the most, I think."

"Well, best you're not close to them now, not with that crazy bastard out there. They're probably safer for it."

He was right. They were better off with me not in their life, and that hurt. I put my hat back on, adjusted my pack, and cleared my throat.

"Let's go back now, huh?"

"Oh, yeah," he said, pulling his pack tight and heading down the hill. "Duty is critical, but I want to see my woman."

"Me, too." Both of my girls were waiting for me. I knew Jai Li was going to break my heart someday. But for now, I could share my life with her.

Sixty

EVERYONE WAS THRILLED WHEN WE GOT HOME. BUB EVEN hugged me. Frick and Frack just loved all the excitement. Jai Li had gone suddenly shy. Katie gave me a shrug when Jai Li stood off, arms crossed over her chest.

I went to her and knelt down. "Hey, kiddo. You miss me?"

She shrugged and turned her head, but Bub nudged her from behind.

"Did you have a good time while I was gone?" I asked.

"Give it to her," Bub said.

I looked up, and Katie shook her head and shrugged, again.

Jai Li ran into the living room and pulled a piece of paper out from under a stack of blankets and pillows; then she ran back and handed it to me.

I unfolded a picture of Jai Li standing and holding both my hand and Katie's. Around us was a big flowery heart.

"It means she loves you," Bub said, smug as can be. "She let me help."

There was a distinct difference in the work Bub had done and the work Jai Li had done. Together it looked like something a six-year-old Picasso would've done.

I reached out and hugged her. "Thanks, kiddo." Before he could get away, I pulled Bub in as well, hugging them both. "You're both pretty amazing."

Frick and Frack toddled over and fell against us, and we all tumbled to the ground, laughing. Jai Li had a sweet laugh, which seemed to surprise her. I bet she didn't laugh a lot at Nidhogg's place. Not tolerated.

Funny how quickly she'd found her way into my heart. If we didn't end up keeping her, I wasn't sure what I'd do. Move on, I guess. But I didn't want to find out.

Jimmy hit the showers first and then unpacked his gear while I showered. Katie didn't join me, which was a relief and a disappointment. I'm not sure if I could've handled it with the kids in the house.

By the time I was dressed in clean clothes, Katie had whipped up soup and sandwiches. I sat down with Jai Li on one side and Bub on the other. Deidre and Katie had Frick and Frack in high chairs pushed up against the table, and Jimmy carried a big pot of cheese and beer soup to the table. That and several loaves of homemade bread and a gallon of fresh coffee had me feeling warm again for the first time in days.

"Good food," Jimmy said, pushing back from the table. "Makes me want to take a nap."

"Go ahead," Katie said. "We'll take the kids out to play in the snow, let you get some shut-eye."

Deidre winked at Katie and faked a pretty big yawn.

By the time we had the kids bundled up to go out, Deidre was practically shoving us out the door.

"Keep your pants on," I said as she nudged me with her wheelchair.

"Not likely," she said under her breath.

Katie laughed, and we headed out into the snow.

The troll babies had pretty thick skin and didn't seem to mind the cold. Jai Li was hesitant at first, having likely never seen snow in real life. I wanted a full rundown from Qindra someday. I was willing to bet everything I had that Jai Li had never set foot out of that house before she ran away to find me and rescue Qindra.

We managed to build a snowman and a snow fort before the kids began to flag. Bub entertained the kids by melting the snow in his hands, on his head, even with his feet. He didn't actually burst into flame as I'd seen before, but he definitely was burning hotter than the rest of us.

While the kids frolicked, Katie told me about Rolph's call. No surprise that Jean-Paul had his talons in this necromancer bullshit. He had been a foul little dragon. Just made me want to kill Justin all the more. And I'd be damned if I was hiding from the bastard. He could have Gram when he could pry her from my cold, dead hands. Gram wasn't made to be hidden. She was all action.

After an hour and a half, Katie called a moratorium on snow and directed us all back into the house. "They've had enough time for a nap," she said, stomping the snow off her boots. "My ass is cold."

I know we had to sound like a herd of buffalo heading back into the house, but neither Jimmy nor Deidre stirred. We got the kids changed into dry clothes and plopped them down at the table with hot chocolate and cookies.

"I'm kinda beat myself," I said, yawning. "I could use a nap."

Katie looked at me, serious and sultry. "You'll get your nap later."

"Okay." I think I had a pretty good idea that Jimmy just wanted to sleep, but Katie and Deidre had changed the meaning of the word "nap" while I was gone. I'm sure it would be good for me, but I went and lay down on the couch anyway.

Deidre woke me up a couple of hours later. The kids had all

sacked out in front of the television, though it was off. Katie sat at the kitchen table with her head on her arms, fast asleep.

"I think you should take her home," she said, pointing to Katie. "She needs some loving."

I sat up, stretching and yawning. "Well, as tempting as that sounds, I can't leave Jai Li overnight without being here myself. Besides, it's safer here."

Deidre had her arms crossed and, I realized, was wearing Jimmy's shirt.

"The kids will be fine here. You and Katie need a night alone. She's been missing you. Jai Li is fine here. She's enjoying herself. Go home and rock Katie's world. Make some noise, break some furniture. I have a feeling it may be awhile before you get this chance again."

She had a point, though I was hesitant to admit it. Still, all things being equal, I wanted some quality alone time with Katie.

I got up, stepping over drooling troll babies, and squatted by Jai Li. I brushed her hair, and she rolled over, blinking up at me. "Hey," I said, smiling at her. "Katie and I need to go to our apartment for a while. Do you want to go with me, or would you like to stay here with the other kids?"

She reached up and touched the side of my face, then pointed to her chest and then to mine.

"Yes, I love you," I said. It was a powerful thing to say, but I realized it was as true as my love for Katie, if different on almost every level.

She nodded, patted me on the arm, and rolled back over, pulling the blankets over her head.

"There you go," Deidre said. "Free and clear. Now please take Katie home and do things to her I don't want to know about. She's too wound up."

"What, are you her pimp now?"

Deidre chuckled and rolled her chair back, turning it toward the kitchen. "Come on, sleepyhead," she said, bumping into Katie's chair. "Time to go."

Katie sat up and looked around, dazed. "What?"

I walked into the kitchen and stroked her hair. "We're leaving Jai Li here and heading home," I said.

"No," she said, rubbing her face. "We have responsibilities."

"Yes," I said, eyeing Deidre. "And tonight our responsibility is to go home and have some grown-up time."

"She'll be fine here," Deidre said. "Sarah already cleared it with her."

Katie looked at me, then looked into the living room, where the kids were all sacked out. "They'll be up half the night at this rate."

"Don't you worry about it," Deidre said. "Go home."

I grabbed our overnight bags and headed out to the truck. When I got back in, Katie had her shoes on and was hugging Deidre. "Call if something comes up."

Deidre shooed her out of the house, and we ran to the truck through freshly falling snow.

The long driveway already had a couple inches of snow from the night before, but the way the snow was blowing sideways, it looked to add a few more before long.

We stopped on the way home. I picked up flowers, candles, and wine, while Katie picked up some bread, salami, olives, and cheese. The ride from Bellevue to Kent crawled by in a haze of anticipation and snow. The flurries were brutal, cutting visibility and turning the other drivers into complete idiots.

Luckily, at this elevation, the snow wasn't sticking. We got home long after dark, and we were both starving. Lunch had been way too long ago.

We carried our supplies into the apartment and turned up the heat. We hadn't been home for a few days, and the place had that abandoned feeling.

Katie took the food into the kitchen and cut up the bread, salami, and cheese, while I cut the flowers down and placed them in these small vases Katie had. Soon I had a dozen bright points of flowers scattered around the room.

Katie went through the bedroom and took a shower while I lit all the candles. It was the winter solstice—the longest night of the year—and I wanted to fill every dark moment with Katie.

I put Led Zeppelin's *Physical Graffiti* on the stereo and poured two glasses of wine. She came out in nothing but a bathrobe. Her hair fell down over her shoulders, and she'd put on a touch of makeup. I handed her a glass of wine and sipped my own. She drained the glass in one long pull, sat the glass on the bar, and let her bathrobe fall to the floor.

She reached out and took my glass of wine, dipped a finger in it, and traced it down her throat and across her left breast. I didn't interrupt her, just watched her play. She dipped her finger in the wine again and drew dark swirls around her aureoles, then tipped the glass against her chest, dribbling it over her breasts and down her belly.

I leaned forward and licked the side of her neck, tracing the path of the wine. She grabbed the back of my head as I licked my way across her breasts, taking first one, then the other in my mouth, nibbling and suckling until her nipples were hard as stones.

Her breathing was coming in shorter gasps as I kissed my way down her stomach and swirled my tongue in her navel to get all the wine. Finally, I trailed my kisses lower, thrilling at the smoothness, tasting the way the tang of the wine mingled with the slick wet heat of her.

She leaned back against the bar as I grabbed her with both

hands, pulling her tight against me until she filled the apartment with the guttural cries of release.

Afterward, we danced to "Kashmir" and made out like teenagers. She pulled my clothes from me as the song's rhythmic pulse bore into us, driving us to the next round of passion.

I surrendered to her need, letting her drive the show. We made love with a fevered urgency that spoke of both fear and release. We finished a second bottle of wine, fed each other to keep up our strength, and filled the world with our exaltations.

The long black of the world slid away to the light of passion and love. I didn't care that a predator hunted me. I was safe with the woman I loved, naked and satiated. At least until the food was gone and the passions flared into the next inferno.

Sixty-one

Trisha sat up, the memory of passion echoing from her dream. Justin sat before her, dressed in leather and pain.

"Are you ready for the power?" he asked, tapping a thin bladed dagger against his naked thigh. "Ready to embrace the raw strength you so crave?"

She hesitated, caught between the feeling of utter helplessness and the intoxicating allure of power. "I'll be strong?" she asked, eagerly. "Strong enough to protect them, protect the children?"

Justin grinned at her. "Stronger than you can imagine."

She looked down at her naked body, the ropes criss-crossing her most intimate points. He had given her so much already, passion and love. And she'd seen him bring the doves back to life, seen him work the blood magic. She knew he reveled in giving pain, but she didn't care. At least when he cut her she could feel something.

"Yes," she whispered.

"I'm sorry," he said. "I can't hear you."

She straightened as far as the ropes would allow and spoke with a surety of purpose that she'd lacked since Bob and Chloe had been killed by the giants.

"I need the power," she said, her voice growing firmer. "I want it; I deserve it."

He rose, bringing the blade to her. "Yes, I think it is time."

"We must do one more thing," he said, cutting the binding from her hands. "One more step on your path to transformation." He held his hand out, helping her to stand. "Will you take that next step with me?"

"Of course," she said, smiling. "Lead me to glory."

They tended her cuts and dressed. He grabbed a pack from behind his bed while she tied her shoes. "This will be a night beyond your wildest dreams, this much I promise you."

She felt the thrill of the unknown rush through her.

They left his apartment in Sultan and got in her car. "Where to?" she asked him.

"Take me to your home," he said, patting her on the thigh. "The most powerful magic can be found there."

At his touch a wave of warmth flooded her, easing the last of the worry. He'd take care of things.

Deidre had the twins for the weekend and the rest of her crew was out of town. The other units would either be on duty or in transition. She could sneak him into her place easily enough.

The drive from Sultan to Black Briar wasn't really that far. The roads were getting bad, though, so she took it slow and careful. He seemed impatient, frustrated by the delay. She wanted to please him—for him to be happy. Something niggled the edges of her brain. Why did they have to sneak into Black Briar? Why were her thoughts sliding out of focus?

She breathed a sigh of relief when the long drive to Black Briar came into view. She turned onto it, slowing on the gravel. They'd gone about thirty yards down the long drive when Justin spasmed.

He beat the dashboard with fists. "Stop!"

She slammed on the brakes and the car sluiced to the side, skidding on the snow. Justin rolled out of the car and stumbled back up the drive. He fell to his knees and vomited.

Trisha threw the car in park and ran to him, leaving the doors open and the car running.

"Justin?" she called to him over the bitter wind. She fell to her knees at his side, placing her arm over his heaving shoulders.

"Protected," he gasped, pushing himself up onto his hands and knees. She helped him stand, and he regained a bit of composure.

Her thoughts were muddy. What was protected? "I don't understand."

"Watch," he said. He reached into a pocket and withdrew a bit of ash, flicking it into the air. "Dust of the grave," he told her.

A barrier crackled in front of them. The car was parked just on this side. "If I'd gone any further, I'd have been killed."

She looked at him, confused. "Why would the farm be protected from you? You aren't a threat to anyone here."

"Stranger," he said, coughing. "I'm unknown and I have power. The protection sees me as a threat."

Trisha hugged her arms to her chest, shivering in the wind. "What can we do?"

"I need to find a break in the fence," he said, pacing east along the road. "There is something nearby, a booster of some sort."

After a few more feet he stopped and picked up a rock. "There," he said, pointing. He threw the rock, and it struck a snow-covered post about two feet high and as thick as his wrist. "That is one of the nodes."

He turned to her, took her hand in his. "How badly do you want this?"

She looked from him, then to the post. If that protected Black Briar, then it kept her family safe. But he loved her. She'd given more than her body to him. If she couldn't trust him, then she had no reason to live.

"What do I do?"

"This is crude," he said, "but it is effective." He lowered his trousers and squatted in the snow. She didn't turn away.

He stood after a minute, buckling his pants. "Take that," he said, pointing to the steaming pile he'd left behind. "Smear it on the post, making sure to cover the top especially."

She looked at him, then down to his refuse. "Seriously?"

He grabbed her by the shoulder. "You clean diapers; you wipe up shit every day. Are you going to let something this minor stand between you and your rightful transformation?"

"Of course not."

The feces acted as a short in the system. The post shook for a moment, and she backed away just before it burst into flames.

"Excellent," he said, stepping toward the burning post. "I can work with this." He stepped past the barrier and walked several yards toward the house.

Trisha wiped her hands in the snow, scrubbing them with great handfuls of the thick, wet slush.

"Let's go," Justin said, stepping back onto the drive.

Trisha jogged back to the car and got in. "If it's all the same to you," she said, putting the car in gear and pulling the door shut. "I'm still gonna wash my hands when we get to the barracks."

They parked the car between the big house and the road. It was after dark, but probably no later than nine. The night had a long time to run. She led him to the barracks, where she cleaned up and then grabbed a camping kit, including sleeping bags and a tent.

The barracks were emptier than usual with the twins up at the big house. She wanted to see them, to kiss them good night, but she knew she needed to do this thing. To be able to protect them was paramount.

Justin paused at the burned-out barn as they made their way to the back of the farm. "There is power here," he said, marveling at the ashen ruins and the way they looked with the snow driving down around them.

"The snow won't stick to the wood," Trisha said. "Too hot still."

"Truly?" he said, stepping forward and reaching his hand out to the gaping doorway into ruined barn. "I can feel the energy that lingers here. I can feel the echo of his power." He stared, sightless for a moment, and she waited, giving him the moment he so obviously needed. Strange that this should hold his attention. Was he enthralled by the dragon taint?

After a bit, he shook himself and looked at her, smiling. "So much power to be had," he said. "You have no idea."

They walked hand in hand past the outbuildings, northward through the battle zone. She wanted to take him to the clearing she'd found. The energy was nice there, peaceful.

He stopped her halfway across the field, where the battle was fiercest. "There are spirits here," he said to her, his voice full of joy. "Can you feel them?"

She paused, letting his hand drop. "We lost good people here."

It took him a second to notice she'd stopped.

He turned, his face impassive. "And their loss will feed you, help you grow into your own."

"I don't know," she said, images warring in her head. Bob died here. Chloe and all the others. A pain throbbed in the back of her skull. Her thoughts were muddled. "This doesn't feel right."

He cupped her cheek with his hand. "Do not fear, dear one. You will be transformed."

A glow flared from his hand, red and violent. For a brief moment she made to pull away.

"Shh," he whispered. "Be calm."

She shook, as if with a seizure. Her breath fogged between them in stuttering gasps. After a minute the pace lessoned, and she grew calm once again.

He lowered his arm. "There now, all better?"

She smiled at him. Why had she been concerned? His eyes were so amazing, the depths of them held secrets she'd only dreamed of.

He took the first of the sleeping bags and opened it, laying it with the protected side down, but he let the fleece be exposed to the falling snow.

"The spirits of the dead provide a different form of energy, a different flavor of magic," he said. "Blood is quicker, hotter, filled with the raw energy of life. The essence of the dead is colder, harder." *He was talking to himself,* she thought. He did not look at her. "Magic fueled by the spirits of the dead is hard, longer lasting, but brittle. Blood magic is powerful, explosive."

She looked around, amazed at the possibilities. He knew so much, was willing to show her so much. She was honored and awed.

"Let us begin the ceremony," he said to her, smiling. "Make yourself ready for me."

She nodded and knelt on the sleeping bag—removing her clothing. The night air sent shivers through her body, and her skin grew taught in the cold. It was so cold her nipples ached when she removed her bra, exposing herself to the elements. He removed several silk ties from his pack and knelt beside her, taking one wrist. "With this bond, I link us, body and soul."

She let him tie her once more, only this time the knots were different. On one hand he used very few lengths of silk and tied her in a way that allowed her the ability to move and react to his touch. That is not how the game had been played before, and she realized that this was significant.

The magic he wove flashed around them in muted colors of pain. She gasped at his first touch and arched her back to the sky at his kiss. When he made love to her, she gave herself to him, relinquishing her fear.

After he'd finished he climbed off her and stood naked with his arms raised to the sky, a supplicant to a frozen god.

"Come to me, brothers and sisters," he said, pulling the spirits around them. "Come to me and bind her, make her mine now and forever."

Trisha began to buck as the spirits of the fallen pressed upon her, smothering her in their longing. When she stopped moving, he wove a final spell, painting a rune of binding on her with blood and semen. The silk ties that had bound her faded into her, leaving her body marked with their passing.

"Rise," he commanded her. "Rise and do my bidding."

Trisha gasped, one long, clean breath; then she rose, her mind a fog of need and desire. She had to please him, needed to please him. His touch would release her, allow the shuddering orgasm to flood over her and shatter the world.

"Get dressed," he urged her, putting on his own clothes. "Time is short and there is much yet to do before the sun next rises."

As she dressed he took out his cell phone and made a call. He described the breach in the protective barrier and bade them hurry. Trisha watched him, her mind filled with the buzzing of honeybees.

They abandoned everything but his pack as they made their way to the house. "I need an item within," he said to her. "You have described it to me, a ring with a green stone."

"Yes," she said. "I've seen it several times."

"Bring that to me. Nothing else matters. No one in that house must stand in your way. If they do, kill them." He handed her a knife, and she stepped toward the house.

"And the children?" She looked at him.

"Bring them," he said. "We'll keep them safe."

Half a dozen bundled figures approached the house across the long swathe of white between the house and the road. Four large vehicles idled behind them on the distant road.

She stood quietly, gripping the blade in her hand. *Get the ring; get the children.* She waited for Justin to tell her when to go. Only his word mattered now. Only he could help her get the power she needs to keep them all safe.

The largest of the newcomers broke away from the rest and crossed to one of the power poles that ran out to the main grid. He carried a large axe. She just stood there as the tock-tock of chopping echoed across the farm.

Why does no one hear that? she wondered, bemused. They shouldn't be doing that. Jimmy wasn't going to like it. She should be worried, maybe do something to stop the man with the axe, but Justin had said to wait, so she waited.

With a loud pop the pole buckled and fell, dragging power lines with it. Two lines snapped away from the house and danced along the ground like snakes spitting lightning. "Now," he said, motioning for the intruders to move toward the house. "Trisha is to retrieve the ring. No one else is to touch it, do you understand?"

The first figure threw his hood back and nodded. He was a rakish man with thinning hair and pointed ears. "We understand," the elf said. "And we honor our bargain."

Some of them snapped on headlamps and drew blades before sprinting to the dark house. Trisha gripped her knife and jogged after them. She knew where to get the ring. Jimmy kept it in a box on the mantle these days. There was no need for blades. This was a safe place. She paused, glancing back at Justin.

"Bring the children," he called. "They are in danger here. Let no one stand in your way."

She turned back toward the house. *Get the ring; protect the children.* Somewhere in her mind she warred with herself. This was not right. But Justin was so insistent. He would keep them all safe. Make it so she could be strong. She ran to the house, ran to stay ahead of the nagging doubt and fear.

Sixty-two

ANEZKA WOKE WITH A START. "STAY STILL," GUNTHER SAID from the doorway. She could see him, a shadow among shadows.

There was a crash in the kitchen. Anezka scrambled from the bed and pulled two blades from between the mattress and box springs. She'd hidden these a week ago, two short swords she'd smuggled out of the barn. Never know when trouble would show up.

She slid up behind Gunther, pushing the handle of one blade into his hand.

He grasped it with a grunt. "I won't ask why you have swords in your room."

"Good," she said. "A girl's gotta keep some secrets."

He reached back and squeezed her arm. "On three. Just don't stick a friendly." He counted and threw the door open, lunging into the hall.

The house was in chaos. People with headlamps were moving forward, like Navy SEALs. They were throwing books from shelves and knocking over cabinets. Deidre shouted as sounds of fighting erupted from her bedroom.

From the front of the house the children began to shriek.

Gunther rushed ahead of her, toward the children. An assailant darted out of the bathroom to their left, knocking into Gunther, who bellowed in pain. Anezka saw the flash of a blade as it slashed across Gunther's abdomen and he fell to the floor.

"Gunther!" Anezka yelled, leaping over him to swing at the assailant. "Eat that, bitch," she screamed when the blade connected with muscle and bone. Whoever it was stumbled forward, their headlamp falling to the ground, splashing Gunther in a broad beam of light. He lay on the ground, his hands at his sides. The hall was slick with blood.

"Go," he grunted.

She hesitated. "Don't die!" she ordered, and turned after the invaders.

Anezka screamed as she ran over broken glass, several pieces cutting into her tender feet. She stumbled against the wall.

They'd broken the mirrors.

She pulled a large piece of glass from her foot, and stumbled onward, ignoring the throbbing pain with each step.

They were fleeing the house. She loped through the kitchen. The last of the attackers ran ahead, knocking aside the kitchen table and chairs—scattering them in front of her. She dodged a chair and threw herself forward, catching them by the legs.

They hit the ground hard.

Anezka scrambled forward, stabbing downward with her short sword. The hooded figure grunted as the blade pushed through the thick muscles of the back, only to be stopped by the tile floor beneath them.

Anezka jerked the hood off the man as she stood, pulling her sword out of the kicking body.

"Move, people," a voice echoed from the outside the house.

Justin's voice.

She stepped over the dying man and flung the door open. "Justin!" She shouted and limped out onto the deck. "Show yourself, coward!"

Five individuals were running across the snow-covered grounds. They carried the children. Jai Li was fighting the man who carried her, battering him with her fists, ripping his hood off and biting him. He cuffed her once, and she went limp. Trisha carried one of the twins, and a woman with long, flowing black hair carried the other.

"Trisha," she called, and the woman slowed for an instant. But then the other woman passed her, and Trisha moved again, keeping up with the other twin. She never looked back.

That made no sense.

The deck was icy and treacherous, but Anezka didn't slow down. She jumped the last two steps, shouting. "Justin!"

One of the figures skidded to a halt thirty feet away. "Anezka? Is that you, lover?" Justin called back. "How did I miss you here?"

She stalked out into the yard wearing only Gunther's shirt. The cold of the snow numbed her feet, dulling the pain of the cuts. "Come back and face me," she sang out. "You candy-ass piece of shit."

Justin laughed at her. "Another day, lover," he called and sprinted away.

She chased after him, punishing her wounded feet on the ice and snow. They had vehicles waiting, big four-wheel-drive trucks. Trisha's car sat across the drive, its doors opened, abandoned.

Each truck had a driver, and the engines idled. Trisha and the others bundled the children inside one of the vehicles, and three pulled away. A fourth vehicle waited. Justin reached the final vehicle, and a hulking brute stepped out. He had a club in his hand, and the ground shook as he ran back toward her.

"Ignis," Justin called out, and Anezka fell to her knees, the blood in her body burning, boiling.

She rolled in the snow, losing the sword, and another voice roared into the night. Jimmy came sprinting across the grounds.

He slowed, fired a shotgun, and sprinted forward again. The blast rocked the huge man.

Justin climbed in the last truck, and they drove away.

Jimmy fired a second blast from the shotgun into the oncoming brute, but it only slowed him. Anezka screamed in frustration, rolling to her feet once again.

She ran forward, impotent rage coursing through her body. She'd never catch the truck. She looked toward Trisha's abandoned car. Maybe she could catch Justin.

Unfortunately, whoever the big guy was, two shotgun blasts weren't enough to stop him. Jimmy was staggered back by a glancing blow of the huge club. The shotgun flew from his hands as he fell.

She abandoned the hope of catching Justin in that instant, ran forward, and snatched up the shotgun. The brute smashed his club on the ground, barely missing Jimmy, who rolled to the side at the last possible moment. He was dazed and couldn't avoid the club for long.

Anezka knew this gun. It belonged to her. The stock was carved with runes that kept it working, even when magic disrupted other mechanical tools.

She pumped the shotgun and fired, swearing at the top of her lungs.

The blast staggered the brute. She fired again and again. Jimmy scrambled away, as the hulking attacker turned his attention to Anezka.

"Come on, motherfucker," she yelled, pumping the shotgun and firing again. He went down to one knee, dropping his club. Anezka fired over and over, walking forward, until the shotgun clicked on an empty chamber.

"I think he's dead," Jimmy said, pushing himself to a sitting position. "You can stop shooting him now."

Anezka turned to him and held out a hand. "Just making sure, boss. Can't tell with some of these bastards."

Jimmy took her hand, levering himself up onto his feet. He wobbled a little, but had his wits about him. Glancing blow, after all.

"Gunther's hurt," she said, handing him the shotgun. "How's Deidre?"

"Fine," he said, turning back to the house. "But they took the kids."

"Yeah. Wrecked the place. What was that about?"

"Not sure," he said, turning toward the house. "But I'm sure as hell gonna find out."

"Time to call in the cavalry?" she asked.

"Aye. Fucking DEFCON one. We'll go after them as soon as we can get moving."

They hobbled back to the house. Maybe Bub knew something.

Sixty-three

KATIE SCREAMED, AND I SAT BOLT UPRIGHT. THE CANDLES were nearly spent, and the house was suddenly cold. "What the hell's going on?" I asked, letting the blankets fall to my waist.

"Get up, get up," Bub shrieked. "They've taken the children." He pulled on my hand, trembling. "They raided the house, blood everywhere. You must get up."

"What the hell are you talking about, and how did you get here?" I asked, pulling the sheet back up to my neck.

"He's come to the farm," Bub said, staggering to the side. I dropped the sheet and caught him. He shook violently, near to collapse. "The accursed one. He's taken some item of power. I felt it. Someone has helped him invade Black Briar. Even now he speeds toward our home."

Katie was already getting dressed when Bub fell on top of me. I rolled to the side, letting him lay in the spot I'd just vacated. "Hang on, big guy." His eyes were shocky. "Did you port here from Black Briar?"

He nodded, but did not speak.

Holy crap. I got up and ran into the kitchen, naked and freezing. "Call Skella," I shouted as I grabbed the remains of the bread and salami from the counter. I dodged back into the living room and held the food out to Bub. Teleporting that far was beyond anything I'd ever seen or heard of him doing. It had to have taken it out of him. He ate the bread and salami in two great gulps and then accepted a pitcher of water.

Katie was tossing me my clothes, which were scattered all over the living room and kitchen.

"Call Skella," I said, pulling a T-shirt over my head.

"No use," Bub said, shivering. "They've smashed all the mirrors."

I knelt by him and rubbed his head. "We'll head to Chumstick," I told him. "How much head start do they have?"

"Minutes," he said. "They took Jai Li." I could hear the shame in his voice.

"Not your fault," I said, looking over to Katie. "She was supposed to be safe there."

"Fuck," Katie said into her cell phone. She ran into the bedroom, yelling. She came back out with her guitar slung over her back and a short sword at her belt. "Bike?" she asked.

"Yeah, faster. Hope you can keep us warm."

She nodded and handed me Gram. I finished getting dressed, slung Gram in her shoulder rig, and went back to Bub.

"You rest here," I told him. "You've done enough. We'll go get them."

He grabbed my hand, his claws digging into the back. "He means to kill her," he said and passed out.

"Damn," I said, standing. "You ready?"

Katie tossed me my helmet and went to the door. I grabbed my saddlebags from behind the couch, feeling the comfortable weight of my hammers inside.

"Which her?" she asked as we locked the door behind us.

"No idea."

Her phone rang, and she answered it right way. "Jimmy," she said to me. "Yeah, Jim. What the hell's going on?"

She relayed the information to me as we exited the building and ran around back to where I kept the bike parked. "Gunther was stabbed," she said to me, "and they took Jai Li and the twins. Deidre was roughed up, spilled out of her chair, but she'll survive. Power is out at Black Briar." She listened for a few seconds while I tied down the saddlebags.

I started the bike, and Katie cupped her ear, screaming into the phone. "It'll take us two hours. Get Skella. You've got to beat them to Chumstick. We're on our way."

She slammed the phone into her pack and climbed on the bike behind me. I waited long enough for her to strap down her helmet and grab me by the waist. Then we ripped through the streets of Kent doing a hundred and twenty before we passed the second light.

Sixty-four

FREDERICK TOOK THE ELEVATOR TO THE TOP FLOOR AND MADE his way to the stairwell and the roof access. No one stirred this late at night—nearly midnight. Once on the roof he carefully disrobed. No point in ruining the Armani. He dropped the cell phone on the pile of clothing. He no longer needed it. There would be no further communication. The orders had been clear enough.

He walked to the edge of the hotel and looked down the twelve or so stories to the street below. While the hotel slept, the city did not. He saw no other recourse. The transformation was quick. One minute, he stood there, naked and seemingly vulnerable; the next, his skin began to bubble and stretch. First, his back elongated, and then his limbs twisted and grew. He fell forward, catching himself on his hands and knees while the talons burst forth and the great wings unfurled from his back. As he transformed, the lights of the city waned. He drew in the power, a bite of the whole, aiding his metamorphosis.

He stretched his broad wings, beat them against the night sky for three beats, and leapt into the sky, his scream of anger echoing off the surrounding buildings. Before the city had time to react, the cold waters of Lake Washington were already slipping below his scaled belly. He avoided the bridges, preferring the dark, open waters between.

His instructions had been crystal clear: if he wanted to see Mr. Philips alive again, all he had to do was come take him.

"Come in all your glory," the snotty voice had instructed him. "Let the world quake at the sight of your true form."

Then the phone had gone dead. He hadn't hesitated. There was no more important action than this. He feared no man, not even one steeped in magic. He'd destroyed wizards before, paltry humans with visions of grandeur.

Once he'd transformed he could feel it, smell it in the air—a diseased point north and east. North of Leavenworth, they'd told him, but he needed no markers for this trip.

And when he got there, he would kill them all. No one attacked him, not even through his thralls. The barista had been an insult, but an expendable pawn. Mr. Philips was personal.

How had that happened? he contemplated as the mountains rose before him, cold as his heart. He flew northward along the ragged crust of the earth until the stench of corruption grew strong enough to turn him east. There, he would face this Dragon Liberation Front and its blight.

Mr. Philips, his able servant and stalwart companion, needed him, and he was surprised to realize he needed Mr. Philips.

He would enjoy killing this lot, would revel in the rending of their flesh and the smashing of their bones.

And the cold night slipped under his wings, carrying him forward to rage and glory.

Sixty-five

Skella ran through the dark of Stanley Park, heading to the place Gletts kept the mirrors. She promised Jimmy she'd meet them at the Starbucks out on Interstate 2 west of Gold Bar, in the little town of Startup.

When she entered the cave, she was surprised to find the mirrors smashed and the shrine Gletts had built to Sarah wrecked.

"What the hell?" she asked, and something heavy hit the side of her head.

Jara, the clan leader, knelt over her, feeling her skull.

"Does my remaining grandchild live?" Unun asked, her face hard and angry.

Jara looked up, "Yes, Unun. She will live."

"Good," she said, her voice tight. "Put her in her bed and destroy that infernal artifact of the humans," she said, pointing to the dropped cell phone. "They will no longer use her as they will. We are a proud people. Their interference is done."

Jara lifted Skella from the cold ground, and they walked back through the pitch night.

"Interference has only brought us pain," Unun said, though Jara did not respond. "I will not lose her to mad folly as well."

Sixty-six

WE CROSSED THE PASS AT SNOQUALMIE AND CUT NORTH ON U.S. Route 97. The snow was heavy in the passes, but once we were across, the road was merely wet and slick.

Katie sang the whole way, enveloping us in a bubble of heat. She ran through a dozen love songs, spacing them out, their magic fading slowly as the road crawled under our tires. The roads were rough, yet we managed to stay upright. I have no doubt it was her magic. She started shaking, nothing too severe, but I noticed it over the vibration of the bike. While I hoped it was just the cold, I feared the music was taking a toll on her.

I missed the winged horses at this point more than anything. The Ducati flat flew, and Katie's singing helped keep us stable and warm, but it still seemed to take forever.

Every second, every heartbeat put our people in danger. Jai Li, bless her. How terrified was she? And the troll twins? So much tragedy already in their lives.

Gram sang in my head. *Kill them all.*

Save the children, yes.

The bad guys would get no mercy.

Luckily, Justin and his evil minions didn't know we were coming, and if they dallied at all, we could beat them out there. Not likely, but Bub had bought us a good deal of time.

We screamed through Leavenworth, catching the attention of one of the local cops. I didn't even slow down as I caught the gumball machine on the top of his car kick in and his siren warble into the night.

Come on, you bastards, I yelled in my head. We can use all the help we can get.

The road out to Chumstick twisted and turned up into the mountains and was bad for speed. I dropped it down to eighty, then sixty, just to make sure we didn't end up roadkill. The sheriff or one of his deputies—I didn't get a good look when he started after us—knew the roads better than I did, and he or she slowed way down. By the third curve I had it down to forty, and the cop had disappeared two bends back. I could see his lights flashing across the clouds, reflected off the mountain, though, so I knew he or she was still coming.

Once we got through the wide spot that's Chumstick, we roared around one final curve and saw a second cop car parked across the road, lights flashing, door open. Two burning trucks blocked the road in front of Anezka's place, which loomed large on the right side of the road.

I slammed on the brakes. We skidded sideways. I barely kept the bike upright with the speed and slush. Katie, bless her, kept a death grip around my waist and didn't fly off.

She did get off the bike fairly quickly once we'd come to a stop. I can't imagine how I'd have kept the bike upright in my trainers. My Doc Martens were golden, though the soles may be missing a layer or two.

The dome over Anezka's house glowed a sickly phosphorous green, casting strange shadows from the puppet show within. Things were moving inside the dome, some of them big.

We were walking over to the police cruiser when a civilian car came screaming around the curve from the north. Katie and I ran to the side as the driver saw the burning trucks, too late. He pulled hard on the wheel, trying to avoid the trucks. With the short distance, his speed, and the ice, the little sedan flipped and rolled several times, smashing into the burning trucks.

I ran forward but was blasted back as the vehicle exploded. I doubted they'd survive that, much less be identifiable by anything other than dental records.

Katie climbed to her feet and crossed over to the police car. I limped after her, shedding gravel and mud as best I could. Luckily I'd landed on my knee, so it only hurt a lot.

The car was empty, but there were shell casings scattered around and blood on the snow by the car. Shots fired, officer down? Was the deputy following me, or responding to a call?

The second sheriff car came to a skidding halt fifty feet back down the road from the way we'd come. They cut the siren, but left the bubbles flashing.

I went to the bike and walked it off to the side of the road in case someone else didn't notice the huge burning pyre of smashed metal or the flashing lights of the abandoned cop car. I pulled the hammers from my saddlebags and settled their familiar weight into the holsters at my hips.

"Got any of those energy bars?" Katie asked. She looked pretty pale.

I dug in the saddlebags and brought out a bar and a bottle of water. Katie took them, her hands shaking.

I watched her as she wolfed down the protein bar. I'd have to keep an eye on her; using her music was draining her after all. I didn't like the implications.

Katie downed the bottle of water, and we headed back to the second cop car, hands in the air. There was only one officer in the car. He'd gotten out and had drawn his revolver, aiming at us from behind his open door.

"Stay where you are," he yelled.

We stopped.

"Look," I shouted. "You followed us. We have friends stationed out here; we need to check on them."

"Don't move," he called. I could see he had the radio in his right hand and the pistol in his left. We didn't move, waiting for Johnny Jump-Up to come to his senses. We could hear his radio squawking. After a few minutes, he threw the mike into the car and came out from behind his door. He held the pistol on us, shoved the car door closed with his hip, and started walking toward us.

"We're with Black Briar," Katie said, motioning to Gram over my shoulder. "We're looking to see if our people are okay. The sheriff knows about us."

He lowered his pistol when he got closer. "Yeah, he told us to cut you folks some slack," he said. "But dispatch says the sheriff was out here. You seen him?"

I shrugged. "Only got here a couple a seconds ahead of you, officer." With shots fired, all that blood and no body, I figured he was already dead. What really surprised me, though, was that we hadn't seen anyone here associated with Justin and his crew yet. The deputy was a young guy, Katie's age, maybe, and scared out of his mind. This was normally a pretty tame beat. Mostly drunk and disorderly in town and some speeding when the tourists were in town.

"You need to let us check on our friends," Katie said.

It sounded like she was giving him a command. Either way, he nodded and motioned with his gun. "I need to check on the sheriff. Hang on."

He went to the abandoned car. I looked past the burning vehicles and into the area up into the hills. We'd been so busy not crashing, we hadn't noticed the fires burning up the hills beyond

Anezka's place. If I stepped away from the burning trucks, I could just make out people milling around up there. Not that far, few hundred yards at most. What was keeping them?

The cave had to be that way, and if I were Justin, that's where I'd be taking the hostages. He had some plan that likely involved sacrifice and blood. We had a little bit of time, but not much.

The junior officer reached into the sheriff's car and picked up the mike. He radioed in to headquarters.

"Kelly, this is Cam. Sheriff's missing, shell casings all over the place, and a hella lot of blood. Can you call in the state boys? I'm here with a couple of the Black Briar folks, over."

He motioned with his head, giving us permission to go look for our people. We jogged over to the Black Briar encampment. It was smashed: tents rent open, honey bucket overturned, and two bodies down.

One was ours, but not the second. Katie checked our guy, but he was way too dead. They'd taken his fingers.

The second was facedown, dressed in a hooded cloak. I guessed a guy by the build, but a dead one by all the blood. I flipped him over. He had a couple crossbow bolts in his chest. I pulled his hood off his face and found quite a surprise. It was an elf. Son of a bitch!

"Katie," I called to her. "It's one of Skella's people."

She stood and walked over. She had tears on her face, but she was pissed. "Anyone we know?" she asked.

I looked at the guy again. Being dead changed the way your face looks in general, muscles all relax, blood pools, that sort of thing. Still, I recognized this guy. I didn't really know him, but he wasn't in the Sarah and Katie fan club.

"He was one of those that kept staring at us the last time we were up to Vancouver, remember? He was chopping wood when we walked by. Skella said he didn't like that she brought us into their village."

"Hope that means Skella is still on our side," Katie said, stepping around the bodies. "They butchered Lonnie, cut off his fingers."

I shuddered. Why the hell would they cut off someone's fingers?

"We waiting for Jimmy?" I asked. I know what my answer was. There were three more of our people out here. Where were they?

"No," she said. She pulled her guitar off her back, took it out of the case, and strummed a few chords. "Let's try that new song you found me, huh?"

She began to sing the eerie little ditty. On the one hand, it made you want to tap your toes and snap your fingers, but on the other, it made you want to look over your shoulder for the monster you didn't see coming.

Almost immediately, her nose started bleeding, but she sang through it twice. It showed us two things. One was a trail going off into the mountains, a glittering path of phosphorescent contrails that marked the passage of a large group. The second was another of our crew, dead. We hadn't seen her—Abrielle was down a slope, fifty feet away from the main camp. She'd run, by the looks of things, not that it helped her. She'd fallen down an embankment, looked pretty broke up from the top side. It would take some climbing to get her, but she wasn't moving.

I was debating on how to climb down to make sure she wasn't still alive somehow, when the sound of several vehicles came roaring from up on the road.

We scrambled back up the slope to the camp and saw Jimmy and Stuart with a dozen of our people decked out in armor and weapons. Three pick-ups total.

They went around the first cop car, slow enough to make sure no one was inside, and pulled up near the wreckage, where the deputy stood beside the sheriff's car.

The three trucks rolled to a stop and folks piled out. Jimmy went straight for the deputy, who had taken the scatter gun from the sheriff's car and was watching across the road.

Katie went to intercept Jim, and I headed for Stuart. I was pleased to see that he had some veterans with him, including Kyle George. Stuart nodded at me and got the crew into a skirmish line. Never know when the attack was gonna come.

I pulled Stuart aside, gave him the rundown on what I knew. He was surprised we'd beat them out here, but when I pointed to the Ducati he just shook his head.

"So, we figure either they have Steve and Jayden, or they were out on patrol and are hiding somewhere. Not like anyone could miss all this," I swept my hand to encompass the still-burning vehicles, "unless you were already dead."

"Lovely," he said, scrubbing his face. "Deidre's calling in the rest of the troops, and they're trying to figure a way how to get them out here. Skella was a no-show."

Damn. I told him about the one cultist we'd found, and he followed me over to the camp. He knelt and examined the body. "Good shooting, at least." He looked around. "That Lonnie?" he asked, pointing to the body nearby.

"Yeah, and Abrielle's about fifty feet that way," I pointed to the slope, "and another thirty down."

He winced, but didn't go look. Instead, he straightened up and walked back to the troops. Jimmy was there with the police officer.

"Okay, people," Jimmy was saying. "We have at least six bad guys and four civilians in the general area. We anticipate a lot of bad shit."

Katie shook her head. "That should narrow it down," she said, where only those closest could hear her.

"I want a defensive position here; use the terrain, but I'd rather we were on the farside of that mess," he pointed to the burning vehicles, "and away from that dome."

I pointed up the mountain, toward the burning fires. Jimmy and Stuart walked around the wreckage and up the hill. "Damn," he said. "That's a whole lot of people."

"What you reckon?" Stuart said. "Fifty? Hundred?"

I looked over at the small group of us. Counting the deputy we had seventeen known fighters. That didn't include Steve or Jayden. They were just MIA. Seventeen against a hundred. We were screwed.

Stuart began barking orders, and the crew double-timed it around the wreckage and began setting up a line. Two runners moved the pickups over to the line and began unloading supplies. For getting out here as fast as they did they had a lot of stuff—boxes of crossbow bolts, pole-arms, and guns. Guns had a tendency to stop working when magic was around, but if they only worked once before the magic shut them down, then we were up on the game.

"I want snipers here." Stuart pointed down the road about fifty feet, where an embankment gave an elevated view of the road coming up and the rocky terrain along the north side of the dome. "And here." He pointed over to a good size elm tree that had a decent view of the dome and the road back toward Leavenworth.

Jillian ran to the truck, took out a sniper rifle, a crossbow, and a messenger bag full of bolts. She slung them over her shoulders and headed to the elm. She was petite but had an eye for long-range work.

Kyle grabbed his kit, a rifle, crossbow, and sword and headed to the embankment.

The rest of the crew got in a nice skirmish line partway into the ditch along the side of the road north of the dome. They could hold that pretty well with the pole-arms and crossbows. None of them drew their firearms, but each had a pistol at their side.

I was impressed.

"Guess it's up to us now," I said, nodding to Katie. "We have two friendlies unaccounted for, as well as the hostages."

"Aye," Katie said, dropping the case from her guitar by Jimmy's truck and slinging it over her shoulder for easy access. "And you know the folks up the hill know we're here. We aren't surprising anyone."

"There's another wrinkle," Jimmy growled. "They took the ring."

"The Valkyrie ring you boys have been studying?" Katie asked.

Jimmy nodded. "We still don't know what it does. But Stuart and I were discussing it. Might be some sort of dark magic. Maybe we were supposed to keep it away from evil bastards like this group." He jerked his thumb toward the mountain. "Just keep an eye out for it."

"Hell, Jim," Katie said, with grim determination, "if the brain trust hasn't figured it out, maybe it wasn't taken on purpose. Maybe one of 'em thought it looked cool. They did take the time to snatch the kids. That's more likely what they were after."

"We gotta go," I said, tugging at Katie.

Jimmy nodded at me. "Scouting only," he said. "Do not engage the enemy."

I pulled Gram free of her sheath. Flames erupted from the blade, but I felt no heat. "Right. Scouting." I winked at Katie, who smiled.

"Wabbit time," she said, picking up a crossbow and slotting a bolt home.

Part of me should have been more concerned, especially with the gleam in Katie's eye as we headed off. But I was too busy with the song the sword sang in my head. We were going to battle. What could be better?

Sixty-seven

Trisha watched the tableau before her, eagerly awaiting her transformation. She could feel the power here, like a vibration through the soles of her feet. Justin had promised her great things—a chance to make a difference.

Justin stood atop the outcrop, looking down on the road below. To his left, Anezka's home, his home for a while, glowed the shade of decayed flesh. An altar stood before him, the intricate grooves cut into the stone to channel the blood to either side, where receptacles waited to catch the sticky red offering.

To his right, a brazier burned, the coals glowing a red and yellow panorama of pain. Several utensils hung to the side, ready to be placed in the fire, to enhance their already-craven utility.

Trisha stood behind him, naked, her face a contorted mask of jubilation. Jai Li and the troll twins were being held in the cave behind him, the entrance masked by his intricate spells. "To keep them safe," he'd told her. "Safe from this offal who willingly serves the great beasts."

Mr. Philips sat on the ground before her, bound with twists of barbed wire and his head covered in a leather mask. She knew his kind, the bootlicker who served a monster rather than being a man in his own right. She knew he would die screaming like a pig. That was the thought that buoyed her. This man would die to draw out his master, and then Justin, her lover, would bring down another of the fell beasts. And she'd help. She'd be like Sarah, a hero, someone who saved her loved ones, not someone who lay wounded on the battlefield while those she cared about were savaged by giants.

This was her moment of redemption. Her mind buzzed with possibilities. He promised her power, promised her glory. All in the name of protecting, she told herself. For the children.

"Do you see the maggots before us?" Justin asked, pointing down to the road below them. "Our enemies gather to thwart us, to prevent you undergoing your immaculate transformation."

She could not see who they were, the tiny figures below, but she knew they meant to harm Justin, to prevent his actions, and that made them her enemies. If only she could go back to the children, for just a moment, to comfort them. How hard it was to think beyond Justin and his words. Those were clear as the sun. Everything else fell to shadows.

Sixty-eight

KATIE AND I SLIPPED AROUND THE DOME, IGNORING THE SHAPES that moved within. They were off radar at the moment. As long as the dome held, they were harmless. At least in theory.

We'd covered a couple hundred yards and were coming into real rocky elevation when we caught sight of Steve and Jayden. They flagged us down, and we ran to where they hid.

Jayden was wounded, and Steve had lost his crossbow.

"We took out three of those bastards," Jayden said, grimacing against the slash on her leg. It had a field dressing, but the bandage was soaked with blood.

"They attacked the camp while we were out on patrol," Steve said. "They didn't know we were out here, I don't think. Let us get the jump on a few of them."

"How long?" Katie asked.

"Not too long after we got here. Eleven-thirty, maybe. They arrived in those two trucks. Loaded a bunch of crap up the mountain path there, before they set them on fire."

"Just blocked the road, as far as we can tell," Jayden said. "We sniped at them a bit, but the second group caught us by surprise."

Steve looked over at Katie, abashed. "They had kids with them. We had to be careful. Only managed to take out a couple of them. Couldn't get to the kids."

"You did your best," Katie said, patting him on the shoulder.

"We were checking those we killed," he motioned to a pile of bodies about twenty feet away, behind a stand of scrub, "when one of them stabbed Jayden."

I glanced at Katie.

"Not dead," Jayden growled. "Only faking it. Steve took care of the bastard."

Steve shrugged. "They've sent a couple patrols, so we've been sniping at them, moving around."

"Were the kids okay?" Katie asked.

"Seemed okay," Jayden said. She looked away.

"Trisha was with them," Steve said, his voice bitter. "Just followed them up the hill here, carrying the twins like she was going to a picnic."

Jayden spat. "I think he's got her under a spell or something," she said. "That freaky dude in black."

I sat down on my heels. Holy crap. "Was it a blond guy, about thirty, with a scar on his face?"

Steve shrugged, but Jayden nodded. "It was her boyfriend. I saw them once in town. She didn't know I saw her, but they were out at dinner one night and me and Cole were picking up takeout."

Katie looked pale—shook her head. "Wait a minute. Trisha is dating Justin . . . the fucking necromancer?"

I rubbed my temples. This was fucked up. And she voluntarily carried the kids? Was she how they got into Black Briar?

Sixty-nine

Originally, Justin had only hoped to draw forth a powerful spirit to bend to his will. This had exceeded his expectations. The witch's dome just added to his available resources. Did she realize the gift she'd given him? Now he had the power he needed to do something he'd only dreamed of. Drawing Frederick Sawyer here had been child's play. The vanity of his kind had always been easy to manipulate. He would rip out Sawyer's still-beating heart and eat it, claiming the drake's power as his own. But first, to take care of the riffraff.

From a dripping sack he pulled a handful of severed fingers and cast them into the brazier. The words fell from his lips like honey. "Blood seek and bones crack." The fingers blackened in the flames. "Spirits of pain. Cover this valley with dread and woe."

Gray smoke billowed from the brazier and flowed down the side of the mountain. He watched it roil out over the valley before him, obscuring the greenish glow of the tainted dome. On the road below, the enemy panicked. Their screams of anger and dismay rose to him, filling him with delight.

"Slaughter them," he called as the few dead that lay below rose up. "Let no one stand before us." He turned to his cultists. "Soak the ground in their blood."

They screamed as they descended the side of the mountain, spirits flowed with them, drawn by the gray smoke, diverted from the quest for the dome.

Seventy

GRAM THRUMMED IN MY HAND, ALERTING ME TO DANGER. I stood, stepping out from the overhang where we were hidden. A wall of gray rolled down the main trail from above.

"Uh-oh," Katie breathed. Spirits rode in the thick fog, sucking the heat from us as they passed.

As soon as the fog hit the cultist's bodies, the ones Steve and Jayden had killed, they started moving, broken and twisted as they were. It was like when we'd been trapped inside the house.

"We have to get them out of here," I growled. "Down to the line."

Katie nodded, and we stood. Steve got Jayden in a fireman carry while I moved ahead, keeping the stirring dead in my sights. Katie darted out onto the path a little ways ahead, making sure the way was clear. The fog was not as thick here, but it gathered more the lower it rolled. Then, several figures came screaming from the stones around us, cultists with daggers. One jumped at me, and I stepped to the side, bringing Gram around to slash at the masked attacker.

Katie sprinted up the next hairpin turn, swinging her guitar around and belting out a song. The fog cleared around us. The first cultist fell at my feet, his chest pulsing with rising blood. A second dodged past me, thrusting a dagger at me as she passed. I blocked the wild blow with Gram, and she performed an intricate gesture, flinging power in my direction.

Flames erupted around us, a wall separating me from the others.

Katie countered with a song about rain, and the fire fizzled. She stumbled and went to one knee. *Too much*, I thought. She's gonna overdo it.

I sprinted forward as the cultist began a second spell, but I cut her off, literally. Gram caught her just below her right ear, severing her neck and sending her head bouncing down the rocky slope. Never send the casters out without a tank. These people were idiots.

The body fell forward, following the head, to land in a bloodied mess a dozen feet below. Then, as we watched, the corpse rose and began making its way down to where Black Briar had its skirmish line.

"We can't afford to kill them twice," I growled to Katie as I caught up with her, pulling her to her feet. "We need a better plan."

Steve was in damn good shape, but Jayden was heavy, and the trail was rotten with mud and ice. We skittered our way across the uneven ground. Half a dozen walking dead were between us and our crew.

We heard the crack of a single gunshot, and a bullet ricocheted near us.

"Hope we don't get shot by our own troops," Jayden said.

Steve just grunted and hunched a little lower, dancing down the rocky slide.

A dozen more cultists came screaming down the hill toward us. Too many for us to handle. I fell back to give Steve a chance to make it to flat land. Katie stopped as well, sending several crossbow bolts up into the pursuing cultists. One stumbled and fell, but the others just jumped over the fallen, screeching like banshees.

I waded into them, swinging Gram for all I was worth. Two went down as the black blade cut through muscle and bone. Several cultists fell back, giving me a wide berth, but several dodged past me, sprinting toward Katie, Steve, and Jayden.

They stumbled onto flat land before the cultists could reach them. The Black Briar line parted to let them in. The cultists didn't slow. The walking dead, as well as the living, crashed against the shield wall, many impaling themselves on the halberds.

More gunshots raked the enemy, and they fell back, only to surge forward once more. Our line was anchored on the right by the burning wreckage, but that didn't deter the dead. Several plunged into the flames and emerged as walking infernos. Black Briar scattered, breaking into squads as they'd practiced, falling back across the road to the second ditch.

I hit the cultists from behind as a second wave rolled down the mountain and onto the road. Three cultists went down under my blade before I got to the first burning dead.

It turned to me, a hulk of a man, with several crossbow bolts in his chest and his robes on fire. I danced back, swinging Gram at one outstretched hand. The blade cut through the burning meat, and the bastard lumbered forward, grabbing my sword.

I reached down and pulled the hammer from my right side, slipped my hand through the loop. At that moment, another cultist swung a dagger at me. I yanked Gram back with a muscle-wrenching pull and swung the hammer, smashing the dagger aside.

The burning dead guy clubbed my shoulder, and I staggered. I spun around, bringing Gram through the cultist's arm, severing it above the elbow. She fell back, screaming as blood sprayed in a wide arc. I hit the flaming man with the hammer, smashing the side of his already-mutilated head. He dropped to the ground, kicked once, and did not move.

Seventy-one

A young woman struggled as Dane and Tobin dragged her forward. She kicked at them, shouting with a voice cracked from exhaustion. They dropped her, sobbing, at Justin's feet.

He knelt, cupping her panic-stricken face. "You do have a certain beauty," he said, turning her head from one side to the other. "I should allow my compatriots a moment or two with which to entertain you, but alas."

He waved his hand in the air, and the brutish cultists stepped forward once more. She thrashed against them until they slammed her onto the altar before Justin. She squeaked as the breath was knocked from her.

They lashed her feet and hands to the corners of the altar, pulling her spread-eagle against the stony surface.

Justin glanced back toward Trisha. "What do you think, lover? Will this one bring the dragon to us? Will her life's blood be the sacrifice we need to bring you to your glory?"

Trisha did not answer. She stared forward, her eyes glazed and with a vapid smile on her face.

He chuckled and turned back to the altar.

"Please," the nameless girl begged, her tear-stained face turned to Trisha. "What have I done?"

"Done?" he asked. "My dear, you have done nothing. It is a

shame, really, that you are of no more value than the blood that flows in your veins." Justin drew a long dagger from his belt. The blade twisted, serpentlike, to a needle-fine point. He bent, tracing the blade across her shoulder. She whimpered as a line of blood followed the tip.

"How I wish we had time to play," he said, lowering his face to hers. She gasped as he shoved the blade into her, kissing her open mouth while she kicked beneath him.

When she stopped moving, he rose, holding the dagger aloft. As he began to chant, the blood that flowed from her rose in a fine mist. Within seconds she lay before him a shriveled husk. He stood back, clothed in a robe of her blood.

"Come to me, Frederick Sawyer," he called into the skies. Lightning flashed skyward from his outstretched hands. "We await your vengeance."

From the cliff wall above him, a metal scaffold reached out over the plateau. There, Mr. Philips rose, feet first by a length of chain, his body wrapped in barbed wire. Blood covered his body from dozens of cuts and the constricting bands. Below him a dozen women pulled the chain through a series of pulleys, ratcheting him upward one halting step at a time.

"Does the bait not suit your taste?" Justin asked the sky.

The red-robed cultists, Dane and Tobin, cut the bonds that held the corpse to the altar and tossed the remains onto the growing pile of leathery skin and bones that littered the plateau.

"No reply yet?" he asked, shaking his head. "One more, I think." He snapped his fingers. "Then your moment of glory will be upon us, my sweet."

Trisha moaned quietly, then fell silent once again.

Seventy-two

THE SHERIFF'S DEPUTY STOOD ON TOP OF THE CAR, FIRING HIS riot gun into the oncoming horde. He managed three rounds before the gun exploded and he was flung backward, out of sight. Katie disappeared behind the Black Briar trucks so I rushed forward, taking down another cultist. Ahead of me, where the terrain rose back toward the mountain, another wove a spell. I ran forward, knocking a dead guy aside, but I couldn't get there in time. The caster brought her hands together, falling to one knee. A sonic boom broke over the area, knocking everyone to the ground.

My ears were ringing when I climbed to my feet a couple of seconds later. I'd beaten most of the rest to their feet, so I sprinted forward, stepping on a rising cultist, springing off her back and landing next to the spell caster.

The gunfire had quieted. The magic had to be interfering with the mechanisms. Luckily, Gram had no such limitations.

The spell caster retreated several steps, and another cultist flung himself in front of me, taking six inches of Gram into his gut, allowing the caster a chance to scramble back amid the knife wielders.

I kicked the cultist, pushing him off Gram with my boot, and assessed my next target. The caster was running up the hill, and a dozen knife fighters stood between her and me. I stepped forward, grinning.

A noise I'd only heard once before rent the air—the sound so horrible even the cultists fell to the ground covering their heads.

Dragon.

The world slid into slow motion. I looked up, searching for the source of that cry. High in the night sky, amid the parting clouds, one of the stars separated itself from the others and fell toward us—a glowing ember that grew larger by the millisecond.

It was a dragon, glorious and horrifying. One I hadn't seen before. I shuddered, stepping back from the cultists. They stood frozen by that cry, their faces awash with terror.

Gram throbbed in my hand, in my brain. I rushed forward, smashing through the line and cutting down the caster. Then I was past them, running to meet that dragon. It fell from the sky like an eagle—wings thrust back and long neck straining forward.

Gram sang in my head, a song of victory and death. She needed to drink this beast's life force. He—she told me—this new dragon was definitely male. He was beautiful and deadly, beyond even Jean-Paul, who had been black and sleek, a stealth bomber, bad-ass, killing machine.

The memory of Jean-Paul paled next to this new dragon, who glowed as he fell, the magic of Gram amplifying the light around him. The better to kill him, I supposed, but it lent him an aura of power beyond Jean-Paul's might. If I could just look at him, appreciate the way the light glinted off his scales, at the varied colors, greens and blues, more dark than light, then I would have been content. Part of my brain wanted to marvel at his beauty. But the rest was locked up, panicked. All the crocodile brain could register was a lot of very large teeth.

For the briefest of moments there was no other sound in the world but the cry erupting from him, a sound that cracked the bones of the mountain and sent shattered stones falling from the heights above.

Seventy-three

THE DRAGON PULLED OUT OF HIS SCREAMING DIVE AT THE LAST
second, his claws out like landing gear, and shredded two of the
cultists in his first pass. I was nearly knocked to the ground by
the force of his passing, but I managed to stay on my feet. The
world stopped for a brief instant as he passed within a few yards,
one great golden eye boring into me. I shuddered at that scrutiny
but did not falter. There was an intelligence behind that eye, an
appraising. I had the strongest feeling he knew who I was.

He flipped his tail around and smashed the burning trucks,
sending flaming debris scattering across the road. He circled us
once and rocketed toward the mountain, flying over the enemy.
Where his shadow crossed, friends and foes fell to the ground,
holding their hands over their heads—all but the walking dead.
Our boys fired a few crossbows' bolts at the dragon, but they just
bounced off his scales.

I glanced back. The Black Briar crew had reformed beyond
the ditch on the farside of the road, but their line was ragged.
I debated going back to bolster them, when I heard Katie's voice
rising above the din. It was a song I recognized—one she sang
when I sparred. The fear that permeated everything began to
ebb back, allowing a hint of hope to creep in. The line firmed up,
and the crew brought down several of the dead.

None of the dead were ours, not yet. I didn't want to think how they'd react to face one of their friends brought back from the dead.

Okay, Katie was safe, the line was holding, and a dragon was sweeping toward the enemy encampment. Time for me to do something radical. I had to find that cave. If I could get to the shield—remove it from the ley line—maybe I could short-circuit some of Justin's power.

I sprinted forward, cutting my way through the stunned cultists, following the dragon's wake. I'd take advantage of the chaos he caused and get to the cave. Maybe we'd get lucky and this dragon would eat Justin. That wouldn't suck.

Justin's voice echoed down the mountain, amplified by magic somehow. I didn't understand the words he used, but the hair on my neck did a little dance, and my stomach tightened like I was going to throw up.

I ran past a large bonfire, jumped over a pile of bones, and scrambled onto a trail that doglegged up the mountain. Here, everything was cast in the green tint of the glowing dome. The light from the fires below did not reach this high.

At the first bend I could see that the Black Briar line was holding back a wave of cultists and a few remaining undead. They had us outnumbered but hadn't overwhelmed the line yet. It was like they were teasing us, playing for time. Justin had a plan of some sort and a quick kill of our side wasn't in the cards. He wanted us alive, for a while at least. I bet it was the fear he needed.

As the sky opened and freezing rain pelted down onto us, two cultists ran at me out of the shadows. One leapt at me from the switchback above, missing me by inches. The second skidded around the end of the turn and came at me with a long blade. I caught it against Gram, and sparks shivered into the eerie green glow from the dome. It was like fighting inside one of those old

CRT computer monitors. I spun around, ducking a blow from the first cultist who'd found his footing, and kicked out, knocking the second to the side. I punched Gram forward, stabbing the first cultist in the shoulder, and he dropped his blade. The second grazed my right arm, sending a line of burning pain across my bicep. I punched him with Gram's pommel and then landed a bone-crunching blow with the hammer in my right fist. Not my strongest weapon, but enough to send him reeling back into his partner. I slashed forward with Gram, cutting the first man open, his guts falling to the ground, then lunged over him to skewer his buddy in the throat.

I didn't wait, just ran around them, leaving them to their dying.

At the next bend I could see the altar on the plateau above. A young woman in a fast-food uniform fought against two men in red. Justin stood above her, dagger in hand, appealing to the heavens. Three bolts of lightning struck the blade, flashing down the length of his body. Power strobed about him as he struck, slashing the young woman's throat.

"You bastard!" I growled, rushing up the last bend.

Justin's voice rose in a great crescendo. "Arise, mighty one. Let us cower beneath your might."

As I crested the final landing, a wave of energy flashed across the mountainside, casting the world in frozen images of black and white.

I held my hands up against the nova that blossomed on the plateau. At the center, a lone figure rose, its body arching and its head thrown back. An anguished wail broke from the figure, and in that instant it transformed.

Those on the plateau fell to their knees as a huge dragon materialized in their midst. The great beast reared back on its hind legs, unfurling its massive wings, and shot a column of green flame upward into the falling rain and snow.

My heart thudded in my chest as adrenaline coursed through me. Gram throbbed in time with my pounding heart. Holy crap. Another one? I squatted down with my back against the side of the path, Gram across my knees.

The dragon crashed down onto all fours, shaking the mountain. In that instant I knew it was a she. Once again it was Gram who knew. The runes on my scalp and leg flared, driving spikes of pain into me, focusing my mind.

The new dragon stretched her long neck over the edge of the plateau and roared. I covered my ears, and still my head felt as if it might rupture from the ferocity of it. If I'd been able to stand in that moment, I could've touched her, could have driven Gram into her neck, but I had no strength in my legs. The smell of her was horrible, like fetid carrion, and she glowed a vibrant green like the flames that splashed down onto the road.

She was the dragon from my dreams—all those months ago—before I killed Jean-Paul. I crawled to where I could peer over the edge of the plateau again. Justin danced among a scattering of dead bodies. A dozen cultists stood behind him, against the mountain, but they were an afterthought.

The green dragon rose on her hind legs once more and beat her great wings, driving rock and dirt down the mountain in a wave of grime. I turned my head to protect my eyes and watched as those who were standing downwind covered their face against the grit, many stumbling farther afield.

This beast had a wingspan greater than Jean-Paul's. He'd been big—forty feet from nose to tail, with a wingspan twice as wide. This monster made Jean-Paul look like a Chihuahua. I'd guess a wingspan of a hundred and twenty feet or more. I wasn't sure how something that huge didn't collapse under its own weight.

She screamed and jumped from the mountain, falling like a

747. The field was lost. Both Black Briar and the cultists were scattered on the buffeting beat of those great wings.

I took a stuttering breath, despite the stench of her passing, and ran onto the plateau. The male dragon appeared from the blackness that surrounded the plateau and buzzed the cultists, sending them scrambling.

Why two dragons? Life just sucked sometimes.

The plateau was huge—a couple hundred yards deep and twice that wide—a semicircle pushed up against the mountain. Altars and braziers burned in a wide semicircle facing the valley below. Three huge bonfires rose high into the sky, casting enough light to see but creating deep recesses of shadow. This light warred with the green from the dome, giving the living the pallid complexion of the dead.

Justin's maniacal laugh echoed off the mountainside, but I could not pick him out any longer. Cultists milled around in several groups, and many individuals ran pell-mell through the pools of light.

The male dragon flew toward the mountain. I followed his path and saw a large scaffolding jutting out from the side of the mountain. A body dangled below it, eighty feet or more above the base of the plateau.

As the dragon smashed into the scaffolding, grabbing the hanging body in one of his great talons, a dozen cultists suddenly flared with pulsing magic. They raised their hands, channeling a dozen threads of golden light. In a blink, they formed the threads into a net of energy, slamming the dragon against the mountainside, wrapping his wings in the twisted bands of light.

"He's taken the bait," Justin shrieked, pumping his fists into the air. The dragon roared, pinned against the side of the mountain, as the cultists chanted in unison.

Gram thrilled at the captured dragon, urging me to kill it while it was trapped. But if the cultists wanted to capture that dragon, I knew I needed to help it. Psycho, huh?

I sprinted out onto the plateau, dodging several burning braziers, and set Gram back into the sheath over my shoulder. Then, I shifted the hammer from my right hand to my left. When I was about thirty feet from the cultists, I let fly.

"Eat this," I barked.

The hammer arced up, then came down with a muffled thud against the back of one of the twelve, who flew forward against one of his compatriots. Two of the beams flickered and failed. The dragon roared, struggling against the rest.

Justin yelled from somewhere to my right. I didn't hesitate. I pulled Gram from her sheath once more and slashed the closest cultist. Apparently, keeping the dragon pinned required their full attention.

A blast of energy exploded at my feet, sending me careening over a pile of broken bodies. Justin ran toward me, glowing with anger, the rage on his face a lovely sight. Bastard.

I didn't even get to my feet, just rolled to the side, swinging Gram at the nearest target. I slashed one of them across his knee, a serious enough wound to divert his attention. And another thread in the net vanished.

"Kill her," Justin called, and knife wielders rushed toward me. I staggered upright and ran at those holding the net. I bowled over two others, and the net dissolved altogether. The "oh, shit" factor was off the charts. I was deep into enemy territory with nine really pissed-off casters concentrating their attention on me. Ten, if you counted Justin. Plus a whole slew of others who wanted to stab me a lot.

Luckily, the male dragon had plans of his own. He fell forward, catching his bulk on his wings, and strafed the plateau, sending most of the cultists scattering. One of the casters was too slow, and the dragon grabbed him in his free claw. He had managed to keep the body from the scaffolding.

The dragon banked west over open territory and flung the screaming cultist into the mob below. The enemy on the ground had fallen back to the mountain, avoiding the rage of the green dragon, who held court below.

I put some distance between me and the cultists, running to the western edge of the plateau, above the switchback trail, following the male dragon's path. I saw him land far to the west, near the original Black Briar encampment, and gently deposit the figure he'd taken from the scaffolding. He was really close to our guys. They must've fired on him because he buffeted them with his wings, driving them back, and he launched himself skyward once more.

Had he just delivered the body to us? Who was it? I wondered.

As the first dragon crossed the road again, heading toward the plateau, Justin screamed out. "He is here, my sweet. Your vengeance is nigh."

The green dragon roared an answering call, shedding broken cultists like lice. She unfurled her humongous wings and pushed her bulk skyward.

The male dragon strafed the plateau once again, spewing a column of dragon fire against a clump of cultists and knocking several others aside in his wake. The remaining eight channelers had changed tactics and were drawing thick columns of green power from the dome. They funneled the trapped spirits toward Justin, who seemed to grow as the power surged into him. This couldn't be good.

I cheered as the male dragon swept around again, snatched a fleeing cultist in his enormous claws, and tossed the broken body against the mountainside as he banked back south. He was so focused on the channelers that he didn't notice the other dragon until it was too late. The green dragon smashed into him, her talons the size of long swords.

Her momentum carried them upward, where they crashed into the side of the mountain, sending a shower of rubble down onto the plateau. Twice the male bounced against the rocks before he got his wings under him once again. The two drakes tore at one another with flashing talons and snapping jaws. Blood rained down, black and green in the glow of the fires. Justin stood in the downpour, arms stretched skyward as the acidic rain vaporized against his glowing skin.

"Kill him, lover," he cried to the green dragon. "I will cut out his heart and we shall eat it together."

I stumbled to my knees, struck suddenly with the truth. The runes along my scalp burned as I dragged my bloodied hand across them. I needed clarity. The fog of battle was confusing me, making me jump to conclusions. The green dragon rolled in the sky, falling earthward with the male in her talons. In that split second, I saw the ring. It was huge against the thickness of her claw, and everything fell into place.

There was the Valkyrie ring. That had been the lie. The Valkyrie statue had misled us. This was dwarven magic—Fafnir's ring.

"No!" I shouted, running toward the cultists, cutting one of them down, breaking the surge of energy. Justin stumbled, and the remaining cultists turned on me, knives flashing. I suffered cut after cut, but I felt none of them, allowing the beserker to consume me. I knew the green dragon. She was one of us.

The ring had come down from legend, its story intertwined with that of the sword in my fist. Gram had been forged to destroy the dragon Fafnir, who was also a dwarf. The ring allowed this dwarf to shape-shift—gave him the means to terrify a kingdom. Only he was really a she. Had to be. Black Briar had figured out it was magic tuned to women. Her tragic tale was directly linked to the misbehavior of Loki and the injustices he had meted out on Fafnir's clan. And our Trisha had taken that ring with Justin's help and somehow unleashed its power.

I don't know how many of them I killed, five, seven? But more seemed to appear from the mountain itself. There were too many. A blow struck the back of my head, and I fell forward onto my knees. The world swam, but I kept Gram clutched in my fist. I gulped in air—my heart thudding against my chest. My head throbbed and my eyes stung with sweat.

"So, you have come to me, finally," Justin said. He floated across the ground, his feet six inches above the rock. The green energy held him aloft.

"I'd hoped to use your blood in this evening's rituals," he said, raising his hands to his chest. "Instead, I had to take many others." He flung his arms out, encompassing the dozen or so bodies scattered around the nearest altar. "Such a waste."

His boot caught me in the head, flipping me over onto my back.

"That," he barked, spittle flying from his enraged face, "is for taking my fucking motorcycle."

He raised a long blade and lunged at me. It was a bleeder like the one he'd used to kill Mary Campbell's horse, Blue Thunder. Nice for sacrificing, I supposed. None of that messy clotting to slow down the flow of magic.

I rolled, tucking Gram to my chest. On the third revolution, I swung my knees under me, surged to my feet, and ran toward the mountainside. Several of the cultists grabbed for me, two caught me with blades, slicing in my left arm and my right hip. Hurt like hell, but I was out of Justin's reach when I turned.

He screamed obscenities, flinging bursts of energy at me, smashing rocks above my head, and raining hot fragments down on me. I flattened myself against the stone, trying to avoid falling debris, but I passed right through and fell ass-over-teakettle into the mountain.

I flipped over, doing a reverse summersault, and landed on my chest, winded and without a sword. I'd flung Gram behind me as I tumbled. I could hear her skittering down the steep passage behind me. I tried to rise, but slipped in the rock and dust that had blown into the cave with me. I rolled over, sat up, and slid on my ass, deeper into the mountain. I plowed into the stone wall at the bottom, smacking my head on the hard stone floor.

The world spun for a moment. I tried to sit up, but a cultist came skidding down the passage on his feet, sword flashing toward me.

I grabbed a handful of gravel and flung it at him, rolling to the side. The passage opened that way, and I dropped five feet into an open cavern.

"Sarah?" a voice called to me. I scrambled onto my hands and knees, looking for the voice. It was Qindra, or rather, Qindra's spirit.

"Hi," I said, shaking my head. "Have you seen my sword?"

She pointed to my left, and I lunged that way as the cultist jumped from the opening. He landed, catlike, and swung where I'd been. I grabbed Gram in time to deflect the blow. He grinned, stepping toward me. This was not going well.

He raised his sword over his head, and I scrambled backward against the wall. "Damn it," I bellowed, and he froze.

I waited a second, and, when he didn't move, I scrambled to my feet, putting distance between him and me. Qindra had reached out and touched him, paralyzing him.

I leaned against the wall, letting my breath slow before nodding to her. She let him go, and the cultist swung his sword on the original trajectory, only I wasn't there anymore.

I whistled at him, and he turned, surprised. "Sorry, dude," I said, lunging forward. He dropped his sword as Gram slipped between his ribs, puncturing his left lung and heart.

He fell over, grinning. I hated these guys.

I looked down at myself. Everything hurt, and the knees of my jeans were shredded. I liked these jeans, too. It's so damn hard to find good jeans that fit.

"Fancy meeting you here," I said and fell over.

Qindra knelt over me, smiling. "You always were into drama, Sarah. Can you do nothing simply?"

"I'm here to rescue you," I whispered. "And get the shield out. There are two dragons up there, and my people are getting their asses kicked by cultists and the undead."

"Jai Li is here, is she not?" she asked.

I shuddered against the rage. I couldn't succumb—had to keep control. "Yeah, somewhere," I choked. "That bastard Justin has her somewhere. He's killed a lot of people." I had to believe she was still alive.

"Perhaps it is time for me to let this go, then." She waved her hand, leaving a phosphorescent contrail. "I have been fighting him all evening. He has done something I cannot see, infected the dome somehow. He is very powerful."

"I need to get the shield," I said, trying to sit up. "That'll put a knot in his tail." The world swam, and I couldn't do it. My head was really pounding.

"Here," she said, passing her hand over me. The pain in my head subsided, and the cuts and bruises eased—like I'd been healing a few days.

I stood, amazed again at her power. If she worked for the good guys, we'd totally kick the dragon's asses. I glanced around the room. It really wasn't very big, but the shield floated where I remembered it. I strode to it, watching the way the energy crackled off it.

"What do you think?" I asked.

A shout brought me around, and two more cultists jumped down from the ledge, rushing at me. I sidestepped the first one, throwing him to the side, into the ley line.

He shrieked as his face melted off. Very Indiana Jones. The second guy paused to stab at Qindra, who only smiled at him as his sword passed through her.

Spirits began to slip into the room, and she stepped back, putting up her shield once more—the crystalline force wall that kept the spirits from her.

"Yo, scumbag," I called.

The cultist turned to me, raising his sword, and attacked.

We exchanged a few strokes, steel crashing on steel, when the spirits turned to us. I kicked him, sending him backward, and several of the eaters fell on him.

He screamed as they bit into him, ripping out chunks of his spirit.

I took the opportunity to turn back to the ley line and the shield that blocked its natural flow.

Okay, Sarah. Treat it like flame. Get the shield out without burning yourself.

I reached out with Gram and touched the shield with the tip of the blade. Power arced off the ley line, ricocheting around the cavern, killing several of the spirits that had fallen on the struggling cultist before fizzling out.

Nice. I took a deep breath. Nothing held the shield there except the force of the energy flow. I should be able to knock it out of the way.

I pulled Gram from the flow and looked around. Three spirits were feeding on the writhing cultist. It was nothing to slash through them. The cultist wasn't dead, but nearly so. I grabbed him by his robes and dragged him onto his feet.

"Come here, be useful." He staggered with me, not sure of what was happening, and I shoved him against the shield.

He screamed as the skin flayed off his bones, but the shield careened into the middle of the room. I was flung backward. Qindra moved to me, encompassing me in her magical field.

"Are you unharmed?" she asked, once the light in the cave dimmed back toward normal human spectrum.

I sat up. "Yeah, I think so." Gram was glowing like nothing I'd ever seen before. She'd absorbed a lot of energy from the ley line, and she vibrated at a higher pitch than I was used to.

Qindra nodded grimly. "He's been wresting control of the dome from me for hours. I think I'm going to let it go, relinquish the magic. Maybe it will rebound on him, fry some of his cronies."

I looked up at her. "Careful, I need you to come out of this alive."

"Then you'd better come get me from the house," she said. The smile on her face was bittersweet. "I don't think I can walk."

The ground shook. Rocks and dust fell into the cavern. Qindra's energy shield vanished, and she faded, waving. "Go," she said, her voice trailing away.

I got to my feet, picked up the shield and tossed it up onto the ledge, laid Gram up there, and hoisted myself up. A large chunk of rock crashed into the room behind me as I picked up the sword and shield. Time to go.

Halfway up the passage I found a cutoff I'd missed on the way down. It ran to the left, toward where the house was. The up passage led to the necromancer. "Left," Qindra's voice spoke in my head. I scrambled left, running along the undiscovered passage. Behind me, the cavern began to collapse.

Dust and debris rolled out of the cavern ahead of me, choking me as I emerged into the night. The whole mountain shook, and I stumbled out, coughing.

Seventy-four

Katie leaned against the sheriff's car, catching her breath. The dragons had been battling between the dome and the plateau when the dome exploded. The smaller dragon was flung back onto the road, but the green dragon, nearly twice his size, had taken the brunt of the explosion.

Shattered scales and green blood splashed against the car where Katie had hidden. Most of her people were down. Jillian still sat in the elm tree, sniping at casters. Her sniper rifle had quit working awhile ago, but she was damn good with a crossbow.

Jimmy and Kyle were on the other side of the battlefield, and they still had a working rifle by the echo.

There were bodies everywhere, some moving, some not. Cultists were getting to their feet, and, as they did, the dead rose around them, moving at their commands. Katie swung out from behind the car, her short sword out, and cut one magic-weaving son of a bitch down as she ran past, cleaving through his skull while he concentrated on raising the dead around him. As soon as he hit the ground, the undead around him fell as well.

Others weren't doing so well. Stuart and a group of others had been knocked down when the dome exploded, and not all of them were getting up. Stuart had his great axe out, clearing a path to the fallen, regrouping near the deputy's car, farther back down the road.

Only they were seriously outnumbered. As the magic casters began weaving their spells, the dead around them rose up, including some of our own. It had only been a matter of time, Katie knew. She did not want Stuart to have to kill his own, even if they were already dead.

She sprinted down the road, sheathing her sword and swinging her guitar around. She slowed as she approached the back of the crowd of cultists and dead. Stuart and his crew were surrounded, and time was running short.

She thought a minute. If the dead weren't a problem, they'd be doing okay. Then the idea hit her. The song she began was slow and melodic, filled with deep thrumming notes that reverberated across the open ground.

Take 'em home, me boy'os
Return him to his mother
let her cast the posies
atop his cairn
and we'll drink him into heaven

It was a funeral dirge—a wake song she'd heard a long time ago at a ren faire. One of the regulars had passed, and the filking group sang this. Katie had been young, maybe fifteen, but the song came back to her as clear as if she'd just heard it.

The music flowed from her, and her nose began to bleed. The music, when used this way, was taking more and more from her, but she couldn't let her people die. As the music touched them, the dead froze where they were, becoming statues of flesh and bone. The cultists noticed and stopped their charge, confused.

One of the cultists reached out, giving the nearest undead a shove, and it crumbled to dust.

Stuart and his surviving squad rushed forward and cut their way through the dead until they reached the living, and Katie drew her sword to meet them.

They came together, she and Stuart, as the last cultist in the area fell beneath their blades. He hugged her, shaking. It had been too close for comfort, but they'd made it. At least some of them.

The rain pelted down harder, and these dead began to dissolve.

"Damn powerful singing," Stuart said, looking at her. "Care to tell me how you pulled that off?"

"Nope," she said, smiling at him. "Just started happening." She staggered, and he caught her. Her face and chest were covered with blood.

"You're wounded!" he growled.

"Nosebleed," she said. "That's new, too." She leaned against him, trying to get her balance.

He helped her back to the deputy's car and gently sat her down. "Tilt your head forward a bit and squeeze the bridge here," he said, placing her hand on her nose.

"Yes, sir," she mouthed. It had been pretty damn close. She'd almost collapsed. It was only adrenaline that had kept her on her feet. Too many of his crew were down. Only four others remained.

"How's Jim?" Stuart asked.

"Saw him and Kyle shooting up the farside of the battlefield but didn't see anyone else."

"Jillian's still doing good from her perch," he said, looking around. His four were not all whole. Two were wounded. But they all were alert, keeping an eye out for bad guys.

The smaller dragon hadn't moved in a while, not since the dome exploded. The green had turned away, taking the fight to the house.

"They're toying with us," he said, his voice bitter. "They're stalling, doing something."

"They brought in a big-ass dragon," Katie said, smiling, her mouth and teeth limned with blood. "I figure, if it wasn't for that second one, the one that dropped a package back by the camp, we'd all be dragon poo by now."

Stuart grunted and stroked her hair. "Take a breather; I'll look around."

He stood, glanced around, and talked to each of the survivors with him.

Things are pretty damn grim, she thought. Where the hell was Sarah?

Stuart squatted back down by Katie. "The green dragon has flamed the house and seems to be fighting something there."

Katie thought. "Statues, maybe. There was some haunted shit in there last time I visited."

"Great," he said. "Maybe they'll kill the freaking dragon before we have to get involved."

Katie smiled, then sat up. "Wait, did you say she flamed the house?"

"Yeah," Stuart said, standing. "Green flames, like the world's worst Saint Patrick's Day float."

"Qindra's in there," Katie said.

"Damn it," he grunted, looking over the hood of the car. "Really?"

Katie nodded and started to stand, pulling herself up the car.

"Here," Stuart said, giving her a hand. "You look like hell."

She shrugged. "Could eat a horse, but I'll live."

"I can help there," he said, swinging his pack around. He pulled out an energy bar and a bottle of water. "All I got," he said. "But you need it more than me."

She thanked him and worked her way through both. When she dropped the water bottle into the back of the cruiser, she felt about a thousand times better.

"Guess all that special singing requires some serious fuel."

He eyed her. "Just be careful. We need to tell Jimmy about this, you know."

"Yeah, sure. After we get Qindra, right?"

He hesitated, debating the witch's worth. "We'll need light," he said, reaching into the deputy's car and retrieving a large flashlight. "Let's roll, people," he barked. "Bobby, you take Eddie and fall back. Make your way to Jillian; she's doing pretty well from that perch."

The two wounded guys headed off.

The air hummed with the din of battle and the booming roar of the green dragon. Spirits erupted from the grounds around the house—rolling, eating masses just like she'd battled before.

"Let's see if I can clear us a path," Katie said, dashing off a chord, encompassing them in a golden glow. The lyrics felt sweet on her lips.

"I'm coming for you, lover mine . . ." It was the song she'd sang going to rescue Sarah. It worked before.

Spirits parted before them, avoiding the golden circle that sprang up around her. "Let's go save us a witch."

Paul and Marla didn't argue, just padded behind them, crossbows locked and loaded. Katie was sure they'd have followed Stuart into hell. Of course, the way the house was burning, it could be a matter of semantics.

They took the scenic route, avoiding the dragon, and swung around the south end of the place, coming by the smithy. She kept the singing to a minimum, but the spirits were coming thick and fast. With the dome down, they were stunned at first, but now it was a feeding frenzy. Luckily, the dragon and cultists appeared to be equally valid targets for their hunger.

The dragon was smashing haunted statues and ghostly critters, ignoring Katie's small group. They fought their way across the grounds, taking down one of Anezka's metal warriors near the carport.

"Don't go out back," Katie said.

Paul froze, his hand on a door to the back of the property.

"Trust me."

He shrugged, dropped his hand to the haft of the crossbow, and stepped back from the door. Something roamed back there. They could hear it. "We going in or staying here to guard the exit?"

Stuart looked into the house. "Rearguard's a good idea," he said. "No heroics, though. If something big and nasty looks this way, you duck and cover."

Marla stepped to the side of the house and rested her crossbow on a stack of overturned shelves. "I got the yard," she said, glancing back at Paul. "You keep an eye on my six." She leaned over the shelves and wiggled her backside.

Stuart harrumphed and shook his head.

Paul grinned at her. "Anytime."

Katie rolled her eyes. If they weren't already messing around with each other, that was a pretty obvious invitation. Crazy what near-death experiences did to a normally quiet person.

Stuart waved Katie to the side and kicked in the door to the kitchen. The interior of the house was full of smoke.

"I got this," Katie said. She hunched over her guitar and began a low, thrumming speed chord. Stuart watched her, anxiously waiting for something to happen.

"We going in or what?" he asked.

She looked at him out of the corner of her eye, grinning. The chords got louder and faster until she straightened up and let out a wild howl. *This is getting awesome*, she thought.

A ten-foot cone of heavy metal music blasted through the house with such ferocity that the walls on either side of the doorway splintered inward. Those battling out on the road all turned as a column of solid sound rose, blasting a chunk of the roof into the sky with contrails of dragon fire. The smoke in the house followed, sucked upward in the vacuum created by the music.

Stuart looked at her, his jaw hanging open and his ears ringing.

"Come on!" she shouted as the chord began to fade. She slung the guitar back across her shoulder and ran into the house.

Stuart followed, his great axe bouncing against his back.

The house was a wreck, but the back rooms remained intact. The roof in that area hadn't burned through, and nothing moved in the darkness. Stuart pulled out the big-ass flashlight and shone it down the hall.

"Last room on the right," Katie said, pulling her short sword from the sheath on her hip. She crouched, leading with her sword, and ran down the hall. Stuart held the flashlight high, keeping the light shining in front of her. They paused at the first rooms—bathroom on the left, utility room on the right. Both were devoid of the living and the unliving. At the end of the hall, Katie took a hard right into the empty room where she'd last seen Qindra.

"Bedroom behind me," she said to Stuart. Flames flared outside the high windows, but Qindra stood in the corner, untouched. She looked thinner and haggard, but she still mumbled, still held her wand in front of her, the flicker of blue coming from the tip.

"Bedroom is all clear," he said. "Smashed all to hell, but no bogies." He stepped into the hollow room and stopped with a whistle. "She's still there, after all these weeks."

"Yeah, we have a problem," Katie said. "Last time we were here, Sarah touched her, and her spirit was sucked into the sideways, down to the cavern where Qindra's spirit is holed up, protecting the joint."

"Dome's down," he said. "She's not protecting anything at this point."

A huge crash shook the house. Katie stumbled, but Stuart steadied her.

"Dragon!" Paul shouted from outside.

They heard the distinctive sound of a firing crossbow and a roar that split the night.

Stuart dodged back into the hallway, shouting. "Go! Get to safety!"

The house shook again, and flames shot across the opening in the roof.

"We gotta go," he yelled, stepping back into the room.

Katie stood, the guitar out and her sword sheathed. "I think we gotta risk it," she said.

"Fine," Stuart bellowed and ran into the room. He grabbed Qindra by the waist, spun her around, and flipped her up over his shoulder. His arms bulged with her weight. For a moment, Qindra remained rigid, but as he turned to leave the room she went limp. He didn't pause, didn't slide into the ether like Sarah had done.

"Let's go," he growled. "She's heavier than she looks."

As they left the room, Qindra dropped her wand, and the house groaned.

Katie knelt, snatched up the wand, and sprinted after Stuart. *She'll be wanting that when she snaps out of this*, Katie thought.

The front of the house had vanished. The dragon smashed her shoulder into the house once more. Stuart stumbled but kept running through what was left of the kitchen. Katie skidded to a halt. The dragon swung her head down through the gaping roof, her great eye—the size of Katie's head—blinking with a wet, schlorping noise.

"Oh, shit," Katie breathed.

Seventy-five

THE PATRONS OF KELLY'S BURGER PIT WATCHED IN AMAZE-
ment as three dozen men and women in armor and carrying
swords and spears emerged one after another from the restroom.
They each nodded to Kelly, who stood behind the counter, a slice
of pie slowly sliding off her pie server.

Skella apologized as the last of them emerged and fled up the
stairs behind the militia. She stood to the side, waving at the gawp-
ing patrons. One sleepy-eyed kid waved back, and Skella grinned.

Deidre was the last out of the restroom. Skella held the door
open as she wheeled to the stairs. Two burly men trotted back
down the stairs and grabbed either side of her chair.

One of the women in the restaurant stood and pointed. "She's
got a gun," she said.

"Part of the show," Skella said. "Nothing to worry about." She
turned to Kelly, who didn't look half as confused as she might've.

"You off to Anezka's place?" Kelly asked, wiping her hands with
a rag.

Skella nodded. "Aye. Hope we aren't too late."

"Go," Kelly said. "Don't worry about this lot." She waved her
hands toward the customers.

As Skella raced up the stairs, she heard Kelly offering the
patrons free pie.

By the time she pushed through the door at the top of the stairs, the Black Briar crew had commandeered a bus. They hustled the elderly passengers off and handed the bus driver a wad of cash to take them into the pub and wait. Then they all loaded the bus and drove north toward the highway.

"Think they're okay?" Deidre asked as Skella settled in a seat next to her wheelchair.

"With Sarah and Katie, I'm sure they'll survive."

Deidre caressed the shotgun with one hand and rubbed her eyes. "What a total cluster fuck."

They pulled onto Highway 2 and were waiting at the turn to Chumstick when three ambulances came screaming up behind them.

"Melanie and Dena made good time," Deidre said, holding on to the bar by her chair as the bus made a hard left turn. "Let's hope we can save some of our people."

Skella sat with one hand holding the side of her head. Jara had been afraid to hit her too hard, so she'd come to as he carried her out of Gletts's secret cave. The freezing rain had also helped to revive her. She'd known Sarah needed her and had fought him.

Unun's voice had followed her as she ran through the woods, praying she could make it to the golf course before they stopped her. Good people had probably died because of her family's growing xenophobia.

She stared out the window watching lights flashing in the distance—fire, magic, worse . . .

"I just hope we aren't too late," Deidre said, taking Skella's hand.

Seventy-six

By the time I could stop coughing, I realized I'd come out of the mountain behind Anezka's property. There were no bodies here, no spirits, cultists, or anyone. I could see the fires out on the road, and to my left Anezka's house burned. The flames were green. No question what that was. The flames would lick the sky until dawn finally sapped them of their magic. Basically, the whole place was a loss.

And Qindra had been in there. The thought hit me like a brick. I ran to the house, but it collapsed before I got close enough. Burning ash and choking fumes washed over me. I fell back, holding up the shield, and the heat was diverted. The shield glowed slightly around the edges, pushing back the night.

"Damn it," I shouted, watching the house burn. "Qindra?"

"Here," a voice answered. To the far left, along the back of the burning house, two figures rose from the shadows. I ran forward. It was Stuart and Qindra.

"You were too late," she said, smiling faintly. "This charming man and your Katie came for me. I'm glad you made it out."

Stuart lowered her to the ground, breathing in gasps. "Katie was back there," he said. "I don't know if she got out."

I stood, taking a step to the burning house, but Qindra touched me on the leg as I passed. "Hold," she said. I turned, kneeling down to her. "She lives, but is seeking you. She will find you; do not despair." She looked around and motioned past me with a trembling hand. "There. Take me there."

Stuart grunted as he lifted her again, smiling when I helped him stand. "I'm getting too damn old for this," he groused.

We moved to the back of the house, and I saw the dragon Anezka had built. The metal gleamed menacingly in the glow of the green dragon fire.

"That will do," she said. We moved forward. I kept Gram clutched tightly, expecting the damn thing to move. It had stalked the grounds right after the spirits had taken over, back when Qindra had first become trapped in the house.

"The necromancer has stripped the spirits from this place, siphoning them off to perform his dark magic," she said, wearily. "I have an idea. Help me stand."

Stuart lowered her feet to the ground and steadied her. She leaned forward, grasping the dragon by its great metallic jaws.

"Sarah, if you please?" She held her hand out, grasping mine when I offered it. "Stand here."

She positioned me to the opposite side, our arms interlinked through the open jaws of the intricate machinery. The gears were intact, and the mechanisms were undamaged.

"I believe," she said, looking at me with an intensity I'd come to associate with fever or psychosis, "if we pool our resources, we can use this to our cause."

I nodded, unsure of her choice, but she reached forward, wiping the blood from my forearm and spreading it across the broad snout of the metal dragon. "Your sword?" she said, pointing. I held Gram up and she gripped the end, cutting her palm and adding her own blood atop my own.

"Grip the side of its head," she said, placing her hands on the metallic housing on her side. "Now, if you can do it, push it with your will. Command it to waken." She looked at me, grinning. "Think of it like you would when working a piece of metal. You are a maker, Sarah. Use that."

I concentrated, thinking of the way the metal felt beneath my hands, how I wanted it to waken, like Gram had, I realized.

Qindra pulled back, stumbling a step, but Stuart held her upright. I stepped back as well, and she smiled, lifting her bleeding hand, and spoke several words I did not understand. Light flared from her bleeding hand and my bleeding arm, arcing to the dragon, setting its head in a glowing sphere. Neither of us moved for three beats; then, the dragon lifted its head.

"The necromancer," she said, straining. "The one who stole your life. He must be stopped."

The beast turned its head toward her, closing its jaws with a metallic crash.

"And protect our people," I added.

It swung its head to me and took a step forward. I backed away, and it took another step.

"Go," Qindra said. "Seek the foul one. Claim your vengeance."

It took several more lumbering steps, and then its movements became more fluid, like it had found its footing.

"I'll be damned," Stuart said, wiping his face.

"Some of the spirits he killed were trapped within," Qindra said. "They just needed a bit more energy to get moving."

I ran around to the side of the house and watched the metal dragon running toward the enemy. The green dragon, Trisha, stood between it and Justin.

And she wasn't passing up the challenge.

"Damn," I said, running forward. "Not the dragon. Get the necromancer."

"Sarah, wait," Stuart called to me, but I had to do something.

I didn't want her to be killed. Stupid woman. How the hell had she gotten into this mess?

Seventy-seven

KATIE WATCHED THE CULTISTS REGROUPING BEYOND THE shattered house. They fell back to the steep mountain trail, calling up more of the dead and sending them at the Black Briar line in a shambling scrum.

She emerged from the ruins of the smithy. The green dragon had eyed her, blinking several times, but hadn't attacked. There was a moment there where Katie thought the dragon knew her.

She clutched her short sword in one hand and Qindra's wand in the other. She should probably make her way to Jimmy and the survivors, but she wanted to go to Sarah, to find her. She didn't think she was dead. No way. So she was out there, somewhere. Probably up on the plateau, fighting the damn necromancer. Maybe she'd risk that secret song again, see if she could get a clue without passing out.

She slipped her sword back into its sheath, put Qindra's wand behind her left ear, and took up her guitar. She strummed a few chords, then began the secret song. Immediately, she fell forward, her intestines cramping, and vomited. Scarlet splashed against the churned mud and snow. Okay, maybe not, she decided, heaving again. She tried to rise but only got a couple of steps in before the world spun and she fell, the sound of the last chord echoing in the night.

Seventy-eight

NEITHER TRISHA NOR THE METALLIC DRAGON FOUGHT WELL. Jean-Paul would've eaten them both alive. He'd known how to use the assets he had. As it was, Trisha just batted the mechanical to the side and did not follow up with tail or wings. Really missing a lot of chances. She didn't want to fight it, I realized. It was a distraction. Something else had her attention. Something I couldn't sense.

I skirted the edge of the rocky incline, watching as the remaining cultists made their way up the trail, back to Justin and his altar.

Then I heard it.

"Mama!"

It was the cry of a small child. In the midst of the retreating cultists, I saw them. I have no idea where they'd been keeping them hidden. There, being carried by the panicked, retreating bastards, were Jai Li and Frick and Frack.

"Mama," one of the troll babies called.

Trisha turned aside, her great head searching for that cry. I knew what I had to do. I ran in, dodging the metallic dragon. Didn't want to get stepped on. When it rammed into Trisha's huge bulk, Trisha spun, smashing it with her tail, sending it staggering back a dozen paces. She turned and launched herself into the air. I was buffeted aside by her back draft. I crouched down, my hands over my head, protecting my face from the flying debris. Goggles next time, I thought. Not the coolest, but I needed something to protect my eyes.

I blinked rapidly, trying to find her through watering eyes. She dipped down, buzzed the fleeing bad guys, and smashed several cultists off the trail. Those farther up the trail forged ahead even faster. They had the children. Those farther back on the trail hesitated, unsure whether or not they should move ahead. Trisha banked and swung around for another pass. The lower group separated. Most fled back down toward the lowland, but two ran ahead, ducking low, carrying a body between them.

I had no idea who they were carrying, but if it was important enough to risk their lives against the green dragon, it had to be somebody I didn't want them to have.

"Back up the trail, Sarah," I said, breaking into a run.

The dragon wheeled and soared across the plateau, roaring her displeasure. Trisha was pissed. I hoped it was bad news for Justin and his flunkies.

Seventy-nine

OUR PEOPLE WERE DOWN, OUT OF THE FRAY. I HAZARDED A glance back toward the last place I'd seen them, but I couldn't see anyone. I hoped they were just hunkered down. Jimmy and Stuart would hold them together. I was just stressing about Katie. Girl had cajones. I just wished I could hear her singing.

By the time I got to the trail, the dozen or so cultists below had scattered north, away from the house and the fires. *Good riddance*, I thought. Keep running, fuckers.

I sprinted up the trail. Okay, big-ass dragon; necromancer; a smattering of tired, worn-down cultists; and some kids. I was feeling old and busted myself, but somebody had to stop them. I had a crazy glowing shield, one hammer on my hip, and Gram over my right shoulder. What I needed was a couple of giants or something. My ass was tired, but I was gonna rock Justin's world . . . or die trying.

No one stopped me. I made it all the way to the top, running out onto the plateau, before anyone even looked my way.

Justin had Trisha backed up against the mountain, her long neck curved down to rest at his feet. He was chanting something, sending magic flowing into her. She whimpered, her eyes darting to the side. He was holding her there; it was obvious by the way her whole body vibrated.

I followed her gaze and saw that two red-robed cultists held Frick and Frack. The kids were struggling with a fervor only infant trolls could muster. It would've been almost comical if they hadn't been standing near the altar amid the broken bodies.

Their intent was clear enough. They were going to sacrifice the kids. I was seriously outnumbered, but no one had noticed me yet. I had to figure this out. Too many targets, too much that could go wrong.

"It will free you, my dear," Justin crooned, his voice still strangely amplified. "You do not need these vermin."

Smoke curled from her jowls and her whimpering grew louder, but she didn't move. The corded muscles along her neck stood out as she strained.

"Kill Sawyer first," he said, the strain obvious in the way he stood, like he was trying to hold her down physically.

Wait. Sawyer? So, he was the second dragon. Fuck me.

Two burly men in cloaks jogged to the altar, carrying a limp and bloodied Frederick Sawyer. He looked so small and broken. Nothing like the powerful predator I'd met. The red-robed cultists did not move aside, however. "We kill these first," one called. "You do not have enough power for the ritual, otherwise."

Justin rocked to the side as Trisha lurched, raising her head a few feet off the ground. He grunted, holding her head, pouring more magic into his binding. I could see it flaring from him, washing over her.

"Your power ebbs," the second red-robed cultist called out. "These will bolster you, give you the power you need for your transformation."

Justin did not turn, just looked into Trisha's nearest giant eye.

"It is for the best," he said, pushing once more, flooding the plateau with light. I could see the binds on her, then—glowing ropes that twined around her great bulk. Ropes that ran from her to him in an intricate braid.

He twisted his hands, his physical metaphor tightening the magical bindings. Her movements slowed to a stop. The additional bindings were too much for her to overcome. Justin stepped back, his body shaking. "Quickly," he said. "She is stronger by far than we anticipated."

He turned toward the two in red, looking at them with his hands on his thighs, his breath labored. "You are correct. I do not have the strength to take Sawyer's heart, not properly." He straightened. "I'll slay the children myself." He motioned for them. "Tobin—" a lithe elf stepped toward the altar, holding a struggling Frack. "Dane—" a burly man with rough features had Frick in a vicelike grip. The child's struggling was much less.

Nu uh, I thought, running forward, finding my target at last. "Hey, douche bag," I cried, pulling my second hammer. "Catch!"

To kill them and save the children, I would have to be in two places at once. Instead, I decided to even the odds.

Okay, there comes a point where you realize your life is way beyond anything you'd ever imagined. When things go beyond surreal and enter the sublime. The runes on my scalp pulsed, and I could see the trajectory for the hammer like a heads-up display on a Blackhawk helicopter.

I let the hammer fly.

Justin turned his head toward me as the hammer arced over the plateau. His rage was instant and terrifying. For a moment I saw something deeper in him, a glimpse of his true self, the horror he'd become.

The two goons holding Frederick dropped him and ran at me. I pulled Gram from her nest and bellowed my best war cry as time slipped a few beats. One of them faltered, but his fellow pulled a blade from his belt and let a feral grin creep onto his face.

I ran forward, each step hammering a spike of energy and pain through the runes on my leg, driving the beserker to the fore.

I danced with them, dodging the first, pushing him aside with the shield, and brought Gram up to block the overhand blow from his partner. I spun, brought the shield around sideways, and clipped the second with the edge, breaking his arm. He fell back, cursing. The first turned, swinging his short blade at me.

I leapt back, instinctively sweeping his thrust aside, passing his blade inches from my chest, and brought the shield up, smashing him in the face. As he staggered back, I stepped forward, thrusting Gram into his throat. His eyes widened in surprise. I flicked my wrist. Gram tore through the cartilage in his throat. Blood sprayed in a wide arc.

I spun around, catching the second as he swung his blade at my back. I struck him twice, first slashing his arm with a passing slice. Then, I stepped to his right, driving Gram into his abdomen.

He stood there, rigid as the pain flooded his brain. I jerked Gram back, letting him drop to the ground.

And the hammer fell.

It struck the altar with a thunderclap, shattering it into several pieces. The red-robed cultists were blasted off their feet.

Frack landed hard, crying out; his captor, Tobin, sprawled on his back. The second cultist, Dane, didn't lose his grip on Frick, but fell with the young troll under him. I didn't hear a cry. That wasn't good.

Justin staggered as the concussion rippled over him. The funneled, processed, and purified energy stored within the altar sputtered from the ruin. He ran forward, hands out in supplication, attempting to scoop up the wasted power.

I reached him, swinging the shield forward, and smashed him in the side. He stumbled, falling over a chunk of altar.

Before I could kill him, however, Tobin rolled to his hands

and knees, drawing a dagger from his crimson robe. He looked from Justin to me to Frack and lunged at the baby troll. Bad choice. I sprang over Dane's facedown form and drove Gram into the bastard. Tobin fell, kicking. Several feet away, Frack screamed like only a healthy toddler can.

Trisha stirred. The magic that fed her bonds no longer had a reserve. Justin was on his own, bleeding away his personal store.

I spun around for my next target. Justin had the second cultist, Dane, pulled back by the hair and dragged a blade across his bearded throat. The blood that splashed forth covered an unmoving Frick, but a thick pulse of energy rushed into Justin.

He rose, reaching for Frick. I darted forward, swinging Gram wildly.

Justin fell back, cursing. Several of his remaining cultists came forward at his beckon, throwing themselves at me, daggers out. I cut the first one down but realized they were beyond their own will. He was controlling them, whether literally or through coercion.

I batted the second aside, knocking the blade from her hand and kicking her feet out from under her. I turned Gram to the side and clocked her with the pommel. Maybe she'd live.

In the meantime, another of the remaining cultists scuttled forward and grabbed Frick by one leg. The cultist lurched away, carrying the child like a broken doll.

I froze. He drew a dagger as he ran. It wasn't a bleeder like Justin's, but it looked pointy enough to kill a wee one.

He slashed wildly as he ran. Frick screamed.

That was the tipping point. Justin vanished behind several of his people, intent on something they guarded, but the threads that bound Trisha had begun to fall away.

She rose, roaring her displeasure, and swung her mighty head around, snapping at the cultist who had Frick. The bastard flung the toddler into the air, waving his arms wildly as he tried to avoid Trisha's bite.

He failed.

I dove, dropping Gram on one side, and swung the shield around, belly-up, catching Frick before he hit the ground. Unfortunately, I hit the ground on my arms and chest, knocking the wind out of me and jarring both sets of elbows and shoulders.

Frick was screaming even more. I couldn't tell how badly he was hurt with all the other blood over him. I dragged him to my chest, hugging him and making soothing sounds. I stood with him, snagging the shield with my right hand.

Half of the cultist who had stabbed Frick fell to my left with a squelching plop. I looked up and Trisha was over me, her mouth inches from us, her horrid teeth grinding.

"He's safe," I said to her, holding the child to me.

Smoke rose from her snout and she sniffed loudly, raising the hair on Frick's head. She twitched, pulled her head away from us, and roared into the night.

Only there was an answering roar.

This one from high above the plateau. I looked up, past Trisha's bulk, to see a white dragon perched on the mountain's peak, gleaming against the sky.

Holy mother . . . Nidhogg.

Eighty

THE REMAINING CULTISTS FLED, SCREAMING. EVEN JUSTIN'S charisma and power could not keep them with him. Nidhogg, the mother of all dragons, fell from the mountain, casting a swathe of fear so strong two of the cultists threw themselves off the edge of the plateau, screaming.

She unfurled her ancient wings to catch the wind, soaring toward us like something out of Revelation. Da would be wetting himself about now. I cringed as the fear rolled over me, but I could not stop, could not panic.

I rolled, holding Frick to my chest with my shield arm, and scrambled back to pick up Gram. Trisha, who'd swung her head upward at Nidhogg's call, turned back to me, roaring. She lunged, her great jaws clacking shut a foot from me.

"Come on, Trisha. I know it's you."

She swung one wing forward, missing me by a mile, but it gave me an idea. I ran forward, getting inside her weapon zone. She was a lousy dragon fighter. She barely realized she had a tail. I'd have been clobbered if I'd tried that move with Jean-Paul. As it was, I was inside her extended danger zone.

Nidhogg pulled up at the last second, clipping Trisha.

Trisha roared, falling to her knees. One great wing bent, broken.

She turned her long neck to bite at Nidhogg, who was already gone, circling around for another pass.

I took my chance. Even carrying Frick, I had to risk it. I figured I just had this one shot. If I screwed up, Nidhogg would kill her.

Trisha whimpered and struggled to her feet. A dragon whimpering is a pretty pathetic sight, let me tell you. I took my chance. I placed Frick on the ground and said a quick prayer. As I ran forward, Gram beat a rhythm inside my skull. *Kill, maim, destroy.*

I shuddered, willing my hand to do *my* bidding, not the blade's.

Trisha fell, smashed to the ground by Nidhogg. I lunged forward, swinging Gram with both hands, and cut through the talon on Trisha's paw, just above the ring.

The world exploded.

For a minute, I couldn't hear anything but the ringing in my ears. Then I heard Frick screaming and tried to sit up. I still clutched Gram in my fist. Trisha lay a dozen feet away from me, naked and human once again. I went to her, knelt to her side, and felt for a pulse. She wasn't breathing.

"Come on, damn it!" I yelled, shunting Gram into her sheath. "Wake up."

I straightened her, tilting her head back, and gave her two quick breaths. Then, I slid over and placed the heel of my palms between her breasts, just above her sternum. I hated giving CPR. Thirty cartilage-crunching compressions with "Staying Alive" echoing in my head, then two more breaths. Nidhogg didn't attack, and Justin was nowhere to be seen, bastard.

Trisha had to live.

I was on my third set when she kicked once, then vomited. I turned her head to the side, pulling her shoulder off the ground. She retched a second time, then fell back, panting.

Her eyes fluttered open, but they did not focus. "Babies," she whispered, and I laughed out loud. "They're alive," I said, squeezing her shoulder. "Let's just hope we make it out of here."

She coughed, and I rolled her onto her side, pushing one of her legs out to keep her from rolling over. Her wing had been broken. Now that she was human again, I didn't know how that translated. Broken ribs, maybe? Her spine? Crap—and I'd moved her. Piss-poor first aider I was.

Her left hand was butchered, however. The last two fingers on that hand were gone, cut away by Gram, but in the transformation, she wasn't bleeding. The hands looked as if the fingers had never been there.

I went to Frick, picked up the crying child, and took him to Trisha. She held him to her and wept.

Nidhogg roared from above us, and I looked over. She landed on the far side of the plateau and nosed down, pushing Frederick Sawyer's body with her snout. He twitched. He was not dead after all. I didn't know whether I was disappointed or relieved.

I climbed to my feet and went to get Frack. Gram screamed in my head, begging, pleading me to attack the dragons. I ground my teeth and hunched my shoulders against the pressure.

No! You're not the boss of me.

Frack had his head buried in his hands, quivering with fear. I knelt next to him, ignoring Nidhogg. Having Nidhogg at my back was one of the hardest things I've ever done. But Frack needed me. I cooed to him, reaching out. He didn't lower his hands, but he didn't fight me. I picked him up and stood.

Jesus, he was heavy. Trisha must have arms like a power lifter.

My neck itched as I ignored Nidhogg, but I needed to get these kids to their momma; that was my new mission. I just hoped Frick wasn't too badly wounded.

I took Frack to Trisha and placed him in Trisha's arms, next to his brother. He calmed almost immediately.

Nidhogg growled, and I looked up.

Justin was backing toward the edge of the plateau with Jai Li in his arms, a dagger to her chest. He'd been going so quietly, he'd have gotten away if not for Nidhogg.

I stood, picked up the shield, and drew Gram.

"Let the girl go," I said.

Nidhogg roared behind me.

"She dies," he said, his hands shaking. "I have not come this far to be thwarted by you meddling fools."

Thwarted? Seriously. Does being an evil SOB make you talk like Snidely Whiplash?

I stepped toward him, and Jai Li cried out. It hurt my heart, that guttural cry. "I cannot kill you enough," I said.

He laughed, and I saw a line of blood appear on Jai Li's neck. He was using a bleeder. No matter how slight the scratch, it would not clot, the wound would not close.

"I'll cut you down," I promised him. "I will cut you into pieces and then burn the pieces."

Jai Li stopped struggling, but her eyes flitted from me to the dragon behind me. She was determined, that angel child.

"I love you," I said.

"Fool," Justin barked, his head thrown back with laughter. "She will die, and you will have nothing."

Jai Li turned her head, the dagger pressing into her neck, and she bit him.

Justin screamed, the knife slipping from his hands, and Jai Li fell to the ground.

"No," I yelled, rushing forward. I smashed him with the shield, and he stumbled back several steps before falling. Before I could lunge after with Gram, another form rose above him.

Trisha.

I don't know where she picked up the fallen blade. She had murder in her eyes, and, for a moment, I thought I'd have to kill her to protect Jai Li.

Justin must've thought the same thing for a moment as he reached toward her, a lurid grin splitting his face.

"Bastard," she said, swinging the blade. She took his hand off just below the wrist.

"What?" He pulled back the stump, confused. "Trisha, help me."

"Oh, I'll help you," she said, kneeling onto his lap. She grabbed the back of his head and held his face upward to hers. "You lied to me; you used me."

She pushed the blade into his abdomen, pulling him to her as if in an embrace. "You should suffer for what you've done," she said, jerking the blade upward.

Justin coughed, blood flowing down the front of him.

"You made me evil, you fucker." She spat on him and stood, letting him fall backward.

He held his remaining hand up to her. "But I gave you power!"

She stepped back, watched him slump over, watched the blood flow from him. When he stopped moving, she stepped forward and brought the sword over with both hands.

I pulled Jai Li to me, keeping her face away.

Trisha hacked him, four, five blows, until she stood with his severed head. This she carried over toward Nidhogg and tossed it at her feet.

"Fuck you and your kind," she screamed, flinging the blade at the great white dragon. "Kill me, you bitch!" And she stepped forward.

Then, the babies wailed. I'm not sure why they'd been quiet up to this point, but the second Trisha stepped into Nidhogg's shadow they let rip.

Nidhogg looked from Trisha to the crying twins. Trisha looked over, torn between her own anguish and suffering and the needs of the children.

"For Christ's sake, Trisha," I shouted. "Go get your kids."

She looked back at Nidhogg once more, who jerked her bird-like head toward the sound of the crying babies.

Trisha stumbled to them, falling to her knees, pulling them to her chest.

Nidhogg looked back to me, ignoring Trisha and the troll toddlers.

I nodded to Nidhogg once and turned back to Jai Li, putting my body between her and Justin's butchered form.

I looked into Jai Li's face, stroking her hair with one hand while blood seeped from her wound. "Hang on," I said, trying to remain calm. I tore a strip of cloth from my shirt and pressed against her wound.

I lifted her, keeping the pressure on the side of her neck while not cutting off her flow of air. "Need to get you to a doctor," I said, hugging her to me. "You hang on."

When I stood, Nidhogg watched me, her birdlike head turning from one side to the other. "Protecting Frederick?" I asked her. "Is he so important?"

She just watched me, turning her head silently.

"Your prerogative, I guess." I kept walking, keeping my head turned toward her. She was not moving, did not attack me or make a move to Trisha. The troll kidlets had stopped crying.

There were seven final cultists, men and women who fell to their knees, hands behind their heads. I ignored them as well. May they burn in hell.

Before I got to the edge of the plateau, several people jogged up, then came to a screeching halt. Stuart, Qindra, and a few others. Farther back, a bloodied and wounded Mr. Philips limped along, leaning on a large branch. He had a dogged look on his face, one that spoke of blind determination and a fervor born of loyalty and love.

Katie was not with them, nor were many of the other Black Briar folks.

"Qindra," I said. "She's been cut. He used a bleeder."

She hurried over and placed her hands on Jai Li's face. The girl beamed, her smile ashen and gray, and her blood ran down my arms.

"Set her down," Qindra said, holding her hand out to Stuart. He helped her kneel, keeping her steady.

I lowered Jai Li to the ground. There was so much blood.

"I need my wand," she said, "but if wishes were horses . . ." she trailed off, looking around. "Does anyone have a gun, some bullets?"

"Yeah," Paul said, stepping forward. He was with Marla, hand in hand, weaponless. He pulled several rifle shells from his pocket and held them to Qindra, who took one. She bit the tip, where the lead was, and twisted it back and forth several times. It was pretty damn hard.

"Here," I said, taking the bullet from her. I lay it on the ground and took out Gram. Cutting through the lead was simple.

She took the bullet and pulled the bandage away from Jai Li's neck. She sprinkled the gunpowder into the wound, which was barely bleeding. Not much blood left, my mind ranted.

"Hold her," Qindra said, looking at me.

I leaned over, placing my hands on Jai Li's shoulders.

Qindra snapped her fingers and a spark of fire erupted. The gunpowder burned quickly, and Jai Li screamed for a second before passing out.

"That should stop the bleeding," she said, her face a sheen of sweat and fear. "She needs a hospital."

"Where's Katie?" I asked.

Stuart shook his head. "Jimmy's looking for her." He had a horrified look on his face. He didn't say more, but my insides did a somersault. He was scared and didn't want me to hear his fears. I kept my hands on Jai Li, afraid if I moved, I may collapse. Katie was okay. She had to be. I couldn't think about that, couldn't let that into my head.

"She'll be fine," I said, swallowing hard. "She's too awesome."

Qindra laughed gently, and it was loving, didn't make me want to punch her in the face. Very much, anyway.

Mr. Philips passed us, glancing once at Jai Li, and turned toward Nidhogg. He didn't pause, just kept his plodding way to his master. Nidhogg growled once, but he kept his head bowed and plowed onward.

When he got close enough, he fell to his knees, examining Frederick.

"You will live," he said. For the first time, I heard a tremble in that always-stoic voice.

Eighty-one

GRAM CONTINUED TO ECHO IN MY HEAD, BUT HOLDING JAI LI seemed to act as a filter. While anger rolled, filling me with fire, I tamped it down. A shudder wracked my body as the anger faltered. My will. My life. I did not need to succumb to the beserker. Not every single time.

"Stuart," I said, looking up. "Trisha's back there," I nodded toward the mountain. "Frick was stabbed, but I don't think very badly. Kid has tough skin."

He motioned for Paul and Marla, who jogged with him toward the mountain. I brushed the hair from Jai Li's face. "Hang in there, kiddo. We'll get you to a hospital."

I slung the shield over my back and picked her up in my arms.

Nidhogg made a coughing sound, and I turned to her. "We're safe," I said to her. "Borders secured."

She watched me with that oddly birdlike flutter of her head.

"Sleep, mother," Qindra said, striding forward. She began to sing a lullaby. Jai Li gasped, recognizing the song.

"Shh," I said, holding her to my chest. She snuggled against me, mewling.

Qindra had her hands in the air, weaving back and forth, like a snake charmer. Nidhogg followed, her great head swinging from side to side.

The song echoed from the mountainside, filling me with a sadness and longing beyond my defenses to contain. I sobbed once, gasping for air, my throat aching and my eyes burning. A second sob burst from me, and I started crying.

Jai Li patted my arm as I wept, head bowed over her.

The sky above us began to brighten, allowing me to see more clearly.

Sirens echoed off the mountains, and I walked to the edge of the plateau. One of those huge tour buses pulled up to the burning wreckage below, followed by three ambulances. Folks in armor poured from the bus, fanning out across the battlefield. Others left the ambulances, pulling out rolling stretchers, looking for someone to save. The cavalry had arrived. Better late than never.

I walked to the path. I had to get Jai Li down to them. She needed more help than I could give her.

I looked back one last time.

Nidhogg lay down, her wings spread behind her and her long neck atop her forelegs. Qindra closed the final distance, placing a hand against the glowing white scales. Again, it was Gram that caused the glow, but with the fresh light of morning licking against the tops of the mountain, I no longer needed the assist.

"She'll sleep now," I said to Jai Li and began to descend the trail.

Maybe Jimmy had found Katie. If not, I'd begin looking for her as soon as Jai Li was seen to. I needed Katie to be alive most of all—the skald of my hearth and home. Tears leaked from my eyes, but they were beyond my control.

Eighty-two

WHEN I GOT TO THE AMBULANCES, MELANIE WAS THERE WITH Jim and Katie. He'd found her, facedown in the snow, her guitar smashed beneath her. She was unconscious. Melanie got to her quickly, sending her and the deputy back in the same ambulance. They headed to Wenatchee. It had the closest hospital.

She hooked an IV into Jai Li and got her stabilized enough to ride to the hospital. I didn't leave her side. Part of me screamed to go with Katie, but this little girl needed me as well.

The ambulance ride was one of the longest times in my life. I ached—hollowed and hurting with dread. If Katie died, I didn't know what I would do.

I looked down at Jai Li, stroking her hair. She was so small, so weak. How could anything that beautiful and fragile survive in the world we lived in?

Deidre had been there, coordinating the search for survivors. Since we hadn't had a big contingency, it wasn't a long search.

A handful of our folks had stayed back at Black Briar. Skella texted me from Deidre's phone, all the way to Wenatchee. She explained that her grandmother had feared she would get killed mixing up with our kind. She was probably right to be concerned. Skella promised to give me all the details later, but as long as she was on our side, I didn't care too much. The fact that there were elves with Justin, however, that had to be addressed. Later, though. I was too damn tired to deal with it.

Katie came around in the emergency room. They gave her fluids and kept her overnight. Best they could figure was she had passed out from exhaustion and lack of food and water, as there were no wounds. She'd obviously had a nosebleed at one point but didn't need a transfusion or anything. They had her on an IV to get her fluid levels back up and put her in a private room.

Jai Li was in the pediatric ward, where they gave her a pint of blood. They bandaged her neck, but the biggest worry was infection. She'd be staying a couple of days.

Gunther had been stabbed, and Anezka stayed with him until the ambulance could arrive. He had to have surgery but had no permanent damage. He'd have a wicked new scar to add to his collection, though. Anezka had really stepped up, clobbering the cultist who stabbed him and fighting the others off.

I didn't sleep that first day, going back and forth between Katie and Jai Li. When Deidre and Jimmy got to the hospital with the Black Briar survivors, I let her spell me while I went to use the hospital locker room to shower. I changed into scrubs and fell asleep at Katie's bedside. Jai Li was asleep, and Deidre would be there when she woke. I needed Katie to wake up, to say my name.

Did I say that ambulance ride was long? The night waiting for Katie to wake up was longer. Now I had an inkling of what she'd been through after I killed Jean-Paul. And those chairs were not comfortable at all.

Around dinner the next day I was contemplating the fact that I hadn't had any food since the olives, cheese, and salami we'd had in our apartment the night before. The thought of it and the memory of making love to her warred inside me. I needed fuel. Knew I needed it, but if she died, if she did not open her eyes soon, I don't think I cared if I ever ate again.

And I couldn't bear the thought that she'd wake up and I'd not be there.

Skella solved it. I was nodding, trying to stay awake, realizing *that*, too, would take me down eventually.

"Here," Skella said, swinging into the room with two boxes and a case of Diet Coke.

She pulled a hospital table around and placed a box on top of it, flipping open the lid. It was a BBQ-chicken pizza. My mouth watered and my stomach clenched.

"Thanks," I said, but she was already at the door.

"Got to deliver this other one," she said with a wave and was gone.

I closed the lid on the box and slid the table aside. I did take a drink, though, and cracked it open. The first few gulps tasted like heaven going down.

"I'd kill for a slice of that pizza," Katie said.

I dropped the soda, lurched up out of the chair, and practically threw myself onto the bed. I was laughing and crying at the same time.

"About time," I said, wiping my face. "You scared the hell out of me."

She smiled, taking my hand, squeezing it. "You look hot in those scrubs."

That's when I knew she was going to be okay.

Eighty-three

We had twenty-four people in Chumstick counting the hostages. Of the four on duty when the cultists arrived on the scene, Lonnie and Abrielle were killed, while Steve and Jayden survived.

Stuart and Jimmy brought twelve people with them. Paul Aaronson, Marla Stewart, Kyle George, Jillian Brachman, Jimmy, and Stuart survived. We lost Eddie Boyce, Bobby Denton, Daniel Kincaid, Byron Fischer, Aiswara and Victor Tiwary (brothers), Andrew Ohng, Cindy Nguyen, Tila Morgan, Kesha Mahnke, Lorelei Sturgis, and Brook Lefevre.

The bad guys had shown up with some of our folks in tow. They all survived, miraculously. Trisha, Frick, Frack, and Jai Li. As well as Mr. Philips, the manservant of Frederick Sawyer.

Qindra was already there, trapped in the house. She got out alive.

Frederick Sawyer and Nidhogg both arrived after the battle had begun, and both survived. Although a change had happened. Nidhogg had not been out of her house in a hundred and fifty years. The world had progressed a lot in that time. Big changes were on the horizon.

On the bad-guy side, they counted the bodies of eighty-four cultists. Didn't make any sense why they hadn't totally kicked our ass. Sometimes you just had to shake your head and wonder. I know our fighters had trained and used weaponry and terrain to our advantage, but seriously.

About a dozen of Justin's folks were seen beating feet for the hills.

On the plateau, Qindra counted forty-seven murdered civilians. She had a crew come out, but there was no way to cover up that many dead.

The newspapers had a field day.

The sheriff was among the murdered, but the deputy survived, thanks to our folks. He told the story of how we'd broken up a cult, like that Heaven's Gate crowd. They killed a lot of people, burned down a few buildings. We were all heroes. Like I needed more time in the papers.

The elves and, in two cases, trolls, who had been part of the cultists, were handled by a private funeral home that had connections to Nidhogg. Need a body disappeared? No problem. A dragon owning a crematorium. Seemed redundant.

And the seven we'd captured. They disappeared. Qindra wouldn't say anything more about them. I guess I didn't want to know.

Eighty-four

EVERYONE WAS FREE TO GO HOME ON THE TWENTY-FOURTH—Christmas Eve. Jai Li would need to check in with a doctor, but her wound was remarkably light. Qindra had done something to her, I was sure. The scar would be much reduced as well. Her wand had been with Katie when Jim found her. The look on Qindra's face when he handed it to her was amazing. A détente had been born. That was the final handshake in my mind. I'm not sure how we'd all move forward, but Qindra was no longer "them." She was part of "us."

Stuart had stayed with her while she'd taken control of the scene in Chumstick, acting as her personal guard and helper. I'm not sure what happened there, but something. I'd have to keep an eye on that.

Nidhogg's lawyer, Anne Rokhlin, showed up at the hospital as we were checking out. The drive over the pass had not made her any more pleasant.

"You need to take her home," she said, handing me a sheaf of papers. I glanced at them and dropped them on the table in the waiting room.

"Say that again," I demanded.

"With Qindra home again, Nidhogg has formally requested that Jai Li return to her rightful place in her home."

I punched her. Okay, so maybe I didn't have the beserker under control after all. Katie pulled me back. "Sarah, no!"

The lawyer stumbled back against the nurses station, holding a hand to her mouth. "Really?" she asked, looking at the blood on her hand. "I'll tell you this one time, Beauhall. You do not want me as an enemy. If you ever lay a hand on me again, I will bury you." She took a deep breath, plucking several tissues from the box on the nurses station, and held them to her bleeding lip. "I'm just the messenger. Take the girl home and consider some fucking therapy."

She turned, snatching her briefcase off the floor, and stalked out of the ward.

"Nice," Katie said, holding my arm. "Can we not make things worse?"

I took a deep breath. "Yeah, right. We just take her home?"

Katie shrugged. "Let's take her; I'll go with you. We'll talk to Nidhogg, see what happens."

"Fine," I said, snatching up the sheaf of papers.

When we got out into the parking lot, Qindra had already hired a car. It was raining and cold, but I had my bike. We rode in the limo. I'd get my bike later.

We arrived at Nidhogg's place three hours later. Traffic across Highway 2 was miserable as more snow was falling in the higher elevations. Once we cleared Gold Bar, I regretted not stopping there, heading into Black Briar. *Not yet*, I thought. *Business first*.

Katie sat with me, and Qindra sat opposite. Jai Li sat next to Qindra, holding the woman's arm like she was afraid she'd float away, but she kept looking over at Katie and me.

"How you holding up, kiddo?" I asked.

She smiled, giving me the thumbs-up. The bandage on her neck looked huge, but I knew she'd be okay. Well, depending on Nidhogg, I reckoned.

Eighty-five

WE STRODE INTO NIDHOGG'S HOUSE, THE MAIN FOYER EMPTY
and echoing. Jai Li had Qindra's hand in her left and mine in her
right. When the big doors shut, she paused, looked from me to
Qindra, then dropped my hand and pulled Qindra left into the
entrance to her wing. The gate stood across the hall, and Jai Li
pointed at it, then back to me.

"It's quite beautiful," Qindra said, looking back at me. "And
why is this here?"

Jai Li lowered her face but cast me a glance.

"Nidhogg was afraid the children would hurt themselves," I
said. "She asked me to build it, to keep certain urchins," I brushed
my hand across the top of Jai Li's head, "from getting hurt among
your possessions."

"Is that right?" Qindra squatted down, taking Jai Li's face in
her hands. "Weren't you told to never enter my quarters?"

Jai Li pulled her face away, not looking at Qindra.

"Found her asleep in your bed more than once, apparently."

I pulled the key from around my neck, handing it to her, leather
cord and all.

She took it, nodding once.

A sound brought me around. The household had begun to

creep into the foyer, dozens of women and children, each coming toward us.

I saw Zi Xiu standing near the back, her hands over her mouth, crying quietly. The children came first, walking forward to touch Qindra and Jai Li.

Katie and I stepped back toward the front door, letting them welcome their missing home. It was bizarre and heartbreaking. The children especially. They had this desperate look on their faces, like Qindra was a ghost or something.

She stepped into the mob of them, touching each of them, calling them by name. Those she touched fell behind her, hugging Jai Li, then turning back to follow Qindra. Some looked back at me, but most did not. This was not my home; I was not one of them.

After the children, Qindra moved to the adults, saying a word, hugging, touching, making human contact with each and every one. The room swelled with the noise of it, the sheer relief and joy of it.

She stopped in front of Zi Xiu and took the woman's hands away from her face, holding them both in her hands, and said something to her I could not hear. Zi Xiu laughed through her tears, but reached forward and hugged Qindra.

The children cheered. I'm fairly sure this home had not had that form of noise inside the walls, ever. It made my heart ache. Katie clung to me, holding my right hand in both of hers, leaning against my shoulder.

This was a family, not unlike Black Briar. These people loved one another, needed one another. And they lived under the fear of Nidhogg and her erratic moods.

Qindra raised her hands, and the cheering stopped. She was thin, thinner than I liked. By rights she should be in the hospital, but I knew that wasn't going to happen. Her recovery would be here, among her people.

And that was as it should be.

Jai Li hung back, torn between the crowd ahead of her and looking back at me. I smiled at her. "Go on. This is your home."

The huge doors at the far end of the foyer opened, and the noise fell to a hush. Nidhogg stepped forward, dressed in an elegant black dress, her hair pinned back in a series of tight braids, a silver pin holding it all together.

She stood there, leaning against her black and silver cane, surveying the scene before her. First one, then another of the servants fell to their knees, heads bowed. Soon, the rest of the crowd followed, including Qindra.

Only Katie and I stood, on the opposite end of the hall, facing Nidhogg. She looked different, more powerful somehow. Getting out of the house, flying across her land, perhaps that had changed her. Or, maybe it was her daughter's coming home. She walked forward, the cane a staccato beat on the marble floor. First, she went to Qindra, pulling the woman up to her feet, and hugged her.

Those on their knees gasped in wonder. This was unprecedented. Many of them began to cry, whether from joy or fear, I couldn't tell.

When Nidhogg stepped back, Qindra wiped her eyes. "Welcome home, daughter," Nidhogg said. "You have been sorely missed."

"Aye," one of the young boys squeaked. No one else spoke, but Nidhogg laughed. Her voice was paper thin, but the laughter was one of joy. Soon the rest of the room was abuzz with whispers.

Nidhogg turned from gazing at Qindra and raised one hand. The room fell silent. "Jai Li," she said, her voice stern once again. "Come forth, child."

"Mother," Qindra said, her voice quavering, but Nidhogg held up a hand to silence her.

Jai Li strode forward, cutting through the crowd, which shuffled aside to let her pass. She was so tiny.

She stopped in front of Nidhogg and knelt down, her head bowed.

"Do not kneel to me," Nidhogg said, pulling the girl up.

Those kneeling cast glances at one another, and the whispers began again.

Nidhogg did not quiet them, but when she spoke again, they fell silent.

"You disobeyed me," she said, her voice stern. I took a step forward, but Katie held on to my arm.

Jai Li nodded.

"You, who have never once set foot from this house, took it upon yourself to leave here, to do what you thought best."

She nodded once again, keeping her head bowed.

I looked at Qindra, who practically vibrated with frustration.

Nidhogg looked around the room at the upturned faces, each writ with fear once again.

"This is my house, my domain," she said, her voice growing louder. "I rule here. You," she swept the room with her hand, "serve me at my whim."

She dropped her hand onto the top of the cane and looked back at me.

If she made a move toward the girl, tried to hurt her in any way, I was going to kill her with my bare hands.

"You are no longer part of my household," she said to Jai Li. "I cannot allow it."

"But, mother," Qindra said again; the strain in her voice was enormous.

"Silence," Nidhogg said, slashing her hand toward Qindra. "I rule here."

Qindra bowed her head, only the shaking of her shoulders betraying her tears.

"Jai Li," Nidhogg said. "You are banished from this home. Go out into the world and make your way. You have forsaken my bond. You will be casteless, without a master within my lands. I have no claim on you, henceforth."

Others wept then, not caring who knew.

"We'll take her," I said, stepping forward.

Nidhogg stared at me for a long time. No one rose, but many risked glancing back. "She can live with me and Katie. We'll take care of her."

Jai Li looked back at us, her jaw hanging open.

"So be it," Nidhogg said. "Jai Li, you are henceforth indentured to this brigand. You may serve her, at her discretion."

No one moved. I looked at Katie, who nodded to me. "I love you," I said, leaning in and kissing her.

Then I walked through the crowd, following the path Jai Li had taken. When I got through the throng, I nodded at Nidhogg and squatted down to Jai Li.

"Do you want to come live with us?" I asked.

She did not move her head but moved her eyes, first to Nidhogg, then back to me. Very slowly, she nodded, her eyes wide.

"Deal," I said, taking her into my arms and standing. She weighed less than either Frick or Frack. I took several steps back and turned to face Nidhogg.

"I brought Qindra home. My debt to you is cleared."

She looked at me, and I held her gaze. There was more power there than I'd ever seen, ever imagined. She could call down fear and fire so quickly my shadow would be forever burned into the marble floor at my feet.

"The balance swings to your favor," she said, finally.

I stood rooted. Did she just declare a debt to me? I was confused.

"Back to your duties," she called, stamping her cane onto the
floor.

People scattered to all four corners of the house.

Nidhogg turned and strode back into her cathedral-sized
room, and the great doors swung shut. Only Qindra remained
standing there.

"I knew you were brave," she said. "But to challenge Nidhogg
like that. That took some chutzpah," her voice was quiet but firm.

I shrugged. "My da taught me to stick up for myself." It was
true, another item for the plus column.

"You are definitely strong willed," she said, grinning. "Take care
of Jai Li. She is more precious than you know."

Katie walked into the main hall and took Jai Li from my arms.
"You could come and visit her," she said. "You're welcome in our
home."

Qindra raised one eyebrow, studying her. "My thanks," she
said. "While the child is no longer Nidhogg's concern and there-
fore none of mine, I would still very much enjoy the ability to
check in on her from time to time."

I glanced back, and Jai Li was stiff in Katie's arms, nodding in
affirmation.

"It seems that would be amenable."

Jai Li wiggled until Katie set her onto the floor. She ran over,
glancing at me as she passed, and flung herself into Qindra's arms.
She held the witch tightly for several long moments before pulling back. She laid her hand on Qindra's cheek and kissed her.

Then she stepped back, bowed once, and turned, taking my
hand.

"Time to go?" I asked.

She nodded, pulling me toward the door.

"Take the car," Qindra said. "Since getting home on foot would be bad in this weather."

I stopped, let Katie take Jai Li, and turned back to Qindra, holding out my hand.

"You're good people, Qindra. If you need my help, you're welcome to call."

"Funny," she said, grasping my hand firmly and jogging it several times. "I was going to say the same thing."

Eighty-six

THE CAR TOOK US BACK TO BLACK BRIAR. JAI LI CURLED UP IN
the seat next to me and went to sleep.

"You know what's funny?" I asked, the memory suddenly flashing into my mind.

"Hmmm?" Katie asked, looking away from Jai Li's sleeping
form.

"Frederick Sawyer said something about my mother. The last
time I saw him in his"—I made air quotes—"human form, he
said something about my mother."

Katie sat up straighter, taking my hand. "You said he saw her
at your old place."

I nodded. "Yeah, but there was more to it. He was amused
when I blew up at him. Told him my mother was off the table."

"Oh, Sarah," Katie said, patting my thigh. "He was probably
messing with you. It's what he does."

I leaned back, closing my eyes. "Maybe."

We spent the rest of the trip just being a family. It was peaceful.
It was also Christmas Eve.

When we got back to Black Briar, the clan was decorating the
farm for the holiday. Jimmy looked at me when I carried Jai Li
from the car, but he didn't say anything. Deidre was pleased,
though. Damn happy. She took Jai Li from me, riding her into

the living room on her lap. Frick and Frack were there, staring, stunned, at the flashing lights over the fireplace. She sat Jai Li on the couch with Trisha, who was stringing popcorn and cranberries for one of the three trees they have on the farm—one in the barn, one in the barracks, and one in the big house.

Deidre began to sing Christmas carols, and Katie joined her, taking off her coat and heading into the living room. The house bustled with Black Briar folks, and most of them seemed to be getting in the mood of the holiday.

"It's not that we've forgotten the dead," Kyle George said to me. "Rather, we're celebrating the passing of the dark and the shortening of the night."

Fair enough, I reckoned. Jimmy went out onto the deck, out into the cold, and I followed. "What's up, Jim?"

He grabbed a couple chairs that had been tipped against the house to keep the snow from accumulating in the seat. He spun one my way and sat on his own. Snow fell around the farm, covering the world in a blanket of quiet.

"This was delivered," he said, handing me an envelope.

I opened it, reading the letter inside.

It was from the Order of Mordred. Whoever they were, they were requesting Jimmy to bring Black Briar into the fold. Certain parties wanted to meet with him, to discuss taking over his father's position in the order.

"I've never heard of them," Jimmy said.

"Contact them," I said. "See what they have to say."

"What would happen to Deidre if I disappeared like my parents did?" he asked quietly. "We've seen too much bloodshed. Too much pain."

"And if we'd done nothing?" I asked. "How many would have died?"

He didn't answer.

"Good of you to allow Trisha to come back here."

Jimmy shrugged. "She fell in love with the wrong man, let her pain and anger cloud her judgment. In the end, she loves those troll babies. Loves Black Briar as well." He turned to me and smiled. "Qindra says she can lift the last of the hooks Justin wove into her. We can't lose her, too. She'll have a home here, ya know?"

I smiled. "Island of misfit toys." The metaphor felt right. "We collect the broken ones, give them a place to feel whole."

He nodded, tapping the envelope against his thigh.

"What about the ring?" I asked.

"Stashed away, along with the other relics. Now that we know what it is, we'll guard it, keep it away from anyone who may want to use it."

"Why not destroy it?"

"We'll try," he said. "But if my parents didn't destroy it, they had a reason. I'll keep researching where I can, see if I can pick up the thread they dropped."

"And this Mordred crew?"

He looked back at me. "I've been trying to figure that out. Arthur's bastard son. Why would you create an order around him?"

I nodded. "Good question. Maybe we should find out."

Eighty-seven

FREDERICK WOKE TO THE SOUND OF ANGRY VOICES.

"You cannot bring him here," an elderly voice said, the pitch quavering from fear. "She has no idea of her heritage."

"He requires sanctuary," Mr. Philips's voice rang true and strong. "You are obligated to provide us such."

"You do not understand," the old man responded. "He called for Ignacio."

The quick indrawn breath of Mr. Philips drove Frederick to sit up. "You told her?"

The old man squeaked, dropping the lantern he held.

Frederick could make out Mr. Philips in the shadows. The second man, the elder, was harder to place. "Did you say Ignacio?"

"Yes, my lord," the elderly man said, bowing toward Frederick.

"Get up, man. Bring the abbot to me."

"We have not seen the abbot since he went to rouse her, my lord."

Frederick tried to push himself up on his elbows, but failed. In a breath, Mr. Philips was at his side, kneeling beside him.

"Do not rise, sir. You are gravely wounded. I fear you may yet falter at death's door."

"Foolishness," Frederick said. He made no further attempts to rise. *Bravado*, he thought. He felt near enough to death. "Where are we?" he asked when the blood did not seem to rush so to his brain.

"We are at the abbey," Mr. Philips said. "Per your prior instructions. If you were ever to fall, to be near death, I was to bring you here. I assumed this was a place of healing, a place where you would revive."

He couldn't help it. The chuckle escaped him. Mr. Philips rocked back on his heels. The man was wounded himself, and yet he sought to follow the most dire of contingencies. The last possible of Frederick's commands.

"Has she been awakened?" he asked, finally.

"That is what I was saying," the elderly monk said. "The abbot went down to her cell. Your orders were explicit. The fires are raging. There is no going back."

"Who?" Mr. Philips asked, grasping Frederick's arm. "Who is this Ignacio?"

"It is code," Frederick said, letting the finality of it overwhelm him. "In the event of my passing, I could not let the kingdom go to another. I had to have a safeguard."

"I do not understand," Mr. Philips said. "What have they done?"

"They . . ." Frederick paused, the thoughts a riot of uncertainty. "They have hatched my daughter."

Eighty-eight

LATER, AFTER THE KIDS WERE ALL BEDDED DOWN AND MOST of the adults had gone off to sleep, Katie wandered back into the kitchen, where I was writing a letter by the light of the Christmas tree.

"What are you doing, baby?" Katie asked, sliding her hands over my shoulders and kissing my neck.

"Writing to Megan," I said. "Not her fault I can't get along with Da."

Katie nodded.

"Oh, and Deidre found these," I said, holding out a long, thin strip of pictures.

They were pictures from one of those photo booths, with four pictures of me and Katie, laughing and kissing.

"And I have these," I said, opening my wallet. From inside, I pulled out a similar strip, folded and creased like they hadn't been looked at for years, which they hadn't. "Forgot I had these, but when Deidre showed me those, I remembered."

The other was a strip of pictures showing me and my sister Megan.

"We took those at the state fair, right before I left for college," I said. "I wanted her to know I kept them."

"It's sweet," she said, massaging my shoulders. I leaned back into her. God, I loved it when she touched me. I closed my eyes, letting her work the kinks out.

"Trisha gonna be okay?" she asked.

I looked across the room to the trolls sleeping at the foot of the couch, where Trisha lay. "Jimmy says Qindra can peel away the last of Justin's bonds on her. But the magic from the ring may have interfered. It may not be a clean fix."

"She's got Frick and Frack," Katie said quietly. "And we have Jai Li," she said, lowering her cheek next to mine.

I glanced over to the Christmas tree, where the young girl lay in a nest of blankets and pillows.

"She won't stop staring at the lights on that tree," Katie whispered.

"She's never had Christmas," I said. "She's not used to all this."

Katie sat down next to me, picking up the pictures again. "I think it's a good thing, you contacting Megan. Let her know you still care about her."

"Not sure she's open to it," I said. "May be too late. But I'm willing to try."

I sealed the envelope with the letter and the pictures inside. Then I pulled Katie into my lap and watched the people lying scattered around the room.

This is family. The family we choose.